# THE PACKAGE

## An International Thriller of Conspiracy, Murder and Betrayal

BRYAN QUINN

A NOVEL IN THREE PARTS

ISBN: 978-1-64438-468-8



Published by BookLocker.com, Inc., St. Petersburg, Florida.



Booklocker.com, Inc.
2020

Second Edition

## About the Author

Bryan Quinn, a life-long student of history and comparative theology, earned a BA in American History & Politics from McGill University and a Computer Electronics Diploma from Herzing College which comes in handy when he needs to troubleshoot inevitable computer problems. Yet, despite his expertise with digital technology, he still relies on his wife to operate the coffee machine. Bryan lives with her on planet Earth.

Bryan won an Honorable Mention Award in the worldwide 85$^{th}$ Annual Writer's Digest Short Story Competition in 2016.

Follow Bryan on Twitter: *@AuthorBryan.*

## Facts

The Byzantine Empire (330-1453) was the successor state of the Roman Empire. It ruled large swathes of territory, which ranged from present-day southern Spain to North Africa, from Italy to Turkey and from Egypt to Syria. A shadow of its former size, the empire fell in 1453 to Mehmet the Conqueror, sultan of the Ottoman Empire. Constantinople (present-day Istanbul) was the capital city of the Byzantine Empire.

The Ottoman Empire (1299-1922) defeated the Byzantine Empire in the Battle of Constantinople in 1453. The Ottomans subsumed all of the territories of the Byzantines with the exception of southern Spain and Italy. With the defeat of the Byzantines, the Ottomans went on to capture present-day Bulgaria, Hungary, Arabia, Iraq, western Iran, the Crimea and southern Russian territories. Istanbul was the capital city of the Ottoman Empire, which collapsed in the First World War and ceased to exist shortly thereafter.

# Lexicon

*Deep State* is a cabal of billionaire bankers that control the U.S. via the privately-held New York Federal Reserve Bank. This elite monied ruling class is supported and legitimized by its lackeys in Congress, the judiciary, the media, academia, think tanks, intelligence agencies, defense industries and the Pentagon. This cabal dictates U.S. foreign and domestic policy, regardless of which political party is in power, to its sole financial advantage.

*Fatwa* is a ruling on a point of Islamic law rendered by a qualified judge.

*Hamam* is the Turkish word for bath.

*Müezzin* is the Turkish word for the caller of the Muslim faithful to prayer five times a day.

*M'sheekha* is the Aramaic word for Messiah.

*Overton window* defines a range of opinions acceptable for public discussion by pundits and politicians.

*Sella* is a three-legged wooden Roman stool.

*Yeshua* is the Aramaic name of Jesus.

## Acknowledgements

Producing a novel is not a solo endeavor and so the many contributors must be acknowledged.

First, my loving wife who supported me in every way. Next, Todd Engel for his brilliant cover design. Then, my publisher Angela Hoy at BookLocker for packaging my novel and putting it the hands of book retailers.

I also extend a special thank you to my editors and to the following person and organizations:

- Dr. Laurence Brown, D.D., M.D., for his scholarship on the Trinity
- GNS Science in New Zealand for its radiocarbon-dating expertise
- New America Foundation (www.newamerica.org) for its data on U.S. domestic terrorism
- Human Rights Watch (www.hrw.org) for its July 2014 report, *Illusion of Justice: Human Rights Abuses in US Terrorism Prosecutions*. Copyright © 2014 Human Rights Watch. All rights reserved.
- Mass Shooting Tracker website (www.gunviolencearchive.org/reports/mass-shooting) for its data on U.S. mass shootings

## Beginnings
## Istanbul - Present Day

Leave *now* with the package or end up dead like the other two.

Delivered moments ago by his terrified friend, the grim warning haunted Marco Arrigoni as he scrambled to plot an escape route across a crumpled map of Turkey he had smoothed out to the edges of the kitchen table. So much for this day being one he wanted to remember rather than one he wished to forget. But remembering or forgetting today paled in importance to surviving it, and there was no guarantee he would—all because he had pinched from a sacred tomb a holy relic he probably shouldn't have.

So now here he was, holed up in his apartment like a common fugitive, cowering from a vicious killer who hungered after the stolen relic. Hungered after it badly enough to gun down two innocent men last night—one of whom had been his friend's lover. A sure sign the killer was close on his heels.

Or maybe he was a tad paranoid.

Perhaps. But paranoia didn't waste those unlucky victims, Marco reminded himself as he struggled to concentrate on the map.

If nothing else, he now understood how a fugitive must feel—an understanding he would gladly give away in charity if he could, generous soul that he was. Beyond that, Marco knew diddly-squat, and not knowing so unnerved him he couldn't stop himself from flinching at every ominous *thump* and *creak* while he studied the map in the confines of his tiny kitchen which seemed more animated than usual. Time was short—he expected a private courier to collect the packaged relic at any moment. Then he would skedaddle, preferably before the shooting started.

Funny thing how the passing decades had tamed his wild side. Back in the day, he had cut a broad swathe through his feral Bronx neighborhood cracking skulls and breaking bones. But twenty-plus years of shilling sermons on turning the other cheek had dulled his fighting edge. A guilty consolation to him. Guilty because he earned his daily bread preaching a philosophy of life totally at odds with his less-than-stoic behavior of the moment. So what? Failing to walk the walk wasn't the end of the world. A desperate killer was stalking him after all. So his friend had warned. Reason aplenty to excuse this minor episode of backsliding and cut himself some slack. Besides, practicing what he preached wasn't his strong suit. Never had been. Especially the practicing part.

Done justifying his skittish behavior to himself, Marco tore his eyes away from the map and flicked a nervous glance at the clock suspended high on the opposite wall. A double-take, a hard swallow, then fear and anger soared in tandem. The blasted courier was late. The odds of the relic falling into the hands of the gunman shot higher.

His mind in turmoil, Marco sat gaping at the timepiece while the rotating second hand ratcheted up his sense of doom. Just then a horrible awareness rocked him.

If I'm killed, the secret of the relic will die with me.

His senses reeled.

The shooter can't win.

Too much is at stake!

Not one to panic at the first sign of disaster, Marco showed anxiety the door and rallied himself. When you get out of this jam alive, you're gonna buy that backstreet courier the biggest damn clock in the city and chain him to it. Let him then dare lose track of time again. Bong! Bong! Bong!

Despite his dour mood, a sly grin stole over his kisser.

Doubt if the courier will find it funny.

Tough.

As much as he wanted to flee, running from danger wasn't listed in the code that governed his conduct. (A double-check confirmed this.) If he did, his conscience would plague him like an incurable itch. Nah, he'd rather grapple with a psychotic cage fighter than tangle with his nag of a conscience. He had promised to deliver the package, so despite the potential threat to life and limb, deliver it he would.

This wasn't the first time Marco's take-it-to-the-mat sense of moral obligation had placed his life in jeopardy. He simply ached for it to be the last. It had better be. At forty-eight, "Dead Hero" wasn't an epitaph he hankered after, but it might come to that since he wasn't packing a weapon.

Except.

He flexed his scarred ball-peen-knuckled hands and examined them as though seeing them for the very first time…Fingernails could stand a trim…Not solid enough to stop bullets but strong enough to break bones. Better than nothing, he conceded. Marco hadn't clobbered anyone since becoming a priest over two decades ago. But that's not to say the impulse had vanished altogether. Uh-uh. He had lost count of the number of times he felt like hurtling himself through the flimsy latticed divider in the confessional to knock some sense into the heads of wayward congregants committed to perpetrating the same debaucheries again and again, and who then possessed the gall to wonder why the outcomes were no different from the last. The insanity of it all. Luckily for them, he feared prison more than he loathed the priesthood. Retirement couldn't come soon enough.

Marco's lapses of compassion aside, his fists and hard-earned street smarts had rescued him from countless scrapes in his past. And then some. He possessed the scars to prove it. Scars or no, the wary voice in his head, the one that had kept him alive in the mean streets of his youth, reminded him he was going to need his fists and his wits if he expected to outfox the hitman. Once more, consequences be damned, he'd trust in his weapons fashioned from flesh and bone to live beyond the end of the day. What else could an unarmed priest do?

Pray?

He mentally shook himself and turned his restless attention to the bulky package positioned at the edge of the map. It drew him as a wave drawn to the shore. Unable to look away, he regarded it with awe. For the truth was alive in there, with a capital *T*. That much was certain. Unbidden, his hand whispered over the map to the packaged relic and awarded it a gentle pat.

So many innocents slaughtered across so many centuries for the sake of some well-spun lies. Never again! he vowed. The message in this package will expose the biggest hoax ever foisted upon huma—

"Enough!" He glared at the window, and if looks could shatter, the glass would've burst.

Shrill for the time of day, unusual since rush hour hadn't yet slipped its straining leash, the din of traffic flaring up from four stories below sprang him from his chair, sending it crashing across the linoleum floor into the fridge. He rushed to the window to investigate....

Lined up bumper to bumper, cars crept past his building in horn-blaring protest. Farther down the road he spied a double-parked car, its taillights flashing.

"Way to go, buddy," he yelled into the noise. "Those flashers will speed things up real fast." He ducked in and slammed shut the window. "Takes just one selfish jerk to cause a stretch of chaos."

Too preoccupied with the fix he was in to latch onto the illegally parked vehicle as a harbinger of something more than a mere case of self-centred behavior, Marco spun away from the window, none the wiser.

"Damn natives have got nothing better to do than pound on their horns," he griped as he went to retrieve his chair. If time permitted, he would've liked to pound on the drivers just to hear *them* wail.

He shoved the chair home with his foot and plunked himself down in it. Powerless to stop the manic traffic noise, he rubbed his hands through his wavy jet hair then let them flop onto the table, and another glimpse at the burning clock did little to cool his annoyance.

He grunted in frustration. To distract himself, he ranged through the rudimentary escape plan he had devised. He could find no hiccup in it. Must be perfect. Like him. Stealing a final look at the location he had circled on the map, he thought, Should be a quiet refuge to hunker down in until things blow over. No one will think of searching for me there. Any place is better, not to mention safer, than this crib. And if it isn't, well, I'll discover that soon enough.

The escape route Marco would travel to reach the secluded Sümela Monastery in the northeast part of the country settled, he gathered the crumpled map, refolded it after several maddening attempts and finally rammed it into his back pocket for future retrieval.

A futile expectation he would later discover.

With nothing left to do, he stared out the filmy kitchen window at the Hagia Sophia, its massive brick-and-mortar dome seemingly propping up the leaden sky like a giant umbrella. His gaze turned inward while his fingers probed the jagged scars on his knobby knuckles, the crude braille of a troubled past etched in his flesh, if not in his soul.

How did the shooter get wind of the relic? he asked himself and not for the first time today. Only three other people are aware of its existence. Two of them are trustworthy. They wouldn't say a word. Would they? But the third. Could he have informed the gunman from jail…? But how?

He would give much for the answers to these questions. Even his vows? Worth considering. Too overwrought to think straight, he let the matter drop. The answers wouldn't change his predicament anyway.

The horns blared on, but Marco's gaze did not waver.

*Steely* you might call it. And you'd be right.

Doing his best to ignore the shrill protest percolating up from the traffic-snarled street thirty-feet below, and containing his gut instinct to lay down some scuffed-up shoe leather and beat a path to safety, he sat tight and willed the courier to materialize. Only then would he put shoes to pavement and disappear. And with no trail to follow, perhaps the unknown killer would too.

He hoped.

That was the plan. Such as i—

The doorbell went off, detonating the tense atmosphere in his apartment. Marco bolted upright in his chair.

Must be the courier. So he deigned to show up. About damn time.

Hurrying toward the front door, he welcomed a surge of relief.

It didn't last.

An obvious question rattled his brain: What if it's not him?

Marco froze and time with him. The living room seemed to shrink and fade away until nothing but the front door loomed before him. If he remained still, maybe the caller would give up and leave.

The buzzer detonated again; he jumped out of his skin.

Caught in the amber of indecision, Marco fixated on the door, knowing there was no going back once he opened it.

His senses on full alert, he found his courage and reached for the deadbolt with utmost effort, as though in a nightmare, and at that same moment a shudder ripped through him—the fuse on the most explosive secret in history was about to be lit.

The time for him to skedaddle had come.

He didn't know how wrong he was.

His ordeal wasn't over. It hadn't even begun.

# Part I

*The cultivation of percipient doubt is the greatest hindrance to the spread of falsehood*

# Chapter One
## Roman Province of Judea – Early First Century CE

An ill wind crept through the hushed streets of Bethany, which lay dark and deserted beneath a cold, moonless sky, while a silent murder of crows surveilled with fierce black eyes a sacred dwelling from atop the highest perch in town. The scribe held his emotions in check as he watched the retiring figure of his teacher depart through the doorway one last time without so much as a glance back. Despite having learned he had been sentenced to die in the cruelest of manners by his enemies, his teacher had left their meeting in high spirits. Unremarkable that. Because his teacher knew what his enemies did not. And now so did the scribe. But what he didn't grasp, nor could he, because he would be long dead before the event would ever come to pass, was that the secret shared by his teacher this evening would surface one future day and expose the carefully crafted lies concealing his teacher's actual fate.

Out of respect for his teacher, the scribe waited for the door to his room to close before letting out a cavernous yawn. His drowsiness momentarily subdued, he laid aside his quill and writing palette with a sense of release. Seated cross-legged on the tiled floor in a dim pool of light cast by the oil lamp, he stretched his arms and aching fingers before him, listening to them crack. Bleary-eyed, he gazed with wonder upon the scroll lying before him. Done transcribing the message of his teacher, a message of peace preserved for prosperity on calfskin, he acknowledged the futility of his accomplishment. Three onerous years of preaching this message by his teacher throughout Judea had brought neither him nor his community any peace.

In its stead, the message had ushered in a period of social and political unrest in danger of descending into violence. Not an unusual state of affairs. Whenever the authority of an entrenched power felt threatened, reprisal was in the offing for the source of this threat. It would be no different for his teacher.

But the scribe was not worried. The enemies of his teacher could scheme and conspire all they wanted in hopes of putting an end to the supposed source of this unrest. But their schemes, like their hopes, would be in vain. For their Lord was the best of the planners.

He gingerly turned his head left and right to relieve the painful kinks in his neck and noticed the faint glow behind the curtained window on the opposite wall had faded to black. Night had fallen. When? He couldn't begin to guess. After many hours of transcribing, he was oblivious of time. But it must have been long ago because his limbs were heavy with fatigue and the house lay in deep silence. If not for the rhythm of his steady breathing, he heard no other sound in an atmosphere layered with tension.

He remembered his companions had gone to their beds earlier than usual, the teacher's sermon on the mount having taken its physical toll on them. So would have he, but his conscience, obsessed with fulfilling his solemn duty, would not surrender to the irresistible need for sleep. And now his exhausted body screamed for rest.

There will be time for slumber, he reassured himself. Not now. But soon. Very soon.

He puckered his cheeks, blew out the guttering flame in the oil lamp and crabbed over to his wool bedding. Alone is his room with only the oppressive darkness for company, he stretched out on his back, cupped his hands behind his head and stared holes in a ceiling he couldn't see, only imagine, his mind at work. My teacher's enemies have convened in secret and rendered their tainted verdict. Before long I, too, shall convene in secret. But it is history who shall render its impartial judgement! Hardly had he formed this intention when his inner voice whispered to him this moment was at hand.

That quickly, he rolled onto his side and pushed himself off his bedding, brimming with anticipation. The time for waiting was over. Nervous exhilaration rose in his breast and his nerves tingled. Everything rested on the success of a secret meeting he had planned for tonight. Destiny was at hand. Though his cause was fraught with risk it was also freighted with reward, and the triumph of his cause would depend in significant part on his character and wits. But he also believed success was dependent on the will of his Lord.

Disoriented by the utter dark, he stood still and felt for the bedding with his bare foot and concentrated. Mindful now of his whereabouts, he picked his way to the opposite wall without kicking over the ink pot he had been using earlier and congratulated himself. He slid his hand along the smooth, cool surface of the plastered wall until it brushed against the curtain which screened the solitary window in his room. A cold draft snatched at him as he drew back a corner of the heavy fabric, a warning to him to dress warm tonight. He ignored the chilly air and surveyed the canvas of high velvet sky above. The patch of the heavens he scoped from his location was thick with stars, moonless. Relief washed over him.

A good omen. My movements will be harder to detect beneath a cover of darkness, he told the night.

Gratified, he released the curtain, snuffing out the feeble starglow. He turned away from the window and eased his way back to his bedding to retrieve an object vital to tonight's meeting. He concealed the bulky object beneath his garments. Careful not to disturb his companions asleep in adjacent rooms, he clothed his sandals and cloud-stepped out of the two-story home.

A shock of frigid air greeted him outside which bid his lingering drowsiness farewell. He bunched his shoulders and drew his thick woolen robes close to himself. A crow cawed a cautioning note. He glanced up. Worry lines deepened on his face.

Evil is astir this night, he warned himself.

Alert now but still wary, he paused in the recessed doorway that fronted the unlit street prepared for danger. I seek protection with God from the accursed devil, he prayed, a prayer he never failed to invoke whenever he departed a dwelling. For only brigands roamed the streets at this hour, desiring to ply their wicked deeds under the veil of night.

Unsettled by the malevolent charge in the atmosphere, he leaned forward and cast furtive glances up and down the murky street from the safety of the doorway. Long liberated from the noisy daytime parade of beast and man and from the pall of churned-up dust that hung heavy in the air like a depthless fog, the street appeared to be empty, his eyes attentive to the slightest of movement in the shadows.

At length, satisfied with his inspection, he straightened up and inhaled deeply. The air tasted fresh, perfumed with night-time odors and scents. Then he exhaled slowly. He repeated this breathing exercise several times. Little by little, he felt his anxiety depart in plumes of frosted air.

Revitalized and his guard up, he scanned the street one last time. Still empty. He took one more sober pause and a sense of conviction stole over him. You can do it. But his nerves were telling him something else. He ignored them. There was more to life than succumbing to one's fears. Confident no one lurked in the darkness, with his staff in hand, he steeled himself and rushed into the deserted streets of the town with only the glint of stars to light his way. He was committed now.

How different his neighborhood appeared at night. Details had vanished and colors had transmuted to shades of black as he slipped by darkened homes and shuttered shops, their owners sleeping the sleep of the overworked, unaware of the desperate plot unfolding in their midst. He scooted along dirt lanes like a whisper of air, forming the briefest of acquaintances with the darkest of shadows as he forged toward the clandestine meeting site with unexaggerated caution, his eyes constantly sweeping his environment for danger and his ears alert for the sound of pursuers. And despite his best efforts to be noiseless, his footfalls, muffled by sackcloth tied around each leather-shod foot, made soft thumps against the ground in the narrow passageways.

So dark and so still, he observed. Like a graveya—from nowhere the anguished braying of a tormented donkey shredded the tranquility of the night, setting off a chorus of bays from watchdogs in stone-walled yards surrounding him. Startled by the sudden commotion, he froze and terror stabbed at his entrails. He tensed and glanced around. An urge to quit this place, to abandon his duty, seized him. If not for his faith and his self-discipline, he might have succumbed to fear. But there was no turning back. Too much was at stake! Instead of retreating, he darted next to a stone building and squatted, unsure if he had been seen or heard.

With nothing to do but wait, he rubbed his cold hands together, damp with anxiety, and a bead of sweat trickled down his back despite the cold.

Cursed dogs might draw a Roman foot patrol to this area. That is all I need.

Waiting was no easier for him than for anyone else, but patience, a virtue he possessed in large measure, was his ally this night. On edge, he listened while his apprehension mounted.

Households awakened. Angry shouts for quiet rang out in the dark and, but for the odd mutter, the four-legged friends of man, their guard duty loyally performed, called it a night and turned in. With quiet restored, he snuck a peek around the corner of the home concealing him. His vision by now adapted to the darkness, the vicinity seemed safe, as best he could tell, and he heard nothing. Emboldened by the silence, but still on edge, he grabbed his staff, jumped to his feet and dashed off.

Cautious, though it was the depth of night, he kept his identity shielded with the cowl of his woolen robe as he snaked his way through the winding streets. He could not be found in this neighborhood in possession of what he carried beneath his layers of clothing. His teacher's enemies would kill him for it. Invisible and propulsive, the fear of capture drove him to fulfil his duty while there was still time.

Racing around a street corner, he heard the tramp of marching feet carried on the quiet night air grow louder. His heart banged against his ribs, blood chilled in his veins. He skidded to a stop.

Roman foot patrol, his ears reported. "Cursed dogs!" he hissed.

Where to hide? No place for concealment. In the gathering peril, an inspired ruse lit up his mind. Quick-thinking is the ally of the frightened. He began tapping his staff on the ground in a steady cadence and repeating in a measured voice, "Alms. Alms for the blind and the poor. Alms."

The footsteps grew closer until they were almost upon him.

"Halt!" someone in authority ordered.

The scribe ceased begging and came to a standstill as did the foot patrol.

"Who goes there?" the one in charge challenged.

"Samir the blind beggar, centurion." He gave the speaker a lofty title to inflame his pride.

"It is past curfew."

"I have no reckoning of day or night, good sir."

The lead soldier approached him and whipped off his hood. He stood still, peering without attention at his unlit surroundings. The soldier then raised his hand and made to strike him, but he did not recoil, continuing to study his environment with an unfocused gaze. He seemed to have passed some kind of test for the leader said, "Go about your business, you fool. A thief's dagger will skewer your flesh before this night is through."

A sharp order spoken, the stamp of many feet faded away into the gloaming behind him. He let out a long slow breath.

Calm restored to him, he replaced his hood and set off again. Guided only by his memory, it came as a surprise when he found himself across the street from the secret meeting place, an unremarkable one-story, stone-built home similar in construction to its neighbors. He savored the sight of it. He caught his wind and offered up an unspoken prayer of gratitude. Done, he listened while he looked both ways before approaching his objective. The narrow street was devoid of life. Thanks to God. He could not be seen here for its owner was a senior member of the Sanhedrin as well as a secret follower of his teacher's way. There was no telling what the High Priest would do to the owner if his double life was discovered. The scribe advanced on the stout iron-strapped door in the thrall of anxiety and tapped out a series of knocks, a signal to the owner of his safe arrival.

Hurry, he willed, the tension a palpable sensation in the dark.

Nerve-wrenching moments later the door opened without a sound and beyond it stretched a black emptiness. He plunged through the entrance with the silent words "In the name of God" on his lips and was swallowed up by the dark void. The door closed silently behind him.

Solid as it was he knew the wooden planked door offered scant protection from enemies determined as those who had his teacher in their sights. Nonetheless, he expelled a heavy sigh and the burden of worry that weighed on him sprang from him like a boulder from a catapult. His success up to this point was worthy of celebration, but he was not in a triumphant mood. For he was preoccupied with a far-reaching decision he had to make. A decision that would safeguard the truth about his teacher's ultimate fate.

He swept back the cowl of his robe in a fluid hand movement and stood in silence for several heartbeats to gather himself. The warmth of the room thawed the ice in his veins and the air, laced with the elusive traces of—cinnamon? nutmeg?—delighted his nose. Temporarily blind but alert, he heard the rustle of garments and the slap of sandaled feet on the tiled floor pass by him in the dark and come to a halt several cubits away. Clicks and clacks of metal on flint made him start. Sparks flashed to his right. A wick made of sheep's wool dipped in a clay pot filled with olive oil sputtered then flamed in its niche. Shadows, brought to life once more, swayed on the uneven stone walls. The soft, flickering light cheered him, the darkness driven to the corners of the snug room.

An expression of relief on his face, the host, clothed in a similar long-sleeved, ankle-length garment padded across the softly lit room towards him with arms outstretched, clasped his cold hands—his eyes widened briefly—and extended to him the traditional greeting: "Peace unto you, brother. Praise to God the Almighty who guided you safely to me."

Squeezing his host's warm hands, "Unto you peace, as well, brother," the scribe replied in kind, his lips parting in a shy smile. "Thanks to the Almighty for His protection," he added.

"There is a dreadful chill in the air this night," the host said, making polite conversation.

"In more ways than one," the esteemed visitor replied, and the host seemed to wonder at his remark.

A sella was offered him. Thanking his host, the scribe raked his fingers through his shoulder-length, dark, curly hair and, with care, lowered his sturdy frame to the seat, unsure of its ability to support his weight. Seated, and his eyes by now adapted to the weak light, he inspected the spartan room, taking in the sparse furnishings and bare stone walls. A man of immense wealth and yet he lives modestly. He nodded his approval. Good. For this humble abode might one day be taken from him, if he accepts my plea for help. Loss is the essence of sacrifice. But the reward for sacrifice is greater than the loss, if not in this life, then surely in the next, he believed.

They sat opposite one another now, their faces half-hidden in shadow. Finished wandering, his eyes came to rest on his host, who sat expectantly on his sella, palming his knees. Curly salt-and-pepper hair crowned his head and from beneath caterpillar-like brows, a pair of keen black eyes peered back at him, likely wondering why this hasty meeting had been called.

He held the other's gaze in the faint light. "I feared my secret message might not have reached you earlier today."

"And I was worried you would not make it here. But God did not forsake us," the host replied.

Without warning, the scribe shot forward and spoke with urgency: "Brother, the die is cast. The life of our dear teacher is at stake!" He couldn't help but notice the visible effect of his words on his companion.

The host went rigid on his sella, firm resolution on his face. "God willing, I shall do everything in my power to save him from his fate, O scribe of the M'sheekha," he said, no false courage in his tone.

The scribe sat back in silence and smiled his pleasure at the host's brave and spontaneous response. It will require more than your resolve, Most Beloved, to save our teacher's life. Much more than you could imagine. And you will soon discover just how much.

## Chapter Two
## Istanbul – Present Day

Alone in his mental space, the hum of the city sounded far away while Marco Arrigoni stared out the open window of his office located on a quiet leafy side street. Experiencing a bout of writer's block, he sought inspiration in the view from where he sat. Lack of original ideas seemed to be affecting him more and more these days. Burnout must be just around the corner.

He focused his eyes on the slender minarets of the Blue Mosque, named for the profusion of blue Iznik tiles that adorned the interior walls of this archetype of Ottoman sacred architecture. The cylindrical columns of stone crowned with cone-shaped caps poked high above the red-tiled rooftops, stark against the bowl of blue sky. Not unusual. Minarets were as common a site in his adopted homeland as steeples were back home in New York.

The stone-built minarets alternated between a pale beige and bluish-grey, depending on the position of the sun, or maybe it was the intensity of the sun. He wasn't sure which. They sure beat staring at his computer screen all day. Today they were bluish-gray.

For close to seventeen hundred years, the Golden Horn, the strategic peninsula where he toiled away week after week, had been the imperial seat of three empires: Roman, Byzantine and Ottoman. Then, in well less than a century, the drums of war gave way to the beat of commerce, and Istanbul metamorphosed from imperial capital to holiday mecca, following the dissolution of the Ottoman Empire in 1922.

Although he couldn't see them or hear them from his office window, and though he wasn't a gambling man (provided his raise came through next month, otherwise, all bets were off), he'd wager that at this very moment, with summer still in full swing, tourists in their multitudes were thronging the covered laneways of the Grand Bazaar—one of the oldest shrines to shopping in the world. Begun in 1456 by Mehmet the Conqueror and expanded in subsequent years, the Grand Bazaar housed close to four thousand shops. A shopping mecca second to none.

Marco, however, rarely paid tribute to Mammon in that cathedral of commerce. Shopping wasn't his thing. But if it were, he wasn't paid enough to relieve the ennui of life with shopping excursions. Most of the time he was too consumed with work far more spiritual than commercial in nature (at least that's what he told himself). Unavoidably so. He was the parish priest of Santi Giuseppe Church, a church which enjoyed a celebrated status among his flock. Legend had it, his church had been built over the tomb of a holy man sometime in the late tenth century when Istanbul was called Constantinople, the Second Rome, named for Constantine, the first Christian Roman Emperor. The local Catholics believed the holy man would protect them so long as his tomb remained undisturbed. Father Marco didn't put much stock in the legend. Like his faith, it was just so much folklore.

Just then *she* popped into his head. He pictured his friend in his mind's eye…Her smile. A fixation of shiny white teeth and glossy rouge lips, that smile...But her smile imparted friendship, not romance...So far as he could tell...Why do you torture yourself with thoughts of her? How many women fall in love with a priest? The answers wouldn't come to him. He blinked and her image dissolved, the neural equivalent of a puff of smoke before a gust of wind. Once again he was alone in his mind, staring off into the distance.

Inspiration not on offer in the vista before him, he turned away from the window with a tic of discontent. Best get back to the daily beans-and-wieners routine, he urged himself. Working at his desk in frustrated industry, papers and reference books piled without care on its cluttered surface, he reread the text on the computer screen for the fiftieth, hundredth time? He had lost track of how many times. He was cranking out the Sunday sermon, his most important weekly task, and it was giving him trouble. Composing each sentence on the page was excruciating, like excavating a fossil. And he knew this firsthand because he dabbled in archeology in his spare time.

His brow knit in concentration, Father Marco struggled to express in words a middle ground between faith and modern life, the theme of his sermon. His parishioners, blighted souls one and all in his opinion, were constantly wrestling with the conflicting demands of the secular and spiritual realms. (Wallowing in the muck of sin was more precise, but who was he to judge?) Thus, they were in constant need of practical guidance to help them navigate the stormy shoals of modern life. Between him and the wall, a slap upside the head would be more effective, but then a priest has to conduct himself within acceptable social norms. Ever the optimist—or masochist, take your pick—he believed his sermon would deliver this essential navigation and, with the help of God, prevent his flock from running aground in the moral shallows. They needed all the divine help they could get. Deserved or otherwise.

So absorbed in his work, he didn't sense at first the faint motion of his padded seat. But as it grew in strength, he could no longer ignore it. His concentration broke, and his eyes drifted from the computer monitor, concern in them. Rumbling's too strong for a passing truck, he gauged. Icy fingers of alarm crept up his spine and his flesh crawled. In the next moment reality hit him.

Earthquake!

He dove beneath his desk with only his stomach-churning dread for company, and the rattling increased to a terrifying racket. While he huddled in terror on the bone-jarring floor, the acid taste of fear in his mouth, his thoughts vaulted back to memories of the last major earthquake that had stricken Istanbul.

When was that? he asked himself as he quivered on the floor...August 1999, he recalled after a rapid heartbeat or three, answering his own question.

That earthquake had been a powerful one. A 7.9. Thousands of people had died in it. The epicenter, which had been farther east, on the Asian side of the city, had caused significant damage to Istanbul's infrastructure. As items crashed to the ground around him, adding to his already considerable distress, he prayed for divine deliverance from such a fate.

Not ready to pass through the Pearly Gates just yet, my Lord.

His prayer (and the prayers of many others) must have been answered because, as if on cue, his office became eerily quiet and the floor ceased shuddering, the giant jackhammer pounding the earth stilled by a mighty hand. Car alarms wailed in the distance and dogs bawled. Still wary, thinking what could have been, he poked his head out from beneath his desk, unsure if it was safe to leave his improvised shelter.

Now he knew how the bells on a Turkish belly dancer must feel. Actually, he knew exactly how they felt, but it was best if that peccadillo stayed within the confines of the confessional.

Still on his knees, he took stock of himself. Shaken and dishevelled, he was otherwise unscathed. He stood up, brushed off his black soutane, combed back his dense, charcoal hair with his fingers, and expressed an unspoken prayer of gratitude.

Exhilaration infused his central nervous system, like an athlete mounting the winner's podium. He had won. He had cheated death—unharmed! But not his office he noticed; his features tweaked in displeasure. A bookcase, which he had meant to level but hadn't gotten around to doing, was face down on the stone floor next to the desk, its contents strewn about, and framed items, which once graced the bare stone walls, now lay shattered on the floor. And a bust of Lincoln, his favorite president, lay in pieces, mixed in with the books and shards of glass, too small to glue back together. An edgy stillness hung over the room.

Then his eyes fell upon a framed picture of his mother and sister lying atop the debris. Somehow it had survived intact. He blew the dust off the glass and stared at the picture, forgetting himself for a moment in a memory of the past. He graced the picture with a kiss before placing it back on his desk.

He glanced around and nodded in satisfaction. *Appears we lucked out. Hope the rest of the church did too. I can't afford any downtime. My damn sermon isn't going to write itself…Unless procrastination succumbs to desperation and I slip an old sermon past them.* The mischievous idea brought a grin to his face, but it was quickly erased by concern for his church.

A weekday afternoon, the nave was most likely empty of parishioners making devotions. No surprise there. Nevertheless, Father Marco strode from his office with urgency in his step, the chance of injury, even death, still a possibility. He marched through the north transept into the crossing aware of the thump of his racing heart, and the echo of his thick-soled shoes on the ancient flagstone floor worn smooth by centuries of use telegraphed his progress into the cavernous nave, the main body of the church.

He entered the nave in a state of apprehension while motes of dust floated on blades of sunlight which pierced the lancet stained-glass windows above, decorating the vast open space in a panorama of colorful stripes.

Holding his breath, he completed a quick survey of the church. Much to his delight, only the pews were dislodged and a few unlit candlesticks on the high altar table had toppled over. He permitted himself a long relieved sigh; the tightness in his chest relaxed. The church, based on his cursory inspection, seemed to have withstood the tremor undamaged.

Appears I'll have to finish my damn sermon after all.

He didn't see or hear any injured worshippers flailing or wailing about and his heart swelled with gratitude for small mercies. The sight of blood distressed him even though he had seen plenty of it in his former life. Hands clasped behind his back, he rocked on the balls of his feet and, in spite of his irreverence, soaked up the visual splendor of his church in solemn silence what thousands of other awestruck worshippers had likely done over the ages. The very grandeur of the space mocked whatever out-sized measure of self-importance he possessed.

Every architectural detail in sight proclaimed the power and glory of the Almighty. A gilded coffered-ceiling, framing ornamental rosettes in bold relief in its recessed panels, soared high above him, and successive rows of lofty yellow and white marble columns, ramrod at attention, flanked both sides of the nave from front to back, while faithfully-rendered biblical scenes, exploding with color and exuding a deep degree of spirituality, painted with adoration on the far walls left and right, carried his thoughts to another dimension. A visual symphony of form and function exceeded only by that of Saint Peter's Basilica in Rome he felt compelled to ad—

Intruding upon his meditative state, almost beyond the range of earshot, he heard off to his left a groan. Now what? he thought with barely concealed irritation. He turned toward the direction of the eerie sound, cocked an ear and deliberated whether the church itself was the source of it. He caught the moan again, in the right aisle, among the rows of columns.

Evil spirits? He stiffened and fingered the large crucifix dangling from his neck. I wonder if the crucifix can ward them off…He stole across the nave as if he were about to be pounced on and peered between the shadowy columns.

To his surprise—and relief—he spied the feet of his custodian beside a column, sticking up on the cold floor next to an overturned footstool. No evil spirits after all!

"Dimitri," Father Marco cried out.

In a flurry, he dashed between the columns, nearly tripping on the hem of his soutane. He had forgotten about the cranky caretaker. Which was difficult to do most days. For good reason. Nonetheless, sickly guilt pinged his conscience.

Kneeling on the floor beside him, Father Marco said in Turkish, his voice raised, "Dimitri, my dear. Can you hear me...?

He stirred and his eyelids fluttered.

DI-MEE-TR—"

"Don't yell. I'm not deaf."

"I wasn't yel—"

"What happened?" Dimitri said as he brought his hand to his head.

"You don't remember?"

"I'm just asking for the helluva it."

Father Marco's mouth flopped open, then it clamped shut for a beat. "An earthquake hit us. But not a bad one, thank God."

A brief smile flickered at the corners of Dimitri's mouth. Father Marco wondered at this. But not for long because Dimitri then said, "See what I have to suffer for this job."

"No one—" he held his tongue, and not for the first time "—Never mind. Are you hurt?"

"I was meditating before you interrupted me," he snapped. His eyes adopted a searching look as though he were taking a mental inventory of his body. "My head hurts."

Father Marco was tempted to ask, “Can I knock some sense into it?” but let it pass and opted for “May I examine it?”

Dimitri moved his head in a sluggish manner which Father Marco guessed—correctly—was a gesture of consent. With a delicate touch, he examined Dimitri’s pumpkin-sized head and felt on the back of his skull a small knot beneath mousy hair.

“Hmmm,” he intoned with the gravity of an ER doctor.

“What?”

“It’s never been done before,” Marco said out loud, pretending to be in deep discussion with himself.

Dimitri became agitated. “What’s wrong?”

“I think we have to amputate,” he said in a serious tone.

“Amputate?” Alarm showed in Dimitri’s eyes. “Amputate what?”

“Your skull,” and he let go of the laughter he was suppressing.

Dimitri’s alarm flipped to anger. “Now that you’ve had your *fun*, help me to my feet.”

He managed to get Dimitri into a sitting position.

“Don’t be rough with me.”

Father Marco rolled his eyes heavenward.

Little by little, he helped Dimitri, a stout man, rise to a standing position, requiring no small amount of effort on both their part. Once on his feet, he swayed like a sailor after a night on the town—make that several towns.

“Take a seat,” Father Marco advised, indicating a pew, “while I go scrounge for something cold for that bump.”

“Don’t trouble yourself, Father,” he said, slumped in the pew.

“It’ll reduce the swelling.”

Dimitri palpated the bulge with his fingers. He winced. “The bump isn’t big.”

“It will also numb the pain,” Father Marco added as an inducement.

“It doesn’t hurt much.”

“It’s what’s best for you.”

“I said—” He stopped himself short, realizing who he was addressing. “If you must,” he relented.

"Don't move. I'll be right back." Father Marco turned away. Touchy, touchy. What's biting him? He never pretended to fathom his crankier-than-usual colleague in any depth though they had been working together going on twenty years. His custodian liked to keep to himself. You'd think the old grouch would show some appreciation for my concern, he grumbled as he made his way to the small kitchen. Maybe a kick in the pants would straighten him out. The notion of corporal punishment lightened his mood while he prepared the icepack on the counter.

He returned a few minutes later and presented Dimitri with an improvised icepack wrapped in paper towel. It was the best he could do under the circumstances.

Dimitri pulled a questioning look at him. "Yogurt?"

"Don't worry. It's frozen—and it's fat-free." Unlike that head of yours.

He backed down and mumbled, "Well, you did say it was fat-free." He grabbed the frozen container and set it against the lump..."Thank you, Father."

At an age when most men were well into retirement, Dimitri was one of those rare men who worked and stayed active. Why was anyone's guess.

"Did the church suffer any damage?" Dimitri asked.

"It's still in one piece as far as I can tell."

"So now you're a stone mason?"

Father Marco caught himself before replying. "I suggest you take the remainder of the day off, my dear," he said, hoping his paternal tone masked his exasperation.

"Let me rest a bit. This wooziness is only temporary."

"You shouldn't push yourself."

"I've been in a lot worse situations."

"But you're not a young man anymore."

"I could still give you what for," he said with a cocky air.

Weeks later, fate would give him his chance.

Father Marco allowed himself a grin. If only you knew. "No one said you couldn't."

"Made your diagnosis haven't you?"

"You know it. And you should let a doctor inspect your head." Preferably by one schooled in psychiatry.

"Let's sit here a while longer," he said to stall.

Father Marco joined him on the pew and they made small talk.

Dimitri finally gave in. "Think you can manage this place in my absence?"

"It'll be difficult without you."

Tone-deaf to Father Marco's sarcasm he said, "Don't let the church fall apart while I'm gone."

"We'll miss you."

Dimitri rode a taxi home instead of a bus. Later that day, passengers on the bus celebrated their good fortune.

Father Marco spent the remainder of his day rearranging pews and putting his office back in order. When done, he sprawled out in his office chair, his energy spent. He hadn't felt this drained since chasing frisky nuns around at the start of his ministry.

Aah, the advantage of youth. Age is gaining on me. No matter how much I exercise or how well I eat.

His eyes coasted over his messy desk and noticed a pile of folders he had stacked on it during the cleanup. His chin dropped to his chest and he heaved a weary sigh. You should put those files where they belong. They aren't going to get there by themselves. Maybe the angels will do it for me. Dream on.

Still too beat to move, he resisted the urge to rise. Minutes ticked by; his eyelids grew heavy. Better move or you'll fall asleep, he prodded himself. Hands on the armrests, he pushed himself to his feet, gathered the files in one arm and trudged to the stairs that led to the archives.

The air grew cooler with each step he descended on the stone stairwell into the depths of the medieval church and it revived him. Upon reaching the landing, he strode along a narrow, weakly-lit passageway tailed by his shadow on the rough stone walls, his footsteps ringing out in the subterranean space. He stopped before a secure metal door and keyed himself into the archive with his free hand. A rush of cold, musty air grabbed at him. He groped for the light switch on the wall to his left and flicked it on. While he stood transfixed in the doorway, gripped by a scene of mayhem that stretched to the far wall beyond, he felt a curtain of despair zip across his face. Filing cabinets and shelving units lay toppled over, their contents vomited onto the stone floor.

He groaned inwardly, overcome by the chaos. Now I have to clean up this kuffing mess, pronouncing the gerund of a popular profanity backwards. I'll never finish my sermon on time.

Snapping out of his funk, he picked his way to the center of the archive and unburdened himself of the folders he was carrying. The groined vault room being quite large, the naked overhead bulb laboured mightily but failed to illuminate the entire storage space, surrendering to the shadows in the far corners.

In the feeble light, at the rear of the archive, he noticed a lone filing cabinet leaning at an odd angle. It nabbed his attention. What gives? His curiosity aroused, he crossed the floor to investigate, but halted abruptly several feet away from the cabinet; it had sunken into the floor.

Ho-*lee* Mother! The floor isn't built on solid rock. He puzzled over this for a few beats…Too late to sue the builders, I bet, and he grinned at his own humor.

Out of an abundance of caution, he approached the cabinet on cat feet, testing the floor with each footstep. Assured the floor was firm, he tried to shove the cabinet onto solid ground. It wouldn't budge, not even an inch.

Dammit. Now I'll have to empty it. Like I don't have more important things to do with my kuffing time.

With an air of resignation, he got down to the unenviable task of clearing out the cabinet's drawers of their precious contents, mostly birth and baptismal records and marriage and death certificates, the milestones of people's lives chronicled for posterity on reams of paper and parchment. He spent precious minutes stacking items in neat piles, cursing all the while under his breath. All but the bottom drawer were emptied.

I should be able to budge it now. Here goes…

He gave the metal cabinet a good shove, and it screeched in protest against the friction with the floor as it escaped the hole's maw which had attempted to scarf down more than it could chew. He sniffed at the musty air, then stooped to peer into the gaping cavity. Nothing was discernible in the gloom.

I wonder what's hiding down there. Buried treasure? he kidded himself. Well, you won't discover anything without better lighting.

Possessed with visions of treasure and the opportunity to wrest it from the pit, he ignored the disorder around him and went to fetch a flashlight from Dimitri's storeroom.

With flashlight in hand, he returned to the archive room, chockfull of excitement and with a spark of adventure in his eyes. He knelt before the void and shined the powerful beam of light into the darkness. Dust floated on the conical beam of light which illuminated large chunks of rock on the floor of the cave directly below him. Deciding they were unworthy of further scrutiny, he swung the light beam to his left but failed to discover anything of special interest over there. His initial excitement began to wane. He played the flashlight in the opposite direction, ever hopeful that something of value would be captured in its beam…Nothing…Wait a sec. He ducked deeper into the cave.

"What the hell!"

Without warning, he reeled backwards, almost dropping the flashlight into the hole. Bug-eyed with fright, Father Marco frantically crossed himself, more out of reflex than conviction.

"The legend is true," he murmured aloud. "By God."

## Chapter Three
## Roman Province of Judea – Early First Century CE

The beloved disciple projected an outward appearance of calm. He sat on the edge of the sella, his full attention focused on his visitor, his expectation almost tangible.

"Most Beloved," the scribe continued, "our teacher's life is in mortal danger even as we speak."

He sucked in his breath. "You already received news of the Sanhedrin's decision?"

"I heard it from the teacher himself."

The host threw him an astonished look. "How does he know?"

"The All-Knowing God informed him."

"Of course. How senseless of me."

He gave him an understanding nod. "Our teacher has been accused of sedition, the most serious Roman crime, in revenge for speaking truth to power. He will now suffer the ultimate Roman punishment."

"Crucifixion," the beloved disciple said almost to himself. "We must stop this evil from coming to pass."

The scribe, seeing his fellow disciple's distress, couldn't avoid saying what needed to be said even though doing so would increase his anguish. "Our teacher's sentence is final so we have to accept it."

"There must be something I—we can do. We cannot sit here while our teacher's life remains in jeopardy."

"Our teacher's fate is the will of God."

The beloved disciple sagged on his stool. "This is a heavy burden to bear. All is now lost."

"No," he corrected him. "The revelation cannot be crucified," he said. "The revelation is greater than one man."

"They can kill a righteous man but they cannot kill the message."

"You understand."

The beloved disciple exhaled audibly and his expression suggested he had resigned himself to this fateful outcome. "But how can people be so blind?"

"People put their trust in the 'wisdom' of their leaders instead of seeking the answers themselves because it is easier to have someone else decide for them."

He mulled over these words.

The scribe clapped his hands. "Let us not dwell on these matters any further. They are beyond our control. Let us turn our attention to the matter of this meeting."

"Which is...?"

"You must take a test."

Inclining his head, he said, "A test? What kind of test?"

"Knowledge of the Gospel," was the scribe's plain-spoken answer.

The beloved disciple's throat bobbed, and he shifted his weight on the sella. It was too late to back out.

"Your anxiety is misplaced, Most Beloved. You underwent this examination once before with our teacher in Jerusalem at the outset of his mission. God willing, you shall do well again," he said to encourage him. "We shall cover the fundamental points of Divine Legislation. Time is short. I must be certain a decision I am compelled to make is the correct one."

"What decision?"

"Patience, brother," the scribe counselled him. "Shall we begin?"

"I am ready," he said, but his fretful expression betrayed his true feelings.

The questions came in quick succession, the beloved disciple's answers concise and precise.

"Behold, Most Beloved. Your learning is commendable."

He nodded, but there was no time for self-congratulation because the rapid-fired questions continued. Then the scribe paused, signalling the end of the interrogation was near. Soon enough, he posed the final question. "Lastly, what is the Good News of the M'sheekha?"

The beloved disciple gazed past his interrogator at the fluttering shadows on the walls, silent witnesses to his testimony. "A prophet named *The Praised One* who shall be a mercy unto mankind. From the House of Ishmael he shall come. He shall confirm the M'sheekha's message and his prophethood." Finished, he returned his focus to his brother in religion.

"Well done, Most Beloved. You are ready." The scribe appraised his brother in religion. Praise God. My teacher's ministry will endure through this righteous man. If the M'sheekha's followers cling to the Divine Guidance like a drowning person would a rope and cleave to his way like sheep would a shepherd, Heaven shall be theirs, God willing.

The disciple's shoulders relaxed. His head bowed in humility, he said in a low voice, "Praise to the Almighty for my success." Filled with enthusiasm, he looked up and asked, "So, what is next?"

"Your reward," the scribe replied. He straightened his legs, rubbed them down and then drew them back, talking all the while. "All the mightiest messengers of God left behind a written message to steer their disciples toward the right path. Our father, Prophet Abraham, left the Scrolls, Prophet Moses left the Torah and Prophet David left the Psalms." He paused, but his lips moved without speaking, and the disciple fidgeted, his anticipation irrepressible. Then the scribe locked eyes with him. "The M'sheekha is no exception. You are his most beloved disciple and you offered to help him with no regard for your own safety. I am bequeathing to you his message."

The beloved disciple drew a sharp breath and jerked upright. "The M'sheekha's message." He spoke these words almost in a whisper, but the wonder in his tone was clear and unmistakable.

## Chapter Four
## Istanbul

Father Marco sat on his rump on the cool paving stones deep in the bowels of the church, leaning against a cabinet and thinking, Hell of a shock to find a corpse lying in an ossuary beneath what is supposed to be a solid floor. He stared into the near distance, waiting for an explanation to dawn on the horizon of his mind. The corpse should've been laid to rest in the crypt. But wasn't. Very weird. Mystified, he struggled to make sense of his astonishing discovery.

The answer came to him in a flash of intuition, and he felt pleased with himself. This church must have been constructed over the tomb unknowingly, its location long forgotten, he decided. But his period of self-satisfaction was brief. Not so fast. Someone must have known of this tomb's existence. The legend proves it. This supposition only provoked his curiosity further. But what happened to this knowledge?

Early evening had fallen, signalled by the melodic tones of the *müezzins* soaring high above the profane clamor of the city from a multitude of minarets in swelling waves of sound from every direction. A majestic acapella of otherworldly verses calling the Muslim faithful to the worship of God for the fourth time that day

Allaahu Akbar, Allaahu Akbar
Laa illaaha illallah....

So much history had occurred since the church's construction in the late tenth century people must have forgotten the tomb's location. The Santi Giuseppe church had once belonged to the Greek Orthodox Church before it came under the control of the Roman Catholic Church. This, most likely during the Fourth Crusade of the early thirteenth century when the Crusaders of Catholic Europe, on route to the Holy Land, invaded and sacked Constantinople, the seat of Eastern Orthodox Christianity. The city never recovered as a regional power from this military assault.

And since it was once common practice for Greek Orthodox Christians to store the disinterred bones of their departed loved ones in ossuaries, or bone-boxes, the ossuary's presence beneath his church made historical sense.

Then a couple of centuries later, Constantinople, the imperial seat of the Byzantine Empire, which by this time had been reduced to a mere city-state, was invaded again. In 1453, Mehmet II, the Ottoman sultan, at the youthful age of twenty-one, captured the city after a siege of fifty-three days in behalf of Islam. After this martial victory, he changed the city's name to Istanbul, which became the capital of and the crown jewel in his empire.

With armed conflict roiling through the land across so many centuries, it's no mystery why the location of the tomb was lost in the mists of time.

I wonder whose bones are lying there...Those of a long-forgotten saint? His thoughts drifted and he found himself dreaming a vision of rivers of pilgrims from far and wide streaming their way to his church. But a cold splash of reality doused him, rousing him from his dream state. He turned to the hole and felt a strong urge to investigate. He stared at it, hypnotized. The tomb wasn't deep, about ten feet he estimated. If I lower myself into the tomb, how will I climb out? I don't have wings, so I'll need a ladder. There's one in the storeroom, but Dimitri will have to help me lug it down here.

Stymied, he cycled through feasible methods of accessing the tomb. But it soon dawned on him that his analysis was stuck in a circular track with no clear solution in sight.

Unmindful of the swift passage of the day, Father Marco checked his watch for the first time since the earthquake had struck. Caught unawares by the lateness of the hour, he called it a day.

So damn close and yet so far. Best get my carcass in gear.

Sighing, he rose from the floor with great reluctance and brushed the dust from his soutane. He cast a final look at the mess and told himself tomorrow's another day. I could pray to have the angels clean it up…Who am I kidding? He trudged to the entranceway, flicked off the light, locked the door and made his way upstairs.

While it pulled mightily at his curiosity, the startling discovery he had stumbled upon temporarily lost the tug of war in his mind to yearnings for dinner, prayer and a firm, warm bed. And performing his night-time run, which was long a part of his daily routine, was dismissed outright. He secured his office, eager to go home, the stressful day having taxed him both mentally and physically. As he sped on foot toward his apartment, the strains of the day seeped away. And in spite of the many responsibilities competing for his attention, he couldn't help but revisit the highlight of his day.

I wonder if I should contact the Vatican...Maybe I should wait until I know who's buried in the tomb. Leaves stirred in the evening breeze while he raced along the tree-lined street washed with faint electric light. Yeah. No sense stirring an empty pot. Wouldn't want those bone collectors in Rome to slobber over nothing. The deceased was likely nobody important anyway.

## Chapter Five
## Roman Province of Judea – Early First Century CE

Time seemed suspended while a tense silence gripped the dimly-lit room. The scribe let the silence stretch as he reached into the folds of his clothing and retrieved a thick scroll while the beloved disciple, watching with unbridled anticipation, squirmed on his sella, eyes riveted on his visitor. The scribe looked down at the scroll with adoration.

"You carried our teacher's message in your heart these past few years. Now you shall carry it in your hand." Without solemnity or ceremony, he held out the scroll to the host who gawked at it with what could only be reverence.

"Do not be afraid. Take hold of it," he urged, relief detectable in his tone, glad to unburden himself of a heavy charge.

Overcoming his trepidation, the beloved disciple wiped his sweaty palms on his cloak and accepted the roll of vellum, so humble in appearance and yet so inestimable in value.

"The M'sheekha is the final prophet and messenger of the House of Israel and so his message is recorded for posterity," the scribe said while the beloved disciple, in the thralls of religious awe, handled the scroll delicately, a priceless treasure, almost too precious for the touch of human hands. "We cannot allow the M'sheekha's message to be corrupted, as what happened to the Torah and for which purpose the M'sheekha was sent by God to denounce and correct."

Though distracted, the host followed the flow of conversation. "This is an enormous responsibility. I'm-I'm honored you have chosen me bu—"

"Brother, you are more than equal to this task." He held his tongue to let his brother in religion process this unexpected development. To this praise, he added, "You are the most beloved disciple. You have believed in our teacher since his declaration of his being the M'sheekha. Thus, you have been entrusted with this responsibility."

He beamed with appreciation. "May I always be worthy of such trust, if God wills." Then he posed an obvious question. "What am I to do with this scroll?"

"You are the Keeper of the Revelation now and so your sacred duty is to guard it. With your life," the scribe said and, with these ominous words, he hoped to convey the enormity of what was expected of his fellow disciple.

"With my life," the beloved disciple repeated, his countenance grave. He lowered his head and affected to scrutinize the scroll.

The scribe missed nothing. "Trust in the Almighty and seek His help." As an afterthought, he instructed, "Do not read the scroll until after our teacher's crucifixion."

The beloved disciple signaled his obedience, then he sat up straight. "O scribe of the M'sheekha, why do the people reject our teacher and his message, a message that is so lucid to us?"

The scribe stared at the writhing shadows projected on the far wall, pondered the statement, then returned his gaze to his host. "The burden of tradition lies heavy on people's consciences and a blinkered trust in their religious leaders deters them from the straight path. It is no easy undertaking to forsake the beliefs and customs of one's forefathers," he answered.

Demonstrating that he understood, the beloved disciple said, "To walk the familiar path is always easier than to take the path unknown though it might be the right one."

The scribe struck his knees with his hands. "Yes! That is why our Lord sent us the M'sheekha—to show us the right way."

He considered this. "But one requires a good dose of courage and effort to follow him."

"If you wish to have peace in this life and the next life, be on good terms with your Lord. Believe in Him, His prophets and master your desires."

"What is to happen to us after...after—" His voice cracked, the words wedged in his throat.

"After his crucifixion?" the scribe asked.

"Yes," he breathed out.

"You and your brethren are to preach his message to the House of Israel in every nation."

"*Truly?*" He couldn't believe his ears and his mood brightened. "Our teacher's mission endures!"

"Do not be disheartened that your fellows will scorn you," the scribe cautioned. "Your sole duty is to convey the Good News to the people of Israel. It is God who leads hearts to His way."

"You can lead a camel to water but you cannot make it drink."

"Precisely." He weighed his next words carefully. "Most Beloved, please do not divulge this information. Our teacher shall inform our brethren in due time."

"What about our enemies? Won't they remain a nettle in our path?"

"You and your brothers should have nothing to fear from them. It is our teacher with whom they are fixated."

"Why does our teacher not flee Jerusalem to save his life? Moses fled Egypt to escape the Pharaoh."

"The M'sheekha is not like Moses. God has a different plan for our teacher and it will be accomplished before the coming Sabbath."

"Our teacher's enemies cannot triumph in this matter," he said.

"Time is short. Our teacher's days on this earth are not long." Noticing his brother's despondency, he leaned forward, grasped his shoulder and said to him in a cheerful tone, "All shall be well, God willing. Trust in the Lord thy God. He who is without faith is lost and empty."

The beloved disciple hung his head. "O scribe of the M'sheekha, it stings my heart to know our teacher's passage on this earth is soon at an end."

"He does not do his own will but the will of the One who sent him."

"We must trust in God's wisdom however inscrutable it is to us," and he sniffled.

"May God bless your tears for they are shed not for your sake but for God's prophet."

He shook off the scribe's sympathy. "The shedding of tears is better than the shedding of blood."

"All who take the sword will perish by the sword." To console him, the scribe asked, "Do you recall our teacher's lesson on Father Abraham's aborted sacrifice of his first-born son, Ishmael, in the sacred valley of Bakkah?"

"How could I forget it?" he replied as he dabbed his tears with the sleeve of his garment.

"Hold on to it." He further counselled, "Though the water's surface may appear placid to our eyes, we do not know what peril lurks below it. Trust the word of the good person but verify the word of the evil person. You shall tell the difference by the fruits each one bears."

"There is plenty of rotten fruit in our midst."

Changing subjects, the scribe said, "I require your help with vital arrangements for the crucifixion."

"God prevent me from denying you any request." Once he heard his brother's wishes, he pledged, "God willing, all shall be ready when the hour is full."

He pointed to the beloved disciple's heart and said, "The M'sheekha shall always be with you in here." Then he rose from his seat in a hurry. "It is late. I must leave now," he announced.

The host's eyes turned up to the scribe. "So soon?"

"Dawn is nearly upon us. I cannot be seen here for both our sakes. So I must take my leave."

"Of course." With great reluctance, he got up and extinguished the lamp with a strong breath of air. Once more, darkness pounced and reconquered the room. He sidled to the door and opened it wide enough to poke his head out. He withdrew it and whispered, "The passageway is clear."

They approached each other in the murk and embraced. Instead of a brief clinch, the scribe held his brother in a tight hug and breathed puffs of warm air into his ear as he rasped: "Most Beloved, wicked men shall strive to destroy the message of the scroll for it is the Divine criterion for distinguishing good from evil and it identifies the final prophet to come before the Day of Reckoning. Keep it close and protect it with your life. Seek the Almighty's help in adversity *and* in comfort." The scribe released him and parted with "May God be with you." No time to spare, he whirled and set off, not waiting for a reply.

While the scribe scurried down the road, his retreating figure merging with the somber night, the beloved disciple, crestfallen with the knowledge of his teacher's imminent demise, ducked back into his home and bolted the door.

The die, indeed, is cast, he thought.

The silent darkness of the room and the scribe's dire warning still buzzing in his ears set him off. He paced back and forth in a pall of gloom to calm himself while he unscrambled his thoughts. Then, he must have realized he still clasped the scroll in his right hand for he stopped pacing and raised the scroll to eye level. Although he couldn't see it, he beheld it with a mixture of reverence and fear.

More—much more—than mere words scrawled on a length of parchment, the scroll was holy revelation from the Eternal One. A Divine corpus of numinous verses whose untold power could lift a man to the heights of heroism, or lower him to the depths of depravity. Verses that people would die for—and kill for!

His disquiet aroused, he sensed unstoppable forces had been set in motion. And he was caught up in their momentum, powerless to escape it. Where the momentum carried him to, he could not imagine. One thing he did know: this was only the beginning and whatever lay ahead—danger, wickedness, even reward—would arrive in its own time, according to the Almighty's own plan.

# Chapter Six
# Roman Province of Judea – Early First Century CE

Clouds broiled and scudded across the somber gray-metal sky above while wind-churned dust blew in strong gusts over the barren hilltop below called *Gol'gotha*—the place of the skull—a desolate wasteland where any hope for an immediate and merciful termination of life was doomed to die aborning. As a matter of custom, death by crucifixion was administered in this bleak locale, but on this auspicious day, Heaven and Earth were silent witnesses to an act of calculated barbarity unique in its savagery. A savagery not remotely joined to the word justice, neither in its meaning nor in its dispensation despite receiving the legal sanction of both secular and religious authorities.

It was a day that tested mankind's faith in a just God as it was a day in which God tested man's belief in what was just. Rome's demonstration of its monopoly on violence expressed through an act of brutality was on bold display for all to see, a warning to those who housed sedition within their breasts. On the peak of the hill, three criminals were cruelly affixed to crosses and a hostile mob had gathered to condemn the crucified. The man suspended in agony from the center cross drew the lion's share of the spectators' rage.

For several hours, participants in this violent spectacle taunted and jeered the "King of the Jews" but the man studiously ignored their hostility for he was consumed by a vision of his reward in Heaven promised him by his Lord. But for his fettered hands, he desired to reach out and grasp the otherworldly vision he saw before him. Longing for his Lord filled his weakened heart. At the limit of his endurance, he strained to raise his heavy head one last time and his blood-caked lips parted as he gathered his remaining strength to voice a final prayer. His lips moved but the sound of his words were carried away on the wind, known only to his Lord.

The tortured man on the Cross uttered a death rattle and died, a peaceful smile upon his beaten face. Taunts and jeers soon faded away to a sullen, merciful end. His tormentors moiled while the wind howled and the dust swirled. The spectacle ended, their pent-up bloodlust apparently sated and with nothing more to do, the once-hostile multitude dispersed. Above the constant shriek of the wind, the crunch of countless feet on the gravelly landscape could be heard as the army of tormentors filed off the hill into ignominy.

All the while, at a remove from the crowd, Nicodemus and Joseph of Arimathea, secret disciples of the M'sheekha, their cloaks billowing, their hair blowing and their eyes stinging from wind-borne grit, stood, observing the pitiless tableau before them, pretending to be impartial spectators. The bloodied, battered body of their teacher now sagged on the wooden cross, his life force liberated from the wanton humiliation and persecution he had so stoically endured.

Nicodemus blamed himself for his teacher's fate. As a member of the Sanhedrin, he had recommended to the High Priest that Jesus be given a trial. The High Priest heeded his recommendation. But it hadn't been enough. The trial had been a mockery of justice. And now this sacrilege.

"Peculiar."

"What's peculiar?" Joseph asked.

Realizing he had been thinking out loud, Nicodemus gave him a self-conscious look. He returned his gaze to the crowd. "I do not see any disciples in the front ranks of the mob. Do you?"

Joseph, the taller of the two, peered intently at the boiling mass of humanity. "I do not see any of our brethren present. It is just as well. That bloodthirsty mob is a danger to any supporter of our teacher."

"Peculiar all the same," he said, mystified. He let the matter drop.

They remained rooted in place until the summit emptied of their teacher's cruel and vicious persecutors. But a shrouded woman lingered behind, and the hood of her modest robe covered her head, hindering disclosure of her identity. She approached the body impaled on the center cross in small steps and halted before it. With a trembling hand, she reached out, then stopped in mid-air. But her desire for consolation overcame her hesitation, and she caressed the bloodied feet of the crucified man. Her head bowed in prayer, she stood a few moments in this pose. Her head tilted up to him one last time, her expression perhaps a mask of pain and sorrow, then she ambled away.

Nicodemus and Joseph crept toward the cross, eyes on the ground, afraid a bolt from Heaven above would strike them dead for not rescuing their teacher in his hour of need. However, in spite of their fear of Divine retribution, they reached the Cross in safety and stared up at their crucified teacher, his peaceful countenance belying the dreadful torment he had borne with bravery and without protest.

They bowed their heads together in prayer and beseeched the Almighty to accept the martyrdom of their teacher. Having secured permission from Roman authorities in advance, they set about the difficult task of removing his lacerated and lifeless body from the Cross, their effort little short of heroic. They worked on in silence, each lost in his own private fugue.

With delicate fingers, Joseph, in a state of profound anguish, pried the crown of thorns from the M'sheekha's head and flung it away as though it were cursed. The barbed circlet tumbled along the flank of the hill when, unexpectedly, a strong updraft snatched it and carried it away into oblivion.

Done, with tenderness in their hearts, they wrapped their teacher in fine white linen. Their mouths set in a grim line, befitting the mood of the scene, Nicodemus and Joseph glanced around one last time at the desolation in their midst, and their red-rimmed eyes met over the corpse, expressing the silent affirmation that a grave injustice had been committed. An injustice they had been powerless to thwart. Focused once more on their task, they lifted the shrouded body of the M'sheekha and, with solemnity, carried it off the all but deserted hill for the journey to its final place of eternal rest.

So they witnessed. So they believed.

## Chapter Seven
## Istanbul

The alarm went off in his head like a siren and jolted Father Marco awake from a deep sleep. He groped around for the off button and pressed it. Once more, silence reclaimed its rightful place in his peaceful domain. He was usually up before the alarm sounded, but he had gone to bed late last night to put his home back in order. His apartment, particularly the kitchen, had received a good rattling courtesy of the earthquake.

He lay in bed, stretching and yawning, and he wrung from his body the final vestiges of sleep. There had been dreams, vivid dreams. Memories of skeletons chasing him faded as his mind cleared. He whipped off the sheets, swung his long legs onto the floor and sat on the edge of the bed in his underwear while he waited for his blood circulation to stabilize. Yesterday's discovery seemed far away and had lost its sense of urgency.

The early morning sun was tracing its predictable amber arc in the sky and so thin yellow sunlight peeked around the edges of the bedroom curtains, providing ample glow for him to discern his surroundings. Still not fully awake, Father Marco, chin in his hands, appraised his spartan room. A bed, a bureau and a night table. He was, like this room, a modest man shorn of finery. And pretty much everything else. Such was the life of a priest. But, overall, he was content with his lot. His primary needs of food, clothing, comfortable shelter and meaningful life's work—scratch that—and a job were met. Anything more was superfluous...and worth pining for in moments of weakness.

Done commiserating with himself, he got out of bed and stretched to limber up his lean, muscular frame. As always, he started his morning workout with a hundred push-ups, varying the width of his arms at specific intervals to alter the impact on his pectoral muscles. After a short break, he performed fifty sit-ups. Then he did a hundred deep knee bends, widening his stance every twenty-five reps to stress his quadriceps in different positions. Hanging from a bar he had installed in the doorjamb of his room, he finished his exercises with sets of chin-ups. Through with the calisthenics, he wrapped up his exercise program with multiple series of Kung Fu kicks and punches and their combinations, pretending to strike invisible enemies with his quick hands and feet. Never know when a parishioner might take issue with something he had preached. His workout completed, he shuffled toward the bathroom.

A brief shower refreshed him and a foamy shave pruned the salt and pepper whiskers which had sprouted like tiny cactus needles overnight. He wiped away the condensation from the mirror, his neutral reflection stared back at him. He studied his face. Several white hairs colored his temples and faint frown lines creased his forehead. Not bad for a middle-aged man, he judged. Stop it! He thought about reciting a brief prayer of repentance but dismissed the idea. A little vanity never hurt anyone.

Ever conspicuous, a long pink scar on his left cheek, a mark of honor he had once called it when he was a member of the 167 gang, named after a street in the Morrisania section of the Bronx, had earned him the nickname Scarface. Though decades had passed, the incident was still fresh in his memory and, without warning, his ruminations drifted back to that fateful day.

"Marco," his mother called to him. "Marco," she called again, but louder.

"What is it, Mama?" he asked as he entered the bright, cheery kitchen adorned with floral-patterned wallpaper. The spicy aroma of simmering pasta sauce pervaded the air and an oldies tune played on the radio. His mother spent most of her time in this cozy space whether she was preparing meals or not. Maybe it was because she and his father used to sit here while they enjoyed a glass of home-made vino after most dinners. A place where they talked and laughed and occasionally argued—typical behaviour of a married couple. While his father had been alive. Good memories. But just memories now. His mother said she often felt his presence in this room, the supposed heart of their home. If this were true, then she was the vital force that gave life to this heart.

"Why didn't you answer me the first time?" She was much shorter than he. Her glossy black hair, now streaked with silver, was tied in a ponytail which was the way she wore it while cooking. Age was taking its inevitable toll on her. The passage of time had etched wrinkles into her smooth, fair complexion like moving water carving lines on a sandy shoreline. She was still pretty, though.

"I was watching the Lincoln movie.

"Again?" She stopped chopping carrots and looked at him with amazement. "You've watched that movie so many times you should be able to recite it from memory."

"I can't get enough of his speeches. I wish I could write like him."

"We don't have the money to send you to college."

"I will prepare and someday my chance will come." He put his arm around her. "At least I earn enough money from my job at the warehouse to keep us alive."

"You're a good son."

He gave his mom a squeeze before releasing her.

"It's time to bring Maria home from the church. Her catechism class finishes in half an hour," she said without looking at him, her attention returned to chopping the carrots on the wooden block.

"I can tell *time*. You don't have to remind me."

"No cheekiness, young man."

"Sorry, Mama."

"It's a long way, so you should get moving."

"I suppose," and he bent over to kiss the cheek she offered to him.

In the short hallway off the kitchen, he grabbed his jacket from the hook on the wall before he exited the apartment. He didn't need it to protect himself from the elements but to serve as a warning to those who weren't members of his notorious 167 gang. The colors of his jacket enjoyed an intimidating reputation in the neighborhood but they also conferred a sense of belonging. His gang was a band of brothers who watched each other's back. Oddly, his gang didn't deal in drugs or petty crime. It dealt in retribution.

A few years ago, he and his friends from the local martial arts club had formed a gang to keep drugs out of their neighborhood after the sister of one of them had OD'd. She was only seventeen at the time. In spite of their do-goodism, the 167 wasn't above breaking the law. A rival gang's drug den burnt to the ground for no explicable reason. Gang-bangers awakened from a beating to find their arms or legs broken. Unofficially, the 167 were championed by the police who were stretched thin in the Bronx. The aluminum screen door banged shut on his way out.

He rounded the corner of his street and hustled north on Park Avenue, which formed the western border of the 167's turf. Few rivals dared cross it. His long legs ate up the distance between his home and the church beneath a robin's-egg blue sky dotted with cotton-candy clouds. Along the way, he passed many childhood landmarks, but they were grittier, grayer, much like the people in his neighborhood, who yearned for something or someone to rescue them from further decrepitude. He soon arrived at a set of cement stairs, which rose to the stout, weather-beaten oak doors of The Our Lady of Fatima Church, where he plunked himself down and waited.

He hadn't attended Mass in several years. After his father passed away, he stopped attending. Why was anyone's guess. He wasn't able to explain it to himself let alone to his mother, who pestered him about it on occasion. Maybe he was angry with God. Father Tony had counseled him and his sister to pray real hard to the Virgin Mary for his father's recovery. Their prayers had been in vain. His father died of lung cancer, anyway. So much for the power of prayer.

A familiar voice called to him, interrupting his reminisces. Just his luck. He shifted sideways. "Hi, Father Tony," he greeted the parish priest over his shoulder. His real name was Antonio, but he never corrected anyone, so the name must be fine with him.

"Marco, how are you, my son?" he asked, sincerity in his tone. He stood by the open door while the young catechumens scurried out of the building as though it were on fire.

"I'm fine. How's church business?" he kidded.

"The Lord is offering a special deal with no expiration date. In exchange for belief in His son, Jesus Christ the Redeemer, He will reward you with eternal life. You should consider it," Father Tony said above the clamor with a toothy grin which belied the concern he held for Marco.

"Let me think about it, Father," he replied with no intention of doing so.

"Marco," his sister squealed at the sight of her big brother as she spilled out of the church onto the wide front concrete porch. Maria, almost twelve, outfitted in a girlish floral-printed dress, was dearest to his heart. He gazed upon her with fraternal affection. She resembled their mama when she was that age. Her dark, curly, shoulder-length hair and long eyelashes were hallmarks of a future packed with pimply wannabe boyfriends. He didn't look forward to that day. He did his best to keep his little sister safe ever since the death of their dear father.

"Hi, Sweet Peach," he replied, using the pet name he had given her years ago.

"Take care, Father Tony," he said, and Maria echoed the same words of farewell.

Marco took his sister's small hand in his own and they began their journey home. Maria prattled on about the catechism she had learned and commented on the antics of her fellow catechumens. His mind wandered and his sister's monologue faded in and out of his reverie while they meandered the length of the avenue at the pace of her short stride. A tug on his arm broke his dreaming.

"Marco," she whispered. "Are you enemies with those two scary-looking men on the other side of the street? They're following us."

She was about to point to them but Marco spied the "men" out of the corner of his eye and stopped her short with a stern warning. His sister referred to any tall boys as men. He appraised them without drawing their attention. They could be young men, but in his world, *punkheads* was the proper term to describe the two satanic-looking individuals shadowing him from across the avenue.

He affected not to notice them and paused in his tracks. His well-honed street smarts, always on alert when he tramped the mean streets of his neighborhood, were clanging like church bells on Christmas day now. The punkheads also stopped walking, and their Mohawks, assorted tattoos and painful-looking facial piercings projected evil vibes.

Thinking quickly, he invented an excuse to convince his sister to return to the church without frightening her. "I'll meet you there in a few minutes." He watched her stroll away. The church was only a city block back in the direction from which they had traipsed. Maria twirled around a few times to wave; he waved back at her. In his peripheral vision, he saw the punkheads cutting across the avenue toward him, each Mohawk knifing the air like the scimitar of a great white's dorsal fin slicing through water.

Looks like trouble coming my way. Damn. I'll have to teach it a hard lesson. All. Over. Again.

He didn't recognize them, and he congratulated them for their nerve, or stupidity, or both. Whatever. They had made their choice to cross an invisible red line in the neighborhood. Maybe they were aware of it and maybe they weren't. Either way, it didn't matter. They would pay the price for their trespass in a currency possibly foreign to them: pain. Unluckily for them, no refunds were permitted in this transaction and he intended to do his damnedest to ensure this outcome. He had never run from danger in the past and he wasn't about to now.

Let them move first, he decided. Self-defense is the best offense in a street fight.

"Yo, salami breath," the taller of the two called out to him from a few yards away, his lips curled back in a snarl, and his spiked hair—bright green tipped with orange—betrayed a repressed desire to be reincarnated in the guise of a man-sized DayGlo porcupine.

Marco ignored the taunt and instead focused on their non-verbal communication. Man, what a dentist would give to have a go at this mutt's rotten chops...? His first born?

"Yo, spaghetti breath. You deaf *and* dumb?" the other said, trying to catch his attention, which wasn't too difficult since he suffered from the same disorder afflicting his pal.

And definitely his second born to tackle this gapped-tooth black-holed orifice. Must be the sidekick, Twiddle Dumb.

They approached contact range when Marco replied, "I'm neither deaf nor dumb, you mutants. I was struggling to decide which one of you is the freakiest." He broke it to them politely. "Sorry. It's a tie." His sarcasm caused them to halt inches beyond the range of his feet, not that they were paying attention to such things. Probably not. Their bravado vanished. Their tactics of intimidation (if that is what they were) were having no outward effect on him. But it was two against one and these odds typically emboldened bullies.

"Whatcha doin' in our hood, salami breath?" the taller one asked, cracking his knuckles.

Marco stood his ground, not saying a word, never taking his eyes off them. He adopted the fighting stance learned at the club.

"Arencha gonna answer, spaghetti breath?" the shorter one challenged over the shoulder of his larger partner.

Marco didn't react. He stared at them, his silence making them jittery.

Done with posturing, the taller one lunged and spat out the words, "I'm gonna teach y—" but Marco lashed out with a vicious right circle kick to his aggressor's left knee trailed by a devastating right palm strike to the left side of his skull to cut short the threat. The thug punctuated his interrupted threat with an agonizing scream before he crumpled bonelessly into an unconscious heap.

"With malice toward none, with charity for all—except you." Marco returned to the fighting stance.

The shorter one, aware now he was no match for Marco, opened a switchblade, and advanced on him, slashing the air with the knife.

Marco danced around, desperate to keep his distance from the lethal weapon. Unexpectedly, someone screaming his name broke his concentration. Out of reflex, he torqued his head in the direction from which he heard his sister's shrill voice. He realized his error and turned back to square-off with his opponent. Too late. The knifepoint approached the left side of his face in slow motion, and he tilted his jaw to avoid the blade but the tip caught him, cutting his face from cheek to chin.

His assailant dithered, guessing Marco was done for. That was the second mistake he had made in his sad short life. Being born was the first. A spinning reverse round kick to his skull was the last thing the shorter one saw before a shroud of darkness descended upon him.

"Here's a news flash, you worthless scumbags. I hate salami," Marco bellowed at their unconscious forms, adrenaline surging through his arteries with each beat of his heart.

Something burned and tickled his left cheek. He threw his hand to it, which felt warm and slippery. He withdrew his hand, smeared with blood. The cut was deep, but it hadn't sliced through his cheek. He ran toward his sister, leaving a trail of bloody blotches in his wake on the cracked and weed-choked sidewalk.

With a few yards remaining, he staggered toward the church steps where he collapsed in pain, the adrenaline receding in his bloodstream. Maria ran to get Father Tony while Marco lay on his back and stared upwards, wondering why the blue sky above was becoming darker by the moment. He experienced the weightless sensation of falling backwards down a deep, dark hole as he watched the circle of light above him recede to a pinprick. Then all was black.

A car horn jerked Father Marco and recalled him from his contemplation of the irretrievable past. In hindsight, he acknowledged the street fight had been a catalyst for something good. It had been one of those incidents whose consequences shoved his destiny onto a different and, ultimately, more life-affirming vector. So it seemed at the time.

From that day forward, his life advanced in a more constructive direction, not in a spurt, but in half-starts. A constant reminder of his former gang life, the scar was also a touchstone of when he had been saved…and almost carved up like a Christmas turkey. He smiled at himself in the mirror, pleased with what his Creator had fashioned.

A face only my mother could love. May Our Lady's blessings be upon her soul, he prayed.

Done reminiscing, he combed his springy hair into place, wielding his comb with deft strokes to put the final touches on his morning ritual. The result was…He had trouble putting a word to it…Satisfactory came to mind. Satisfactory? Why not handsome? he judged after critical appraisal.

Fresh-faced and revived, he donned his faded plaid bathrobe and padded his way barefoot to his cramped kitchen, slippers unnecessary in his penny-wise world. The space was aglow with amber sunlight.

No curtains were hung for no neighbors fronted his apartment. Heated by the sun's gilded rays, the floor felt toasty beneath the soles of his bare feet.

He flicked on the radio and prepared his usual breakfast fare while listening to the morning news. With a full cup of coffee in one hand and a plate in the other, he walked a couple of steps to the table, pulled out a chair with his foot, set down his cup and plate, sat, crossed himself, and hungrily tucked into his morning feast, the aroma of fresh coffee, fried eggs and raisin toast having sharpened his appetite.

He attacked the food on his plate as though he were a prisoner on death row eating his last meal. Several minutes later, the hunger in his belly satisfied, he sat back and gazed at the empty chair across from him, a vacant look in his eyes.

Quit dreaming, you deluded fool. So long as you wear a priest's robe, you'll never see *her* in that chair.

He blinked and dropped his gaze to the yellow stain on his plate, the stain's color fading as it hardened. Dishes here I come. He sighed and moved away from the table. The dishes washed, he left them to drip-dry in the rack. Drying them by hand was such a waste of precious time.

He paid another visit to the bathroom where he took care of dental hygiene. Done, he returned to the bedroom and made his bed. That out of the way, he changed into his clerical attire, a traditional black soutane, ready for another day of managing the affairs of his church and congregation.

He was about to leave when he remembered the lunch he had prepared last night. Revisiting the kitchen, he grabbed the paper bag from the fridge. The *Hürriyet Daily News* was waiting for him when he opened his door. He tossed the bundled newspaper inside, secured his apartment, and descended the stairs to the street. He opened the main door of his residence and his senses awakened to the commotion of his city as it roared back to life.

With long quick strides, he made his way on foot to his church which was several blocks west of where he lived. Try as he might, he found it impossible to stroll. Whenever he walked, he felt he was racing, but against who or what he couldn't determine. Despite his characteristic hurry, he enjoyed the ritual of his morning walk. The best part of his day he called it. Because it was that part of the day he wasn't working.

He used the brief walk to reflect on the day ahead and to savor the pulsing energy and splendid sights of his adopted city. Engines, big and small, heaved up and over the clogged and hilly streets of Old Istanbul, a familiar, if not frenzied, racket in the morning punctuated by the beep of a vehicle or the lowing boom of a horn bellowing from one of the many freighters he could see plying the busy shipping lanes in the choppy Sea of Marmara a few hundred yards south. In the sunlit sky above, gulls hovered, squawking like a bunch of crybabies.

Nothing a round of birdshot couldn't silence.

He smiled and nodded at several men sitting on footstools on the sidewalk in front of their tourist agency enjoying a smoke. Despite the Islamic prohibition on smoking (it was considered a form of slow suicide), Turks were heavy smokers. He guessed no one had informed them. They returned his greeting, taking no notice he was a priest.

Although Turkey is a Muslim country, religious pluralism is a fact of life here. Say one thing about the Turks, they aren't religious fanatics. He never worried about his church being firebombed by racist locals or being terrorized by well-armed, red-neck bikers like mosques were back home. Only a country descending into fascism could consider the latter a form of free speech. Those who deny freedom to others deserve it not for themselves. Stomping jackboots on parade can't be far behind back in the homeland.

In his twenty-odd years in Istanbul, he had seen plenty of changes. When he first arrived in the late nineties, he could be forgiven for thinking Turkey wasn't an Islamic country. Not a hijab was in sight on the streets of Istanbul. Turkish women dressed every bit as nakedly as women back home did. Curious how the less clothing a woman wears the more liberated and empowered she feels. Progress! He shrugged his head as if to say, "Woman, thy name is Mystery."

With the election of Ordekan, first as prime minister in 2003 then as president in 2014, the country began a slow process of Islamicization. Modest Islamic dress and morals came back in vogue. Father Marco couldn't help but notice female Turkish Muslims dressed more like the depictions of the Virgin Mary than did the women of his own Catholic flock.

If he had to guess, he'd say over fifty percent of women now wore hijabs in Turkey. And those that didn't chose to dress modestly. It was quite a change for a supposedly secular country. And it was a change the old guard from the former military dictatorship tried to undo in the U.S.-backed coup several years ago. The U.S. regime, pumped up with hubris and shoddy intelligence, underestimated the mood of the Turkish people when it tried to overthrow their democratically-elected leader, President Ordekan. But the wily president outfoxed the disloyal leaders of the coup and roared back to power on a wave of popular support, both military and civilian. There was no going back to a U.S. puppet regime.

The Turks admire their economic prosperity and democratic rights which they attribute to the return to their country's Islamic roots. Father Marco planned to stay in Istanbul when he retired. It was a green and modern cosmopolitan city. He had no interest in returning to a racially and politically-divided banana republic ruled by a clique of merciless plutocrats who pulled politicians strings behind the scenes.

Halfway into his walk, Father Marco passed a tall row of Ottoman houses squeezed together like books on a shelf. No matter how many times he passed by them, he admired how these nineteenth-century structures were grounded on a bottom floor constructed of stone atop of which were built one or two stories fabricated from wood that projected out over the street or sidewalk. This unique architectural feature, called a *çikma* (pronounced chikma), offered an enclosed balcony whose windows were covered with wooden lattice covers, or *kafesler*, so female occupants of the house might enjoy the fresh air without passersby below observing them. This, to preserve the Islamic strictures of modesty. Too expensive to maintain and insure by private individuals, many of these homes had been repurposed as boutique hotels.

His appreciation of Ottoman architecture was interrupted, for rounding the final corner of his short journey, he came in sight of his hulking church. It soared high above the adjacent buildings, and its weathered hand-hewn stonework blackened by centuries of polluted air spoke to its antiquity. An exemplar of the traditional Byzantine basilica plan, the church's aesthetic comprised an apse, a transept, a nave, side aisles, a narthex and an atrium courtyard. Everything about the church's architecture imparted a devotion to a higher purpose.

The central building was two stories high with a gable roof bracketed by one-storied wings topped with sloping roofs. A pleasant vista, both visually and spiritually, it was his sanctuary from the brass ring bandwagon race of the secular world.

Father Marco entered the church from a side door in the north transept, which gained him quicker access to his office. He noticed the lights weren't on and deduced Dimitri had followed his advice and booked a sick day, or he was playing hide-and-seek. Father Marco bet on the former.

I'm glad he listened to me. But this means I'll have to delay my archeological quest for at least another day, he grumbled. A selfish inclination infected his mind. You could always call Dimitri and try to make him feel guilty. He did insist on staying yesterday. The more Father Marco thought it about, the less he hated himself. In the end, he counseled himself to be patient. Since the ossuary wasn't about to disappear, he went to work on his Sunday sermon.

The routine activity of pastoral work distracted him and soon he forgot about the unidentified corpse reposing nearby. The morning hours passed like minutes. He glanced up at the clock on his office wall and reckoned it was time to check on the state of Dimitri's health.

Don't want him to assume I've forgotten him. Though there are times I'd like to.

Retrieving the phone from its cradle, he dialed Dimitri's number. He tapped his fingers on the desk while the phone rang. Several ringtones later his wife answered.

"Hi, Anna."

"Father Marco?"

"The one and only. How's Dimitri?"

"He's resting right now. He has a headache. The doctor said he suffered a mild concussion. Nothing to worry about. A few days' rest should help him get well. Is this a problem for you, Father?"

He detected a nervous edge in her voice. Heaven's no. I have a corpse in the archives of my church I'm dying to investigate but can't because *your* husband took an untimely spill. "Please tell him to rest and return to work when he's ready. May Our Lady bless him with health and healing."

She expressed her gratitude to him then whispered in confidence, "Between you and me, Dimitri's afraid of losing his job."

"Seriously?"

"He worries you might judge him too old to manage the church."

A clairvoyant flash lit up Father Marco's mind. "So that explains wh—" He caught himself.

"Explains what, Father?"

Explains why Dimitri didn't want my help after he took that tumble. "Uh, nothing important. I was thinking out loud. Please tell Dimitri his job is waiting for him."

"He'll be so reassured when I tell him."

He heard relief in her voice. "Anything else I can do?"

"Please pray for Dimitri's recovery, Father."

"I most surely will. God be with you, Anna." He cradled the instrument. I guess my wish to be Indiana Jones will to have wait, he chuckled to himself. Remembering Anna's comment about Dimitri, he made a note to himself to compose some confidence-building words he would say to him when he returned. Words such as: Keep your balance. Stay on your feet.

He resumed editing his Sunday sermon.

That should do it and he withdrew his hands from the keyboard. A glow of contentment on his face, he leaned back in his chair, elbows resting on the armrests. As was his habit, he steepled his fingers and seized the moment to reflect. Lord, may my work be pleasing to You and may it resonate with the needs and concerns of my congregation. And if not, well, too bad.

A rumbling in his stomach communicated he had missed lunch. He retrieved his bag from the fridge and arranged its contents on his cluttered desk. His meal was a modest affair, comprising two chicken and lettuce sandwiches, an apple and, for dessert, *sekerpare*, a round Turkish pastry with an almond on top, his one indulgence. He stared absentmindedly at his computer screen, listening to the sound of crispy lettuce being masticated.

Several bites into his sandwich later, the email icon on the computer taskbar blinked, indicating the receipt of new messages. He roused himself from his gastronomically-induced trance.

What now?

Father Marco clutched the mouse and clicked on the icon to restore the application window on the desktop. The email program, a proprietary software program that encrypted incoming and outgoing messages, protected the communications of the Holy See. He entered his password and personal identification number to gain access to his Inbox. He scanned the list of messages, seeking those that required his immediate consideration.

An email *monitum*, or warning, issued by *The Congregation for the Doctrine of the Faith* grabbed his attention. This august dicastery, or department, of the Roman Curia is the oldest and, many would opine, most notorious, for its original name was *The Supreme Sacred Congregation of the Roman and Universal Inquisition*, founded by Pope Paul III in 1542. In the late 1580s, Pope Sixtus V, a doctrinaire theologian, expanded the powers of this dicastery such that ordinary Italians of his era joked he wouldn't pardon Christ himself.

Established to spearhead the violent Counter-Reformation begun in 1545 against Protestantism, this department now promotes orthodox Catholic doctrine and safeguards the integrity of the

Catholic faith from heresy, both within and outwith the Church. Words, not swords, are now its weapons of persuasion.

Reluctance and curiosity vied for Father Marco's attention. Curiosity won. He clicked on the email link.

"Dear Brothers and Sisters in Faith" it began.

> The sacred mission of the Congregation for the Doctrine of the Faith is to propagate and protect Catholic doctrine in the whole Catholic world. To this end, the dicastery is committed to ensuring the doctrine upon which the Catholic faith rests is practiced and promoted, both in words and in deeds, by Church officers.
>
> Catholic doctrine has come under attack from both within and outwith since its adoption. And the Church has withstood these attacks whether through renewal or refutation. Once again, the Church confronts a grave crisis, a crisis that undermines the doctrine of our faith. The crisis is this: Our faith rests upon the doctrine enshrined in the epistles of St. Paul, the Apostle of the nations. The integrity of this doctrine has been challenged in the past but without lasting nor damaging effect. Until now. Michael Giltmore, a pre-eminent American professor of theology at the University of Thomas More in Indiana, has published a book titled: *The Destruction of the Second Temple: The Fall of Judaic Christianity and the Rise and Triumph of Gnostic Paulianity*.
>
> The book's theme is not original. It has been studied by scholars, both Catholic and Protestant alike, without undermining the veracity of Catholic doctrine. This time is different. Professor Giltmore proposes a new method of biblical criticism, which he has coined

"criterion of divergence." This method seeks to authenticate New Testament writings through their concordance with the continuity of the message transmitted by the Old Testament prophets and by our Lord Jesus Christ.

Professor Giltmore's book wrongly asserts St. Paul's message diverges from the message communicated by the Old Testament prophets and by the Nazarenes with respect to monotheism such that St. Paul should be crowned the founder of Christianity and not our Lord Jesus Christ. In the same vein, this work cunningly reinterprets the Great Commission of our resurrected Lord Jesus Christ, throwing the Church's mission into serious doubt.

A television interview of Professor Giltmore discussing his book can be viewed here (hyperlink).

It is our duty to defend and preserve the integrity of the Faith. We will work together in a spirit of collegiality and dignity to refute this latest attack on the Catholic faith. We encourage you to seek guidance from the Almighty Lord. May the Lord Jesus guide us in protecting his Church.

We must remain steadfast in evangelizing our faith in the Lord Jesus, the wellspring of our abundant joy, and not let our enemies sow dissension in our communion of fellowship. We must call upon our Lord Jesus, who was persecuted for spreading the Gospel, for inspiration to combat attempts to undermine the foundations of the Catholic faith. The enemies of the Church never slumber and neither shall we. We must remain ever vigilant to protect the Holy Church and its missionary mandate.

> I wish to thank you for faithfully serving the Church's missionary commitment. Our faith is reinforced when shared in an ecumenical spirit with our fellow men and women.

It ended with "Dear brothers and sisters, May the Lord Jesus bless you and Our Lady protect you."

Father Marco sat and stared at the computer screen while he tapped his index finger on the desk. This is most unusual. Stunning even. Thomas More is a Catholic university. Maybe I'm mistaken but this might be the first time a sitting professor at this university has challenged the Catholic faith from within this institution. A courageous but potentially career-busting move. I'm sure better minds than mine will conceive an adequate response to this attack on our contrived faith.

He scrolled up and clicked on the hyperlink to watch the interview with Professor Giltmore, relishing a chance to cheer on this Bible scholar from the private comfort of his office.

## Chapter Eight
## Roman Province of Judea – Early First Century CE

Bone-tired but unmolested, Nicodemus and Joseph reached without incident a clearing that fronted a secret rock-hewn tomb in a garden luxuriant with trees and bushes and perfumed with the fragrant aroma of wild flowers. The area was deathly calm as though Creation itself was observing a period of silent mourning. With sorrowful hearts, they laid the limp body of the M'sheekha on the ground patterned with crooked shadows cast by the setting sun burning through the protective cover of foliage. Lined up near the tomb, Nicodemus spied the bundles of linen and vessels of water he had been asked to position there by the scribe.

"Per our customs, we must wash the M'sheekha's body before we entomb him," Nicodemus urged. "But we must work fast. The Sabbath is almost upon us."

Joseph bobbed his consent, still too grief-stricken to speak.

They made preparations then they unwound the blood-stained linen from their teacher's body while they invoked prayers over him. When finished, they laid the corpse on fresh white linen then, with trembling hands, they dabbed at the lacerations that had hardened into ragged purple ridges with moist cloths.

Conflicting emotions stirred Nicodemus' troubled conscience. He understood what had transpired was the Almighty's will, but the ire brewing in him for the ignoble, agonizing end to which his mentor had succumbed was difficult to keep in check.

Grant me understanding, Lor—

Nicodemus' head jerked up, the hairs on the nape of his neck bristling. He glanced around the clearing. The woods withheld their secrets.

"Did we forget something?" Joseph said.

"No, no. I sense we are being watched."

"It is just an irrational feeling."

"Perhaps." Quiet reigned, but he couldn't shake his paranoia. Must be a case of jangled nerves. He shrugged and resumed his ministrations. Beset with melancholy, he couldn't help but reflect on the lessons he had learned at the foot of his beloved teacher. Without warning, a snippet of a lesson submerged deep within the well of his subconscious surged to the surface of his mind, unbidden.

What was that lesson about? Nicodemus anxiously sifted his memory. Of course! His talk makes sense now. "Brother Joseph. Something is wrong. What do you perceive?" he asked, pointing to the M'sheekha's face.

"I see nothing but the bloodied face of our dear teacher," Joseph sniffled.

"Peer closer," Nicodemus implored.

Joseph regarded him strangely. "Brother, I am tired to the marrow of my bones. I cannot think straight. What am I supposed to see?"

His voice dropping to a whisper, Nicodemus said, "Listen to what I have to say." He rushed through the recounting of the story about Prophet Abraham's dream.

Joseph pulled a confused expression. "I cannot fathom what bearing Father Abraham's aborted sacrifice of his first-born son has to do with the M'sheekha's crucifixion."

"Did the Lord not substitute a ram in place of Ishmael to carry out His will?" Nicodemus said.

"Yes, bu—"

"But what? God tested Father Abraham's faith and he succeeded. In hindsight, our teacher was communicating the Almighty would not forsake him."

"Maybe our Lord planned a different fate for the M'sheekha," Joseph proposed, though with weak conviction.

"The sole purpose the crucifixion of the M'sheekha could serve is to disparage and diminish the Almighty's omnipotence for failing to protect one of His mightiest messengers," Nicodemus reasoned while Joseph weighed his words. "Listen, brother. Did the Almighty not rescue Prophet Jonah from the belly of the big fish and deliver Prophet Moses and our ancestors from the land of Egypt?" Nicodemus said. "And what about Prophet Lot? Did God not save him and his immediate progeny from the destruction of Sodom and Gomorrah?"

"Yes, He rescued these prophets and destroyed their deniers but how do you explain the likeness of the M'sheekha who lies dead at our feet?"

"Striking resemblance aside, this dead man is not the M'sheekha," Nicodemus said with self-assurance.

Joseph visibly stiffened. "You are not making any sense, Brother. If this dead man lying here is not our teacher, then who is he?" he demanded.

"Your Lord knows who he is and that is sufficient," a voice rang out from behind the veil of trees.

## Chapter Nine
## New York

With his long silvery leonine mane brushed back from his high, regal forehead, Professor Michael Giltmore, tall and trim and broad in chest, still projected a powerful air—a veritable lion in the winter of his years. Clad in a bespoke navy blazer, white shirt and cuffed gray dress pants, belying the trademark image of a rumpled, tweedy academic, Giltmore glanced at his puck-sized analog watch yet again and fretted. His moment of fame was almost upon him.

Yet fame wasn't his ambition. The quest for truth—as he perceived it—was a fixation for him before he took his retirement. It was what he had strived for during his entire academic life but had failed to achieve until now, in his estimation. It was his own fault. During his lengthy career as a Bible scholar, he had bunted when he should have swung for the fences. Life is full of should haves, could haves and would haves—the trifecta of never-has-beens.

He knew better now. But, early in his profession, he understood challenging, not toppling, the status quo was the key to advancement in academia. He could rock the foundations of scholarship provided they didn't crumble. And he could push the boundaries of knowledge, but not beyond the point where they exceeded the parameters of acceptable discourse per the Overton window which dictated the narrow range of issues tolerated in the public arena. *Pre-emptive thought-policing* he had baptized this institutionalized practice.

The past was prologue for this his final act. His latest (and likely final) book proved he still possessed a scintilla of intellectual honesty. That he still possessed integrity expositing biblical truth. That he still possessed the ability to hit a homerun in the cutthroat field of biblical criticism. Which was why the spotlight of notoriety was focused on him.

Fidgeting in his seat, his bright blue eyes fixed on the abstract painting on the wall opposite him, Giltmore never pictured his waiting in the guest lounge of the most popular conservative talk show in America.

He had toiled away in obscurity these past three decades as far as the average Jane and Joe was concerned, and now here he was on the other side of the television screen ready to battle a know-it-all right-wing host who took no prisoners. Life is like the wind; you never know what's going to blow your way.

He admired this show for its no-holds-barred, take-it-to-the-limit debate format. But, despite his edginess, he savoured the grilling for which the host of this talk show was celebrated. Giltmore wasn't easily intimidated nor was he one to shrink from a contest of wills.

Tonight, someone's goose other than my own is getting cooked, he predicted, feeling cocky. Let the feathers fly.

He wasn't naïve though. He knew why he had been invited here. It was for one reason only: controversy sells. And nothing was more controversial now than he, or more accurately, his book. The show was simply cashing in on the uproar generated by it.

The show can hitch a ride on my bus, but it's in for a rough ride, he vowed.

If his critics, who were having an unchallenged dialogue over his book, supposed they had escaped unnoticed, their day of reckoning had arrived. Tonight represented his singular chance to respond to these critics and defend his book in the arena of public opinion.

I'll go kicking and screaming into that dark night if I have to.

He deemed his work a *cri de coeur*, a sincere and principled appeal to the hearts and minds of those who loved truth for its own sake. His book was also a polemic against the Catholic Church. Predictably, the Holy See had listed it in the *Index Librorum Prohibitorum*, which only shoved his book deeper into the consciousness of the reading public.

"Professor Giltmore," an attendant said, her pleasant tone drawing him out of his reverie. He faced her. "Please come with me."

Show time! He stood up. A tremor vibrated through him and the knot in his stomach untied itself. There was no turning back now. His brain worked quickly. Subtracting commercial breaks, he calculated he had maybe, at best, three-quarters of an hour—not more—to shake up the world.

She led him to an area of the stage hidden by a heavy curtain. A red warning light flashed nearby. Then an upbeat musical introduction began while he waited in anticipation in the darkness.

"Good evening folks and welcome to *The Last Word*. I'm Adam Nashton, your host. Tonight we have a distinguished guest with us. Please give a warm welcome to Professor Michael Giltmore."

A stage attendant drew back the curtain. He paused to gather himself before stepping into the glare of publicity.

Think of the audience as students in a lecture hall and you'll do well, he told himself. And remember, Ol' Boy, debate Adam in the best of manners.

To the sound of enthusiastic applause, Giltmore coasted confidently from the wings onto the well-lit stage, the stark lighting making him blink. Adam Nashton, short in stature but long on bumptiousness, outfitted in a casual but expensive dark suit, which sported an oily sheen like snakeskin, his brown hair impeccably groomed, stood behind his desk to greet Giltmore. A feral smile fixed on his lips, Nashton held out his hand to shake.

"Good to meet you, Professor Giltmore," Nashton said with what might be a hint of sincerity. "Don't expect me to go easy on you tonight just because you're twice my age," he said with a wink.

Spare me the superficial bonhomie, brother. Giltmore grasped the outstretched hand and squished it like a bug. Nashton winced and his eyes watered.

"There may be snow on the roof but there's still fire in the belly, Adam. Consider yourself warned," Giltmore said in his stentorian voice, an iron smile on his lips. He released Adam's squashed appendage and plunked himself down in the armchair beside his host, coolly resting an ankle on the opposite knee.

The battle lines drawn, their gloves lying on the floor, no mercy was on tap tonight.

Giltmore acknowledged the exuberant audience with a wave, soaking up the goodwill he expected to be short-lived while Nashton rubbed his sore knuckles, waiting for the applause to fade away.

Nashton resumed his introduction. "Professor Giltmore is a resident scholar of biblical criticism in the Department of Theology at the University of Thomas More in Indiana. He is the author of thirteen books on Christian theology and religion. His latest book, and maybe his last book, if we have anything to say about it, is titled: *The Destruction of the Second Temple: The Fall of Judaic Christianity and the Rise and Triumph of Gnostic Paulianity.*" He laid down a copy of the book he had been holding up for the audience's benefit.

Turning to Giltmore, he said in a sneering voice: "Because you're the dean of Bible scholars, your work cannot be sidestepped. Though we can't ignore your book, we can do our best to drop-kick it."

"Give it your best boot," Giltmore said, daring him with his frostily blue eyes.

"You're somewhat of an iconoclast at Thomas More aren't you?" Nashton said, the question more of a verbal jab than an inquiry.

"Only until recently. In a former life, I was a respected professor of biblical criticism."

"Does this mean your colleagues don't agree with your latest scholarship?"

"In a manner of speaking. Not that they speak to me with proper manners anymore."

"So, is it safe to say your book has caused quite a stir in your department?"

He uncrossed his leg and leaned toward Nashton. "A sandstorm is more apt. You see, Adam, an academic department is akin to a sandbox. It has its own rules and strictures managed by adult children. If you don't abide by them, then your colleagues kick sand in your face. This is how they express their displeasure with heterodoxy."

"So what compelled you to go where angels fear to tread?"

"Here's the thing. So much of what we believe about Christianity is premised on tradition and not truth," he answered. "Unlike my colleagues, I was prepared to differ with the foremost minds of Christendom. They aren't willing to travel down that desolate path. They don't want to risk professional suicide. I view myself as a modern-day Galileo, unafraid to risk the ire of hide-bound traditionalists."

Snickering, Nashton said, "Your book advances many controversial interpretations and startling conclusions that overturn what most academics claim to be settled Bible scholarship. Considerable heated debate has been generated by it, here and abroad. Let's find out then what all the fuss is about."

"Go ahead, Adam," he said, steel in his teeth.

"Your book adopts a theoretical approach that is imaginative as are the conclusions derived from it. For the people sitting here and at home, please explain your theory of 'criterion of divergence.'"

"The criterion of divergence isn't a theory," Giltmore said, crossing his legs again. "It's an original method of biblical criticism I developed which seeks to position the message of Paul in the continuum of biblical prophecy and chain of prophethood," he elaborated. "This method strives to answer the question: Does the message of Paul diverge from that which Jesus and the Old Testament prophets propagated?"

"Okay. So playing the devil's advocate, what does it matter if one prophet's message differs from another?" he asked. "After all, the prophets lived in dissimilar eras and likely encountered unique tests and trials that dictated different messages," he said, raising his brow.

"No. The principle theological message of all the prophets was the absolute oneness of God and the condemnation of idol worship," he informed the host.

"Thank you for this explanation, Professor," Nashton said without emotion. "Why is Paul's message so at variance with earlier dispatches from the Divine?"

Warming to the topic, "From Adam to Jesus, the prophets preached a consistent doctrine of the unity or oneness of God and the worship of Him alone," he said. "Paul preached the duality of God wherein Jesus shared the Godhead with his presumed father. He—"

"Wait a minute, Professor," Nashton broke in, holding up his hand. "Are you suggesting Jesus preached the unity of God and not the Trinity?"

"Adam, I'm *asserting* Jesus preached unitary monotheism," he answered. "To wit. 'Hear, O Israel, the Lord our God, the Lord is *one*. Love the Lord your God with all your heart and with all your soul and with all your mind and with all your strength.' Mark 12, verses 29 to 30.'" He continued with, "And in Mark 10, verses 17 to 18, we read one of Jesus' strongest declarations of monotheism. When a man addressed him as 'Good Teacher,' Jesus replied, 'Why do you call me good? No one is good but God *alone*.'"

"Catholics and Protestants believe there is only one God and that He has revealed himself as the Trinity."

"Cite for me the verse of Scripture that proves your contention."

"The First Epistle of John chapter 5, verse 7," Nashton said, a tone of triumph in his voice.

"I'm disappointed in you, Adam. You didn't do your homework," Giltmore informed him. "Nevertheless, I'm grateful you introduced this passage of Scripture. To the people in the audience here and at home, I want you to listen carefully," he said, shifting to the edge of his seat. For the next few minutes, he explained to his listeners how verses 7 and 8 in chapter 5 in the First Epistle of John began their life as marginalia but ended it as Scripture, having been inserted into this epistle by a cardinal in 1515. None other than Sir Isaac Newton discovered this trickery. "Biblical exegetes call this trickery *interpolating*. Lawyers call it *tampering with the evidence*."

The jibe drew laughter from the crowd, and Nashton's face scrunched up in fury, sporting a look that insinuated "Someone's gonna pay for my humiliation."

Giltmore shifted back in his seat and locked his hands. "Don't kid yourselves, folks. Church authorities are aware of this fact. These verses of the First Epistle of John don't exist in any foundational biblical document."

He detected an atmosphere of incredulity in the studio, but could only guess at the reaction of those watching at home. A mental image of raging fundamentalists hurtling their remotes at their TV flashed by and made him want to duck for cover.

Nashton sat there fuming, incapable of mounting a credible defence against the verbal blows raining down on him. Unable to verbally extricate himself from the corner into which he had talked himself, Nashton responded with the throwaway line "That's your opinion."

"No it's not," Giltmore said, leaning forward. "If you don't believe me, then let us inspect two approved Christian sources and see what they say about the Trinity," he proposed. "*The New Westminster Dictionary of the Bible* evinces—and I'm paraphrasing here—the word *trinity* is not found in Scripture. And the *Harper Collins Encyclopedia of the Bible* baldly claims the doctrine of the Trinity is not revealed in either the Old Testament or New Testament." Giltmore sat there, telegraphing triumph.

"Then why is the Trinity the cornerstone of Christianity?" Nashton said in a taunting voice.

"That's the rub, isn't it?" Giltmore shifted his weight, trying to find a comfortable spot. He wasn't used to sparring intellectually from a chair. "Adam, the Trinity, like Santa Claus, doesn't exist in reality but only in the fertile imaginations of misguided souls. It is a doctrine proclaimed by human inspiration and not by Divine revelation," he argued. "Christian authorities took four long centuries to hammer out the Trinitarian Creed, which was finally ratified at the Council of Chalcedon in 451 CE. Imagine. Four. Long. Centuries," he repeated for emphasis.

"I'm sure there's a sound explanation for this," Nashton lamely said.

"But wait, Adam. There's more. Just when you thought the ink was dry on the Trinitarian Creed, in 1993, the Anglican Church recommended the *Filioque* clause be removed from the creed for the sake of ecumenical unity. This clause has been a long-standing issue of contention within the Orthodox tradition," he said. "Unbelievable. Here we are, over fifteen hundred years after the Council of Chalcedon, and religious leaders are still tinkering with the definition of Jesus and the Godhead. If the Trinity was derived from Divine inspiration, why are Christian leaders still debating it?" he said, shoving his argument home with brutal honesty.

Realizing he had lost this round of verbal jousting against an opponent who parried every thrust with frustrating ease, Nashton changed tactics. "Regardless of whether the Trinity is true or not, the main point of your book's thesis boosts Paul as the founder of Christianity, not Jesus. Describe for us how you arrived at this unconventional conclusion in as few words as possible," Nashton demanded.

"This issue ties into your original question about the divergence of Paul's message, but before I further demolish his message, I put it to you Paul did not have the apostolic authority to preach to the Gentiles. In fact no one did," he stated categorically.

"*Really*? Show us your proof."

"In Matthew chapter 10, verses 5 and 6, Jesus commanded his disciples to stay away from the Gentiles and Samaritans and preach 'only to the lost sheep of the house of Israel,'" Giltmore said, deflecting Nashton's line of questioning.

Perched upright on his chair, Nashton was on the verge of responding, the words dangling on the tip of his tongue, when Giltmore, anticipating his host's rebuttal, got the drop on him and said, "Before you fling Matthew 28, verse 19, my way, the verse where Jesus commands his disciples to make disciples of all nations, what the Church refers to as the *Great Commission*, we have to harmonize this verse in light of what Jesus directed his disciples to do in Matthew 10, verses 5 and 6."

The wind taken out of his sails, Nashton sat back listlessly, like a boat becalmed.

Giltmore resumed making his case. "I adhere to specific rules when I analyze the Scriptures. The principle rule I stick to is: one verse of Scripture explains and interprets another," he said. "A Bible scholar such as myself, unlike a minister or priest, won't interpret Scripture out of context on purpose since I don't have a personal stake in propagating Christianity."

"Fair enough, Professor. Do proceed," an embattled Nashton said.

Giltmore acknowledged his host and picked up where he had left off, his voice effusing professorial fervor. “With this principle in mind, when we examine those verses in Matthew 10, we remark Jesus did not restrict his disciples to preach to the Jews in Judea only. He knew there were Jewish diaspora communities dispersed throughout the Roman Empire,” he said, advancing his argument. “For example, Alexandria, Antioch and Rome. He also knew his mission was short-term. Logically, then, he gauged there was no time for him to preach to the Jews living in those distant cit—”

“That’s conjecture, Professor,” Nashton said because he couldn’t offer a counter-argument.

Giltmore feigned not to hear him. “We can argue Jesus was ordered to tell his disciples to profess his mission to the Jews and not the Gentiles if we explain verse 19 of Matthew 28 with Matthew 10, verses 5 and 6 in the following way. ‘Go therefore and make disciples [of the lost sheep of the house of Israel] of all nations, baptizing them in the name of the Father and of the Son and of the Holy Spirit.’” he concluded.

“Clever interpretation, Professor, but you’re late to the game.”

“Wait. I’m not finished,” Giltmore said. “This interpretation binds both verses together in a logical and coherent narrative, compared with the interpretation propagated by Christian authorities wherein Matthew 28, verse 19 abrogates Matthew 10, verses 5 and 6. The Church’s tortured interpretation of these passages of Scripture suggests God changes his mind which isn’t possible since Numbers 23, verse 19 reads: God is not a human being that He should lie, or a mortal that He should change his mind.”

Backpedalling furiously, Nashton said, “I understand why the Vatican banned your book. You’ve put the whole mission of the Church into doubt.”

Giltmore grumbled, “I’m not here to defend the Church. Perhaps the emperor—I mean the Pope—shouldn’t parade around in public with no pants on.”

Splutters of laughter erupted from the audience.

“So what does the Church gain by claiming a mission to the Gentiles not sanctioned by Jesus?” Nashton said casual-like.

"Christianity was and still is a tax-free business, although not as profitable as it once was," Giltmore replied. "Paul was soliciting donations from wealthy Gentiles which were remitted to the Jerusalem congregation. This is why the party of James allowed Paul to proselytize the Gentiles on his terms. We can conclude the Great Commission was a business decision adopted by the Jerusalem congregation irrespective of doctrine. Inarguably, the mission to the Gentiles has been profitable to the successor Catholic Church. Does anyone doubt the vast wealth controlled by the Vatican?" he asked.

Defeat haunted Nashton's eyes and yet the battle had only just begun. "Are you insinuating the Catholic Church is nothing more than a *business*?"

"Initially, yes," Giltmore said, standing his ground. "Notwithstanding the charitable good works of the Church, which is purely a gesture of corporate social responsibility, I'm sure you're aware the Protestant Reformation was a direct response to the Catholic Church's selling of indulgences for the remission of sins. And the brutal Counter-Reformation was launched not for reasons of doctrinal differences, which were nothing more than an intellectual smokescreen, but to safeguard the Church's financial interests which had suffered incalculably," he said.

"Yes, I'm aware of this unpardonable episode in Church history. However, I wasn't aware of the financial dimension you dished up. Anyway, it's old news. The Church cleaned up its act," Nashton said with a dismissive flap of his hand.

"It did, but not completely," Giltmore shot back.

"What're you inferring now?"

"What I'm trying to get at is despite Catholic churches closing left and right around the world, there's still enough money in the collection plate for parasitic archbishops and cardinals to afford million-dollar mansions and apartments both here and abroad. The Church is nothing but a vehicle for wealth redistribution, from the bottom of the congregation to the top. Whatever happened to the vow of poverty?"

"Well, uh, I guess, these clergymen know how to invest their earnings."

"And have you heard about the new cult growing exponentially in Latin America that is centered on the worship of *la Santa Muerte* or *Our Lady of Holy Death* whose likeness resembles the Grim Reaper?" Giltmore asked.

"The Vatican condemned this cult as a blasphemy against religion."

"That's rich. An institution that sanctions and promotes the worship of images and idols of the Virgin Mary is in no position to judge other idol worshippers. Anyway, this cult has at least twelve million adherents." Surprise lit up Nashton's face. "This cult's growing success is supposedly due to the fact they don't solicit donations from their adherents, who, it is claimed, have taken issue with paying for the Catholic sacraments. It's apparent this cult's cohort is voting with its feet. I reckon the Church still has lessons to learn."

"We've gone off on a tangent. We were discussing the divergent character of Paul's message. Put us back on course, Professor Giltmore," Nashton snapped.

"Sure, Adam." He paused a moment to catch his second wind as an aging pugilist would to marshal strength for further battle. "Contrary to what Jesus taught, Paul preached Jesus was the son of God."

"But Jesus *is* the son of God," Nashton insisted, and he tried to curb the desperation he heard in his own voice.

"Get real!" Giltmore said. "The Egyptians, the Romans, the Persians and the Babylonians believed their leaders were divine. Up until 1945, the Japanese believed their Emperor was the Son of Heaven. What makes your claim more valid than theirs?"

"The Bible says so."

"Your contention is not buttressed by Scripture."

"Nonsense. In John, chapter 3, Jesus professes he is the only begotten son of God," Nashton said, slamming his fist against the armrest of his chair for emphasis.

Indifferent to his host's angry outburst, Giltmore said, "I'll come to this passage of Scripture in a second but first I want to mention God also had *sons* in the Old Testament, and the word *son* wasn't capitalized because the languages of the Old and New Testaments were written in lower case letters." Shaking his head, he said, "It's contemptible how Christian authorities go to fraudulent lengths such as capitalizing words in English to hoodwink their flock into believing the New Testament is the inerrant word of God. Suffice to say, *son of God* means one who is close to Him. I don't have time to pursue this side issue any further but you can read more on this subject in the second chapter of my book."

Nashton bridled. "How dare you impugn the inerrancy of the Holy Bible, you heathen?"

Giltmore rolled his eyes and mouthed *o-kay*. Unruffled, he replied with as much tact as he could. "Your statement is so full of holes it's nothing but the rhetorical equivalent of Swiss cheese. When you start with a false premise such as 'Jesus is the son of God,' then you have no choice but to invent doctrine to maintain this premise."

"I want proof of this claim," Nashton screeched.

"Verses 16 through 21 in John 3 are an interpolation. So Jesus didn't preach to his disciples this absurd tale about God and His only begotten son," he said without rancor. "God is *the* Creator, not a common procreator. You want further proof? In the Gospels of Matthew, Mark and John, Jesus frequently refers to God as *your father* when he addressed the people. Most decisively, in John 20, verse 17 Jesus says, 'I am ascending to *my* Father and *your* Father, to *my* God and *your* God.' How much clearer does Jesus have to be?" he said in an exasperated tone.

Nashton sat there dumbfounded, staring at his guest, unable to rebut him.

"This Johannine verse puts to bed any notion of an exclusive paternal relationship between Jesus and God," Giltmore said with finality. "And the notion of God impregnating Mary, as the Gospel of Luke suggests, recalls the story of Zeus, the supreme god in the Greek pantheon, impregnating the mortal, Leda. In consequence, the pagan Gentiles were predisposed toward the Christian version of Jesus' conception."

"The Gospel of Luke suggests no such thing," Nashton protested.

"I'll say this. If Jesus didn't teach it, Paul can't preach it."

"But Paul said he received his Gospel from Jesus," Nashton said, his voice breaking, a sure sign he was losing the debate.

"And the tooth fairy left me a dime beneath my pillow when I was a child but nobody believed me," Giltmore complained. "This is another point of divergence. Paul claims in First Galatians he received his revelation from Jesus. Paul is professing he is a prophet."

"What's wrong with that? Didn't Jesus say in John 14 and 15 verse 26 he would send an advocate or helper? Doesn't Paul fit this role?"

Pouring cold water on this line of enquiry, Giltmore answered, "Everything, yes and no. It's curious *and* disturbing none of Paul's Epistles reference this verse. In fact, Paul's Epistles make no mention of the Gospels at all. The reason for this is obvious: the Gospels were written after the fall of Jerusalem in 70 CE, almost a decade after the execution of Paul. Did Jesus forget to tell Paul in his 'vision' on the road to Damascus that he was Jesus' advocate? Moreover, Paul doesn't fit the role of a prophet. He diverged from the religion taught by Jesus. The Book of Acts, chapter 15, records a contentious meeting between Paul and members of the Jerusalem congregation, a meeting which historians have called the Council of Jerusalem."

Not wanting to be dismissed as a complete philistine, Nashton jumped in and continued the line of thought. "This council, which occurred around the year 50 CE, was convened to discuss allowing Gentiles to convert to Christianity without undergoing ritual circumcision and without having to abide by the majority of the strictures in Mosaic Law."

"Adam, you took the words right out of my mouth." He let Nashton bask in the glow of his easy victory.

"And it's no coincidence this issue was championed by Paul, the apostle to the Gentiles," Giltmore said. "Though a conservative wing of the Jerusalem congregation vigorously opposed this dispensation, a compromise was reached to the mutual satisfaction of Paul and the congregation as I mentioned a short while ago."

"The early Church encouraged Gentiles to join because Jews resisted becoming Christians. This decision was a necessary compromise for the survival of Jesus' mission," Nashton said.

Giltmore suppressed a snort of derision. His brow arched, he replied, "*Really*? A compromise? Who is Paul to make compromises with the divinely revealed words of the Messiah? Did Jesus not say in Matthew 5, verses 17 and 18: 'Do not think I have come to abolish the Law or the Prophets. I have not come to abolish them but to fulfill them. I tell you the truth, until Heaven and Earth disappear, not the smallest letter, not the least stroke of a pen, shall by any means disappear from the Law until everything is accomplished.'" He added, "Adam, I may be getting on in years, but my powers of perception are still sharp, and, as far as I can tell, Heaven and Earth still exist, unless we're living in a parallel universe."

The audience, unable to restrain itself, hooted at his wisecrack.

Unfazed, Nashton ignored the laughter. "True, but Jesus inspired Paul to change his message," Nashton said, raising his voice above the boisterous laughter.

"So he says." He noticed Adam was becoming agitated, but he couldn't stop now. "Let's be clear about Paul. He was born a pagan Greek in Tarsus. He converted to Judaism to win the hand of Popea, the beautiful daughter of the High Priest of Jerusalem. She rejected him and became an actress in Rome where she caught the eye of Emperor Nero. Long story short, Popea became his mistress and eventually his wife."

Nashton had a stunned look on his face, having never heard this story before.

"It was about this time a dejected Paul began preaching a Law-free religion mingled with the Greek paganism and philosophy of his upbringing. Maybe his rejection of Judaism and his invention of Christianity was a slap in the face to the Jews, Giltmore suggested. "It must be said: Paul was an opportunist. He appropriated a Jewish sect, dressed it up in Hellenic attire and paraded it before the Gentiles as a new Law-free religion. It was a Trojan horse which let loose a host of fictions and fabrications upon a Greco-Roman world ripe for a new religion. I admire Paul's showmanship but I likewise condemn his altering the Word of God. His advocacy of antinomianism was an evil act *par excellence*," he said, delivering praise by faint damnation.

An uproar arose in the studio. Basking in the glow of the firestorm triggered by his incendiary remarks, Giltmore grinned with satisfaction, surveying the horde of hostile expressions, enjoying his ability to light a fire under people and awaken them from their intellectual torpor.

"People who play with matches sometimes get singed."

"It's okay. I have insurance," Giltmore fired back. "The fact is, Adam, few people read the Bible critically nor do they understand Christianity is an invented, not a revealed, religion created by the minds of men over centuries rather than disclosed by the mind of God."

The audience reacted feverishly, shouting insults at Giltmore.

I hope no one is carrying a cross. "Did I say something inappropriate?" he asked in mock innocence.

Nashton glowered at him. Regaining his gladiatorial bearing, he tried redirecting the professor. "So you reject the message of Jesus?"

Bait and switch. The tactic of scoundrels on the verge of defeat. I'll take the bait and throw it right back at him. Giltmore said, "I eschew the Gnostic Gospel of Paul. His writings are the fundamental doctrine of mainstream Protestant and Catholic churches."

"Gnostic Gospel of Paul?" Nashton said with an incredulous look.

"Appears you didn't receive the memo in Sunday school, Adam," he said. "Jesus preached salvation was achievable through the works of the Law and faith. In Luke 10, verse 25, Jesus is asked by a lawyer what he has to do to inherit eternal life. Jesus replies, 'What is written in the law?' The lawyer replies, 'The first commandment and to love your neighbor as yourself.' Jesus replies, 'You have given the right answer. Do this and you shall live.'"

"Yes, bu—"

Cutting him off, Giltmore concluded, "There's no mention in Jesus' reply about believing in the mysteries of baptism, the Crucifixion, the Resurrection or the Eucharist to achieve eternal life. Paul preached these mysteries and so do the Protestant and Catholic Churches. Mystery is synonymous with Gnosticism. Another divergence in doctrine. Moreov—"

"Slow down, Professor. You're running off at the mouth a mile a minute," Nashton broke in.

Giltmore paid him no attention. He was in the zone now, the words gushing out of him in a torrent. If a normal brain had five gears, Giltmore's was in tenth. "This leads me back to my former point. Paul spoke of secret knowledge, or *gnosis*, in his epistles to the far-flung congregations of Asia Minor. He wrote only he was privy to this knowledge which had been kept secret from the Old Testament prophets and from Jesus' disciples. How preposterous," he said. "And this gnosis was the sacrificial death of Jesus and his consequent resurrection both of which were necessary to fulfill the Pauline concept of vicarious atonement."

"Professor, you spewed quite a mouthful. Give us an abridged version," Nashton said.

"Sure. Jesus did not teach his disciples about dying on a cross for mankind's sins, but Paul did. End of story."

"Now, hold on."

Ignoring him, Giltmore resumed his discourse. "The notion of vicarious atonement is another divergent doctrine of Paul's. Every prophet up to and including Jesus taught repentance for the forgiveness of sins. The belief that someone else can bear the sins of humankind contradicts Scripture, specifically Ezekiel 18, verse 20, which reads 'The son shall not bear the iniquity of the father, neither shall the father bear the iniquity of the son.'"

"Timeout," Nashton sputtered, waving his hands. "If vicarious atonement contradicts Scripture then what about the crucifixion of Jesus?"

"Let's call a fable a fable, Adam," Giltmore said, his voice calm but commanding. "The Church's portrayal of the crucifixion of Jesus was nothing more than an elaborate Greek tale. Jesus was crucified because he chased the usurious moneylenders out of the Temple. Money has always been a prime motive for murder, or crucifixion in Jesus' case. Banal but true."

He continued building his case, buttressing it with one argument at time. "The redemptive nature of the Crucifixion was a later innovation concocted to appeal to the pagan Gentile conditioned to believe in the propitiation of an angry god through ritual sacrifice of a human virgin. Although the Greco-Romans had ceased practicing human sacrifice, it was still an integral part of their tragic mythology."

Adam tried to break into Giltmore's monologue but was rebuffed with a flap of his hand.

"Belief in the forgiveness of sins through the sacrificial death of an innocent salvation deity in exchange for an eternal life of bliss held abundant appeal in the Greco-Roman world. The Crucifixion possessed the essential elements and manufactured cachet of a Greek tragedy." He sported a satisfied expression. How he loved to expose people's cherished illusions masquerading as received Divine wisdom.

The agitated crowd hissed, never having had to confront such a thorough deconstruction of its belief system.

"Despite your assertions, Jesus died for my sins and yours," Nashton blustered.

Giltmore shook his head as if to say, "Great. Now we're making progress." Then he levelled his gaze at his tormented host. "Come on, Adam. Is that your best shot? I anticipate your saying something wise one day, but only after you've exhausted the canon of ill-conceived comments. I have a long wait ahead of me, I suspect."

Nashton cut him a quizzical look, not sure if he had been insulted or complimented.

"Adam, there's no biblical proof for your belief. The sole rationale for Jesus dying for our sins is to give the Church a role in mediating the expiation of sin. This role is the *raison d'être* for the existence of the Church. No Crucifixion, no Church."

Hearing the anger emanating from the audience, Nashton shifted the conversation to a safer channel of discussion. He glanced at his notes and attempted a different tack. "We've gone off on a tangent again, Professor. Let's circle back and clarify for our viewers what Gnosticism is and why you stress Paul was a Gnostic."

"Gnosticism comes from the Greek word *gnosis,* usually translated as *knowledge*, a knowledge both rational and empirical. Gnostics, however, define gnosis as *insight* or *inner illumination*, which is derived from inspiration, the source of which is supposedly God," he explained. "Paul asserted he received his secret gospel from God, but this poses a problem. Only prophets receive revelation from God. Paul was not a prophet. So what was he?" Answering his own question, Giltmore said, "We must conclude Paul was a false prophet and so the founder of the false religion of Paulianity."

Nashton sat with an exasperated expression on his face. Giltmore's seamless speaking style prevented him from even getting a word in edge-wise. He threw up his hands as if to say, "Who the hell is in charge here?"

"Did Jesus not warn his disciples to be aware of false prophets who preach in his name, specifically Matthew 5 end of verse 19? 'Anyone who breaks one of the least of these commandments and teaches others to do the same shall be called least in the kingdom of Heaven, but whoever practices and teaches these commandments shall be called great in the kingdom of Heaven.'" Giltmore tossed common sense around the studio like confetti at a wedding. "Paul abolished the Law, therefore, he is a disciple of the anti-Christ."

Nashton was at a loss for words. People in the audience hurtled abuse at Giltmore. Pandemonium threatened to engulf the studio. Nashton held up his hand for quiet and the room drained of noise. The audience got the message and settled down.

Now I know the kind of hostility Jesus confronted in his time, Giltmore ruminated.

"Well, you've driven home your point regarding the status of Paul," Nashton said.

"I have one more point to make about Paul then we can move on."

"If you insist."

"I do."

Nashton caved in. “Go ahead.”

“Though Paul is the founder of Christianity, he did not preach the doctrine of the Virgin Birth. Now isn’t…this…odd.” He left this point hanging in the air.

“I find this difficult to accept without evidence.”

He fixed his eyes upon Adam. “Read Paul’s epistles. Not one word about the immaculate conception of Jesus. In fact, in Romans 1, verse 3, Paul writes Jesus ‘was made of the seed of David, according to the flesh.’” He delivered the punch-line in short phrases for emphasis: “So. Very. Thought-provoking.”

“Enough about Paul. The fact remains the Bible is the foundation of Christianity,” Nashton said.

Bait and switch again. “Which Bible?” he asked.

“What do you mean, *which* Bible?”

“It wasn’t a trick question, Adam,” Giltmore said. “Do you mean the Catholic Bible which has seven more books than the Protestant Bible? And let us not forget the Orthodox Bible, which also has a different canon. None of these aforementioned Bibles are exactly the same, nor are the different *versions* of the Protestant and Orthodox Bibles in circulation,” he informed the host.

“Damn you and your irritating intellectualism.” he fumed, ready for a fitting with a straitjacket.

Is that smoke coming out of his ears or am I imaging things? Turning to the audience, hoping to appeal to their sense of reason, Giltmore said, “It is no exaggeration to say there are over 4000 secondary sources for the Bible, none of which agree. From this pile of documents, the majority of the books in the New Testament canon were first compiled by a coterie of doctrinaire religious establishment figures around 170 CE, a compilation called *The Muratorian Canon.* Books were chosen *a priori* for inclusion in this canon for their consistency with emergent Church doctrine and orthodox teaching, which was inconsistent with accepted Old Testament doctrine and orthodoxy, and not for their veracity or authenticity.”

“Anyway,” Nashton interrupted.

“Anyway, the discovery of extra-biblical texts at Nag Hammadi in Egypt points to many other Gospels in circulation during the development of *The Muratorian Canon*. But these Gospels were rejected for dogmatic and, daresay, political expediency, and not for reasons premised on theological integrity and continuity of message."

"For Christ's sake," a combative Nashton blurted out. "What proof do you have for this spurious claim of yours?"

Giltmore appraised his host with sympathy. "We have time for one example. For the longest time, the *Letter to the Hebrews* was rejected by bishops in the West but was considered canonical by bishops in the East. Long story short, in a shady deal reached at the Council of Carthage in 419, this epistle was folded into the New Testament canon," he said, skewering his host.

Nashton stewed in his own juices.

Giltmore resumed speaking but now with verve. "Here's the catch. If the New Testament canon was inspired by God, which religious authorities militantly assert, then the nature of Jesus' personhood and of the Godhead would have been chiseled in stone at the outset of Jesus' mission. Agreed?" he said, addressing no one in particular. "But it wasn't because Christianity was invented on-the-fly!"

His argument jolted the audience, and he felt a wave of anger forming before him. But he couldn't avoid it, so he surfed it.

"There's something else I'll say. The Church has convened council after council since the time of Jesus wherein matters of doctrine are invented then revised, refined and ratified. This practice remains in vogue. The First Vatican Council. The Second Vatican Council. The third one is most likely in the works," he said. He moistened his lips with the tip of his tongue.

"These councils do no such thing, Professor," Nashton said. "They discuss and decide points of doctrine."

"Which they've pulled out of a hat," Giltmore added. "Jesus didn't come to found a new religion. He came to restore Mosaic Law which had been corrupted by the Pharisees."

"Wrong," Nashton barked. "In the Gospel of Matthew, Jesus said he will build his church on a rock."

"Wrong! So-called modern Bible scholars insist on translating the koine Greek word *ekklesia* for the word *church* when *ekklesia* means congregation or assembly. No church, no Christianity. End of story," he said, delivering a strong rebuke to Nashton and cutting off any further discussion. Giltmore could tell he was getting on Nashton's nerves.

"So what is the religion of Jesus, Mr. Know-It-All?"

"The message of Jesus is crystallized in Luke 4, verses 18-19, passages commonly referred to as *The Messiah Manifesto*. 'The Spirit of the Lord is on me, because he has anointed me to preach the Good News to the poor. He has sent me to proclaim freedom for the prisoners and recovery of sight for the blind, to release the oppressed, to proclaim the year of the Lord's favor,'" he recited from memory. "That's it, that's all. Christianity cum Paulianity is a religion *about* Jesus but not the religion *of* Jesus," he said with authority, noticing Nashton's mien of annoyance.

The audience settled down to listen. Giltmore finally had their attention as well as his host's. They sat in their seats spellbound by his erudition.

Taking advantage of their rapt attention, he said: "Curiously, it was not until 1546, during the Council of Trent, responding to canonical challenges arising from Protestantism, that the canonicity of the New Testament, based on Jerome's Latin Vulgate of 384, was approved for Roman Catholicism. On the other side of the biblical ledger, approval of a New Testament canon occurred in 1559 for Calvinism, 1563 for Anglicanism and 1672 for Greek Orthodoxy."

"I'll be damned," Nashton said aloud.

Emboldened, Giltmore pushed on with his disquisition. "Abraham had his scrolls, Moses had his tablets and David had his Psalms. What do we have?" Replying to his own question, he said, "We have contradictory Gospels *according* to so and so, but nothing from Jesus' own pen.

"The New Testament canon, *ex officio* claims of legitimacy aside, is commendable as cult literature but is unfit as the foundation book for a religion. The New Testament suffers from a lack of concordance with Christian doctrine."

"You hurled a verbal salvo at us, Professor," Nashton said. "And you gave us heaps of food for thought, but there's one more item on the menu for discussion before I feed you to the lions," he said half-jokingly.

"Lions are no match for me," he deadpanned.

"The title of your book implies the destruction of the Second Temple in Jerusalem was responsible for the concomitant triumph of what you term 'Gnostic Paulianity' or the 'Gospel of Paul'. Explain this claim of yours."

Giltmore rose to the challenge once more, drawing on his last reserves. "The Jesus movement was centered in Jerusalem. Paul's movement was centered in Rome. When the Roman legions destroyed Jerusalem in 70 CE, the Jesus movement scattered and never recovered from the loss of their base," he verbally sketched for them. "The Pauline movement swooped into this doctrinal vacuum and flourished unimpeded, its main theological competitor having been all but eliminated. Rome supplanted Jerusalem, becoming the hub of Pauline Christianity. Judaic Christianity failed and Gnostic Paulianity prevailed," he sermonized.

"You make it sound so decided, Professor," Nashton said. "I'll have you kno—"

Giltmore shook himself with irritation, like a lion shaking its mane. "Cork it!" he cut across him.

Nashton jumped in his seat, visibly startled.

Giltmore scowled at him. "You possess a mouth and two ears so you can listen more and talk less," he said. "What galls me, Adam, are professional polemicists like yourself who conflate argument for erudition. You're only interested in winning an argument instead of acknowledging the truth of the matter. Your stubborn pride is deafening you and blinding you to the truth. Maybe you like the sound of your flapping lips, but they sound like a loose sail snapping in a stiff breeze. So sit there and listen."

Nashton looked floored. Having never been put in his place before, he was momentarily cowed into silence.

Giltmore resumed speaking at a clip, his mind on fast forward. "That the vast majority of people are oblivious of the doctrinal shift from Judaic Christianity to Gnostic Paulianity is proof of the most audacious conspiracy of silence in the history of the Church," he said. "Religious figures on both sides of the aisle are well aware of everything detailed in my book. It is astounding how they can stand before their congregations each Sunday and spout the dogma of Catholicism or Protestantism with a straight face."

Nashton sat there punch-drunk, having suffered too many blows in the verbal sparring match with Giltmore.

Seizing upon Nashton's dazed bearing, Giltmore delivered the *coup de grace* and knocked away the props supporting Adam's final argument. "It's fair to say the preponderance of Christian practices do not mirror in the least what Jesus practiced. Jesus was circumcised, the majority of Catholics and Protestants aren't. Jesus worshipped his Creator, Christians worship Jesus or Mary or both. Jesus held Sabbath on Saturday, Christians hold it on Sunday. Jesus bowed and prostrated before his Creator, Christians stand, sit or kneel when worshipping Jesus or Mary. Jesus did not celebrate his birthday and his disciples did not deck the halls with boughs of holly, but Christians do. Jesus didn't eat pork, but Christians do. Jesus fasted, all but the Coptic Christians don't. Jesus forbid usury, Christians are drowning in interest-bearing debt. Jesus baptised no one, Christians are baptized. Jesus worshipped God three times a day: morning, afternoon, and evening. Christians worship someone other than God once a week. Jesus was entombed, half of all Christians cremate their dead. The list of contradistinctions goes on *ad infinitum*," he said with a tone of exasperation. The contrasts were as stark as a call girl in a convent.

"Yes, but there are reasons for these differences, Professor," Nashton said but Giltmore was having no more of his evasions.

He flagged from the verbal combat for he didn't have the stamina of a young man anymore. Once more he unspooled the evidence against Adam. "Christianity has no ontological validity because its principal propositions—the Trinity, the Resurrection, and the divinity of Jesus—have no foundation in Scripture. In closing, Christianity's Trinitarian rites and rituals echo the polytheistic paganism of the ancient Greeks—from baptism to cremation, from the Crucifixion to the Resurrection and from the Cross to the Communion. As I argue in my book, Christianity's central story soars to the lofty heights of Greek tragedy with the agony of the Crucifixion, but then plunges to depths of Greek farce with the teleological façade of the Trinity." Giltmore lapsed into silence, hands clasped in his lap, mentally spent by the energy he had expended in the verbal cut and thrust with Nashton.

The audience gasped. "Crucify him," someone yelled, snapping Nashton out of his mental torpor.

"Good idea," Nashton said. He added chillingly, "Lucky for you, Professor, this is the U.S. of A and not Eye-ran."

Unnerved, Giltmore couldn't believe his ears. Am I in New York City or the Plymouth Colony? All that's missing are the felt hats, breeches and buckled shoes.

Off camera, the studio manager signaled Nashton it was time to wrap things up.

"Well, Professor, we're almost out of time. This was a most bruising discussion. It was quite the verbal boxing match. We went toe-to-toe, but we're both still standing," he said. "I have one last question for you."

"I'm all ears."

"Thomas More is a Catholic university at which only Catholics can teach and study. So how were you able to publish this tome which clearly refutes Catholic doctrine?"

"Tenure guarantees me academic freedom."

"I see. Now, in a gesture of goodwill, you may have the *last* word," Nashton uncharacteristically offered.

With a hint of devilment in his voice, Giltmore said, "Thank you, Adam." Turning his eyes to the audience, he wound up. "In his day, Jesus didn't have the time to reveal everything to his disciples due to the brevity of his mission. Similarly, the time constraints of this talk show don't permit me to share with you all that I wished to. Therefore, I say to you as Jesus once said to his disciples. 'Verily, I have much more to say to you, more than you can now bear.' Even so, I give to you three words of advice: Read. My. Book."

Muted laughter broke out in the studio, defusing the emotionally charged mood of the audience.

I won this skirmish. Nashton was prepared to make mincemeat of me but I ate his lunch instead. Just then the cold wind of reality blew in and swept away his hubris. Come Monday morning, though, I'll have to face the music over this interview. He shrugged it off and a crafty smile tugged at the corners of his mouth. Better dust off your dancing shoes, Ol' Boy.

## Chapter Ten
## Roman Province of Judea – Early First Century CE

Nicodemus and Joseph stiffened in shock, not expecting anyone to be lurking in the vicinity so near the time of the Sabbath. Twigs snapped and branches rustled in the shadowy woods. The figure of a man emerged at the edge of the open ground.

Overcome with astonishment, they were momentarily speechless. Then they cried out in unison: "Scribe of the M'sheekha!" They leapt up and covered the short distance to where he stood, forgetting their dead brother, who, mercifully free of earthly cares, was in no position to express disapproval.

"The dead man is not the M'sheekha," he declared.

"But how? Why?" Joseph said.

"You shall know the truth, and the truth shall make you free of doubt. First, we must finish preparing our brother for burial," he said.

They hastened to where their brother lay dead. Gazing upon him, the scribe repeated the words their teacher had once spoken: "Greater love has no one than this, that one lay down his life for his friends." Overcome with compassion for his brother in religion, he wept.

Together, they finished the burial preparations of their brother. They then laid him in the carved-out tomb, his final resting place. The scribe recited the prayer for the dead over him, finishing with the words "To God we belong and to Him we are returned. Amen."

They had performed the rites their religion mandated and now their brother was with his Lord. They retreated from the tomb and rolled the stone in front of the burial chamber to protect it from robbers and the deceased from predators.

The scribe gestured to Nicodemus and Joseph to follow him, and they tramped deep into the woods of the garden to a comfortable and secluded spot. They sat around in a small circle on long grass and the perfume of wild flowers scented the air.

"I am pleased you did not forget the lesson our teacher had taught you," the scribe said to Nicodemus.

"But how did our brother come to be crucified instead of the M'sheekha?" Joseph said.

"A youth from among our brethren stepped forward to take the place of the M'sheekha when Roman soldiers came for him in Jerusalem."

"But how did we perceive the M'sheekha to be on the Cross and not our young brother?" Nicodemus asked in a humble voice.

"God the Almighty placed the likeness of the M'sheekha upon this youth and no one was the wiser."

Nicodemus gaped.

The scribe returned a look that said "Why so surprised?" He paused a moment to think. "The Almighty created Heaven and Earth and everything in between. Convincing the people it was our brother on the Cross rather than the M'sheekha would then be an equally easy affair for our Lord. Are we agreed?" the scribe asked.

"I still have much to learn," Nicodemus said, hanging his head.

"This explains why none of the M'sheekha's disciples were present at the Crucifixion," Joseph said.

"They did not abandon their teacher in his hour of need, in spite of perceptions to the contrary. They remained steadfast with him in Jerusalem," the scribe said.

"God's mercy upon the youth," Nicodemus murmured.

Nodding in agreement, the scribe put in, "We should not feel sad for him for he is now with his Lord."

"His sacrifice is without equal among us. May the Almighty reward him with the highest heaven," Nicodemus said in a spirit of generosity.

"What of the stories about Brothers Peter and Judas betraying our teacher?" Joseph asked.

"Hold fast your tongue," the scribe said in a scolding voice. "You do not appreciate the enormity of your words."

Joseph recoiled. "Forgive me."

"Never trade in gossip and rumors," he advised, wagging his finger. "For backbiters and slanderers will fill the Hellfire on the Day of Reckoning." He shifted his posture. "Now as to your question, Brother Joseph, those *stories* hold no truth. Our brother's body is not yet cold and even now the enemies of truth are sowing lies about the integrity of the M'sheekha's disciples. These wicked liars have no fear of God. And so they cannot imagine the dire penalty for betraying a prophet of God. A true disciple would not dare engage in such hypocritical behavior."

Chastened, Joseph remained silent, giving hard thought to what the scribe had just drilled into them.

"Where is the M'sheekha now?" Nicodemus asked.

"The Almighty raised him up to Heaven."

Nicodemus and Joseph exchanged incredulous glances. "Heaven?" they both said.

"The ascension of the M'sheekha was wondrous." He rearranged his cloak and said, "Sit back and let me relate it to you both."

## Chapter Eleven
## Istanbul

Ho-*lee* Mother! Stroking his facial scar, Father Marco stared past the computer screen out the window as he struggled to conquer the glee percolating inside him. Giltmore didn't just spill the beans on Christianity in his interview, he splattered them over the whole kuffing studio. Father Marco hastily checked to make sure none had landed on him. His soutane was clean.

Close one…The PR flacks in the Vatican must be climbing over each other to contain the damage to the Church. I hope they wiped their feet first.

He recalled another book that had created a stir in the Holy See. In fairness to its author, the novel was a notable work of fiction but merely a hurricane in a handbag compared to Giltmore's scholarly juggernaut. Published over a decade ago, the novel purported to uncover a secret plot perpetrated by the Church to conceal an alleged marriage of Jesus to Mary Magdalene. The book had been roundly condemned and prohibited by the Vatican. No surprise that.

Disregarding the prohibition, he read the book to learn for himself what the controversy was about. An original and thrilling story, the novel's plot was a fanciful tale uncorroborated by Scripture. Giltmore's tome, however, was an unequalled effort of erudition that couldn't be labelled an imaginative work of fiction. Father Marco definitely understood (and secretly applauded) the existential predicament in which the Church now found itself embroiled.

It was true what Giltmore said about the Trinity: three lies for the price of one. The modern Church recognizes there's no textual support in Scripture for the Trinity. The age-old truism of "what's missing" invalidates the Trinity. Because "what's missing" from the Bible is a clear and unequivocal declaration of the Trinity. No Trinity, no Christianity. End of story.

One need only pull on a single thread of Catholic doctrine to unravel the whole fabric of faith because it had been patched together like a computer program. It was a classic case of the whole being greater than the sum of its parts. If one pursued this exercise, why, the official Church narrative would tear apart at the seams. Looks like it might be time to break out the thread and needle.

Father Marco was no stranger to this patchwork problem for he had encountered it in seminary college. There, his teachers repeated ad nauseam how faith and reason were not incompatible but irreconcilable because God in His majesty cannot be apprehended by reason alone. One must just have faith and hold fast to what had been conveyed by the laying on of hands. (And not too few of his fellow priests took this message to heart and persisted on laying their hands where they didn't belong.)

The Church's plan to manage this budding crisis would without a doubt follow the playbook executed for previous controversies. The Holy See would issue a rebuttal, or an apology, context depending, then ignore the matter until it faded from public consciousness. Wash. Rinse. Repeat. This strategy usually succeeded so long as the media lost interest in the issue. "Starve the media beast" was the Holy See's mantra.

This time was different, however. Giltmore's talk raised a host of issues that could overwhelm the Holy See's ability to manage them. Its resources were deep but not limitless. It relied on a few sympathetic media organs. The new media—the Internet—however, was not controlled by biased corporations. Issues assumed a life of their own in the infinite echo chamber of the Web, amplified and multiplied by billions of users. And the constantly erupting child sex abuse scandals diverted so much energy from the Holy See that Giltmore's book might be the catalyst for a complete re-evaluation of the Church.

Could it survive such an exercise...? Do I care...? Too early to tell at this point.

Reflecting further on Giltmore's analysis and harmonization of the verses in the gospel of Matthew which demolished the authority for the Great Commission, Father Marco could not but admire their coherent elegance. The fact remained, however. Giltmore's interpretation invalidated the mother Church's mission! Rome, we have a problem. Mission abort! Mission abort!

While he sat there wondering at it all, the speech of one of his seminarians sprang to mind, quoting Sir Francis Bacon: "If a man will begin with certainties, he shall end in doubts. But if he will be content to begin with doubts, he shall end in certainties." His teachers hyped these tautologies as though they were Divine truths.

His seminary education had begun with many doubts. Doubts about the existence of God, the divinity of Jesus, the immortality of the soul and so on. And the Church provided torturous responses to these doubts. But the old doubts remained. He survived seminary college by regurgitating what his teachers spouted, like a good apparatchik spewing communist doctrine. The things one does to survive. He gave a mental shrug.

A question, forming unbidden in his brain, stirred up old arguments about Catholic teachings. Fearful of giving expression to it, he tried to suppress it, fretting he might slip over the threshold of doubt into certainty. But the more he tried to suppress it, the harder it was to ignore it. So he gave up, realizing his struggle was futile. He resolved instead to put his faith in his Lord.

What if the answers given by the Church were wrong?

The treasonous ring of his question made him shudder with delicious guilt, for disloyalty to the Church and disloyalty to the Catholic faith were one and the same.

He elected to leave the unprecedented question hanging there for now, unanswered. Besides, there was still a mess to sort through in the archive. He needed to organize the files strewn about by the earthquake. To tackle this job, he required his deacon to manage the church in his absence.

I hope he's available on such short notice. If not, sorry. Duty calls.

A quick phone conversation (and a little arm-twisting) resolved the matter. Father Marco leaned forward in his chair, elbows planted on the desk. He unconsciously rubbed his scarred knuckles while he waited for the deacon to show up, giddy with guilty contentment.

# Chapter Twelve
# Roman Province of Judea – Early First Century CE

The sun surged with power and might where earth and atmosphere met, rending the veil of darkness in the eastern sky and pinkening it. Whorls of mist twisted and twirled like tormented spirits in the rising heat, and the chill in the air surrendered without a fight to the fiery onslaught of sunlight. Creatures stirred to life once again, sprinkling the air with a symphony of tweets, buzzes and chitters.

A new day dawned for an unsuspecting people smug in their belief they would crucify the M'sheekha this day as it dawned for a minority of people content in their knowledge the Word of God could never be crucified.

A hooded man rushed along a cobbled street as though he were being pursued, his cloak billowing with each hurried stride, and he came to a sudden halt before the door of a multistoried stone-built home. He tried the door. It was locked. Using his key, he let himself in and recited the prayer for God's protection from the Devil as he crossed the threshold.

He stood in the entranceway to regain his energy. It was cool here, full of shadows…and wonderful silence. The hum of street activity, which had begun to quicken, couldn't penetrate the thick, high walls of mortared stone. He pulled off the cowl of his robe and drifted down the long, tiled, narrow hallway, his sandals slapping the floor, the sound bouncing off the stone walls.

He emerged from the semi-darkness into an open-air central courtyard thick with shadows and stopped to survey it in the rosy morning glow, a setting he never failed to admire. The water in a raised rectangular stone pool, rippled by a soft breeze, glinted with reflected light. In the well-manicured garden, paths meandered through islands of evergreen trees, bushes and flowers of a multitude of colors, shapes and sizes. Birds perched on branches chirped merrily, lending a natural ambiance to the man-made enclosure.

Despite the immense size of the courtyard, it was a private site, a place for meditation, not relaxation.

Done with his appraisal of the botanical splendor laid out before him, he walked the tiled path that led to the overflowing pool refreshed by an underground spring. He performed the ritual ablution of purification for he was to meet his Lord later today and so he must meet Him in a state of ritual purity. Once done, he recited from memory, "I bear witness there is no deity but God. He has no partners. O God, join me with those who repent and join me with those who purify themselves. Amen."

The man heard muffled voices on the other side of the courtyard. He hastened along the meandering path that led toward the hidden speakers. In the cool shade of the portico, he stopped and listened. They are likely in the main room, he decided. He approached the double doors and pushed them open, filling the doorway with his commanding presence. Heads turned. Conversation slowly dwindled away in patches then into complete silence, and he witnessed his disciples gaping at him.

"Peace be with you," the man said, breaking the spell.

"O M'sheekha, Peter cried out with joy and relief. "Peace be unto you. You have arrived from the Temple at last. Praise be to the Almighty for your safe return."

Disciples soon herded around their much-loved shepherd and they peppered him with questions, expressing their happiness at his presence. Hands reached for him, to touch him, to *believe* in him.

Addressing the multitude of his disciples, the M'sheekha said in a strong voice, "I shall be with you a little while longer, then I am going to Him who sent me. You shall search for me, but you shall not find me. And where I am, you cannot come. If you continue in my word, you are truly my disciples. And you shall know the truth, and the truth shall make you free."

The disciples exchanged knowing glances.

"I have told you these things so that in me you may have peace. In the world you will have tribulation. But take courage; I have overcome the world!"

"Praise God, verily indeed you have, O M'sheekha," a disciple shouted out from the back of the room.

"If you keep the Lord's commandments, you shall abide in His love, just as I have kept my Lord's commandments and abide in His love. I have said these things to you so that my joy may be in you, and that your joy may be complete."

"Whenever you are among us, O M'sheekha, we experience the unbounded joy of your company," a disciple close by said.

Murmurs of assent concurred.

"This is my saying, Do unto others as you would have them do unto you. No one has greater love than this, to lay down one's life for one's friends. You are my friends if you do what I command you."

The M'sheekha noticed his disciples were wavering. To shift their focus, Jesus said to them, "Who are my supporters of God?"

The disciples said, "We are supporters of God. We have believed in God and testify we are Submitters."

Pleased with their reply, he exhorted them: "Go to the lost sheep of the House of Israel. And as you go, preach, saying, 'The kingdom of Heaven is at hand.'"

The disciples beamed with overwhelming happiness at this startling news. Someone exclaimed, "The Lord's work is never done."

Yeshua wheeled around and strolled back into the courtyard, and his disciples paraded behind him. The sun was now floating high above in the ocean of blue sky. The M'sheekha halted in the middle of the courtyard and turned to face his disciples who stood before him watchfully, quietly. His mother, Mary, looked down on the congregation from behind a latticed window on an upper floor.

"O children of Israel! Indeed I am the messenger of God to you, confirming what came before me of the Torah, and bringing the Good News of a messenger to come whose name is *The Praised One*.

He was about to speak again when a clamor of voices in high pitch shrilled on the other side of the wall and cut him off. The din caught their attention.

"They have come out with swords and clubs to arrest me as though I were a bandit," the M'sheekha said to those in attendance.

"Who?" asked a disciple.

"Those who hated me without a cause."

The disciples conceived a growing fear for the safety of their teacher.

"Who from among you will take my likeness and thus be killed in my place, taking himself equal to me in rank?"

A youth stepped forward, but the M'sheekha smiled indulgently at him and commanded him to sit. He posed the question again. No one moved but the youth stood up tall and responded with a resolute, "I."

The M'sheekha threw the youth a radiant smile and said, "You are the one."

He addressed them again, saying, "I am ascending now to my God and your God. Peace I leave with you. My peace I give to you. I do not give to you as the world gives. Do not let your hearts be troubled, and do not let them be afraid. It is to your advantage that I go away for if I do not go away the Advocate, the Spirit of truth, will not come to you. But if I go, I will send him to you. He will testify on my behalf. When the Spirit of truth comes, he will guide you into all truth. For he will not speak on his own, but will speak whatever he hears and he will declare to you the things that are to come."

The disciples regarded their teacher inquisitively.

With a sense of unspeakable peace he had never felt this deeply in his life, the M'sheekha gazed heavenwards with palms upraised.

His disciples followed his gaze.

The M'sheekha's lips moved but no words were spoken. Without warning, the sky parted, like scrolls rolled up. A shaft of celestial light burst forth from the opening and illuminated the captive audience congregated below.

A collective gasp erupted as two bright lamps descended rapidly on the ray of heavenly light. When they drew nearer, it became obvious they weren't lamps but angels, and their diaphanous forms glowed in luminous splendor. To a one, the disciples beheld the angels with rapt attention.

The angels, heads bowed, positioned themselves beside the M'sheekha. He gently grabbed hold of a wing of each angel and together they ascended heavenwards to be reunited with their Lord. The M'sheekha and the heavenly hosts of translucent light soon vanished from view. The portal in the cosmic firmament folded back upon itself, blinking out the source of celestial illumination, and the sky resumed its seamless surface.

Their bearing rapturous, the disciples stood still, too stunned to speak. They looked to each other for guidance.

The scribe of the M'sheekha spoke up. "We have been given a command about what to say and what to do by our teacher. Let us not waste time questioning what our eyes have seen."

The disciples dipped their heads in deference.

He added, "Our vision did not deceive us. We saw what we saw. Now let us hasten to spread the Good News to our brothers and sisters in every nation as we have been commanded."

"The scribe of the M'sheekha has spoken so let us do as he asks," Peter said to them.

Just then there was a crash and a troop of Roman soldiers poured into the courtyard with metal swords and shields clanging.

"Where is the one who calls himself the M'sheekha?" the leader called out to the disciples.

The youth, now bearing the likeness of his teacher, stepped forward. "It is I whom you want."

The leader made a gesture and two soldiers seized the youth's arms. "Come along quietly and no harm will come to you," he said.

The youth did not offer resistance, and the leader led his troop of soldiers back the way they had come. They disappeared from view and a cry was taken up by the street crowd. A savage cry, thirsting for blood, which carried over the walls and chilled the disciples' hearts.

"May God's mercy be upon him," the scribe said to his brethren, the knowledge of the grim fate that awaited the youth written all over their faces.

## Chapter Thirteen
## Indianapolis

Monday morning dawned clear and sunny. Giltmore arrived early at the faculty parking lot located off Meighen Drive on the campus of Thomas More, home of the *Conquering Celts*, the pride of students and faculty alike. The parking lot was situated nearest to St. Francis Hall where the Faculty of Religious Studies was housed.

There were two ways to reach his building. He always chose the longer path which passed by the reflecting pool positioned south of the Leacock Library, the usually placid surface of the water mirroring the massive religiously-inspired mural on the library wall which faced it. The watery image was the fixation of countless camera bugs and of many aspiring artists.

It was summer and so the leafy campus was abandoned, but not for long, and he conjured an image of students crawling around the grounds like a colony of ants. He expected peace and quiet at the office. Catching up on email correspondence and other administrative tasks would be the order of the day.

As he approached his building still out of sight, he heard chanting, but distantly. Must be a celebration at the stadium. Kind of early, he judged.

The stadium, due south of St. Francis Hall, was the cauldron wherein many a punishing gridiron game was contested.

As he passed by the south end of the reflecting pool, he spied his building through the leafy trees that dotted the campus. He also plainly saw and heard the source of the chanting now. At the rear entrance to St. Francis Hall, student protesters waved placards and chanted slogans while campus security maintained a semblance of order.

You give one controversial television interview then they come calling for your scalp, he thought.

When he came in view of the mob, it came alive, like hungry hounds caught up in the scent of a fox. The chants grew shriller, more frenzied. The mob smelled blood.

"Jesus died for my sins and for yours...The Bible is the true word of God...Giltmore is guilty of blasphemy," they shrieked.

He scanned the faces of the mob as he scampered down the gauntlet of taunts and jeers. Most were contorted with rage while some others grinned at some private pleasure. With safety in mind, security guards had erected metal barriers on either side of the cement path to allow him to pass unharmed through the hostile passage of surging bodies swinging signs like fly swatters.

Once inside St. Francis Hall, the shrieks grew muted as he progressed toward the bank of elevators, his footfalls clacking on the polished faux-marble.

That was a little hair-raising, he worried, riding the elevator to his office on the third floor of the building. He entered the hallowed seclusion of his sanctuary, a cramped but tidy, book-lined room. Daylight filtered in through cheap venetian blinds which laid a pattern of shadow stripes across his desk. He removed his sport coat and hung it on the wrought iron coat tree situated beside the door. He regarded it curiously for a moment. Wherever did this come from? he wondered for the first time. Strange that I should wonder about the provenance of a coat tree that has been in this office possibly as lo— His musing was broken by the sound of chanting. He squeezed around the desk and peeked through a slit between the blinds. Student picketers had also staked out the front door of St. Francis Hall. He felt like tossing them the one-finger salute but thought better of it.

"Grow up," he barked through the window, but they were too far away to hear his harangue.

Annoyed, he flopped into his chair, his back to the window, and his shadow fell upon personal items precisely arranged on his desk. He flipped open his laptop and logged into the campus network to check his emails which he didn't have time to do over the weekend. The trip he had made to New York last week to attend the talk show had drained him. He groaned when he saw the number of unread emails in his Inbox most of which had been sent by strangers. The emails said oh such witty things as "Burn in hell you pagan" and

"Repent you spawn of the Devil before it's too late" and "Jesus is the Son of God just as surely as you are a follower of the Fallen One."

And so it went. One rant after another with death threats mixed in to leaven the monotony of the tantrum levelled against him. He didn't take the death threats seriously, but he forwarded the emails to campus security, anyway. You could never be too sure.

The sophomoric level of invective hurled against me is dumbfounding. Not one of these emails proposes a counterargument to anything I elucidated on the talk show. Just one uninspired, shopworn epithet after another. In typical fascist fashion, unable to disprove the message, they disparage the messenger instead. Here I am working in one of the premier academic institutions in the world and not one person has attempted to reconcile Christianity with Jesus' religious observances.

He was chagrined by this realization, and it hardened his resolve to retire. The lack of critical-thinking alarmed him for it confirmed a rising tide of Christian fundamentalism discussed extensively in the media these past years.

A knock on his office door interrupted his drudgery. He glanced up from his laptop and he felt his face sag. Wonderful. Arthur Fitzpatrick, the Department Chair, filled the doorway. Fitzpatrick, thick-browed and heavy-jawed, was an imposing figure, stretching over six feet tall and wide as a redwood—a low-center-of-gravity guy. If not for a freak off-season injury years ago, he most likely would've basked in the bright lights of the National Football League. Instead, he had channeled his competitive spirit into the pursuit of academic achievement and succeeded brilliantly where most washed-up athletes typically failed.

"So, the heretic has returned trailing a scent of sulphur," Fitzpatrick said, arms crossed, legs apart, his posture exuding tension. "I guess you bumped into your 'welcome home committees' this morning?"

"I'm too busy to ignore you, Art. Can you come back another time? Like yesterday. Or how about last week?"

Fitzpatrick's jaw dropped. He hadn't anticipated such a snappy comeback.

Score one for me. "And, yes, I avoided the pain and punishment of a burning at the stake this morning," Giltmore said as he leaned back in his chair and swung his forearm in dramatic fashion to his forehead. "The mob prodded me with pitchforks and firebrands, but luckily I escaped serious injury."

Fitzpatrick rolled his eyes at Giltmore's histrionics. "Mike, I'll be candid with you." He glanced at the floor then stared him in the eye, a devilish smile curling his lips. "I've come to warn you the Provost's Faculty Affairs office plans to convene a disciplinary committee to decide whether you breached the university's code of conduct," he said, pleasure seemingly seeping from every pore in his body.

"Because some pencil heads dissolved into a conniption fit over my interview?"

"They're convening this committee because you impugned the reputation and integrity of this department," Fitzpatrick said, bristling like an upended straw broom.

"That wasn't hard to do," Giltmore said, no trace of concern in his demeanor.

"And you insulted my religion. I took offense at several of your statements."

"Thief!" he shot back. "I offered no offense. You took what wasn't yours."

"You're adept at twisting people's words."

Giltmore simpered. "One man's offense is another man's wake-up call. Consider my interview a rude awakening. You should thank me."

"You arrogant—" He stilled his tongue.

"Art, you know as well as I do the Scriptures are not Divine revelation, and the New Testament does not record the historical reality and beliefs of ancient Christian communities. They merely reflect the musings of their authors. It's wishful thinking to believe otherwise."

"I admit to no such thing."

"Of course not. You believe the earth is five thousand years old."

If not for statutes against assault, Giltmore sensed his superior would love to use him as a tackling dummy.

Worked up into self-righteous resentment against the man who had dared to critique his religion, Fitzpatrick blurted out, "You broke your oath to uphold Catholic values you infidel!"

"I hate to burst your bubble, but truth is a Catholic value is it not? Apparently you and your superiors can't handle the truth."

"To hell with the truth. It's about faith—my faith. You ridiculed it!"

"Of course. Why let truth get in the way of a good story?"

Fitzpatrick betrayed no emotion.

Concern creased Giltmore's forehead. "You're not going to go Paleolithic on me now are you?"

Fitzpatrick responded with stony silence.

"You more than anyone should know revelation is to reason what light is to vision. Without light, our eyes cannot see and without revelation, we cannot reason. Revelation is the Divine Light that directs our minds to worship God alone."

"Spare me the insight of your gilded tongue."

"Then how about the tongue of Pope Leo X who said, '*It has served us well, this myth of Christ.*'"

"Don't remind me."

"Art, undoubtedly my talk on *The Last Word* was controversial," Giltmore conceded. "I know I was treading on sensitive terrain and I trod as delicately and politely as I could without giving any ground. Religion is personal, primal. I get it. But Christianity is not evidence-based and so its falsehoods needed to be exposed. I will not withhold the truth from people for the sake of their *sensitivities*," he said in his defense.

"There are many people whose emotions are raw because of your insolent interview. How do feel about that?"

"In a word, bad. In a couple of words, too bad."

"Why you—"

"I will not apologize for supposedly wounding people's *feelings*," he said. "What gets me, instead of worrying about their *feelings*, people should concern themselves with the severe offence they give to God when they breach the First Commandment by uttering blasphemies such as 'Holy Mary Mother of God' or 'son of God' or when they come before a likeness of the Virgin Mary or of Jesus and offer up worship and prayers to them," he finished.

Spots of red anger colored Fitzpatrick's cheeks and a purple vein swelled on his forehead. "Have you lost your frickin' mind?"

"Only my religion, Art, only my religion."

"What are you talking about?"

"People may not have been ready to hear it, but they heard my message loud and clear," he said. "For too long, Christians have been coddled with falsehood. It was time they were confronted with incontrovertible truth."

"What gives you the right to stomp all over someone's religion?" Fitzpatrick bridled.

"Poor choice of metaphor, Art," he said. "I simply examined what Christians unwittingly follow and challenged people to deliberate the so-called *facts* of Christianity." Giltmore sat back, clasped his hands behind his head and calmly inspected the water-stained ceiling tiles. "This affair reminds me of the story about Abraham. Care to hear it?" Not waiting for a reply, he launched into his biblical tale. "When Abraham was a youth, he asked the chiefs of his people why they worshipped wooden statues incapable of speech. The chiefs replied they were doing what their forefathers had been doing. To prove the pointlessness of their idol worship, when the temple was vacant, Abraham, using an axe, smashed all of their idols but the largest one in whose hand he then conveniently positioned the axe. When the chiefs later discovered what had been done to their idols, they asked the people to bring Abraham before them. With their people in attendance, the chiefs asked Abraham if he knew who had smashed their idols. He suggested they should ask the remaining idol who had committed this deed. The chiefs hung their heads in shame, recognizing the foolishness of their beliefs for they realized the idol couldn't speak or act in its own defence. But instead of accepting their folly, they doubled-down on their idolatry. They allowed their pride, their arrogance, to occlude their common sense, and so they plotted to catapult Abraham into a blazing fire to save face. As we know, their plot failed."

"So what's your point," Fitzpatrick asked, leaning against the doorjamb, arms and legs crossed.

He dropped his gaze to look at his boss. "When people are given information that challenges their existing beliefs, their immediate reaction is to demonize the messenger instead of taking the time to consider the validity of the message. Just as Abraham spoke truth to power and was nearly killed for doing so, I sacrificed the golden calf of Christianity on the altar of biblical criticism and now my critics hunger to crucify me. But I won't give them the chance."

"What do you mean?"

"Tell you what, Art. Tell the provost not to waste his time."

"Why should I?"

"Because I was—I plan to retire before the fall term. This should save my pesky persecutors the inconvenience of convening a medieval star chamber."

"The provost would take issue with your conflating a secretive, arbitrary court with an open disciplinary committee," he said, aghast.

"How about a fools' court then? With apologies to fools."

Fitzpatrick slitted his eyes. "Listen, you pagan, you sunk the boat in your television interview. You've upset many people in our community."

Ignoring the insult, Giltmore leaned forward and rested his forearms on the desk. "Regardless of whatever imaginary boat I scuttled, the fact remains the provost choked on his holy water because I pointed out his precious Pope isn't wearing any pants."

Fitzpatrick's jaw clenched and the tendons in his neck threatened to tear.

Score another point for me. He sighed in resignation. "You know what? I've had my fill of this place. My retirement is effective today. Please have the university administration clear out my office and send my personal effects to my home address," he said, business-like.

"So that's it then?" Art asked, deflating.

"Yes. I leave with my head held high *and* intact," Giltmore said, alluding to the head-hunting mentality of the mob he had encountered earlier in the day.

Fitzpatrick huffed. "Fine. You won't be missed. You pushed the line of scholarship too far this time."

Giltmore sat up. "Sooner or later someone needed to point out the Pope's a pant-less apostle. And I was the chosen one because I possess the chutzpah and the chops to do it."

"Your departure cannot come soon enough," he said peevishly.

"But before I depart, there's an urgent health issue we need to discuss."

"Oh. What is it?" Fitzpatrick asked, leaning in, concern etched in his face.

"You need to loosen your *cilice* a notch. It's cutting off circulation to your brain." He rose grinning from his chair.

Fitzpatrick's face dropped and his shoulders slumped like he had taken a hit to the solar plexus. "Go to hell." He wheeled around and stomped out of the office, a dark cloud of humiliation roiling above him.

Sucker-punched again. Walked right into it. Never saw it coming. "Hat trick!" Giltmore wanted to shout but didn't. He stood there and stared at the empty doorway, his fingertips resting on the edge of the desk. His gaze swept the small office, no audience present to congratulate him on his witty wordplay. Then out of nowhere the voice of his conscience pricked him. Way to go, Ol' Boy. Sure taught him a lesson, didn't you? But a lesson in what? Certainly not good character. You need to work on that. Remember, you're a Submitter now. You're commanded to debate in the best manner...Forgive me God. He hung his head in contrition, his self-satisfied grin wiped from his face. So this is how it ends. With a flameout, not a firework. What did you expect? Congratulations? Thank you, Giltmore, for exposing the lies and inventions of Christianity...Most people can't tolerate a challenge to their entrenched beliefs however wrong they are. They double-down on their beliefs out of stubborn pride instead. He heaved a sigh.

With reluctance, he stowed away his laptop and the few personal items used to decorate his office into his shoulder bag. As he shrugged into his sport coat, he glanced around one last time at his workplace of thirty-odd years, and a lump of regret caught in his throat. A single fat tear of sentimentality spilled over and splashed onto the dusty floor. It was worth it, he consoled himself.

Without a glance back, he switched off the light and locked the door. On his way out, he dropped off his office keys at the department's administration counter. The clerk cocked an eyebrow in silent question at him but instead of offering her a clue, he winked at her.

He rode the elevator to the main floor and approached the rear exit of St. Francis Hall with a sense of caution. The silence he heard telegraphed the mob of student protesters had departed, their attempted exorcism a failure. He opened the door warily, still half-expecting to be ambushed. Instead, he saw a lone security guard monitoring the doorway.

The guard spun around as Giltmore came through the door. Recognition dawned on his face. "Awesome show you put on the other evening, Professor. I never heard Christianity explained the way you did. It got me fired up," confessed the young, fit-looking man. Short-cropped brown hair accentuated his angular face. A colorful tattoo on his right arm completed the picture.

Giltmore halted in his tracks. "*Really?*" he said, intrigued.

"Your talk about the Trinity nailed it for me."

"Nailed it?"

"I asked my priest to explain the Trinity to me at church yesterday. The poor guy talked me around in circles. Made my head spin. I was no further ahead after his explanation than before it. What a head trip."

"Mind indulging my curiosity?"

"Sure." He hitched his thumbs in his belt.

"What do you plan to do with this newfound knowledge of the fallacy of the Trinity?" Giltmore said.

The guard reached for his left arm and kneaded the bicep. "Religion isn't my area of expertise. I'm a part-time student here.

I'm studying political science," he said by way of explanation. "Do you have any suggestions?"

"Do you attend mass?"

"Quite regularly. With my wife and our baby," he added.

"What does your wife think about my talk?"

"She dismissed it. Said it was just so much intellectual hair-splitting. We argued about it. In the end we agreed to disagree."

Giltmore nodded in sympathy. "Religion's a touchy subject."

"So what should I do?"

"It's not my place to tell you what to do."

"I know, but I want your advice anyway."

Giltmore weighed the earnest look in the guard's eyes. He took a deep breath as if coming to a decision. "Two things: One, turn off the TV—unless I'm being interviewed—" they both gave a chuckle "—to give yourself time to contemplate your purpose in this life. And two, stop attending church. It's a place of idol worship. Do what Jesus did. Worship and petition God alone."

"Petition?"

Giltmore regarded him as a teacher might a student. "If you desire something from God, ask Him. No one else. Don't call on Jesus, the Virgin, the Pope or a so-called saint."

"That's it?" he said.

"Why so surprised?"

"If it's that easy, then what's the Church for?"

"I answered that question in the TV interview," he gently reminded him.

The guard reflected for a few moments. His mouth twitched. Then his eyes went wide with realization. "Son of a bi—. Sorry. Have to watch my mouth. Gets me into trouble with the wife."

Giltmore smiled sympathetically. "Ask God for help to overcome this personal struggle."

"I'll give it a try, Professor. What've I got to lose?"

"Ask God to guide you. No one else."

"Guide me to what?"

Giltmore smiled. "Hopefully to the path of Submission."

The guard cut him a quizzical look.

"Well, I'm thrilled my interview touched someone. You've brightened my day." He adjusted the strap on his shoulder. "What's your name?"

"Julio Vasquez."

"It's a pleasure to meet you, Julio," and he extended his right hand.

They shook hands.

"Can I ask you a favor, Professor?"

"Sure and please call me Mike."

"Is there some way I can get in touch with you. You know, in case I have other questions."

Giltmore weighed his request. What could it hurt? "You have a pen and paper in one of those pockets."

"I sure do."

"I'll give you my email address."

The guard wrote it down. "Thank you, Mike."

"The only thing I ask is that you don't share my email address with anyone. Agreed?"

"Wouldn't dream of it."

"Well, good luck with everything, Julio, and don't work too hard. Peace be upon you."

"You, too, Mike."

He was about to leave, then stopped himself. "Do me a favor. Buy my book."

Giving him a thumb's-up, "You bet," Julio replied.

Giltmore turned and jaunted off toward the parking lot for the last time deep in thought, dappled sunlight striking his face through the foliage.

Satisfying to know my talk got through to at least one person. Maybe there's hope for my book.

## Chapter Fourteen
## Istanbul

Delighted to discover the lights on when he entered the church Monday morning, Father Marco searched for Dimitri in the nave instead of going straight to his office. Not finding him, he called out to him. Dimitri emerged from the columns on the other side of the nave, a broom in his large hands.

"There you are. Nice to see you. How are you, my dear?" he asked. Hope he's in a better mood today.

"I feel like myself again, Father. Our prayers were answered by Our Lady," he replied.

"So no headaches, no dizziness, no sensitivity to light?" No psychosis?

"No, on all three counts."

"Splendid...While I have your attention, I need your help."

"What now?"

Here we go again. "If you feel up to it, can you help me carry the ladder to the archive room? It's too awkward to carry it there by myself."

"You weak like sheep. Me strong like bull," he said, puffing out his chest.

Yeah, and full of it, too. "Super. I'll put my things in my office and be right back."

"Don't keep me waiting. I have a lot of work to catch up."

"Give me patience, Lord," he said under his breath.

Together they manhandled the extension ladder down the stairs without threatening to kill one another and situated it convenient to the door to the archive room.

"Thanks for your help, Dimitri. I'm most grateful to you."

"So what do you plan to do with it?"

"The earthquake knocked over several tall shelves which I need to restock."

"Why—" He stopped himself.

Many years ago, Dimitri had helped Father Marco's elderly predecessor carry boxes into the archive room which has a low ceiling.

"Why what?" Father Marco prompted Dimitri, seeing suspicion on his face.

"Why won't you open the door so we can put the ladder inside?"

No can do. If I let him in, he'll see quite readily I don't need a ten-foot ladder to restock six-foot tall shelves. "Here's fine. You've been a big help."

"But the ladder is heavy an—"

"Not now!"

Dimitri registered shock.

He softened his tone. "I'm sorry, Dimitri. My nerves have been strained since the earthquake struck."

"You should be. I wanted to help an—"

"And you have. I thank you again for your help. The archive room is a mess," he fibbed.

"You don't need any help to clean it up?"

Shaking his head, "I can manage it alone. So let us carry on, shall we?"

"You plan to leave the ladder here?"

Not unless I make you eat it. "Yes, Dimitri," he said as he struggled to conceal his irritation. "I'll drag it in to the archive later tonight after I have completed this day's work."

Shrugging his shoulders in resignation, he turned on his heel and made his way upstairs with Father Marco tagging along.

He returned to his office and slumped in his chair. Better get a grip on yourself…A grip around Dimitri's throat would feel better.

A lack of proper sleep was having a negative effect on him. He hadn't slept well the past couple of nights, a rare occurrence in his regimented life. The shrouded corpse was always there at the back of his distressed mind, haunting him, taunting him. Work was the sole remedy that brought him a measure of inner serenity.

He checked his daily planner. Besides the requirement to crank out a new sermon, he had scheduled private conferences with several parishioners. One couple required marriage counselling, another parishioner needed spiritual reinforcement for her faltering faith, while still another was struggling with her son's delinquent behavior. They have different problems and they expect *me* to provide the solutions to them. Imagine.

At times he felt lost, like he was stumbling in the dark (not to be confused with those few instances when he sampled too much sacramental wine), seeking answers which might not be there. But that never stopped him before. He just made them up when compelled to. He was wise not to offer money-back guarantees, only guidance. On most occasions it was effective.

It was amazing the trust people placed in priests, as though they possessed a direct pipeline to God. He couldn't blame the people since the Church encouraged such an impression. If only they knew the pipeline was a pipedream and priests were the modern era's shamans. People want to believe in something so long as it isn't demanding or time-consuming. With the help of the Almighty, he did his best and hoped his efforts were sufficient. If not, he couldn't be sued. Thank God for job security.

The day went before he knew it. His appointments arrived. He listened, discussed possible solutions then dispensed advice, like an assembly line, defects and all. So it went. During the breaks, he worked on his sermon, but he wrote without enthusiasm.

Might as well surf the Internet to soak up the time. No sense banging my head against the keyboard.

He clicked on the link to the American News Network (ANN) and the *Breaking News* banner got his attention:

> Iran Quits Nuclear Deal Framework In Response To U.S. Military Strikes. Tehran Hints At Nuclear Missile Capability Within A Month. U.S. Puts All Military Options On the Table. Moscow And Beijing Pledge Full Military And Diplomatic Support To Tehran. UN Security Council Meeting Scheduled Later

> This Week To Avoid Possible World War.
> Stock Markets Plunge.

Kuffing U.S. trying to rule the Middle East. His mood soured. I wish there was something that could put the U.S. Goliath in its place. He scrolled farther down. Another headline grabbed his attention.

Controversial Professor Retires from
University of Thomas More

Father Marco clicked on the link. It read:

> ANN has learned Michael Giltmore, now a former professor of theology from the University of Thomas More and author of the provocative book, *The Fall of Judaic Christianity and the Rise and Triumph of Gnostic Paulianity*, is reported to have retired earlier today. A university spokesperson contacted by ANN stated Giltmore's retirement had been planned months ago. When informed that a trusted source had revealed to ANN Giltmore's potentially facing a disciplinary hearing over his contentious television debate that aired last week on *The Last Word*, the spokesperson merely chalked it up to coincidence. Giltmore wasn't available for comment. This is a breaking story, so check back for updates.

Who do they think they're kidding? he scoffed. There are no coincidences. Things happen for a reason. Thomas More was simply circling the wagons, labouring to minimize the damage done to its reputation. Giltmore was sacrificed to appease the powers that be. He drew first blood and paid the price.

He checked his watch. His last appointment was due in a few minutes.

Mrs. Soylu and her son, Altan, showed up on time. Father Marco greeted them at the front door of the church and led them to his office. It was obvious the boy didn't want to be there. He kept asking his mom when they could leave and he kept making faces at Father Marco. It wasn't long before he decided Altan was a spoiled brat who lacked parental discipline. His mother was of no help. She indulged his every mood with namby-pamby leniency. Father Marco rolled his eyes whenever she wasn't looking.

The mother's disclosures convinced him her son's problem couldn't be resolved at the level of spirituality and faith alone. He really wanted to tell her there was nothing a kick in Altan's pants couldn't cure, but he didn't want to be accused of advocating child abuse. Instead, he advised psychological counselling for Altan whose problem was beyond the realm of his expertise, but not his foot, he wanted to add. Hearing this apparently crushing advice, the mother slouched in her chair. Father Marco informed her he himself had received psychotherapy in his own wayward youth. She straightened up, this bit of personal disclosure cheering her. He told her there was no shame in seeking the advice of a psychologist. Just in refusing to seek one, but he left that part out. As always, he suggested she ask the Virgin for help in guiding her son.

His consultation completed, he escorted mother and son to the front door of the church. He was glad he wasn't a parent. He didn't possess the forbearance to spare the rod in this era of pandering to children's *self-esteem*. Pity the poor child who should ever hear the words "You're not awesome. You're average."

"Goodbye, Father Marco. May Our Lady's blessings be upon you."

"And upon you, my dear." He stood at the door and watched Mrs. Soylu guide her son toward their vehicle. Altan turned around and stuck out his tongue. Father Marco returned the favor, the shock on the boy's face worth it.

On his way back to his office, he ran into Dimitri. "How was your first day back at work?"

"It passed without incident."

"Glad to hear this. If you have nothing important left to do, why don't you go home to Anna?"

"I'm behind on my cleaning, so I'd like to catch up if that's all right with you."

Anna can only take so much of you, too? "Don't push yourself too hard on your first day back at work."

"I'm recovered, Father. My strength has returned."

"Tomorrow's another day."

He pursed his lips. "As you wish."

Dimitri tossed Father Marco a look that signaled awareness of his trying to get rid of him.

"Have yourself a good evening." And don't let the door hit you on the way out. He retreated to his office where he waited for Dimitri to leave. He glanced at his watch. Ten minutes had elapsed. He should be gone by now, he gauged. He crept into the nave on cat feet. It was in darkness. Super.

Back in his office he changed out of his soutane into work clothes and sneakers. He might be in for an adventure tonight so appropriate attire was a must. It wasn't often he wore street clothes—except for his evening run—so it felt a little strange to be wearing pants again. He retrieved Dimitri's flashlight before proceeding to the basement.

He dominated the impulse to race, the sense of anticipation almost uncontainable. I might finally get the chance to learn who's in the cave-tomb. In spite of his self-restraint, he reached the basement quicker than usual. After unlocking the door, he dragged the heavy ladder into the archive room and laid it on the floor with a *clang*. He flicked on the light and swung shut the door. He took a moment to admire the difficult work he had accomplished. Shelves and cabinets and their contents were once again situated in their proper places much to his satisfaction. I didn't need the angels' help after all.

He hauled the ladder closer to the hole. Fortunately, the foot of the ladder was nearest to it. He fetched the flashlight and directed its beam into the tomb and took a stab at calculating its depth. About ten feet, he estimated. He grabbed hold of one section of the ladder and extended it to twelve feet.

Should be long enough.

Hoisting the other end of the ladder, he pushed it forward. The ladder descended bit by bit into the tomb. Once the ladder hit bottom, he positioned it squarely against the edge of the hole so it wouldn't budge. He had correctly guessed the depth of the tomb. More than a foot of the ladder's length remained above floor level. Father Marco congratulated himself with a one-handed high-five.

Let's see the Buddhists top that.

He was ready now. Taking no notice of all the unknowns, a thrill of excitement tingled him. He broke out in a nervous sweat and wiped his clammy palms on his pants. Then he reached around and tucked the flashlight into his pants in the hollow of his lower back. It put uncomfortable pressure on his spine, but the discomfort was tolerable. All I'm missing is a pith helmet, he kidded.

Butterflies danced a Tarantella in his stomach. He hadn't been this keyed up since... well, since he met *her* all those years ago. Now he knew how *she* must feel when on the brink of unearthing an ancient artifact hidden away from humanity for hundreds, possibly thousands, of years. *She* was Aysel Bigili, Professor of Archeology at Koç University in Istanbul, his Armenian friend with whom he had participated on several archeological digs from time to time during his summer holidays and who was rarely absent from his thoughts. Don't get too far ahead of yourself. You haven't discovered anything significant yet, he reminded himself. Still, he was optimistic.

He leaned over and grasped the top ends of the ladder and mounted it. Standing on an upper rung, he shook the ladder to make sure it was solidly planted. Satisfied, he recited a prayer then descended into the tomb, pondering with each downward step how far back in time he was vicariously travelling. He reached the stone floor in one piece. His limbs wobbled and his pulse raced, not from any kind of physical exertion, but from a combination of anticipation and trepidation. His breathing quickened. Like the majority of people, dark, confined spaces spooked him. It was normal to fear in such a space. He crossed himself, the better to be safe than sorry. The air in the tomb was cool, but dry, bone dry. It produced a rabid thirst in him.

I wish I brought water with me.

Deathly silence surrounded him. It was so quiet he could hear dust settling. Remembering the flashlight, he reached around for it and switched it on. The strong beam of light shined like a giant luminescent cone as it swept the walls and ceiling in a jerky motion; it helped tamp down the rising sensation of dread that threatened to overwhelm him. He hummed a favorite hymn while he explored the tomb, fighting to calm himself. Shortly, his heart rate returned to its normal rhythm.

The walls of the tomb were rough and unadorned, unlike the lavishly decorated Egyptian tombs he had often seen in books and magazines. He didn't know why he had formed this comparison. Maybe because Egyptian burial sites were so much a part of the popular imagination.

The conical beam of light came to rest on the ossuary, a crude trench of hollowed out stone. It was uncharacteristically long. Unlike typical ossuaries, which were short in length, the disinterred bones of the skeleton heaped in a bundle rather than laid out end-to-end, this ossuary was full length, like a sarcophagus, though not nearly as substantial.

He approached it warily, not from any superstitious belief but from the anxiety of violating the deceased's sacred space. Unexpectedly, he stumbled. He whipped the flashlight behind him.

"What the hell?"

He bent down and picked up a large and long piece of wood. Inspecting it, he noticed one end was charred. A wooden torch? Odd that this was left behind. Someone afraid of the dark? He gave his shoulders a shrug then set the torch-like implement against the wall of the tomb where it wouldn't trip up anyone else.

The lid of the ossuary lay broken in two against what was a plinth constructed of solid rock. The entire floor had been carved out to create the stand of rock on which the ossuary rested. Father Marco pointed the flashlight on the bottom of the plinth. No seam between it and the floor. What craftsmanship! Pity the poor sods who carved out this tomb.

He pondered the state of the uncovered ossuary for a few moments. Grave robbers? But the shrouded skeleton lay undisturbed in the ossuary. Istanbul had experienced many severe earthquakes in its long history so perhaps the lid fell off on its own. He would never uncover the real answer. Did it really matter?

He shined the light into the ossuary. Coated in dust, the shroud covering the body was in fine shape, having seemingly ignored a protracted passage of time. He played the light beam over the length of the shrouded skeleton, moving from head to feet and back again. If bones could talk, what tales they could tell. He felt the urge to remove the shroud but decided against it. The face of the corpse was not covered and the image of the grinning skull filled his mind and made him cringe inside. Yet the atmosphere was not one of horror but of solemnity.

His inspection of the body completed, he came around to the head of the ossuary and crouched down to inspect an inscription carved into the end of the bone-box he had noticed earlier. The engraving was clogged with centuries of accumulated grime. He retrieved a small paintbrush from his pocket. Holding the flashlight in one hand, and the paintbrush in the other, he removed the crud that had accumulated in the nooks and crannies of the engraving, a simple cleaning technique taught to him by Aysel. How can an apparently airless tomb accumulate so much dirt? he wondered. This mystery wouldn't be solved anytime soon. Father Marco had more important matters that demanded his utmost attention. He blew away the last particles of debris loosened by the brush.

With his index finger, he traced the engraving.

Something's out of joint.

He expected to see koine Greek carved into the ossuary. Instead, he had uncovered Aramaic script.

How odd.

Aramaic had once been the *lingua franca* of the Assyrian Empire, the extent of which was now central Turkey, much farther to the east. This empire collapsed in the early 7$^{th}$ century BCE. He puzzled over this.

Though his knowledge of the Assyrians was limited, he was certain they didn't incorporate ossuaries in their burial practices. With curious excitement he studied the inscription. He was fluent in Aramaic and in koine Greek and paleo-Hebrew, possessing advanced degrees in these three languages. He was also fluent in Latin, Italian and Turkish. Fluency in several languages was just one of the many reasons (not all of them good) for his assignment to Istanbul by his superiors what felt like eons ago.

The crude letters, most likely carved by an iron chisel, required patience to decipher. Tense with concentration, letter by painstaking letter he transcribed and translated what he avidly read. Words began to form, then their meaning.

"O my God," he cried out and reached for the side of the ossuary to steady himself, his brain reeling. "This can't be," and his head buzzed from the blow of discovery.

He stood up for his knees burned with pain, having crouched for so long. He leaned on the ossuary with his hands and regarded the skeleton in the bone-box with veneration. How in heaven? A wave of unreality washed over him and left him shivering in supernatural awe.

"Lord knows how you wound up in this tomb. It's a mystery, but your identity no longer is. Rest in peace, my dear, rest in pea—"

He swivelled around. Every nerve strained for sensory input and the skin on his neck prickled. He shined the flashlight into the dark recesses of the tomb. No ghosts lay hidden, waiting to pounce on him. His rattled nerves under control again, he consoled himself. Just a case of the jiggy-wiggies, that's all. He took one last hasty look up at the opening. Are my eyes playing tricks on me?

He sprung up the ladder, poked his head above the hole and scanned the room. All appeared to be as it was before he got spooked. He was about to descend when he noticed the door to the archive was slightly ajar. Strange. I could have sworn I closed it earlier. Maybe a draft blew it open...You're starting to lose it, he mocked himself.

He descended the ladder, jitter-free, and looked upon the ossuary with a renewed sense of awe.

What a find!

He stood immobile and stared into the distance, eyes unfocused, and his ego swelled with visions of camera flashes bursting like fireworks and reporters hanging on his every word. Maybe they'll make me a bishop. He allowed himself to picture for a moment supplicants bending to kiss his ring. Wouldn't that be an achievement and wouldn't Aysel be impressed. Intoxicated with dreams of fame and fortune, he saw her marvelling him in his mind's eye. Without warning, a scolding inner voice punctured the bubble of his tipsy imagination.

Don't let your ego get the better of you, and he instantly sobered up. Let them try to deny me my raise in salary now.

He contemplated once again the corpse lying in silent repose. Gone was his cockiness—at least for the moment. Here laid the answer to a puzzle that had plagued Bible scholars for two millennia: the identity of Jesus' most beloved disciple! Several possible candidates had been proposed and contested over the centuries, but not a single one had ever been proven. It was just so much hot air.

I not only know the identity of this disciple but I now know why Jesus loved this person so. If the words I translated are authentic, then this discovery of mine will solve one of the most enduring mysteries in Christendom!

# Part II

*Propaganda in the service of unchecked power is the most dangerous enemy truth can have*

## Chapter Fifteen
## Eastern Turkey

Aysel listened to the noise of the angry squall thwacking the walls of the tent. The sound reminded her of an untethered sail slatting in a blustery storm. In spite of the turbulence that thundered beyond the thin but tough layer of canvas, she lay contented on the cot enfolded in the brawny arms of her boyfriend, Baki. Thick in girth, his arms weighed upon her. She liked their heft and solidity. They signified brute power, the power to keep her safe from all perils, both real and imagined.

But she will curse the day she let him into her life.

His presence made her heart thrum and her emotions soar, and she breathed in the man smell of him. He had completed another security assignment and popped in to see her. Private security wasn't a nine-to-five career. He kept odd hours. His job took him away for days and, on occasion, for weeks. Then, with little warning, he would show up on her doorstep—or tent flap, like tonight—sporting a lopsided boyish grin which never failed to relieve the ache in her heart she had borne during his absence.

Generous to a fault, he escorted her to the finest restaurants in Istanbul. They danced in the trendiest clubs. He lavished expensive gifts on her. She had fallen hard for him. Maybe a little too hard—and maybe a little too fast. But he didn't register on her deceit detector so he must be the genuine thing, right? And he's oh-so-easy on the eyes. His curly brown hair and basset-hound eyes made her stomach flip-flop every time she saw him, she sighed, as she turned him around and around in her mind.

Was he too good to be true? She liked the cut of her man's jib but she wondered in moments of solitude whether her yearning to be someone's significant other had compromised her judgement. For the first time in years, however, the roll and yaw of prior romantic entanglements were absent in their relationship. It had been nothing but smooth sailing with Baki at the helm of their vessel of *amour*. She felt like foam on a swelling sea, floating, not floundering like a netted fish. If there's no water in the hold, why sound the alarm? He was her steady rudder now, providing direction in her life with no destination in sight. In spite of her typical need for certainty, she was happy with this uncharted course.

She appreciated his avid interest in her career. Most men were intimidated by her vocation, but not Baki. He admired what she did for a living. He didn't mind getting his hands dirty and often joined her on archeological excavations when he could, performing the grunt work of a novice digger without complaint.

Before Baki (or BB for short) her job had consumed her, but with time, she carved out space in her work for their love affair. And she was glad she had done so for she was now aware of what was missing from her life: passion and tenderness. Baki was both the source of and the salve for the hunger in her heart. How was it possible?

Her girlfriends often griped how much they missed their men when they were away. She could relate to this sentiment now for she was no longer a spectator looking in, nose pressed against the plate-glass window, vicariously experiencing the thrills of romance. Life seemed perfect with Baki. Yet something whose nebulous contours she couldn't define nibbled at the edges of her subconscious.

Maybe it's because I'm Armenian and Baki is Turkish. She hadn't told her mother about him. She was afraid of her reaction. Her great-grandfather had died along with hundreds of thousands of other Armenians in the *Meds Yeghern* or "Great Catastrophe" during the breakup of the Ottoman Empire in the First World War. The Turks were solely blamed for this human tragedy.

War can be evil, but it's the victors' who define what is evil and who assign blame for perpetrating it. In accordance with this rule, the blameworthy always suffer the victors' interpretation of events. The history of the *Meds Yeghern* was written by the West. It's a cliché but truth is always the first casualty of war. There was plenty of guilt to go around. No one's hands were clean in that war. All of them were bloody. She clenched her fists.

"Is something bothering you, Treasure?" Baki asked, nudging her with his muscular arms.

"No," Aysel replied hastily. "What makes you say that?"

"You seem uptight."

He was so perceptive. She loved this about him. "I was musing about my mother."

"How is she?"

"The usual complaints, otherwise, she's fine."

"*So?*"

"I want to introduce you to her, *but…*"

"What's preventing you?"

"Either you're naïve or completely clueless, Baki Cavus. Which is it?" she said with mock seriousness.

"Is there a third choice concealed somewhere in your estimation of me?"

"Two's enough."

"Then I hereby exercise my right to remain silent. I don't want to incriminate myself."

"You're impossible," she said and tapped him on the arm.

He gave her a gentle squeeze. "You still didn't answer my question."

"Don't you get it, you love-besotted fool? I'm Armenian, you're Turkish. We're supposed to be at each other's throat."

"Your mother hates Turks?"

"Can you blame her? She lost her grandfather in the resettlement of our people during the First World War. She never met him. It happened before she was born. But she was raised on stories about him by my grandmother who kept his memory alive. So my grandmother's bitterness became my mother's," she explained.

"There's plenty of hate to go around, Treasure. Armenians massacred Turks in the 1890s to create an ethnically pure Armenia. But no government in the West has made a fuss about it."

"We didn't learn about any massacres of Turks in school."

"Of course not, Aysel. But you would have if you had been educated here. It's a dirty little secret among Armenian politicians. They can't have Turkey accusing *them* of genocide. There's never any moral equivalence between the crimes of Christians and the crimes of Muslims in the minds of Islamophobes. Look at what's going on in Syria right now. Turkey is being accused of genocide against Kurds when it has been sheltering five hundred thousand Kurds since 2011."

"There's a degree of truth to that." She didn't see Baki roll his eyes. "I saw President Ordekan on television the other day," Aysel said. "He claimed Armenian deaths during the war were due to privation and to the consequences of defending Turkey's territorial integrity. Not from any premeditated act of genocide."

"The hatred between our peoples has a long history, but there's also a long history of hatred between Armenians and Kurds. They killed Armenians in the war, too, because they coveted the same territory for a future homeland."

"Agreed. That detail is ignored by Western historians."

"My people bear the brunt of the blame for this crime because of the white man's spectre of the 'Terrible Turk.' This make-believe menace still haunts the fevered imagination of the Western mind. Need I remind you of my *favorite* cowboys and Indians movie to prove my point about the anti-Muslim bias that prevails in the West?"

She contemplated his remark. "I thought you hated *American Sniper*?"

"Sometimes my irony is lost on you, Treasure," he chuckled. "Look, Armenians weren't innocent either. They were insurgents. They collaborated with Russia, our sworn enemy during the First World War. The way I see it, your ancestors were divinely punished for allying themselves with a Godless communist nation."

"But women and children died."

"Collateral damage and human shields."

She twisted and glared at him. "That's sick."

"*No*. It's the sick rationalizations lobbed by Israeli and American journalists and politicians to justify the mass murder of Muslim non-combatants. What's good for the Judeo-Christian goose is good for the Muslim gander."

"That doesn't justify killing my ancestors," she shrilled.

"The Ottoman state possessed the God-given right to expel Armenian rebels from its territory. A legitimate state has every right to defend itself against internal enemies who take up arms against it.

The North waged total war against the South in the U.S. Civil war, did it not? A state cannot make accommodation with traitors. Exile or surrender is the only solution."

"Civil war is a nasty business."

"Did you know twelve million Germans were forcibly transferred from east-central Europe to Germany and Austria after the Second World War?"

"No."

"How many of these twelve million German refugees died en route to Germany and Austria?"

"I don't know."

"Neither do I. And do you know why?" He didn't wait for her to answer. "Because the Allied Powers didn't care and so their deaths weren't recorded."

Aysel was struck mute.

"But I do know over a million regular German soldiers perished in American and French POW camps from state-sanctioned starvation and exposure. That was a clear case of genocide. Westerners can suck a mule's tit. Turkey is for the Turkmens!"

"War's an untidy business, I suppose. The past isn't as transparent as the history books suggest," Aysel said, subsiding back into his arms. She had never been exposed to this side of European history.

But for the buffeting wind, a silence hung over everything in the snug confines of the tent. And there was tension in it.

Baki broke the uncomfortable silence first. "I'm sorry, Treasure...Turkey was fighting for its existence on all fronts. The survival of the Turkish nation was at stake! Russians in the north, the Allied Powers in the west and south and the Armenian insurgency in the east. The Allies blockaded the Eastern Mediterranean which worsened food shortages in Ottoman territories, making the West accountable for the starvation of Armenians and Assyrians. Turkey didn't enjoy the resources nor the internal stability to set up concentration camps for Armenians like the Americans and Canadians did for citizens of Japanese ancestry during World War Two. And let's remember those people weren't engaging in armed insurrection in Canada nor in the U.S. like the Armenians had been during the First World War. If Japanese-Americans had been rebelling, you can bet the gloves would've been taken off. All we can hope for now is God's forgiveness."

Mollified, Aysel's tension unwound. "You have a point. If Latino-Americans were to connive with a foreign power to take back the territories the U.S. stole from Mexico in the Mexican-American War, white and black Americans wouldn't hesitate to annihilate them. That aside, Ordekan took a brave step when he challenged the Armenian government to open its archives, as Turkey has done. Neutral historians, not politicians, should decide whether the crime of genocide was committed. Ordekan offered to pay reparations if such a crime had been perpetrated."

"His offer was an act of political *and* moral bravery. But we wouldn't be having this conversation if the Armenians weren't Christian and the Turks weren't Muslim."

"How can you say that?"

"The so-called Armenian genocide presents a golden opportunity for the Islamophobic court of Western public opinion to charge a Muslim country with the crime of ethnic cleansing, a crime against humanity which the Christian West is expert at."

"You sound so cynical, Baki." She brooded, never having seen this side of him before.

"Do I? The truth hurts, doesn't it? When Muslims kill, it's because we're barbarians. When a Christian country commits an atrocity, it's always a regrettable accident in the furtherance of a greater cause like bringing *democracy* to us savages," he said.

"I never viewed it that way."

"I wouldn't expect you to. Fair and balanced critical-thinking isn't part of your education. You went to Armenian schools, those incubators of anti-Turkish hatred and propaganda."

"Well, the Armenian genocide *is* the third rail of our religion."

"I'll leave it at that. I agree with what the president proposed."

"You do?"

"Of course. Turkey has nothing to hide. The truth should be determined by impartial historians and not by vindictive Armenian politicians who can't even produce the names of those who died in the Armenian resettlement."

"It's a reasonable proposal, but it needs the support of both governments. Armenia is dragging its feet on this issue."

"Ask yourself, Aysel. If Turks are so evil, why are there seventy thousand Armenians living in peace in Turkey and not a single Turk living in Armenia? Who are the real ethnic cleansers?"

"I wasn't aware of that."

"It's ironic Armenians by the thousands are sneaking into this country to find work. I guess they can set aside their sense of victimization and self-pity so long as they get a job here," he said.

"The massacre isn't a bread and butter issue with most Armenians I know. Jobs are."

"Every year, the government of Armenia uses the anniversary of the exile to appeal to its people's sense of tribalism and to generate support for launching a grievance industry like greedy Jewish lawyers did with the Holocaust. Little does it know, Turkey is immune to such financial shakedowns. Plus, Armenia supports the supremacist Zionist entity occupying Palestine, so the Armenian lobby can screw itself."

"I wish this issue would be resolved to the satisfaction of both our peoples."

"It's best to let go of the past, Treasure. Obsessing over it won't revive the dead."

"My mother doesn't see it this way."

"Does your mom have any Turkish friends or acquaintances?"

"I'm not aware of any."

"That's part of the problem. If we remain sealed off in our ethnic silos, we only perpetuate these ancient blood feuds. There's a beautiful *ayat* (verse) in the Quran where God says: *O you mankind! Surely We have created you of a male and a female, and made you into nations and tribes so you may know each other.*"

"What does this mean?"

"It means God created us differently to make us interesting to one another," he explained. "Imagine if we all looked the same, talked the same, dressed the same. Why would anyone want to travel? The world would be such a monotonous and colorless place, don't you think? It's best to honor the diversity of God's human creation by respecting it. We dishonor His Divine diversity with our bigotry, prejudice and racism."

"You're *so* poetic, Baki," she said. "What you're saying is true on a spiritual level. But my mother is an old woman now. If you've been raised your whole life to hate Turks, it would be a real challenge to undo a lifetime of hatred."

"I hear you, Treasure, but hatred is such a waste of energy."

"Let's give it more time." Feeling relaxed again, she nestled deeper into his arms.

Baki loathed to concede he was a complete jerk. But a decent jerk? He wasn't sure. Maintaining the pretense of a loving and caring boyfriend often taxed his conscience. And he did possess a conscience, but he didn't allow it to impact his business affairs. He was fond of Aysel but he *loved* so much more the lucre he earned selling priceless relics on the black market.

Which is why Baki had hitched his wagon to her. She was an unwitting partner in his smuggling business. He didn't join her on archeological digs because he enjoyed swinging a shovel or pick axe. *No.* That was but a means to an end, and the end often generated generous rewards. When ancient booty turned up at one of her archeological sites, a quantity of it wound its way into his possession, then into the greedy paws of rich collectors for which he earned lucrative commissions. The security business held advantages; his connections with the company that provided security for archeological digs was his ticket to early retirement.

Aysel wasn't the sole source of his lucrative trade, though. A good smuggler didn't put all his lucre in one basket. The U.S.-fomented civil war in Syria facilitated the smuggling of Syrian antiquities via the southeastern border between Turkey and Syria which was more porous than ever. And Baki was more than happy to provide a nice, new home for this historic contraband.

Aysel's smartphone burst the silence with its ringtone, startling both of them. She jolted to a sitting position and reached for the phone on the wooden crate, and the cot creaked in protest with her abrupt movement.

"*Merhaba*?"

"Hi, Aysel," a male voice said, gulping into the phone.

"Father Marco," she said, switching to English. "You sound out of breath. Are you okay?" As a faculty member at the English-speaking Koç University, Aysel was fluent in English as well as Armenian, Turkish, Aramaic and Urartian.

"Yes, yes. Are you in Istanbul?"

"No. I'm still in eastern Turkey. My work at the Van Castle took a fascinating twist this summer. We uncovered artifacts which open a window onto the cultural and social activities of the Urartian peo—"

In a burst of eagerness, he interrupted her. "Wonderful. Aysel. How can I say this…? I discovered something—someone—who will shake Christendom to its foundation."

"Shake Christendom? I don't understand."

"I can't tell you over the phone."

"You can trust me."

"That's why I called you. When are you returning to Istanbul?"

"Not for another two weeks. I—"

"Two weeks!"

"Is it urgent?"

"You'll understand why when you see what—who—I stumbled upon."

"One second, Father," she said. Holding the phone to her chest, she turned and asked, "What is it, Baki?"

"Tell Father Marco I say, hi."

"Baki says, 'Hi,'"

"You're with Baki?"

If Aysel could see his face, she'd think he had swallowed vinegar.

"He's here."

"Give him my regards. How about calling me as soon as you return?"

"Sure, Father."

"I'll be waiting for your call, my dear."

"Okay."

"God be with you."

"And with you."

"What's new with Father Marco, Treasure?"

"Don't know," she said, perplexed. "He wouldn't divulge anything over the phone." She shrugged her lips and replaced the phone on the crate.

"Maybe he's found Noah's Ark." His curiosity aroused, he would later ask Cemil, a co-worker of Aysel's in the department of archeology at Koç University and a co-conspirator, to sniff around.

"Be nice. Otherwise, he might put the curse of God on you," Aysel warned.

"He *is* a priest, so I guess I can trust him."

"Is my Baki *jea-lous*?"

"Not of him. Unless he should apostatize due to your irresistible beauty."

Aysel cut an attractive figure. Her well-defined jaw and full lips added to her facial appeal. And she belonged to Baki—provided she remained useful.

"What about you, big boy. Can you resist me?" she purred as she crouched above him, ready to pounce like a cat.

"Let's find out," he said, and he turned away from her in jest.

* * *

Father Marco replaced the instrument with a snort of frustration and tilted back in his chair. The office hummed with silence. He triangled his hands at his lips and pinched them.

Another two weeks! First Dimitri takes a spill and now Aysel is a thousand miles away. The Lord is surely testing my patience. Yeah, but just think. You'll get to spend some quality time with her all by yourself.

The sudden change of heart cheered him up. Just then, sensing someone's presence, he glanced at the empty doorway to his office.

There's that feeling of paranoia again…Get a grip. You're in a holy sanctuary. What could go wrong in a House of God?

# Chapter Sixteen
# Indianapolis

Following his interview on *The Last Word*, the story grew into a firestorm of controversy. Giltmore endured weeks of incessant gossip and personal attacks. He couldn't go anywhere in public without people giving him dirty looks or uttering threats when they passed him. He'd wake up some mornings to find trash on his front lawn. But no burning cross. Yet. Indiana was Klan country after all.

And the hate email poured in. A veritable deluge. Almost biblical. Conservative media outlets piled on, too, interviewing colleagues who all of a sudden didn't have a good word to say about him. Despite the negative pushback, his book sales continued to climb worldwide. He'd be lying if he said he wasn't loving the attention. He was living for it. Not for his own sake but for the sake of disseminating the truth.

Then a representative from the *Sandra Dowling Show* contacted him and plucked him from social exile. Maybe he was more than just another contrarian voice sputtering in the wind. For a second time in his life he found himself in a television studio. His moment of fame (or was it notoriety?) had gone into overtime. He was fine with this. The more publicity for his book, the better.

In this match-up, the atmosphere would be tellingly different. No hostile host or audience awaited him. It'd just be him, two armchairs, a few large potted plants, a circular table and a stunning progressive-minded female host. *This* he could handle. It was rare when he was in the company of a beautiful woman. Between him and the wall, it was closer to never, but that was a carefully guarded secret. Giltmore would do his best to savor this exceptional moment.

He was well aware he now had the nation's undivided attention. He had initiated a national dialogue, sometimes hysterical and nasty, other times reflective and positive, but at least his message was topical. His last TV interview left no room for fence sitters. Based on his social media research, people had split into two rival camps. Those who claimed he was the harbinger of the Apocalypse and those who believed he was doing the world a favor by exposing the inventions of Christianity.

Giltmore didn't pitch his tent in either camp. He was done with camping. He was more interested in stoking the campfires of debate to gratify his newfound calling as a torchbearer of truth. Heated discussion and debate he relished, not for its own sake, but for the sake of the burning truth.

The lights in the studio dimmed. Sandra Dowling, crowned the 'queen of daytime TV,' glided onto the set—five-foot ten inches of polished and proportioned ebony supported on a spiky pair of designer high-heel shoes, which, despite their exorbitant cost, looked uncomfortable. But it was the price she seemed willing to pay to be fashionable. A white silk blouse and a short navy blue skirt hugged her slim figure. Wavy black hair framed an angular but attractive face. Graceful, she exuded the confident demeanor of someone who met the world head on. Sandra strode across the stage toward Mike like she owned it, leaving in her wake a trail of bulging eyes, sagging jaws and lolling tongues.

But her arresting beauty was both a blessing and a curse. A blessing because her looks opened doors for her. A curse because she had to work harder than her peers to be taken seriously. She had to prove she was more than just another pretty face of color. Despite her personal trials, her doggedness paid dividends in the end. She now sat atop the heap of television journalism. And not because she had played it safe. Just the opposite. She had taken risks in her career and the reward was her own show. And although her career had cost her personally, she had never lost sight of who she was or what she stood for, and it was why she possessed such a loyal and adoring fan base.

With her level of success, though, there had been compromises. Wasn't this always the case? When not in front of the cameras, her personal life suffered a train of broken romances. She had plenty of male admirers but she found it difficult to trust them, to determine if they were traipsing through her life carving notches in their headboards or seeking the limelight, or both. Celebrity wasn't something she sought, but it wasn't something she fought against, either. But what good were fame and fortune with no one to share them?

Like many career-focused women, she had delayed marriage and sacrificed her child-bearing years for the sake of her profession. Had it been worth it? She valued her free time—what little there was—so she didn't regret foregoing motherhood. Marriage was still a worthwhile goal, but finding someone her age who didn't have baggage from an earlier marriage was like hunting for a yellow daisy among the dandelions. Of one thing she was certain. She was done with square jaws and chiselled pecs. Someone who was cerebral, someone who could stimulate her intellect and someone who could make her laugh were her criteria now. Was this asking for too much?

Giltmore hoped she hadn't seen him guiltily putting his eyeballs back in their sockets. You're a Submitter now. You're supposed to lower your gaze.

"Hi, Professor Giltmore. So we finally meet." She held out her hand to shake.

He jumped up from his seat so quickly he almost knocked it over. It teetered then righted itself. At his full height, he realized he stood almost eye-to-eye with his host, and he hoped his face didn't have "giddy" written all over it. Her voice was like caramel to his ears. He shook her slender hand. "It's a pleasure to meet you, Sandra." Soft hand but firm handshake. I won—

"May I have my hand back?"

"Oh, sorry."

"Don't worry about it, Professor."

"Please call me Mike. *Professor* sounds too formal."

"Mike it is then," she said, bestowing a friendly smile upon him, her perfect white teeth and pink gums contrasting with her flawless mahogany skin.

"Sandra. We're about to go live," informed the studio manager.

Once again, it was show time. Sandra and Giltmore took their seats. She crossed her legs and tugged and smoothed her skirt into place while he resisted the temptation to follow the movements of her well-manicured hands. The lights grew brighter.

"Thank you all for joining us," she began. "With us today is Michael Giltmore, a retired professor of theology from the University of Thomas More in Indiana. He's the author of the contemplative and provocative book, *The Fall of Judaic Christianity and the Rise and Triumph of Gnostic Paulianity*, which those of you watching might already know, offers a sobering critique of Christianity but also renders many a person drunk with rage. Welcome, Mike. It's great to have you on my show," she said unfeigned.

"The pleasure is all mine, Sandra." You owned me at "With."

Pleasantries concluded, she dove in. "So how are you enjoying your retirement?"

"Well, I spend a portion of my time reading hate mail, mostly of the electronic variety, a task as agreeable as scraping bird crap off the windshield of my car. An—"

She burst out laughing…"Sorry, I couldn't help myself."

"And I'm getting over a severe case of pixel burn from reviewing one too many spittle-flecked YouTube videos excoriating my work," he said without missing a beat.

"You do look a little charred. But before we deal with the backlash to your book, we hope you're prepared to bring an end to the rumors."

"There's more than one?"

"Were you forced into retirement by the administration at the University of Thomas More?"

As part of his retirement package, he had agreed to a non-disclosure clause. His audience wasn't aware of this nor did it need to be. Deciding to have some fun with her, he said, "Since you couched your question in such an opaque manner, I must reply to you in kind. I intended to retire before the commencement of the fall term."

She caught the irony of Giltmore's reply and said, "So the controversy provoked by your book didn't precipitate your hasty retirement."

"Not at all. I planned it months ago. But I advanced it by a couple of weeks out of respect for my employer. My presence on campus was causing security headaches."

She perked up. "What's this about?"

"I received and continue to receive death threats."

"Let's hope these death threats are nothing more than misguided anger. How are the authorities treating them?"

"Police patrols have increased on my street and the FBI is investigating. Emails can be traced."

"Criminal intelligence is sometimes an oxymoron."

Laughing, he said, "Good one, Sandra."

"So the negative fallout from your TV interview continues to rise?"

"I'm wearing hip waders beneath my suit."

Unable to quash a laugh, Sandra paused to compose herself before resuming. His wit scratched her itch. She rubbed her nose and said, "You've adopted a sense of humor in the teeth of this media storm. More power to you."

"Despite my tone of levity, it's a pity my opposition hasn't taken more time to reflect. They went into attack mode right away. The level-headed wisdom I imparted is as beneficial to my detractors as a blank page is to a blind person." He folded his hands in his lap.

"Professor Giltmore—I mean, Mike—you sound disappointed people still believe in Christianity whole hog despite the arguments you raised in your interview on *The Last Word*."

"Not at all. I didn't expect a spontaneous mass exodus from churches. People need time to weigh my words. But my message got through to a part-time student at the university. Julio—that's his name. He and I have been exchanging emails," he said with a smile. "He's probably watching your show."

"You want to say hi to him?"

"Can I?" He looked to Sandra who pointed to the camera he should speak to.

"Hi, Julio." He gave him a brief wave. "That was fun. Thanks."

"So we were discussing the impact of your last talk."

"You know, there's no end to the blinkered credulity of the fundamentalists who fetishize the inerrancy of the Bible in the face of overwhelming and irrefutable evidence to the contrary. Reasoning with such individuals is an exercise in futility. Like trying to slam shut a revolving door. They trip over the truth but get right back up and continue on as though nothing occurred."

A stickler for accuracy, Sandra couldn't resist correcting him. "You misquoted Churchill."

"I did?"

"It was Churchill who composed your simile, but he penned it another way, and I quote: 'Men occasionally stumble over the truth, but most of them pick themselves up and hurry off as if nothing ever happened.'"

"You have a sharp memory."

"I got lucky. I wrote a paper in university about Churchill's practice of using the radio medium to rally the spirit of the British people and troops during the war, so I still remember his most popular quotes."

Wow! Brains and beauty. He held her in wonder.

"Mike?" she nudged. Sandra leaned back in her chair and twirled her long, glossy chestnut-colored tresses with her slender fingers. She looked flattered to have aroused such a reaction in another person.

"Uh, sorry. I was having a senior's moment."

"I won't hold it against you," and they shared a laugh, the audience along with them.

He stared into space for a beat. "The worst lies are the lies we tell ourselves. Behavioral scientists label this state of mind *cognitive dissonance*. I call it stubborn pride. Humans are hard-wired to maintain their belief in falsehoods even when handed overwhelming evidence that proves the contrary. Beliefs trump facts. Neither truth nor fact can put a dent in their convictions. It's baffling how people go to great lengths to reject rational thinking when confronted with incontrovertible truth that threatens their worldview."

"Like those folks who still believe the government's version of the 9/11 attack despite scientific proof steel buildings don't magically collapse at the speed of gravity into their own footprints."

Applause broke out in the studio.

Giltmore sat speechless. A rare event. Did she say what she said? Flumm my ox. "I'm not alone in saying the truth is a fugitive from the captive airwaves in this country. 9/11 was our era's Reichstag fire. A burnt offering to the American ruling class's pagan god and a funeral pyre to inflame the fury of the American people and trigger their snap support for launching an invasion of Afghanistan and Iraq in their name. Just as the German people were sold a whopper about the Reichstag fire, so were Americans similarly gaslighted to swallow the Big Lie about 9/11. But the post-9/11 political repression failed to crush the truth."

"Good point, Mike. It's easy to whip up anti-Muslim hysteria when politicians and the media are marching together in lockstep to the beat of Islamophobia."

"Arthur Schopenhauer astutely noted 'all truth passes through three stages: first, it is ridiculed; second, it is violently opposed; and third, it is accepted as self-evident.'"

"So true."

"Our brains are round so it's easy to get caught in the grip of circular reasoning. Only a sound mind can free us from its grasp."

"Funny. Let's get back to our discussion. You were saying..."

"Right. Most people stay in their comfort zone to avoid the anxiety of venturing beyond its borders because doing so involves risk. But authentic living is having the courage to accept a new perspective when you know you are wrong. This is a sign of wisdom and maturity," he said. "Here's the crux of the problem. In renouncing Christianity, an individual might have to abandon her social group and become an outsider. A frightening prospect from which many would flee. They must suffer the long, dark night of the soul, as I did, and come to grips with the fact they've been victims of the biggest con job in the history of the world."

"Ouch."

"Let me be blunt."

"Don't hold back on us now," and the audience chuckled along with her.

"I'm not here to sugar-coat the truth," he said. "Clergy haven't been pulling the wool over the eyes of their congregants. They've been shearing entire flocks of sheep for God's sake. But what else can we expect? They've perpetrated a gross fraud upon the people.

Catholic and Protestant leaders have a vested interest in maintaining the status quo. Their institutions and vocations rely on perpetuating the theological deceptions I discussed a few weeks ago. These same leaders are guiding their followers to a dreadful destination that smells like smoke and feels like fire. There's even a word for it: Hell."

"So you're in the business of saving souls, are you?" she said, leaning forward in her chair, digging the courage of his convictions.

He held up his hands in protest. "Not at all. I don't possess the temperament to be a preacher. I'm too didactic, too uncompromising."

"You don't say."

Laughter rolled out from the audience.

"But I still have a moral obligation to share with my fellow men and women what I've learned."

"Sharing is caring."

Compassion filled his voice with emotion. "Listen. We're all God's creatures. I consider everyone in the human race my brother and my sister wheth—"

"Do we have a say in this?"

Howls of laughter poured from the audience.

"Afraid not. You're stuck with me." More laughter. "Look. People's houses are on fire, but they can't smell the smoke because the perfume of this life dulls their mental faculties. I feel it's my duty to warn them of the mortal danger they are in. Wouldn't you?"

"You bet I would."

"I harbor no ill-will toward anyone because God is the manager of our affairs. I simply desire for everyone what I desire for myself."

"Which is?"

"Inner peace in this life and Paradise in the afterlife."

"I won't argue with that. So, how can people break out of their comfort zones?"

"Here's the deal, Sandra. People put too much trust in authority. It can be an enemy of truth. Especially when its interests are threatened. People of all faiths should perform their own due diligence when choosing a religion to follow so they don't get conned. Belief should spring from true conviction and not from cultural or tribal affinity. Thoughtless conformity is enslavement. An unexamined faith is not worth believing in."

"What should a person do?"

"First, you must search for the truth yourself instead of blindly trusting your spiritual leaders and, second, you must rid yourself of the age-old fear of What will people think? I struggled with this question," he said. "The pages of history are stained with the tears of regret shed by those too afraid to let go of the safe and familiar. People are loath to rupture their ties to culture and tradition. Is not social exclusion the paramount concern? Only a person of courage can see beyond the wall of fear that hems them in. Family and friends might try to hold you back from seeking the truth. Ignore them. Pleasing your Creator is more important than pleasing them. On the Day of Reckoning, they'll be too preoccupied with their own depositions to cheer you on from the bleachers when you sit in the Judgement Seat before God."

"Sounds daunting."

"Finally, you must admit Christian beliefs have the sanctified odor of truth but are in fact inventions—clever inventions, but inventions nevertheless. It requires a strong dose of personal courage to confess to living a lie one's whole life."

Batting her eyes, she said, "Am I a fool, Mike."

"Only if you take my word for it," he gruffed. Does she expect me to bend over and kiss her feet?

Sandra backpedalled. "The jury is still deliberating." Her attempt at testing his resolve backfired. "What you recommend amounts to a tall order."

"I didn't say it would be easy. People must confront the stark truth about the defining act of Christianity: the torture and murder of an innocent man. Where is the justice, the Divine mercy in this? Do we not condemn the execution of the wrongfully convicted?"

Sandra groped for an answer.

"Someone of stature within the Protestant or Catholic religion needs to step forward and declare the death of Christianity because people tune out intellectuals like me. There's a proven streak of anti-intellectualism a mile wide in this country," he said, spreading his arms far apart.

"How about a modern-day Martin Luther?"

Giltmore shook his head. "Luther protested against the authority of the Catholic Church, but he didn't challenge the basic message of Christianity."

"Then who?"

"How about you, Sandra? You have a huge following. Aren't you a practicing Christian?"

"Yes, bu—"

"But what? Either you believe the arguments I advanced in my book or you don't. If you assent to them, then what are you waiting for?"

She lurched bolt upright and uncrossed her toned legs. She didn't appreciate being put on the spot, so she threw it right back at him. "How about telling us what you're waiting for," she said, indignation in her voice.

He glanced at the floor then he gazed into Sandra's smoldering emerald eyes. "I'm not waiting. While researching and writing my book, I experienced a crisis of conscience—of faith," he confessed. So hard not to. "Judaism doesn't accept Jesus as the Messiah, so I couldn't become a Jew. Christianity isn't the religion of Jesus, so I couldn't remain a Christian. The religion of Submission, however, proclaims Jesus is the Messiah and propagates his monotheistic message. So I became a Submitter a short while ago," he said matter-of-factly, resting his arms on the sides of the chair.

"Religion of Submission? Sounds kind of *kink-kay*," she said, swaying her head.

Giltmore's jaw dropped and a rumble of laughter erupted in the studio and in homes across the country.

"The religion of Submission is the religion of Islam. I used the English word *Submission* in place of its Arabic word *Islam*," he said in a subdued but serious tone.

Sandra sported a mortified look. "I'm sorry for my remark, Mike. Truly. Please accept my apology," she said, laying her hand on his sleeve.

He gaped at the hallowed spot where her hand had lain. There goes an expensive suit jacket. "Apology accepted."

"So you converted to *Islam*?" she said. "*Why?*" And her *why* conveyed a hint of *whatever for*?

Her astonishment didn't faze him. It was a typical reaction. "Because Islam is a comprehensive way of life. It informs every aspect of life, in this world and the next—from the bedroom to the bathroom and from the boardroom to the battlefield and all stations of life in between."

"It couldn't have been easy to switch religions."

"I consider my conversion a miracle."

"In what way?"

"Think for a moment, Sandra," he said. "I embraced Islam in spite of some Muslims behaving badly and in spite of the non-stop campaign of fear and misinformation being waged against the religion of Submission. The message of Islam penetrated the miasma of Islamophobia and moved me to convert. This speaks to the power of Islam to soften hearts, not stab them. Proof that Islam spreads by the word, not by the sword."

"You have a point there," she allowed. "So what do mean you embraced Islam in spite of some Muslims?"

"Behold the ongoing sectarian and communal violence in the Islamic world. Car-bombings, suicide bombings, mosque bombings, ramming pedestrians with cars and trucks, dismembering journalists. Way to go team," he said, his words oozing scorn and sarcasm. He gave his head a weary shake. "These acts are sickening and completely un-Islamic. But, believe it or not, I was able to see beyond this obscene violence and judge Islam by its book and not by its followers."

"So how long did it take for you to convert to Islam?

"My conversion wasn't an overnight affair. It required almost a year of assiduous study and reflection," he said. "I rejected Christianity and Judaism because you won't find the word *Jew* or *Judaism* in the Torah nor will you find the word *Christian* or *Christianity* in the Gospels. A rather serious shortcoming which proves Judaism and Christianity are not revealed religions. And I couldn't help conclude the Islamic creed—There is no deity but God and Mohammed is the Prophet of God—is lucid and rational compared with the wordy Nicene Creed and the tortured Athanasian Creed, a tongue-numbing neoplatonic credo of 660 words that crucify logic and reason on a cross of incoherence. And here's the essential point about these creeds. You will find the Islamic creed written word for word throughout the Quran. But you will not find the Nicene Creed nor the Athanasian Creed in any shape or form in any Bible"

"Interesting. Anything else?"

"Hmm...George Bernard Shaw said the problems of the world would be solved by Prophet Mohammed, peace be upon him, over a cup of tea. The racial strife in this country is one problem Islam would solve overnight. In the Prophet's last sermon, he preached a white man has no superiority over a black man and a black man has no superiority over a white man. That only one's piety determined his degree of superiority over another. He preached racial equality over 1400 years ago and a thousand years before the so-called Age of Reason. True enlightenment began in Arabia. The West has yet to catch up.

"I would also add the impeccable character of Prophet Mohammed, peace be upon him, his hundreds of miracles, his prophecies, his teachings and his mention in the Old and New Testaments as well as the inimitable linguistic miracle of the Quran. Unlike the Bible, the Quran has remained unchanged since its revelation. Every Islamic sect, including the Shia, uses the same Quran unlike the profusion of different *versions* of the Bible that circulate throughout Christendom."

"Thought-provoking. How did your family respond to your conversion?"

He compressed his lips in a grim line. It was an upsetting question but he answered it, anyway. "My brother thinks I'm nuts. He subscribes to the logical fallacy: most Muslims aren't terrorists but most terrorists are Muslims. And my sister believes Muslims are anti-Semites. Another logical fallacy because Arabs are Semites and long before the Hebrews arrived on the scene." He added, "But I don't pass judgement on their opinions. It wasn't so long ago when my own perceptions were, shall we say, less than charitable toward Arabs and Muslims."

"Let's be honest, folks. Muslims are demonized and dehumanized in this country. Negative attitudes toward Islam are premised on a willful ignorance which nourishes an antipathy bordering on the pathological."

Tumultuous applause erupted from the audience.

"I'm grateful for your saying this, Sandra. It has more credibility coming from you than it would from me."

"It really sickens me how Islamophobia has become a social contagion that normalizes the demonization and caricaturization of Muslims much like the anti-Semitism of the Nazi era demonized and caricatured Jews.

Giltmore quirked an eyebrow in surprise. "Islamophobia is the McCarthyism of our age. And like McCarthyism, Islamophobia bestows power in the hands of men and women whose only qualification is a third-rate intelligence of the first rank."

"Like the ogre who claimed on national television, 'Islam hates us.'"

"I didn't know Islam could communicate in human speech." Sandra flashed him a grin before he continued. "Think of the U.S. as an airplane. It has a left wing, representing the Democrats, and a right wing, representing the Republicans, but in the cockpit sits the Deep State, which exploits and manipulates our fear and ignorance of Islam through its propaganda arm, the mainstream media. It plays both ends of the political and media spectrum against the middle. And it's just getting started. Our blinkered ideologies have carried us past the point of sober deliberation to an intellectual dead end. Islamophobes are only listening to opinion-makers who confirm their anti-Muslim biases."

"Propaganda in the service of power is the most dangerous enemy truth can have."

"And we have an adolescent megalomaniac in the seat of American power."

"Any idea what the source of this animosity toward Muslims is?"

"Well, there's an *ayat* (verse) in the Quran where God says: Never will the Jews nor the Christians be pleased with you till you follow their religion."

"Best answer I've ever heard. Now getting back to your sister's remark. *Are* Muslims anti-Semites, Mike?" she pointedly asked.

Her query caught him short and his face tightened. "*That's* a loaded question," he said somewhat riled. "The Islamophobic sectors of mainstream media would have us believe this canard but the truth is otherwise. Fact is, Prophet Mohammed married a Jewish convert to Islam. And the religion of Submission doesn't prescribe or promote any manifestation of bigotry or prejudice whether in word or deed. In spite of these prohibitions, there are anti-Semitic Muslims just as there are Islamophobic Jews and anti-Semitic Christians."

"You got that right."

"What's more, history shows Muslims sheltered Jews during outbreaks of anti-Semitic persecution. In the fifteenth century, the Ottoman Empire welcomed Jews fleeing the burning stakes and torture chambers of the Spanish Catholic Inquisition. And during the Second World War, Muslims in Europe and in occupied North Africa provided safe havens for Jews. I venture to say that if the Ottoman Empire had been extant during the Nazi era, a good portion of European Jewry would have survived the Holocaust by emigrating to Ottoman territory. But unfortunately France and Great Britain were in control of the former Ottoman provinces in that era."

The lion roared and his mighty roar reverberated around the world.

There was dead silence in the studio. Then, like the boy who dared to point out the emperor had no clothes, a brave soul with the moral courage and clarity to see the obvious began clapping. Then another and another until almost the entire audience joined in to express its approval. A few holdouts sat on their hands and scowled.

Giltmore leaned over to Sandra and said, "You started it. I finished it," and he shot her a quick wink. His comment was drowned out by the deafening applause.

She gave him a nod of support. Then she took charge again. "O-kay, folks. Let's continue...Back to you, Mike." The clapping subsided.

He picked up where he had left off. "I want to draw your attention to something devout Muslims commemorate each year. Are you familiar with the Day of Ashura?"

"Can't say I am."

"*Ashura* is the Arabic word for *tenth.* The Day of Ashura refers to the tenth day of the first month of the Islamic lunar calendar when Moses, through the power of God, parted the Red Sea to facilitate the exodus of the Israelites from bondage in Egypt. The Jews commemorate the Exodus with Passover but on a different date because they follow the solar calendar. Prophet Mohammed recommended his followers commemorate this miracle by fasting on this day and on the day before or after it. Now is this a sign of anti-Semitism?"

"It's an eye-opener. So why do Muslims mark this day with fasting?"

"As a sign of gratitude to God for helping Prophet Moses and the Israelites escape from the Pharaoh and his army."

"*That's* revealing."

"It bears pointing out the lamestream media focuses its lens on the atavistic ritual of self-flagellation in which the Shia Muslims take part on the Day of Ashura."

"I take it you're referring to the ceremony where Shiites beat themselves bloody with swords and whips?"

"I am. Now do you recognize how the Western media colonize our minds with false ideas about Islam and Muslims? This ritual of self-flagellation has no basis in the creed of Islam nor in the practices of Prophet Mohammed, peace be upon him."

"It would be akin to the Islamic world broadcasting the Day of the Dead festivity that Mexicans celebrate as an exemplar of Christianity.

"Apt analogy, Sandra."

"Was there anything specific which led you to convert to Islam?" she asked, recrossing her ankles. Sandra was one of those expert conversationalists who drew out people with leading questions.

"Over a year ago, I had an epiphany while writing my book, which steered my life onto a different trajectory. In my line—former line—of work, I read the Bible more times than I could count, and I studied the Scriptures until I could recite them from memory. I don't say this to boast. Studying the Bible was my job...my life's work...my long-term mistress. Please bear with me. I'm coming to my point."

"We're all ears," she said.

"Despite having read the Gospels countless times, I never formed the connection between the following three verses of Scripture and Islam until recently. In Matthew 12, verses 48-50, Mark 3, verse 25 and Luke 8, verse 21, Jesus says, 'Whoever does the will of God is my brother, my sister and my mother'. I repeat, 'Whoever *does* the will of God...is my brother...my sister...and my mother.'

"Now we can agree the verbs *submit* and *do* mean the same thing in English in the context of obedience. For example, if someone tells you to do something, and you obey her, then you are submitting to her. You are a submitter to her authority. Agreed?"

Sandra nodded her head to signal she was with him.

"So if we say, 'Whoever *submits* to the will of God...is my brother...my sister...and my mother' doesn't change the meaning of the sentence does it?"

"No."

"And someone who submits to the will of God is a submitter to the will of God. Right?"

"Yup."

"The noun form of the verb *submit* is *submission.* Correct?"

"No argument from me."

"Now please listen closely, folks. What I have to say next is crucial." Giltmore explained how the Arabic word *Islam* literally means *submission* in English. "Linguistically, Islam means peaceful submission to the will of God. The Arabic word *Muslim* means

*Submitter* in English. A Muslim, or a Submitter, follows the religion of Islam, or Submission. Follow me?"

"Makes sense."

"So when Jesus told his disciples to *submit* to the will of God, he was calling them to the religion of Submission, to the religion of *Islam*," he said, stabbing the air with his index finger. "That is what Jesus meant when he said, 'The submissive shall inherit the earth,' not the meek, which is a mistranslation of the koine Greek word *praus*."

Sandra jolted at his logical and sweeping interpretation. She owned a Bible whose pages were underlined and dog-eared, but this insight had escaped her daily reading of the Scriptures.

"I have to admit you've advanced an original interpretation of those verses, Mike, but wasn't Jesus a Jew and isn't Islam a new religion?"

Shifting his weight in the chair, he said, "I'll answer the second part of your question first. Islam isn't a new religion, Sandra. Submission to the will of God is the religion of every prophet, from Adam to Mohammed. Note that Islam isn't named for a tribe of people such as Hinduism, Judaism and Sikhism are, and Islam isn't a personality cult such as Buddhism and Christianity are. Islam is a religion named by God, not by a man, and this is why it's a universal religion for all of humanity because it transcends nation, race, tribe, ethnicity, class, status, and rank, those pernicious attachments that divide humans."

"So anyone who submits to the will of God is following the religion of Islam."

"You're a quick student, Sandra. But there's a catch. To do the will of God is to worship Him alone and not any falsely partners ascribed to him."

"Please clarify what this entails."

"It means idol worship is forbidden as proscribed in the first two Commandments. You cannot worship statues and stones and people, dead or alive, in place of God."

"Got it."

"Now, to return to the first part of your question. In terms of ethnicity, Jesus was a Palestinian Essene, but in terms of religion, Jesus was not a Jew, just as I'm Irish but not a Catholic. A—"

"Good point, Mike."

He continued, "A Jew could be a Submitter in Jesus' era. As I explained, a Muslim is a monotheist who submits to the will of God *and* accepts every prophet of his era. This meant, during the time of Jesus, a Jew was a submitter to the will of God if he accepted Jesus as the Messiah. He testified so."

"He did?" she asked, tilting her head.

"Absolutely. In John chapter 8, verse 31 Jesus said to the Jews who believed in him, 'If you continue in my word, you are truly my disciples.' And in Mark 14, verse 36 Jesus addresses God, 'yet, not what I want but what You want' and in Luke 22, verses 42 Jesus again addresses God, 'yet, not my will but Yours be done.' In both these verses, Jesus is submitting his will to the will of God," Giltmore said, pressing his fingertips together.

"Do you realize what you've done?"

Her tone made him wary. He glanced around and let out a nervous "*No*."

"You've driven a stake through the evil heart of Islamophobia."

"I want to believe you but it'll take more than my scholarship for the commissars of Islamophobia to get over their anti-Muslim hysteria. Here's the crux of the matter. If a hateful ideology spreads unchecked through the body politic, it will, like a disease, become a social contagion and destroy the host society from within. Look at what happened to the German nation in the 1940s. The Nazis disguised their bid for world domination as a life and death struggle against Jewish-Bolshevism. They wouldn't let go of their anti-Semitism until their country lay prostrate before the Allied Powers. It appears America is venturing down the same self-destructive path of national suicide in its bid for world domination under the guise of fighting so-called Islamist terror."

"A frightful prediction. Now getting back to Jesus calling people to Islam, I don't remember reading this interpretation in your book. Did I miss something?" She sat back and crossed her arms.

"Here's the thing. I omitted this inspired insight from my book," he said, "because it might have undermined its main message. I didn't yearn to be accused of fostering a hidden agenda. Recall the incident of that pugnacious Fox News host who took issue with a Muslim professor of religion for having had the *audacity* to write a biography of Jesus then you'll understand why."

"Wasn't that interview scandalous?"

He communicated his agreement with a nod. "I discussed those three verses of Scripture in my book but in the context of Jesus calling people to submit to the will of a unitary God. Honest truth, I didn't convert to Islam until after my book was published," he confessed. "It was enough for me that Jesus and Mohammed preached submission to the same God as Abraham and Moses did."

"Don't say I didn't warn you, Mike, but your admission will add fuel to the fire on social media and in the mainstream media."

"What gets me is we live in the Information Age and yet we have more ignorance and less critical-thinking. It's a lamentable situation."

"How do you propose to change peoples' attitudes about Islam?"

"I can't do it by myself. We need someone in high political office to denounce the whole war of words and terror against Islam and Muslims," he said. "Sandra, several years ago, we had a Democratic candidate running for president who was accused of being a closet Muslim. Instead of denying he was a Muslim, he should've said something courageous such as 'I'm not a Muslim, but if I were, so what?' He missed a perfect opportunity to prove he was a man of courage and of principle."

"We can't elect paragons of virtue when we select candidates from the frayed edges of the moral spectrum to represent our better natures."

"Regrettably, a majority of us voted for this intellectual lightweight not once, but twice. Talk about the audacity of hope. Audacity of hype would be more appropriate."

"Well, you know what they say about hope."

"Please enlighten me," he said with a sense of anticipation.

"Hope is the triumph of expectation over experience."

"That's so original." How I wish I met you years ago.

He saw her read what was behind his eyes.

"We're running short on time, Mike, so I'm keen to resume discussion of your book."

"So am I."

Sandra glanced down at her notes. "Bible scholars have asserted the historical details in the New Testament canon attest to its probative value. Care to comment on this?"

"You've done your homework, I see."

"Unlike the host of your last interview, I do my own research."

"Getting back to your claim, it's so thin it only has one side," he said, leaning toward her. "I'm not concerned with the invention of the New Testament canon as a product of historical authenticity but as a work of imagination. The historicity of the New Testament is irrelevant. Although it comprises historical documents, historical accuracy is not my primary focus. Scripture dated to the first century CE is immaterial. Doctrinal accuracy and consistency are more important matters for study."

"So, if I understand you, you're stating the historical facts detected in the New Testament aren't proof of its authenticity?"

"Why should they be? If someone writes a book of historical fiction, which is a genre of fiction I adore, the book is not *ipso facto* a book of history."

"True. By the way, I love historical fiction, too," and she flashed her gem-green eyes at him.

"How nice." Her look of disappointment distressed him but it was too late for a redo.

Nonplussed, she pressed on. "You advanced leaps of logic in your book other Bible scholars could have but didn't. How do you explain this gap?"

He pressed his hands together. "Because their reason and courage ends where their faith begins. They have so much invested in defending and perpetuating Christian dogma. They've staked their lives and careers in something that nurtures their identity and provides their source of income. It'd be next to impossible for them to capitulate and admit their mistakes. They're like the prosecutor who knows he's convicted the wrong man but refuses to issue a *mea culpa*."

"This is valid in all facets of life. People are afraid of discarding old beliefs for hard truths. Like quitting no-good boyfriends."

Her comment drew laughter from him and the audience.

"Christianity is an affair of the heart, not the head. In their infatuation with Jesus, his followers have idolized him and transformed him into a god. Much like a besotted lover does with the object of their infatuation.

"Has more than a ring of truth to it."

"My father, an ex-sailor, encouraged me and my siblings to broaden our horizons. He often reminded us—" Giltmore briefly closed his eyes to recall his father's axiom "'—If you want to see what's beyond the horizon, you cannot be afraid to lose sight of the coast.' I weighed anchor on my former religion and cast off for shores unknown with only my faith in God as my compass."

"As you perceive it."

"Precisely."

"The Vatican considers you enemy number one right now an—"

"I'll be damned. I'm proud to be included among luminaries such as Galileo and Copernicus." She's ticked. I cut her off. Dumb habit of mine. He wilted under her withering glare and felt like crawling beneath the table. "Sorry, Sandra. Please continue."

Her eyes narrowed. "As. I. Was. *Saying*. The Vatican considers you enemy number one right now."

He shrugged it off. "The Vatican's animus toward me will achieve the opposite effect."

"In what way?"

"Here's the catch. We live in the Internet Age. We're a virtual global community. The flow of information is multi-channelled. Banning my book is irrelevant, much like the Catholic Church is become with each passing day."

"Them sounds like fighting words."

"I can't help it. I'm Irish. It's part of my DNA," he said, grinning.

She tittered. "A southern pastor promises to burn your book this coming weekend. Anything you want to say to him?"

"I hope he burns more than one copy of my book," he said. "I need the royalties."

Sandra guffawed at his wit. Regaining her poise, she offered, "At least he didn't preach a *fatwa* against you."

"It's likely in the mail."

She continued, "You wrote in your book, 'Contrary to what Jesus preached, the Catholic Church consecrates the rule wherein one cannot be saved by direct contact with God, which necessitates an intermediary role for a priestly caste who manages this contact with Him.' But doesn't Jesus state in John 14, verse 13, 'Whatever you ask in my name, that will I do, so that the Father may be glorified in the son'?"

"Incisive question, Sandra. I'll answer it with another verse of Scripture. In Matthew 7, verse 11, while giving his Sermon on the Mount, Jesus says to the crowd, 'If you then, who are evil, know how to give good gifts to your children, how much more will your Father who is in heaven give good things to those who ask Him.'"

"Sounds like a contradiction," Sandra said.

"Astute observation. We must admit a unified composition of the New Testament was never conceived as such by its compilers. It was the product of many minds, none noble, because a noble mind wouldn't stoop to pass off the Bible as the unexpurgated Word of God. The Bible is not the product of the Divine Mind. It contains revelation, but it is not revelation in *toto*. The New Testament canon is an obvious invention and not a divinely inspired one."

"Strong words, Mike."

"Let me finish," he gently said. "The composers of the Gospels wrote for an audience steeped in Greek mythology. They needed to have an ear for what appealed to this audience. Tragedy, whose essence is pain and suffering, was the apotheosis of classical Greek literature. To capture the hearts and minds of the Greek-speaking Gentiles, the Gospel writers had to embroider the crucifixion of Jesus be—"

"Hold on a sec." She held up her hand to forestall him. "*Embroider*? Are you implying the Crucifixion wasn't faithfully reported?"

"I caution you I possess no textual proof for what I'm about to say, but I have contextual corroboration. With that caveat, all I ask is for you to hear me out and withhold judgement until I make my case."

"Go ahead," she said with a sceptical look.

"The pain and suffering of the innocent lamb of Christianity doesn't commence on the Cross but in the courtroom of Pontius Pilate," he began. "It wasn't enough for Jesus to be crucified. No sir-ree. Before being crucified, he had to endure a decent flogging, but not just any flogging. No sir-ree. Pilate had Jesus scourged with a flagrum, a whip with multiple strands tipped with lead balls or pieces of bone. It was used to lacerate flesh, not lash it."

Sandra grimaced. "How horrific."

"And instead of tying him to the Cross with leather straps per the custom, Jesus was nailed to it to increase his torment. When he was thirsty, he was given vinegar to drink instead of water. We can't have Jesus quenching his thirst. If this weren't torture enough, he was stabbed in the side with a spear."

"He certainly endured his share of agony," Sandra jumped in.

"The story of the Crucifixion could've ended with the tragic but innocent Jesus dying a hero's horrible death—except his death would've lacked the emotional appeal so central to the Greco-Roman world. Gentiles believed their gods were immortal. So the obliging authors of the New Testament bestowed divinity upon Jesus to ensure his immortality resonated with Greek mythology. Jesus became God incarnate to satisfy a pagan religio-literary convention."

"That's an original perspective."

"The resurrection of Jesus serves to bring the tale of the Crucifixion to a happy ending because happy endings were—and still are—essential to storytelling in the West. Similar to the Gentiles, we expect our stories to end on a happy note. It's a compelling counterpoint to the manifold miseries and misfortunes of the human condition."

"Fascinating. Please continue."

"But a problem soon arose. The central story of Christianity slipped away from Church authorities when people began questioning Jesus' dual nature. This is where the story swerves from tragedy to farce. Once you draw back the curtain on Christianity, you need to invent something akin to the Trinity to tie up all the loose and illogical ends. The Trinity functions as the anti-climax to this story."

"They don't teach this in catechism classes do they, Mike?"

He chuckled. "Not the ones I attended."

"You mentioned before the New Testament was an invention."

He stroked his clean-shaven chin. "It's more accurate to call the New Testament an inventive compilation. Medieval Church authorities gathered a subset of the documents that were circulating in Christian communities, massaged them to the best of their ability, assembled them in a book and then proclaimed, '*Voila.* The Word of God.'"

"In your book, you tell the story of how the New Testament was compiled. Please share this enlightening story with our viewers."

"Once upon a time, to check the violent squabbling over the issue of the Trinity which was causing unrest in his empire between the Pauline Church in Rome, the North African churches and the Eastern churches, Constantine, the Roman Emperor, convened a council of bishops in 325 CE in the town of Nicea, now present-day Iznik in Turkey. At this Council the New Testament canon was officially compiled. It superseded *The Muratorian Canon* collected over a century earlier.

"Long story short, the bishops couldn't reach an accord on which of the three hundred or so Gospels in circulation at the time belonged in the New Testament canon. So the bishops piled the Scriptures under a table in the meeting hall and agreed to include in the canon those books that found their way on top of the table via *divine* agency and destroy those that remained beneath it."

"So the bishops *actually* expected God to do their dirty work for them?"

He nodded yes. "The bishops departed the meeting chamber and locked the door. The next morning when they entered it, the pile of

Scriptures had been sorted. By God. So they claimed. The four Gospels and Epistles stacked on top of the table, except for the *Letter to the Hebrews* because someone overlooked it"—sarcasm oozed from his words—"became the New Testament canon and those heaped beneath it were destroyed."

"People at the time believed this tale?" Sandra said with a look incredulity. "It'd be more believable if the key had been locked inside the chamber obliging the bishops to break the lock the next day."

"People had no choice. Religious authorities threatened anyone possessing an unauthorized Gospel with death. Over a million Christians who rejected the doctrine of the Trinity were slaughtered by fellow Christians throughout the Byzantine Empire in subsequent years to enforce belief in the invention of the Trinity. So much for the unity the Council was meant to impose on the antagonistic Christian sects." He shrugged his brow. "This is why the New Testament is contradictory and inconsistent not only internally but externally. It cannot be reconciled with the religion of Christianity. They're as mutually exclusive as chalk and cheese. The New Testament is a book in search of a religion inasmuch as Christianity is a religion in search of a holy book. This is all the proof one needs to recognize the New Testament is not the Word of God and, therefore, cannot claim to be the foundation text for a religion that professes to communicate the Word of God."

"Should we simply toss out the host with the holy water?"

"The Bible is a most earnest book that lacks for nothing except a solid foundation for the truth and Christianity is plated with a patina of truth but, at its core, Christianity is false."

"You're adept at this game of intellectual ping pong, Mike."

"I can play the whole day long if you so desire." If his reading of her was rational and not the delusion of an infatuated mind, then her expression told him he might get the chance someday. He could only hope.

"You mention in your book Jesus never called his followers Christians."

"Strange isn't it? The word *Christian* was used as a term of opprobrium by Gentiles to insult the followers of Jesus who called themselves Nazarenes. Over time, they adopted the name as a badge of honor. Another invention."

"Intriguing. Separately, how do you respond to people who claim Muslims worship another god?"

"Anglo arrogance never ceases to irk me. God did not reveal His revelation in Latin or Greek or English. He revealed it in Akkadian (Abraham's scrolls), Egyptian (Moses' Torah), paleo-Hebrew (David's Psalms), Aramaic (Jesus' Gospel) and Arabic (Mohammed's Quran). Arab Christians call God *Allah*. Enough said."

A shoe dangled on the tip of her naked foot and she asked, "Earlier, you glossed over the Resurrection which you implied was part of the embellishment of Christianity. You discuss this subject in your book, which is possibly the most controversial issue you tackle. Care to let our viewers in on your interpretation of the Resurrection?"

"Sure. Rising above all these issues I've discussed is the issue of the Resurrection to which Church leaders resort when their backs are up against the proverbial wall. They'll toss other touchstones of Christianity under the bus but never the Resurrection because it's the cornerstone of the Christian faith."

"Didn't Paul say, 'If Christ has not been raised, then our faith is in vain'?"

"He did. In Jesus' time, people didn't believe the dead came back to life. But we now have medical evidence proving the *seemingly* dead do."

"This is true of drowning victims, especially young victims."

"Long story short. When Jesus gave up the ghost, a Roman soldier stabbed him in the side with a spear and blood and water *gushed* out. Anyone with a basic knowledge of human physiology knows dead men don't bleed. Blood gushes only when the heart is pumping."

"I read Jesus might've underwent a bout of hypovolemic shock which caused the blood and water to pour out."

"Hypovolemic shock is caused by low blood pressure due to substantial loss of blood. In such a state, Jesus' heart couldn't have pumped with the force necessary to cause blood to gush out."

Scratching her arm, she said, "So what are you saying?"

His way with words was so seductive. He was talking his way into her heart.

"I'm saying Jesus was alive, but unconscious, when he was liberated from the Cross.

The viewing audience uttered a collective gasp.

"The Cross is the *end* not the beginning of Christianity!"

"To be clear, the New Testament provides no eyewitness testimony to Jesus' resurrection," Sandra said. "He was alive when people arrived at the tomb."

"One detail that people miss or ignore is this: Jesus possessed superhuman endurance."

"He did?"

"For forty days and forty nights Jesus fasted," he said. "You and I and everyone else would be dead within half that time or less living under such a strict dietary regimen. Try to picture the kind of person who can survive nearly six weeks without food or drink in the wilderness. It's ludicrous how Christian authorities portray Jesus as a meek and mild man. In my estimation, he was the original Survivor Man."

"Hard to argue against this opinion."

"There's something else I find strange."

Sandra blinked. "What?"

"There is no post-resurrection testimony from either Joseph or Nicodemus both of whom presided over the supposed entombment of Jesus. They both vanish into the void of history and are never heard from again."

"Thought-provoking detail, Mike," she said, changing her position in her chair.

"Did they possess material evidence of Jesus' surviving the Crucifixion that was later expunged from the historical record?" He let the question hang there, pregnant with suggestion.

"There you have it, folks. From Mike's lips to God's ears."

"In the absence of the *Q* document, we can't really know."

"What's the Q document? An ancient recipe for quiche?"

His laughter under control, Giltmore said, "The *Q* is a stand-in for the German word *Quelle* which means *source*." The Q document is hypothesized to be the source for the Gospels of Matthew, Mark and Luke because of their textual commonalities."

"Interesting." Changing tack, she asked, "People are accusing you of bashing Christianity. What's your response to this criticism?"

"This defensive attitude is understandable. One man's critiquing is another man's bashing. Truth is polarizing. Whenever people's cherished beliefs are dissected and discredited, their first response is to attack the messenger instead of taking the time to reflect on the merits of the message being conveyed. For the record, I wrote my book in a spirit of a life-saving intervention."

"Well, Mike, your answer might give people pause for reflection." Deciding to test him, she asked, "So what can people believe about Jesus?"

Giltmore was prepared for such a question. "That he was conceived immaculately and was born a human being. That he was an only child and a Submitter. That he was the Messiah and worked miracles through the power of God. That he preached the oneness of God and the coming of Prophet Mohammed in John 16, verses seven through fifteen. And that he ascended to Heaven and will return to this earth near the end of time to get married and to kill the anti-Messiah and his followers. Anything more is pure fabrication."

"It's astounding how Christianity went from there to here."

"Not really, Sandra. It's called reverse psychology. If you hear a colossal lie so often through multiple official channels you'll begin to believe it because you'll ask yourself: What prominent person would dare tell a whopper at the risk of being exposed and called to account?"

"I guess that's how folks were conned into believing planes could be commandeered by hijackers brandishing box cutters. Machetes? Maybe. Box cutters? *Puh-lease*."

Giltmore played along. "Good thing Saddam's soldiers weren't armed with box cutters. Our troops wouldn't have stood a chance in Iraq."

Sandra carried it further. "Rumor had it Saddam was building a MOAB."

"A Mother Of All Bombs?"

"Uh-uh. A Mother of All Box Cutters."

Saucer-eyed with mock horror, "No way," Giltmore breathed out. "Now I know why the stunted shrub of a president who swaggered like a bush was so desperate to take out Saddam."

Sandra received the signal it was time to wrap things up. "So what are your plans for the future?" She unconsciously moistened her upper lip with the tip of her tongue.

Oblivious, Giltmore sat back in his seat and clasped his hands around his knee. "My book is selling well, but after tonight's revelation, it's anyone's guess. I was planning to donate the proceeds of my book sales toward charity, but I changed my mind. I decided to fund an Islamic institute in Texas that promotes interfaith dialogue."

"The world needs more of this."

"The institute has asked me to host a conference they are convening in Istanbul next month. They've been planning it for months. I can't wait to travel there."

"How exotic. I wish you luck."

"Because I'm a Submitter now, I'll have to obtain permission from the Stasi—I mean Homeland Security," he said.

"You shouldn't joke, Mike. You never know who's listening."

"Screw them Nazis," he said, scratching his cheek with his middle finger.

Sandra smiled. "We're almost out of time. Anything else you'd like to say before we go?" There was hope in her tone that said, "Ask me out for a coffee."

Care for dinner at a restaurant? But his courage was only in his mind and not on his tongue. "Peace unto you and to those who are watching."

"Thank you for speaking with us, Mike."

"My pleasure, Sandra."

# Chapter Seventeen
# Roman Province of Judea – Mid-First Century CE

A sultry day, the heat rested heavy upon the parched land, no breath of wind to cool the air, and the sun, hot and brassy, hung low and swollen on the reddish-hued horizon. Against the infernal heat the beloved disciple struggled to place one leaden foot in front of the other on the sunbaked macadam road, the exertion sapping his energy. Small pebbles, disturbed by his feet, rattled in his path. Consumed with worry, he tried to focus on the journey ahead. It was a difficult time for the true followers of the M'sheekha. The doctrinal foundation of the Jerusalem congregation was in dire jeopardy. Men of faith had been compromised by the corruption of power as much as the faith of men had been corrupted by the power of compromise.

One plodding step after another in his westward march, he withered in the heat of the setting but still molten sun, and he gripped his wooden staff as though it were a lifeline. Has the road to Jerusalem lengthened or have my legs shortened? he complained. The distance between Bethany and the City of Peace, almost fifteen furlongs, was once an easy trek for him, but, like a stealthy thief, creeping age had robbed him of his vigor and vitality, and the wilting temperature was of no help either.

Not much farther, he willed himself.

The steady crunch of his footfalls delivered accompaniment to the beat of his staff he planted with each step. Beasts of burden hauling wooden carts and work-worn people, many of whom carried cloth-wrapped bundles on their bowed backs, their faces drawn and sweat-streaked, shambled by in both directions.

A grayish fog of dust hovered in the air above the arid road, adding increase to his misery, and the dusty air parched his mouth, forcing him to halt on the shoulder. He leaned on his staff and called attention to the hot weather by wiping his shiny brow with the back of his hand, and he rolled his tongue around his teeth to clean them of the grit caked inside his mouth. He spat and watched the fissured ground absorb his dirty spittle like a thirsty sponge.

"Lord, give me strength," he croaked.

Dust-begrimed passersby, their faces lined with the burdens of a hard existence, glanced sidelong at him. He ignored their curious glances. Ahead, in the distance, the Temple Mount peeped above the palm groves, shimmering in the heat-haze, mirage-like, and he drank in the sight of it.

He shook himself and set off again. The Roman road ahead shimmered in the haze. Despite his physical discomfort, he labored to focus his ruminations on the imminent gathering of the M'sheekha's followers. The council of the Jerusalem congregation should have been convened long ago, he fumed. Paul's notion of abjuring circumcision and the Torah of Moses for the sake of the pagan Gentiles had gained unstoppable strength, like a Roman legion joined in battle. The beloved disciple suspected the purpose of this meeting was to formally announce a pre-determined resolution. Peter needs my support to arrest what Paul has set in motion. We cannot allow ourselves to be seduced by the congregation's pointless growth for which this false prophet has been chiefly responsible.

He understood the heady sensation power induced and it is why he had refused a leadership position in the congregation. Too often he had seen men trade their principles, their values, their beliefs for the trappings of power. Why does there have to be men like that, men who champion compromise over conviction? He hoped to sway his fellow disciples from the sidelines. It was the most he could do.

The one who now calls himself Paul shall be in attendance at this council. I hope to meet this self-appointed apostle whose claim to have received secret revelation from the M'sheekha demands further examination. His theology is not grounded in Submission but in Gnosticism. There are no mysteries in religion. His hope was the only force propelling him onward.

"Gnostics shall be the death of our teacher's way," he muttered under his breath.

Paul was accepting uncircumcised Gentiles into the fold of the congregation without permission from the elders. He now sought the imprimatur of the Jerusalem congregation's leadership to forego the ritual of circumcision and observance the Torah to sanctify the conversion of Gentiles. The battle line stark, supporters had formed up on opposite sides to argue for and against these doctrinal changes.

The temperature plunged when the looming wall of the city cast its cool shadow upon him. As always, unable to resist, he lifted his gaze in wonderment as he passed beneath the soaring Susa Gate, one of several that pierced the massive stone wall surrounding Jerusalem. Headed for points unknown, camels, loaded with bundles tied to their humped backs, padded past him through the gate, many quietly, others, led under protest by their handlers, grunting and groaning.

Skirting the Temple, he navigated the streets toward the Lower City and picked his way through the narrow lanes. He dodged knots of rough-looking, rowdy people while mobs of shoeless street urchins and peddlers dressed in rags boiled about him, begging for money or a scrap of food to allay the pinch of hunger in their bellies. His heart went out to them. Stalls of produce and baskets of wares sat in front of the many hovels, seeking buyers, but none were forthcoming. Onward he plodded and the current of humanity flowed to and fro here as it had on the dusty road from Bethany.

Multi-storied buildings constructed from pink Jerusalem stone pressed in on him from both sides while he advanced through the Lower City. The air was cooler now, the man-made canyons of stone providing protection from the blaze of the setting sun. The boisterous clamor of the Lower City faded away as he labored northward. At last, with heavy feet, he reached a non-descript building of stone hidden in the cool shadows of the declining day in the hushed quiet of the Upper City.

It was a large but inconspicuous rough-hewn stone edifice, similar in size to adjacent buildings. Nothing indicated it had been a holy refuge where the M'sheekha sought to reform the religion of a believing people who had gone astray and nothing hinted it would become a den of iniquity where a believing people sought to transform this religion for a pagan people who had long been lost.

The sight of this hallowed chamber flooded his mind with pleasant memories of his teacher and fuelled a desperate longing for him. He stood in the doorway for several heartbeats and shut his eyes to picture his teacher, sitting patiently, instructing his disciples, dispensing a kind word here, a correction there, while exuding an aura of peace and serenity. *O M'sheekha, how you are missed.* He opened his bleary eyes and wished to find himself in the presence of his much-loved teacher.

Instead, he saw rows of heavy benches constructed of hand-hewn planks of wood, the marks of their craftsmen etched in their rough surfaces, lining either side of the outsized meeting hall. A wooden table and two crudely-fashioned chairs now rested on a low platform at the other end of the central aisle, opposite the double doors where he stood. A prosaic backdrop for an imminent historic showdown.

His gaze lifted. The upper shutters were open to let the natural convection of air cool the space. Windows high above allowed the hot air trapped in the ceiling to escape while drawing in cooler air through lower windows. Torches, held fast by angled sconces, had been lit, and their flames wavered in the caress of invisible currents of air, providing a measure of cheerfulness to an otherwise somber tableau.

He dropped his gaze which fell upon a table beside the door laden with vessels of water someone had provided in a spirit of charity. He poured water into a clay cup and quaffed it back. A trickle of water seeped into his beard. He refilled his cup and guzzled it down. His thirst quenched, he dabbed his mouth with the sleeve of his cloak. Thanking his Lord in the silence of his heart for the clean water, he leaned his staff next to the door then traipsed toward the front of the hall, taking it all in before he settled himself on a bench in the first row, beside the dais.

*A seat never felt so fine for these weary legs of mine.*

Disciples and brethren soon trickled in, their leather sandals scuffing and slapping the tiled floor, breaking the silence of this solemn chamber. The beloved disciple nodded to several of them and exchanged greetings with others. People gathered in tight clusters and spoke in hushed voices while others filled the benches. The matter of compromising the way of the M'sheekha for the sake of the Gentiles was undoubtedly on their minds, if not on their tongues.

"Brothers in Submission, please take your seats. If one of you could shut the doors, I would be most grateful," James said in a loud voice, amplified by the acoustical properties of stone and empty space. Tall but slightly stooped, his hair receding and beard graying, he stood beside Peter at the front of the hall before the lone table. Heads swiveled and conversation faded away in clusters. The sound of garments rustling and benches groaning and squeaking in protest intensified in the reverberant hall as the men seated themselves.

"Let us bring this meeting to order. Most Beloved, please ask for God the Almighty's blessings on these holy matters we plan to deliberate."

He stood up. "In the name of God. O Lord in Heaven. We seek Your help and ask for Your forgiveness. We seek refuge with You from the evil of our own souls and from our evil deeds. Whomsoever God guides shall never be led astray, and whomsoever He leaves astray, no one can guide. We bear witness there is no deity but God, and we bear witness Yeshua is His servant and His M'sheekha. O God, please guide us in these our deliberations and guide us on the path of Submission. Amen."

A chorus of "Amen" rose from the assembly of men and ricocheted off the walls of the meeting hall.

"Thank you for the uplifting benediction, Most Beloved," James said.

"I cannot help but raise a voice of dissent," the beloved disciple said, still standing.

"Most Beloved, you shall be given a chance to speak once we have heard from Brother Paul," James said, rebuffing him.

He sat down in a huff and bent his ear to his neighbor on his right who whispered to him. Whatever the neighbor said displeased him for he shook his head in anger and said, "Never."

Peter, tall, gaunt-faced and ruddy-complexioned, his brown hair flat upon his scalp, declared, "My brothers, it has come to our attention Brother Paul has been preaching a doctrine contrary to the message of the M'sheekha. We deserve to hear in his own words what he has been teaching the Gentiles." He motioned to Brother Paul. "If you please."

Paul stood. "My brothers, grace to you and peace from God our Father and the Lord Yeshua. I am a servant of Yeshua, called to be an apostle, set apart for the Gospel of God, which he promised beforehand through his prophets in the holy Scriptures, the Gospel concerning His son, who was descended from David according to the flesh and was declared to be son of God with power according to the spirit of holiness by resurrection from the dead, Yeshua our Lord, through whom we have received grace and apostleship to bring about the obedience of faith among all the Gentiles for the sake of his name, including yourselves who are called to belong to Yeshua the M'sheekha."

Trembling with repressed rage, the beloved disciple sprang to his feet. "Brother Paul, how dare you claim a dispensation from the Almighty to preach a doctrine of Law-less salvation to the Gentiles? God does not speak to mere mortals such as you. He speaks only to His chosen prophets. The M'sheekha received no commission from his Lord to preach among the Gentiles," he thundered, wagging his finger at Paul.

A babble of assenting and dissenting voices exploded in the hall.

With desperate pleas for calm, James restored order among the followers. "Most Beloved, please return to your bench and remain silent until Brother Paul has finished."

He complied but made a show of sitting down.

Paul regaled the assembled men with stories of Gentiles entering the ranks of the believers near and far. "They are eager to accept the M'sheekha as their savior but circumcision is a major stumbling block for them," he said, surveying the crowd.

"What is this heresy about the M'sheekha saving us?" the beloved disciple interjected, hopping off his bench again. "Our teacher was a prophet and messenger of God. He did not save me, he did not save you and he shall not save the Gentiles," he said, waving his hands. "Salvation lies in submission to God the Almighty alone who shall save us from the torment of the Hellfire provided we cleave to the revelation of the M'sheekha," he reminded them, punctuating his protest with his forefinger.

Paul stared back at him, a faint smile on his lips. "You do not speak for everyone in this congregation, Most Beloved." Not a handsome man, his hair receding, one thick eyebrow lining his forehead, his bowed legs supporting a stout frame, Paul was destined to remain single.

"I ask your indulgence, Brother Paul," the beloved disciple dared. "I heard from various sources you saw a vision of the M'sheekha on the road to Damascus many years ago. It is a remarkable story, but before we discuss this matter, please tell this congregation why you were travelling there." He levelled his gaze at Paul.

"I was charged with the authority and commission from the chief priest to arrest anyone in Damascus who belonged to the Way."

"Most interesting. For I was still a member of the Sanhedrin, and we issued no such order to anyone," he disclosed to all those present. "The Sanhedrin of Jerusalem has no jurisdiction in Damascus."

Paul gulped.

"Returning to your vision now, Brother Paul," he resumed. "It is remarkable for your having received revelation from the M'sheekha and not from God or through the arch angel Gabriel, the Holy Spirit. Most unusual. No prophet in the history of our religion ever received revelation in the manner you described." He left the statement hanging in the air, which begged for a response.

Beads of perspiration like drops of dew sprouted on Paul's brow. No one had ever challenged the story of his conversion until now. He swallowed hard. "I was surprised myself, Most Beloved, by the voice that identified itself as the M'sheekha," he replied, straining to conceal the tremor in his speech.

"You heard what you claim to be the voice of our teacher, but you did not witness him."

"It was not possible," he said. "A flash of light blinded me, which my travelling companions also witnessed."

"A bolt from the blue. A voice from the sky. How dramatic. How *theatrical*. What convinced you it was the M'sheekha and not the Devil speaking?" he asked, leaning in. "You were not a disciple, so how could you recognize the M'sheekha's voice?"

"Am I on trial, Most Beloved?"

"Surely you do not object to having your testimonial verified, do you?"

"Not at all," Paul said with well-rehearsed conviction.

"So, I ask you again, Brother Paul. How did you distinguish the Devil from the M'sheekha?"

"Because the voice commanded me in Hebrew to preach salvation is through the grace of God alone and not through works of the Law."

"Behold, my brothers in Submission," he announced, waving his arm toward Paul. "By his own words our brother has proven himself a charlatan."

Paul's backers rose to their feet and harangued the beloved disciple. An uproar ensued. Rival factions almost came to blows. Peter and James implored them to sit down.

"The M'sheekha spoke Aramaic, not Hebrew, and he taught us he did not come to abolish the Law and the prophets but to fulfill them," the beloved disciple yelled above the verbal fray.

"This is true only for the Jews," Paul argued.

The beloved disciple stamped his foot. "Impostor! It is necessary for those who wish to join this congregation to be circumcised and to adhere to the Law of Moses."

"By the grace of God I was chosen to be a minister of Yeshua the M'sheekha to the Gentiles," Paul retorted.

"You have lost your senses."

"I am not out of my mind, but I am speaking the sober truth," Paul said with an appearance of calm, but his mounting terror could not be contained.

"Brother Paul, you claim to have received revelation from the M'sheekha and yet none of your epistles mention his miracles, especially the miracle of his immaculate conception. Instead, you invent a story about his crucifixion and resurrection to attract the pagan Gentiles to your fold."

"God raised Yeshua our Lord from the dead and was raised for our justification."

"That is not true and you know it." Changing course, the beloved disciple said, "Brother Paul, what is that you seek?"

"My heart's desire and prayer to God for the Gentiles is that they may be saved."

"You are leading the Gentiles astray," he baldly stated.

Gasps escaped the lips of Paul's followers in the hall.

"Brother Paul has impeached his honor by calling for heretical deviations to the doctrines of the M'sheekha's message," he said to all those present.

A row erupted among the assembled.

"We thank you, Brother Paul, for attending this assembly," James said to him. Above the tumult of the unruly crowd, he said loudly, "I have reached the decision that we should not trouble those Gentiles who are turning to God. Bu—"

"It is but with the help of the Devil the Gentiles are entering the congregation," someone shouted from the benches.

"—But we should write to them to abstain only from things polluted by idols and from fornication and from whatever has been strangled and from blood," James instructed.

"Brother James," the beloved disciple pleaded, "we do not accommodate the inconveniences of those who wish to join this congregation. The Word of God is not open to compromise. The M'sheekha was circumcised under the covenant of Father Abraham and so were we. Did not our teacher warn us we would lose our way if we disobeyed him? Is our religion not worth more than the polluted offerings of the Gentiles?"

"The Gentiles are growing our numbers," James protested.

"At the expense of the truth," the beloved disciple said with characteristic aplomb.

A hush fell over the chamber. James reddened but remained speechless.

"The M'sheekha never comprised with our people so we should not compromise with the Gentiles," the beloved disciple said to his attentive audience. "But more importantly, we should not preach to them. We have no Divine Commission to do so. Our Lord instructed our teacher to preach to the House of Israel and go nowhere among the Gentiles and Samaritans. Can you not grasp the wisdom of this commandment?" He looked around the chamber and his brothers hung on to his every word. "The desire to gain converts comes at the abjuration of Father Abraham's covenant and the Torah, both of which the M'sheekha practiced and preached. Any innovation in the religion of Submission is misguidance and misguidance leads to the Hellfire," he warned.

"We must have strength in numbers," a supporter of Paul said. "For self-protection."

"God is sufficient for me. We pledged to uphold the truth and to propagate the revelation of the M'sheekha on the Day of the Ascension, did we not?" the beloved disciple reminded the gathering.

Scattered murmurs of agreement were uttered.

"Do you realize the enormity of what is being proposed?" the beloved disciple asked all those in attendance. "The Divine Law cannot be altered by man. The M'sheekha, may the Lord's blessings be upon him, has been gone, what, nigh seventeen years, and now this congregation strives to alter his message? I shall have no further truck with these vile proceedings. If these abominable changes pass, then I shall not remain a member of this heretical congregation." He gathered himself and stormed out of the hall into the cool night air without a glance back.

The beloved disciple rushed out of the building, his cloak billowing, and he did not see the pair of eyes, burning red with hatred, watch him leave.

Disciples followed him outside. They milled around him in the street lit by torchlight, their voices amplified by the acoustical effects of the adjacent stone buildings, while their distorted, disembodied shadows swayed on the rough walls surrounding them, mute actors in a play with no script.

"What shall we do?" one of them asked.

The beloved disciple said, "We are living in a dangerous time. Did the M'sheekha not warn us of an ungrateful generation who would be ashamed of him and his words?" Heads bobbed in concordance. "This time has arrived. If you can, I urge you to leave this place, the sooner, the better. Evil has come to this land. We are helpless to prevent its maleficent spread."

"Where shall we go?" a follower asked.

"I know of a town in the province of Thracia where Jews live in peace with their neighbors. It is across the strait from the city of Chalcedon," the beloved disciple informed them.

Catching his eye, "Most Beloved, may I have a word with you?" Paul asked.

"Quickly."

"Alone."

The beloved disciple pounded his staff, tore himself away from his followers and approached Paul, who had strolled out of earshot, and the tapping of his staff on the cobblestones echoed into the night.

"You wish to talk? Speak your piece." In the dim, dancing torchlight, the beloved disciple saw religious fervour blazing in Paul's eyes and was troubled by it.

Paul smiled but his eyes did not. It was a conceited smile, a smile of victory. "We started our acquaintance on the wrong foot, Most Beloved."

He has a self-satisfied air about him. "Brother Paul, both of my feet are planted firmly in the straight path, the same path the M'sheekha trod."

"Brother James expressed his approval of my mission to the Gentiles," he said with triumphant spite. "We are united in the same mind and the same purpose."

"It is clear winning is of paramount importance to you," the beloved disciple said. "You have permitted your hubris and zeal to cloud your judgement. This meeting was never about *winning*. It was about propagating the true message of the M'sheekha and not the message of Paul."

The false prophet savored his triumph for a few beats then he stepped in, thrust out his jaw and crowed, "I have news for you. Good news. According to the grace of God given to me, like a skilled master builder I laid a foundation, and someone else is building on it."

"You can have your earthly kingdom. I desire a home in the Kingdom of Heaven."

"No one will deprive me of my ground for boasting."

"Your striving has skewed your judgement. Have you no fear of the Almighty?"

"Woe to me if I do not proclaim the Good News."

Narrowing his eyes, he said, "You proclaim false news. There is no forgiveness of sins through human crucifixion!" Calm yourself. Anger will only get the better of you. He took a breath. "I warn you, Brother Paul. Altering the Word of God is an evil affair. It will bring you but to an ignoble end, if not in this life, then surely in the life everlasting."

"With me it is a very small thing that I should be judged by you or by any human court," he scoffed. "I do not even judge myself. It is the Lord who judges me."

"You know very well the M'sheekha was not crucified and he did not die for our sins. We still live in accordance with the Law as must future generations until the final prophet announces himself."

Brushing aside his refutation with a dismissive flap of his hand, Paul said, "If through my falsehood God's truthfulness abounds to His glory, why am I being condemned as a sinner?"

"Because you are not guiding the Gentiles to the truth. You are leading them away from it."

"Each one of us has a particular gift from God."

"What are you implying?"

"I have become all things to all people that I might by all means save some. I wish that all were as I myself am."

He stiffened at Paul's audacity.

"Most Beloved, the hour is late. I must be on my way. Peace unto you."

Speaking to his back, the beloved disciple called out to him, "The M'sheekha told us a person shall be known by their fruits. You offer the Gentiles nothing but poison fruit. Peace unto you, Brother Paul." He stared after his retiring figure. "What can you gain from this?" he asked as an afterthought. "Recognition?"

Paul stopped and spun around. "I think I am not in the least inferior to the super-apostles," he shouted. "I may be untrained in speech but not in knowledge." With that, he turned and hurried away.

The beloved disciple remained rooted, perturbed by Paul's startling boast. He shook himself mentally then rejoined his followers who had observed the whole row from afar.

"Something is afoot, Most Beloved," said a disciple.

"That man speaks evil words, brothers. I advise no further contact with him if you truly love the M'sheekha and fear God."

They regarded one another and nodded their heads, solidarity on their faces.

"May God forgive us for has what transpired here this evening," the beloved disciple said, as much to himself as to those around him. "Go in peace," he bid his companions. Beneath an obsidian sky seeded with winking stars and lighted by a pockmarked pale moon suspended low and large on the horizon, he trudged through the empty streets of Jerusalem with a heavy heart. He exited the city through the wicket, for the huge main gate shut at sundown every day for reasons of security.

Devoid of people, the country road at this time of night was quiet and clear, and, devoid of heat and dust, the air was cool and tasted fresh. Despite being alone, the beloved disciple was not concerned for his safety. For the Lord was his protector and his staff was his protection. He mulled over the events that had transpired in and out of the meeting while he tramped home. How dare the congregation allow these doctrinal concessions to pass? It is sheer evil. O M'sheekha, what have they done to your revelation?

The susurration of the palm tree fronds in the light breeze calmed his agitation while he plodded along the dark road, and insects, hidden in the shrubbery at the side of the roadway, chittered and chattered. Were they warning one another of his presence?

Footfalls approaching rapidly from behind interrupted his ruminations. He glanced over his shoulder and glimpsed the shapes of two men in the moon glow, marching abreast. They were gaining on him. Fast.

This does not feel right.

His spine quivered and his flesh crept. Then self-defense drills he had practiced with an instructor in his youth leapt to the fore which gave him confidence, hope even. When you sense what is coming, a man can prepare for it.

Nowhere to hide, he stopped and pivoted, compelled to make a stand for he was too old to outrun them. Fate had put his life in peril and now he was forced to save it with the Almighty's help. Adopting the proper fighting stance for balance and movement, he positioned one foot in front with the back foot supporting the majority of his body weight, and he bent his knees a few degrees as his instructor had taught him.

Despite the slight tremble of his muscles, he was as prepared for conflict as he would ever be. He held one end of the staff in an overhanded grip and spread his hands a cubit-and-a-half apart while the other end rested lightly on the ground in front of him. To arrest his mounting unease, he took slow, deep breaths to center himself. Tension in the muscles impedes speed of movement and reduces reaction time, the memory of his teacher's voice instructed him.

"Peace unto you," the beloved disciple spoke out in a calm voice to the two men, desperate to conceal his anxiety.

They slowed their pace. He caught a whiff of them on the wafting breeze and crinkled his nose, the pungent stench of their unclean bodies reaching him. His brave stand surprised them. They halted a cubit beyond the end of his staff, their faces registering indecision.

"Will you not return the greeting of peace?" he asked.

Their indecision did not last.

"We do not come bearing a message of peace," the skinny, ferret-faced one said with a tone of malevolence, his scraggly beard and matted, greasy hair betraying an aversion to clean water—much like his bedraggled clothing, more patchwork than original cloth.

"Hear this, old man. We have a message for you," the second one said, tall and burly, his round cheeks prominent beneath his shaggy beard. Sure of conquest his hand went to his side and withdrew the hilt of a gladius from his tattered cloak inch by inch, probably hoping this slow-motion action would instill terror in his aged quarry.

My instincts did not deceive me. Hired assassins! Before the man could complete the movement with his hand, the beloved disciple burst into action. "God is great," he yelled, startling both of them. His sudden outcry caused them to hesitate, thus giving him an extra second or two, which sometimes separates winning from losing, living from dying.

He twisted his hips and shoulders and swung his staff at the knee of the sword-holder. A sound like a dry twig snapping preceded an ear-piercing scream, and the man staggered and fell. He recoiled then sprang forward and thrust the end of his staff into the stomach of the second assassin who doubled over, gulping for air. He followed up with a solid blow to the back of the winded assassin's skull. The assailant pitched face forward into the road, landing with a dull thud, and a puff of dust erupted from the impact and lingered briefly in the unsettled air.

The beloved disciple remained poised, but undesirous of further combat. Taking in the scene, he saw there was no fight left in his adversaries. He let down his guard and took slow, deep breaths, and the tension in his body eased, like a fist unclenching.

He sidled over to the crippled assassin, who was screwed up in agony, and prodded him with his staff. The injured man flinched. He looked up at the beloved disciple, his face a mixture of pain and rage. "I have a message for whoever sent you. Tell him I only turn the cheek toward a true believer," he said. The fallen man glowered at him. He then pivoted and carried on, wearing a gratified expression. O Lord, thank you for delivering me from those two devils.

* * *

"Patience, my husband, patience," she shouted through the door. "Your knocking shall wake up the dead," she scolded as she slid back the bolt.

"Peace unto you, wife," the beloved disciple greeted as he brushed by her. He leaned his staff against the wall beside the doorway then shrugged off his cloak.

His wife, a pleasant-faced, gray-haired, plump woman on the other side of middle age, returned the same greeting of peace. “What has gotten into you, husband,” she asked. “You seem agitated.”

“An attempt was made on my life tonight.”

Her hand shot to her mouth. “Someone tried to kill you?”

“Two hired ruffians mistook me for an old man. I taught them to respect their elders,” he said with a mischievous grin.

“What have you done?” she demanded, hands resting on her hips.

“Wife, I gave them a lesson they shall never forget. We must pack. We have to leave,” he said, distracted.

“Where are we going?”

“It is no longer safe for me—for us. The Devil bared his fangs tonight. Praise God I was fortunate I got the better part of the exchange tonight. I may not be so fortunate next time.”

“Devil’s fangs? What are you going on about, husband?”

He walked over to her and gripped her gently by the shoulders. “Wife! Pack two changes of clothes for each of us and food for a day’s journey. We travel to Ashkelon in the morning.”

She knew better than to defy her husband when he was in one of his moods, so she got busy doing what he had requested.

## Chapter Eighteen
## Istanbul

A battery-powered lantern purchased at a local hardware store illuminated the tomb as Aysel, back from eastern Turkey, inspected the shrouded skeleton, her hands sheathed in blue latex gloves to prevent contamination of the ossuary's contents. Off to the side, Father Marco, his hands similarly sheathed, looked on with something like delight. In such tight quarters, he could smell her alluring perfume; it stirred something forbidden in him.

I'll need to perform the rite of penance later…Must keep temptation in check.

He perceived their time alone, which rarely happened, as a perfect moment to ingratiate himself with her while she examined the ossuary and its swathed remains.

"How's your relationship with Baki, my dear?" Please say, "Kaput."

"I think I'm in love with him, Father," she confessed, peering into the stone cavity while holding a large pen flashlight.

Love? His heart hit bottom with a heavy thud. "Any plans for marriage in your future?" God forbid.

She regarded him with a reproachful air.

Chastened, he raised his hands, palms outward, in a warding-off gesture and managed a weak "Just asking, not judging."

"Honestly, I haven't given it much thought." She stopped her inspection, rested a hand on the ossuary and looked at him. "I mean, I don't foresee children in my life. The window for motherhood is shut tight. So why get married?"

Fool. Don't give her any ideas. "Right. Where's my sense these days?"

"Remember our *entente cordiale*. You don't comment on my lifestyle and I don't comment on the child sex scandals of the Church."

"I haven't forgotten our agreement, my dear. Please forgive me. It's an occupational hazard of mine to dispense moral instruction," he said, guilt planted on his face. How can I make her see the folly of her choice?

"You mean well, Father, but I'm a big girl."

"Can I offer you a piece of advice my mother used to give me?"

"If you must."

"My mother used to say, 'If the milk is free, why buy the cow?'"

"How sweet. But Baki's not that kind of guy. Not even close."

I'd like to convince you otherwise. "So he's with you for the long haul, my dear?"

"You bet he is."

"What makes you so sure?" He wanted to say, "You can do better than him."

"Woman's intuition."

Father Marco wouldn't dare challenge female instinct, so he altered course. "I'm curious. What exactly does Baki do for a living?" he asked, crossing his arms across his broad chest. It doesn't hurt to sow doubt about him.

"Private security."

"What? A bodyguard?"

"Sort of."

"Don't you care?"

"I don't ask him about his job."

"You're not curious about what he does? Where he goes? Who his colleagues are?"

"It's his business, not mine."

"You don't want to know."

His statement must have hit close to home—maybe too close—for something like irritation came over her.

"No," she said, her eyes flaring. "What Baki does for a living isn't terribly important." She changed tracks. "May I ask you a personal question, Father?"

"Sure, but I may choose not to answer it."

"What happened to your mother and sister?"

He started at the question as though shocked by a live wire. He stared into the distance, a haunted look on his face and his lips twitched but no words escaped. Over twenty years had passed since the deaths of his beloved mother and sister, but the lingering pain in his soul was still a gaping wound that festered beneath his layer of consciousness. "They died in a car accident," he said in an inflectionless tone.

"Oh. I'm so sorry."

His voice tinged with anguish, he said, "I was at home when I received the news from the police. Their deaths tested my will to live. If not for the wise counsel of our family priest, I might not be alive today."

"What did the priest say to encourage your will to live?"

"He said, 'We cannot always choose the manner of our death but we can always choose the manner of how we live.'" His eyes stung.

"Wise words."

Seemed so at the time. "I joined the seminary not long afterward."

"A friend of mine once explained death this way. God assigns each soul a certain number of breaths. When the last breath is taken, God calls this soul back to Himself."

"An apt analogy."

"Do you have any family still alive?"

"No. The Church is my family now," he said. A dysfunctional one at that. "It has nourished my intellect. It offers daily tribula—challenges with respect to tending my flock. The Church has given me a sense of sharing in its mission and a sense of belonging to something larger than myself. I have travelled far and wide. The Church has opened many doors to me." And more than a few times novitiates wanted to open my door uninvited. Nothing a solid hook and eye latch couldn't stop.

"I have one more personal question to ask you. It's kind of delicate."

"Ask away, my dear."

"How do you feel about celibacy?"

Much worse than a glutton would feel about a one-plate limit at an all-you-can-eat buffet. "If by that you mean do I experience desire? The answer is yes. However, having never had carnal knowledge of a woman, this desire is inconsequential. It's easier to resist that which you have never experienced. One can overcome desire by avoiding circumstances that produce feelings of lust." Such as being alone with you.

A look of—interest?—lit up in her eyes and then was gone. She paused and gnawed her lower lip. "I was thinking more along the line of the necessity of celibacy."

"Ah. Well, the priesthood is a calling, not a vocation, my dear. Members of the Catholic clergy are servants of God. The Church believes the priesthood can best serve the Lord if it focuses its efforts on submitting to His will rather than dividing its labours between the sacred and the personal." Sounds good on paper, but in practice too many brothers confuse submitting with subverting.

"Good answer."

"So what do you conclude?" he said, noticing she had finished her preliminary inspection of the corpse.

She leaned on the lip of the stone box, her elbows locked. "Regarding the age of this ossuary, I can't say anything definitive at this point. His bones must be analyzed using the accelerator mass spectrometry carbon-14 dating process to determine their approximate age. What I *can* say is this person was once someone prominent in the community."

"How can you be so sure?"

"First, the deceased was buried in a private tomb. Second, he was laid to rest in a full-length stone ossuary. Which means a notable of high status lies here for only such a one could have afforded this uncommon burial practice."

"Your deduction is right on the mark," Father Marco congratulated her. "There's something else you should investigate. I saved the best for last. With a flourish, he removed a towel he had draped over the end of the ossuary."

She came around to get a look. "What's this?" she asked, her voice rising in interest.

"You tell me. You're fluent in Aramaic. Give it a shot," he challenged her.

Aysel knelt to gain a better reading of the inscription, and she tucked her hair behind her ears. Minutes passed. He then heard a sharp intake of breath. She slid smoothly from shock to a state verging on disbelief. "Can this be true?" she cried out.

"I experienced a similar reaction," he grinned.

She stood up and beheld him with a sense of amazement. "Father Marco, this-this is incredible. If this engraving is authentic, you'll be famous," she said, and in her enthusiasm, she lunged at him and hugged him.

He stiffened, statue-like, arms pinned to his sides by her tight embrace. "Or notorious, depending on your perspective," he squeezed out. Embarrassment took hold of him but at the same time a frisson of desire electrified him.

The fragrance of her hair flooded his nostrils, something subtle and feminine and clean-smelling, and he drank in the heady aroma of her. He pushed down on the desire rising guiltily within. The rite of penance is definitely in my future.

Aysel temporarily forgot herself, the thrill of elation taking hold of her senses. A long moment passed, then, realizing her situation, she released him from his imprisonment and stepped back.

She must have realized he was reading her emotions for she looked away, embarrassed. "Uh. Sorry, Father. Please forgive me," she said, cheeks flushed, eyes wide at her own response to the close physical contact. She regarded him in a different light now. She didn't need to say anything. Her heightened color said it all.

"Don't be distressed, my dear. You were lost in the moment." And so was I. Redirecting her attention, he said, "It's quite the extraordinary discovery isn't it?"

She seemed grateful for the deflection. "To say the least. You've been sitting on it for what…two weeks?" she calculated. "It must've been nerve-wracking."

"That's putting it mildly. It was sheer torture," he burst out. "I haven't slept well the whole time. Now that I've shared this excitement with you, I feel less agitated, as if a monkey on my back has been yanked off."

"It's mystifying how this person came to be entombed here in Istanbul."

"My guess is as good as yours."

"I'm curious about the second line in the engraving."

"Go ahead."

"What is the phrase *beloved disciple of the m'sheekha* referring to? My knowledge of the Scriptures is rudimentary."

"Well, in the Gospel of John, this phrase is mentioned six times. Bible scholars say it refers to someone who was an intimate of Jesus. Someone whom he held in high esteem. By God's grace, we have discovered who this disciple is and why."

"So the third line in the engraving is the reason for this disciple's privileged status?"

"What other explanation corresponds, my dear? The Gospel of John concludes with the following description of the beloved disciple: 'It is this disciple who testifies to these things and has written them, and we know his testimony is true.' So who better fits this description, which was literally carved in stone, but the *Keeper of the Revelation*?"

## Chapter Nineteen
## Indianapolis

Giltmore flung his suit jacket on the leather couch. *I'll take care of you later.* He strode over to the patio doors and gazed out the window, hands jammed into his pockets, straining to see beyond his reflection mirrored in the glass. Night had fallen. He walked over to the light switch, flicked it off and returned to the same spot. There still wasn't anything to draw his attention. No swing set or lawn toys. Just a large yard surrounded by a tall, mature cedar hedge, which hid his home from the neighbors, and rarely-used patio furniture. A forlorn view for a man with too much free time to ponder these things.

The life he was living was not the life he had pictured for himself. He remembered his younger years and the unrealized dreams of marriage, of children and of grandchildren. Destiny wasn't someone you could bargain with. He tried not to brood, but his interview with Sandra had stirred up repressed memories which now swirled in his mind like a blizzard in one of those snow globes.

It all began to come back. A wave of unrequited longing overcame him and he forgot himself in the memory of his past. His eyes glistened as he recollected the woman from his youth and how he had let her slip from his grasp because the pursuit of professional success allowed no rivals. Now here he was in the winter of his years and still alone. Sometimes a career can be a cruel and uncompromising mistress, and loneliness was the price you paid for this hard-earned wisdom. He gave his shoulders a shrug and the window fogged briefly before him. The opportunity for happiness at his age was slim to none in his estimation. There was no use torturing himself with guilt. What's done is done. He had grown older and wiser but there wasn't anyone to share this awareness with.

That wasn't entirely true. He tried to dismiss Sandra from his thoughts but he was profoundly curious about her. There was so much he wanted to say to her but words could not express the depth of his feelings for her. He knew so little about her except what he heard in the news, which was so much gossip. *She does like* historical fiction. That much I know. But who are her favorite authors? I wonder what she's doing right now. Who she's seeing. How she lives. What her values are. Remember the words of the Prophet, Ol' Boy. *Marry a woman not for her beauty or status or wealth but for her piety.* Wise wor—

The ringing telephone interrupted his dreaming.

Who's calling at this hour? Giltmore wondered with irritation. He looked at the glowing screen. Private caller, it read.

"Hello?"

"Hi, Mike."

If he could've seen her cringe right after she spoke those words, he would've performed cartwheels.

"Sandra?" Am I hallucinating? His irritation vanished—like a dream upon awakening. His palms moistened and his heart fluttered.

"The one and only."

"Did I leave something behind at the studio?"

"Only your courage."

What does she want? An apology? "I hope my comments on your show didn't cause you any personal or professional problems."

"Don't sweat it. I can handle myself. Bullies know better than to step into a cage with me."

"I'm glad you called."

"You are?" Her mood expanded.

"I was wondering if you received any preliminary feedback on the show we aired earlier today." He didn't know what else to say.

"I took some flak from the suits for my unconventional opinion of the World Trade Center attack."

"It's difficult for some folks to admit to their having being duped."

"They said operational secrecy would have been impossible to maintain if 9/11 was an inside job."

"It's a pithy argument trotted out by people who are either ignorant of history or have a personal stake in shilling the regime's Big Lie. Here are two of many historical incidents to demonstrate how large-scale operations were concealed from the public by governments past. The first, Operation Fortitude. This was a British plan involving thousands of people from the armed services and the government that deceived the Germans into believing a huge army was stationed in southeastern England on the eve of D-Day in 1944. The German High Command didn't catch onto this deception until well after D-Day had been launched. The second was Operation Valkyrie. This was a plot to assassinate Adolf Hitler in July of 1944 involving two hundred core members of the armed forces and the government and thousands of secondary players. Hitler didn't learn of the plot until he was injured in a bomb explosion detonated in his bunker on the Eastern Front by the ringleader."

"Operation Fortitude and Operation Valkyrie," Sandra committed to memory. "Thanks, Mike. I can use those once-secret ops in future debates."

"Those who are ignorant of the deceptions in the past can be easily deceived by the duplicities in the present," Mike said, delivering a succinct truism.

"I told the hollow suits to suck it up if they can't handle the truth. I never back down and I never apologize. It's a game and I play it better than they do."

"You're one tough hombre."

"Yeah, so watch your step," and she laughed.

"Anything else?"

"Well, let's see. Someone posted a clip of our exchange about the Day of Ashura on YouTube. It went viral. Two million hits and counting. You're an Internet star, Mike." He couldn't see her twirling her hair.

"Should I be worried?"

"The comments are mostly positive."

"The people are starting to wake up."

"Could be. So what were you doing before I called?"

"I was admiring my backyard." He turned to look through the glass doors again.

"What's so special about it?"

Beats me. "Um…."

"The Great Silver-Tongued Sage of the Stage is at a loss for words? This is earth-shattering news."

"The cedar hedge needs a good trimming," he said at last.

"I know the name of a good landscaper. He takes care of my property. If you want, I can give you his name."

"Let me get a pen…Okay, shoot." He wrote down the number. "If his work isn't satisfactory, will you refund me the bill?"

"You won't be disappointed."

"I'm a perfectionist."

"I'll take you to dinner if you're not satisfied."

Picturing himself sitting across from her in a restaurant, he asked, "Does he work nights?

"Who?"

"Your gardener."

"Is it that urgent?"

*We're talking national emergency.* "I guess I can wait until tomorrow."

"I was wondering…." Her voice trailed off.

"Have you given any further thought about our interview?" He parked himself on the back of a black leather sofa.

"Mike, I didn't call you to...." She groped for the right words. "I-I…."

*Show insecurity the door and pose the question you big chicken. You have nothing to lose but your loneliness.* "So how do you estimate the Colts' chances this coming season?"

"Huh?" She paused for a couple of beats. "Well, their quarterback is one of the best-rounded in the league. He has one of the best passing games thanks to his terrific arm. He's quick in the clutch and good, strong mobility enables him to scramble in the pocket when he's being pressed by the defense. And let's not forget his fast but effective decision-making ability. All combined that makes the Colts contenders this year. What's your assessment of their chances?"

*Don't embarrass yourself, Ol' Boy. What would she want with the likes of you? Maybe she wants to milk more mileage out of your popularity. She'll think of an excuse to avoid you afterward. Why bother travelling down that path?*

"Mike? Are you still there?"

Drop the damn question. Do it! "Sandra, would you like to go to dinner?" he managed to squeak out. He waited for her response with dread.

"Sure. But with whom?"

His courage all but deserted him. "Me?"

"Forgive me, Mike. I couldn't resist being devilish at your expense. Of course I'd love to have dinner with you."

Love to! "You got me good. I nearly died from rejection."

"What does a woman have to do to get your attention?"

"Hold up a sign that says, 'Call me!' But that would be too gutsy for the majority of us."

"Our egos are so fragile. So when and where do you want to go for dinner?"

"Have you ever dined at *Eddie Merlot's?*"

"Many times. Good choice."

"Are you available this coming Saturday at 7:00 PM?"

"Uh, Saturday evening works for me. Knock on wood."

Knock on wood? "Sandra, forgive me for pointing out this saying is actually an expression of unbelief," he put to her as delicately as he could.

"It's just a harmless expression. Like cross my fingers."

"This pagan superstition suggests one can influence future events by simply knocking on wood. It negates the omnipotence of God through Whose will everything in His creation unfolds."

"I hadn't thought of it in that way. What should I say then?"

"When speaking of conditional or future events, it's best to say, 'God willing' or 'If God wills.' He will be pleased with you when you invoke His name and will reward you accordingly. God willing."

She thanked him and added, "My pastor uses 'knock on wood' on occasion."

"Doesn't surprise me."

"I'll try to remember your advice, *God willing*."

"While we're on the topic of superstition, you know why Friday the thirteenth is considered an unlucky day in Western lore?"

"I haven't a clue, but I bet you do."

"Jesus received the first verses of revelation on a Friday, which happened to be the thirteenth day of the month. Out of spite, his enemies propagated the Big Lie that linked this auspicious day with bad luck."

"Why would they invent such a fallacy?" she asked, her voice strained.

"To poison the minds of believers with the notion that Friday the thirteenth should be a day to dread rather than a day to celebrate the revelation of the Gospel."

"The wickedness of some people."

"Every prophet had his detractors." Noticing the time, he cut the conversation short. "So we're all set for Saturday evening?"

"Seems so."

"We'll meet at *Eddie's*. I'll make the reservation in my name. Okay?"

"Sounds like a plan."

A simultaneously thrilling and frightening impulse plucked at his courage. Dare I? You do. "Can I have your phone number?—In case something comes up." He shriveled inside.

She gave a chuckle. "Sure. But guard it with your life."

He wrote it below the landscaper's number thinking, I should tattoo her number on me so I'll never lose it. "I have one tiny request, Sandra."

"Which *is*?"

"Being a Submitter, I'm not permitted to eat when alcohol is present at the table. Would this be a problem?"

"Fine with me, Mike. I don't drink much, anyway—although my job sometimes drives me to want to drink," she said with a laugh.

That's a relief. "Excellent. So I guess I'll see you on Saturday at 7:00 PM, God willing."

"I'm looking forward to it."

"Me, too!" Easy on the enthusiasm, Ol' Boy. Don't make her think she's the only fish in the sea.

"Take care, Mike."

"You too, Sandra. Bye." Giltmore, you babe magnet.

That was the start of it.

He hung up, a smile of contentment on his lips. Basking in the glow of having conquered his fear, his eyes wandered until they fell upon his suit coat resting on the back of the sofa, and it reminded him of some unfinished business.

Now where are those scissors?

# Chapter Twenty
# Istanbul

Father Marco stood still and remained silent while Aysel paced back and forth. He could sense her mental gears grinding behind her furrowed brow. She stopped and looked at him.

"Any idea why the Bible doesn't identify the beloved disciple?" she asked.

"I've been batting that question around myself these past couple of weeks." He pinched his chin. "And I've hit upon a theory," he said. "But it's not verifiable."

"Let's hear it, anyway."

He crossed his arms and launched into his explanation. "We now know the beloved disciple was so named because he was the Keeper of the Revelation. We also know he was a member of the Pharisees, a group that Jesus attacked for falsifying the Torah. And it was the Pharisees who had Jesus arrested and crucified. If they had discovered one of their own was a follower of Jesus, they might have crucified him, too. It's not a stretch then to claim the author of the Book of John, the only book that references the beloved disciple, kept this disciple's name secret to protect his identity and, by extension, his life.

"Well done, Sherlock. But there's a hole in your theory."

"There is, Watson? Give it to me gently."

"The canonical Gospels were composed *after* the letters of Paul were written in the 50s CE and *following* the destruction of the second temple around 70 CE. So the Sanhedrin would've ceased to exist. It wouldn't have posed a threat to the beloved disciple, if he were still alive.

"Good point," he conceded.

"There's more to this mystery but we're not seeing it."

"I suspect the authors of the Gospels buried the identity of the beloved disciple because he possessed the Truth with a capital 'T', a truth which preserved the original message of Jesus. They couldn't expunge his existence entirely but they did minimize his importance to the Jesus movement."

Aysel stiffened. "What do you mean 'original message of Jesus?'"

"Well, the rite of circumcision and observance of Mosaic Law formed part of Jesus' message. Paul, the Apostle to the Gentiles, claimed God revealed to him the Law was dead and, therefore, one only needed to believe in Jesus as the saviour of mankind and in his resurrection to enter Heaven."

Hands on her hips, she said, "That's it?"

"That's the long and the short of it."

"So the beloved disciple might have disputed these changes to Jesus' message?"

"The Book of Acts, chapter 15, references a contentious meeting of the Jerusalem Church that occurred in the early 50s CE. A conservative group of disciples argued to preserve the rite of circumcision and the Law of Moses. Their advocacy was in direct opposition to Pauline doctrine. The beloved disciple could have been a member of this group. He might even have been its spokesman, bearing in mind his esteemed status."

"Seems plausible." She relaxed, leaning her hip against the ossuary.

"Taking into account he was specifically tasked with the preservation of Jesus' message, the beloved disciple alone had the legitimate authority to mandate what was true revelation and what was false revelation."

"Father, replay what you just stated. You're not singing from the same hymnbook as your fellow priests."

"I'm not?" he said, his eyebrow cocked.

"You stated the beloved disciple might have been the leader of a Pharisaic faction opposed to changes in Mosaic Law proposed by Paul, if I understood you correctly."

He stroked his chin.

"So what are you thinking now?

"Right now my head is reeling," and he gave it a shake.

"Tell me something. Although I'm a Christian—of the Orthodox persuasion—I confess I'm somewhat sketchy about Christian doctrine and the history of Christianity…If there was opposition to Paul's revelation, how come the historical record is silent about it?"

"As the saying goes, the victors write the history."

"But winners don't necessarily document the truth."

"Nor can they blot out the losers' side of the story completely."

"Does this hold true for the Bible?"

"As an archeologist, I'm sure you've heard of the trove of codices discovered in 1945 at Nag Hammadi some of which offer a different view of Christianity."

"That's because Christian doctrine was in flux during its formative years. One man's orthodoxy was another man's heterodoxy and vice versa."

"Bishops destroyed Gospels during the early years of the Church's formation to purge heresy from Christian doctrine."

"Who possessed the authority to distinguish truth from heresy?"

"The early Church Fathers."

"But didn't they argue among themselves?"

"I thought you said you were ignorant of Christian theology," he kidded.

"I said I was sketchy," she replied with a grin.

"To return to your question, yes, the early Church Fathers arrived at different conclusions on matters of Christian doctrine."

"So whose doctrinal conclusions triumphed? The one who shouted the loudest?"

He pursed his lips in a hard line. "Worse. Much worse than that," he admitted. "Theological disputes were often decided with fists. There's a historic account of the Council of Tyre, which convened in 335, where Athanasius, the Orthodox patriarch of Alexandria, assaulted fellow bishops, including dismemberment, torture and false imprisonment. He even torched a bishop's house. These incidents would be ideal grist for a Monty Python sketch." He gave his shoulders an embarrassed shrug.

"Incredible. You can't make this stuff up," she said, throwing her hands in the air. "Isn't Athanasius a pillar of the Church or some such honorific?"

"Both the Catholic and Orthodox Churches consider him one of the four great Doctors of the Church. He's also a saint."

"Hard to believe our Churches venerate such a despicable person," she said, shaking her head.

"Athanasius was instrumental in defeating the heresy of Arianism, so our Churches are forever indebted to him."

"Arianism?"

He smiled at the question. "Arianism was named for Arian, a presbyter from Alexandria, Egypt, who opposed Trinitarianism. He asserted Jesus was not co-eternal with God, therefore, he was not co-equal with, but subordinate to, God."

"Athanasius assaulted his fellow bishops over this issue? Unbelievable," she said, smacking the edge of the ossuary.

"Despite the contemptible actions he committed, theological matters normally came down to a vote, not a punching match, after much learned argument and deliberation," he said, pressing his palms together.

"A vote? How democratic," Aysel said, crossing her arms.

"Do I detect a note of sarcasm in your statement?"

"Not just a note. A whole damn symphony."

"I agree it's an unusual method for defining theological truths, but what else could they or should they have done? Jesus didn't leave a Gospel," and he turned his hands palms up in a gesture of capitulation.

"This reeks of your brethren fabricating Christian doctrine."

If he told her she was right, he'd lose all credibility in her eyes. "Without getting into a broader theological discussion, the New Testament didn't provide detailed explanations on various points of doctrine such as the Trinity, for example."

"Maybe not, but many words of Jesus recorded in the Bible contradict Paul's revelation."

Father Marco corrected her. "Paul was the great interpreter of Jesus' message." Embellisher would be more accurate but accuracy is for mathematicians, not priests.

Aysel stood her ground. "Then why did the Jerusalem Church reject Paul?"

"What was to be their final meeting in Jerusalem, James and the elders accused Paul of preaching a *law-free* Gospel to the Jews. He was telling the Jews not to observe Mosaic Law. This was a severe breach of the accord reached at the first Jerusalem Council convened years earlier wherein the apostles endorsed Paul's mission to preach his Gospel but only to the Gentiles."

"Wait a minute. I can't believe I'm hearing this," Aysel said, exasperated. "How can there be different Gospels for the Jews and the Gentiles? Where's the doctrinal consistency? What's good for the goose is good for the gander, isn't it? Correct me if I'm wrong, Father, but I don't recall Jesus preaching any such doctrine."

Damn. Me and my big mouth. He toed the ground then looked at Aysel. "From the beginning of Jesus' ministry, there were Jews who accepted him as the Messiah without conditions, but their numbers were few. Paul claimed he received revelation from Jesus to preach a Gospel of salvation based on grace and not works.

"What? An update? The Gospel of Jesus version 2.0?"

Father Marco held onto his cards. "The Christianity of today is drawn largely from Paul's letters sent to the churches he had established in his missionary work."

"Has it ever crossed your mind the story of Christ has been burnished over the years?"

Burnished? We're talking cock-and-bull, baby. Not wishing to show his cards, he changed subjects. "What I think isn't important right now. So where do we go from here?" He looked at her expectantly.

She pondered the question a moment. "My work is done here."

"What do you mean done? I need you to assay the age of this skeleton."

"I can't, Father. This skeleton is property of the Turkish state, not the Church."

"Can't you bend the rules a bit?" he pleaded.

She took her time answering him. "Here's what I can do. I'll assay the skeleton but you cannot, and I mean cannot, link me to this discovery. Deal?"

"You have my word. So what do you need?"

"I'll need a bone sample for the AMS dating process."

"Will any bone do?"

"A large bone such as the femur is best."

"Why?"

Aysel patiently explained the need for collagen molecules in the AMS dating process. "Since larger bones contain the most collagen, they're the most appropriate specimens for analysis," she finished.

"Thank you for the lesson in anatomy, my dear," he said without sarcasm. "We'll need to remove this burial shroud then."

"Shouldn't we say a prayer first to absolve our disturbing the dead?"

Father Marco mulled over her suggestion for a moment. "It wouldn't hurt to ask God to forgive us for disrupting the repose of the deceased."

"We should. God forbid He should be angry with us."

Father Marco couldn't decide whether she was kidding. She baffled him at times, and this was one of them. "Our Father in Heaven," he began. "We ask for Your mercy. Please forgive us for what we are about to do. We do this in the name of your son, Jesus Christ. Please bless our work. Amen."

"Amen. With any luck, your prayer should keep the evil spirits at bay."

He shot her a look. "So how do you wish to proceed, my dear?"

"I'll need my trauma shears. They're in my satchel by the lantern." She laid the flashlight at the foot of the ossuary.

"Trauma shears? This patient is beyond saving, doctor," he said as he bent down to get them.

Charmed by his sense of humor, she giggled.

Aysel had never witnessed this side of him before. When he was on a dig with her, she spent little time with him. She was too busy supervising student archeologists.

Father Marco passed the shears to her, handles first. "These babies will cut through almost anything," she boasted. She cut the shroud down the central axis of the skeleton. Then together they separated the cloth and folded a portion of it on each side of the ossuary, revealing the innocent white bones of a man who once walked and talked in the company of the Messiah.

"May God forgive us," he murmured. He couldn't help but glance at the grinning skull whose vacant black orbs stared back at him.

"What's that?" she said, pointing to an object that lay beside the skeleton's ribcage.

He moved, noticing his body was casting a shadow over the ossuary. "It appears to be a scroll," he said, his voice in high register. He reached for the cylindrical object and despite his caution, the bones shifted, and his face screwed up in horror.

Breathless. "What do you think it contains, Father?"

"A letter purporting to have been composed by this disciple was among the documents discovered at Nag Hammadi. Maybe this scroll is the original source for that letter."

"It's a substantial scroll."

"Come around here and help me unwind it."

"Hold it," she cautioned him. "Let me examine it first. If the material is brittle, it might crack."

He handed the scroll to her, and an inexplicable charge of positive energy pervaded the tomb, something that radiated benevolence but also incalculable power.

Aysel froze and her eyes glowed with wonder. "My-My hand is tingling."

He gave her look that said, "What are you talking about?"

"Here, take it."

"The scroll's material is still soft and supple, like it hasn't aged at all," he said as he caressed it. "You're right, my dear. The tingling sensation is a little unnerving. I don't know what to make of it."

"Grab one end and help me unroll it, but be extra careful." They unrolled about a foot of the scroll.

"There's writing. It's Aramaic," he said, his voice rising in intensity. "The writing is so small. Let's move closer to the lantern where the script will be easier to read."

They stood side-by-side like children while they read in silence.

*In the name of God, the Most Merciful,*
*the Especially Merciful*
*God is One,*
*God is Eternal, Absolute*
*He does not beget, nor is He born*
*And there is none like unto Him*

*All glory, all praise, all thanks is for God alone,*
*Who has no partners*
*None has the right to be worshipped but God alone*
*He is Lord of all the worlds*
*To God belongs the dominion and to Him is the praise*
*He is able to do all things*
*He has power over His Creation*
*He is the First and the Last*
*He has no beginning and no end*
*He is Self-Sustaining, the Ever-Existing*
*God is the All-Forgiving, the Most-Forgiving*
*No one but God can forgive sin*
*There is none in the heavens and the earth but shall come to God the Most Merciful as a servant*

"Did you finish, my dear?" He sinfully enjoyed the warmth of her shoulder against his arm.

"Hold on, Father. One more phrase…It's a beautiful prayer to God."

"These verses are unmatched in eloquence. They describe God's grandeur in a way far surpassing any other description I've ever read."

"Even the Trinitarian creed?"

"Most certainly," he affirmed.

"Whoever wrote this didn't have a plural view of God."

"Not surprising."

"Roll your end toward mine, Father, so we can read more of it." Aysel then unspooled more of the scroll from her end.

They read on, mesmerized, heads bowed in reverence. Words, resonating with majesty and power, reverberated across a vast gulf of time and distance, echoing in their minds and stirring their souls. The surreal atmosphere in the tomb, charged with enigmatic energy, vibrated and sparkled. Time and space seemingly dissolved and vanished. The past was present and the present was past. Before and after had ceased to be. The faintest awareness of the here and the now manifested itself. The room spun but no motion was perceived. Fingers trembled and legs shook. Goose flesh budded and hair prickled. Lips quivered and eyes brimmed with tears. They were moved beyond speech in the solemn silence of the tomb. Wonder had supplanted words.

*ABIB 15, 3793*

*The M'sheekha was a servant and messenger of God, and he proclaimed the Good News from his Lord: A final prophet named The Praised One is soon to come who will lead all of mankind to the Truth.*

*And Heaven is promised to every penitent soul who believes in God and in His Oneness and worships only Him and who believes in His prophets, all of them, without distinction.*
*God the Almighty as my witness, this testament is a record of what I saw and heard in my travels with the man who called himself the M'sheekha.*

*In the name of God Most Gracious, Most Merciful.*

*I bear witness there is no deity but God and none has the right to be worshipped but God alone Who has no partner.*

*It has been revealed that your Lord is only one God. So whoever hopes to meet his Lord, he should then do good deeds and should not join anyone in the worship of his Lord.*

*I have indeed been commanded that I worship only God and that I do not join with Him. Toward Him I do invite, and toward Him is my return.*

*I bear witness the M'sheekha was born of the blessed virgin, Maryam, who no man has touched. He was called into existence by his Lord Who said, "Be" and he became. Those who dispute this truth are in manifest error.*

*I bear witness the M'sheekha was not crucified, dead and buried. His persecutors attempted to kill him but they killed him not. The Lord put a likeness of him on the cross and they martyred that man. Those who dispute this truth are in manifest error.*

He heard Aysel's breath leave her and the question that had been haunting him the past couple of weeks suddenly vaporized. The Church is wrong, Wrong, WRONG!, the words ricocheting off the walls of his cranial cavity. By God.

## Chapter Twenty-One
## Indianapolis

Sandra's entry into the dining area of *Eddie Merlot's* made a spectacular splash. Her tight red dress drew attention like a dewdrop of blood in a shark-infested aquarium. The buzz of conversation intensified, heads swiveled and necks craned as hungry eyes sought to glimpse the vision sashaying by. Sandra ignored the voracious stares (and not a few vicious scowls from jealous female patrons) as she and the maître d' weaved their way through tables to where Giltmore was waiting. He stiffened in nervousness at her approach.

"Here you are, Miss Dowling. We wish you a pleasant dining experience with us this evening."

"Thank you, Raymond."

"Hi, Sandra." He shook her hand and the fluttering in his belly increased with the sensation of her touch.

"Hi, Mike." She favored him with a radiant smile, like sunburst on a cloudy day. Her lustrous black locks were wound up on the back of her head and tendrils of hair dangled enticingly the length of her sensuous neck around which hung an emerald-studded necklace matching the color of her eyes.

"Tongues are wagging," she said in an undertone. "Most notorious man in America dines with one of the most famous women in America."

"So that's what that slobbering sound is," he said as he helped her settle into her seat.

"Thank you," she spluttered with laughter.

"My pleasure…Praise God, but you look—delicious," he blurted out. No sooner did the word escape his lips when he pulled a face.

"Delicious?" she said, her eyebrow cocked in mock anger.

Identifying her arched tone, Mike shrank in his chair as Sandra loomed across from him.

"No one's ever dared called me delicious."

"I-I didn't mean it in that way, Sandra. I—"

"Then how *did* you mean it?" she asked.

"I meant you look like…like a sight for sore eyes."

"Are your eyes sore, Mike? If not, they're gonna be real soon," she said, balling her hands into tight fists.

You're a dead man, Giltmore. "No, it's you—I…Please forgive me, Sandra, for my poor choice of words," he pleaded.

"Mike, I'm toying with you."

"You're *good,*" he swallowed.

"I enjoyed watching you squirm."

"You got me," and he laughed.

"The truth is no one has ever called me *delicious* before, but the hunger in their eyes told me what they were *really* thinking. I don't see a ravenous look in your eyes so *delicious* it is."

He broke out into a big smile and sat up straight. "Here's to delicious then," he toasted, raising his glass. They clinked glasses and each took a sip of water.

"You threw me to the mat the other night on the phone," he said before tabling his glass.

"I hope it didn't hurt."

"I wasn't expecting such an informed response to my question on the Colts. You know more about football than most men."

"My older brothers played college ball. Second string. Anyway, as the sole sister in my family, I learned about the game at the dinner table. I'm a season ticket holder now."

"That explains it."

"And you, Mike? Are *you* a Colts fan?"

Her tone intimated he had better be if he wanted to be with her.

"Can't help it. This is a football town. Never played the game though. Didn't have the desire to be knocked on my butt. I prefer to upend people with well-phrased words."

"Did you play any other sport?"

"No. I was—still am—a bookworm. But I work out three times a week." He sucked in his gut.

"Do you belong to a gym?"

"I train at *Life Time Fitness*. Do you work out?"

"*Curves* is my second home. I can train there without men ogling me."

"I hear you. I have the same problem at my gym. Women staring at me all the time. Gets on my nerves," he said with false annoyance.

They held each other's gaze, sharing the same thought, then they both burst out laughing. Their initial nervousness abated; their budding relationship felt more natural now.

The sound of someone clearing his throat got their attention.

"Good evening. My name is Doug. I'll be your waiter this evening. Are you folks ready to order or do you need more time?"

"I guess we should look at the menus first, shouldn't we?" Giltmore suggested, glancing at Sandra then back at Doug. "Please give us a few more minutes."

He nodded his understanding and whisked away to serve other diners.

"You come here often?" he asked, reading the menu.

"I dine here several times a year. I hold my show's annual Christmas party in the private dining space. Since you chose this place, I assume you've been here before?" she asked while she examined the menu selections.

"I've dined here with colleagues from the university over the years. But I don't think such conviviality will happen again."

"I understand your point…So what are you going to order?"

Studying the menu, he said, "I can't eat any non-*halal* meat dish so I'll stick to something fishy."

"*Halal*? What does it mean?" she asked, looking at him over the top of the elegant menu.

He glanced up. "Oh, sorry. *Halal* is the Arabic word for *permissible*. *Halal* meat comes from a herbivore ritually slaughtered in the name of God and in a manner prescribed by Him."

"Forgive my ignorance, but what's the significance of this ritual?"

"I'll try not to be too gory. The herbivore should be alive when its jugular is slit so the working heart can pump out the blood and at the same time the words 'God is the Most Great' should be spoken to bless the slaughter."

"I don't eat meat so this doesn't gross me out. What's the problem with eating bloody meat?"

"When an animal is alive, antibodies in its bloodstream are doing their job killing germs. As soon as an animal dies, the antibodies die and germs begin to spread in the bloody flesh. Every half-an-hour after death, the germs double in quantity. I wouldn't doubt one of the major causes of ill health in the West is related to eating non-*halal* meat."

"Worthy of further investigation. What about seafood?"

"Submitters can eat anything from the sea, and it doesn't have to be ritually slaughtered."

"Interesting. I never fail to learn something when we're together." Her eyes sparkled like the gems encircling her neck.

"If I talk too much, just rap me on the knuckles."

She waved off his insecurity. "I'm hungry. The seafood platter looks yummy." She folded the menu and took another sip of water.

"Good choice. I'm wild about wild Pacific salmon so anchors away…" He paused and interlaced his hands on the table. "This is a little awkward. I haven't dated in ages so I don't know what the *rules* are. Do you want separate bills?"

"That's *so* yesterday. I'm a woman of independent means, so I'm picking up the tab tonight."

"Be advised, I'm cheap, but I'm not easy."

She guffawed.

He was smitten with the sound of her laughter. He hoped to hear much more of it in the future. He could dream, couldn't he?

Giltmore glanced around for the waiter. Making eye contact with Doug, he waved him over. He took their orders and left.

"So I suppose you want to discuss my book."

"Excuse me? Don't be so presumptuous."

"What else have we to discuss?"

Put out, her eyes snapped with anger. "Mike, the last thing I want to discuss is your damn book!"

Speechless, he stared at her for a few beats. "*Really?*"

"Do you think I dress up like this for a business meeting?"

"So this is a genuine date we're on?"

"No. I'm only here for the food."

Uncertainty crossed his features.

She winked at him. “Gotcha!”

Giltmore’s posture relaxed and he beheld Sandra in his eyes and she gazed back, her demeanor welcoming once again.

“A penny for your thoughts.”

“Is that all?” she said, earning him a pretend wounded look.

“If I had a goldmine, I’d give it to you.” A bit rich, Ol’ Boy. Tone it down.

She bet he would.

“So, Mike,” she said, tapping her fingers on her forearm. “Have there been any major changes in your life since you became a Submitter?”

“Hmm…Besides having to worship God five times a day, my eyes have been opened. It’s as if a veil has been peeled back from my vision. I feel like an outsider in my own country now. My religion makes me less of an American in Islamophobes’ eyes. I now have one foot in the privileged-white in-group and the other in the Muslim out-group. And my concerns no longer mirror those of our fellow brass-ring grasping neighbors.”

“In what way?”

“Are you familiar with the hymn, *Amazing Grace*?”

“Somewhat.”

“The line ‘I once was lost, but now am found, was blind, but now I see’ sums up the new me.” He paused, expecting her to get it, but she gave him a vague look instead. He sensed he had failed to convince her. He was stumped. Then his face lit up. “Remember in the movie *The Matrix* when Neo is given the choice between swallowing the red pill or the blue pill?”

“Yup. Neo takes the red pill because he wants to know the truth.”

“Believe it or not, the same sort of awakening happened to me when I adopted Submission as my religion.” He added, grinning, “But none of us is hooked up to a monstrous brain-sucking pod.”

“We should be grateful for small miracles,” she said with mirth. “So enlighten me. What do you see that we non-Submitters don’t?”

Giltmore leaned on the table, supporting himself with his forearms and his face assumed a serious mien. “A Submitter is a servant of God. Once you accept this condition of your humanity…of your reality, you become conscious of how upside down your priorities are in this world," he said. "All this striving and struggling for the ever-elusive American Mirage is so pointless. I was caught up in this matrix of consumerism and careerism that focuses our attention on this life, not on the eternal life to come. But I'm through with such fruitless pursuits. I can now concentrate on serving my Creator."

He was beginning to lower his guard. In spite of her beauty, Sandra made him feel comfortable in her presence. Gone was that sense of ineptness men succumbed to in the company of beautiful women. The boundaries between him and her were blurring, merging, much sooner than expected. He decided then he'd make the most of this occasion even if his reading of her barometer of interest in him might be this side of delusional.

"I sometimes question whether the personal investment in my career is worth it," she confessed. "I have more money than I can spend. I don't have much of a life. My weekends are spent decompressing and preparing for the following week's shows."

"Peculiar. I assumed you led a glamorous life."

"Initially, it was. But the novelty wore off years ago. It's become a bit of a grind lately." A tight-lipped smile crossed her ruby mouth. "I guess I shouldn't complain, considering the Depression-era level of real unemployment in this country."

"We Submitters define success by one criterion. Admittance to Paradise on the Day of Judgement. This is the true measure of success for us."

"Talk about delayed gratification. So you won't know whether you've won or lost the lottery of life until Judgement Day?"

"Pretty much so. The upshot is knowing this keeps us on the straight path. This life is so ephemeral, so impermanent," he said as though he had just unearthed this nugget of wisdom. "We Submitters try not to become attached to it. Instead of accumulating wealth and material possessions, we strive to accumulate good deeds. As Jesus advised, 'He who seeks after the world is like he who drinks sea water; the more he drinks, the more his thirst increases until it kills him.' The sole assets people will take with them when they leave this earthly existence are their beliefs and their deeds, both good and bad."

"This is deep stuff, Mike."

"I hope I'm not boring you," he said, bringing the glass of water to his lips.

"Just the opposite. I feel like I'm sitting at the feet of a wise teacher." She smoothed the tablecloth before her.

"But every student must think for herself so she can judge for herself."

"So true. Do Submitters reject wealth?"

"No need to. It's the pursuit of wealth that's problematic. Wealth is a test for Submitters as is poverty."

"A test? You'd think wealth would be a blessing."

"It's a double-edged sword, Sandra. It can influence a person's behavior in a positive way or its opposite. Psychological studies reveal wealthy people are more callous than their poorer cousins. You're more than twice as likely to be mowed down in a crosswalk by a person driving a luxury vehicle than by a person driving a more modest brand," Giltmore pointed out.

"Fascinating factoid. I drive an Infiniti," she said with an ironic grin.

"And I drive a Lexus. People in crosswalks should feel safe when they see us coming," and he gave her a wink.

"It confirms my belief that money is the root of all evil."

Giltmore was quick to disagree. "Money is just a means to an end. It's our lusts and desires that are the root of all evil."

"That's original."

He resisted patting himself on the back. "Self-indulgence is not a carefree journey toward self-fulfillment but rather a perilous slide toward self-destruction. Think about it, Sandra. Fulfilling our wants isn't free. It takes money, sometimes a lot of it. The bigger the want, the higher the cost, both financial and personal. Some people will go to extreme ends, even criminal ends, to satisfy their desires."

"I grasp now the meaning of the Biblical proverb concerning wealth."

"Which one?"

"It's easier for a camel to pass through the eye of a needle than for a wealthy person to enter heaven."

"Precisely. But God doesn't dislike wealth. He doesn't love a person who hoards it and revels in it," he said. "As Jesus warned, 'No one can serve two masters.' A Submitter cannot be a servant of God *and* a slave to wealth."

"The way the economy's struggling in this neo-Gilded Age, wealth accumulation is the least of our worries. Our economic system is designed to make us debt slaves. Few people can afford a new car or a college education these days without going into debt unto the third generation." She took a sip of water.

"An astute insight, Sandra." He marvelled at her. She seemed to have caught his look for she beamed. "Higher education is the ticket to wealth and professional success in this country, but it comes at an obscenely steep price set by the ruling class to prevent others from joining that exclusive club. It has been this way since the founding of this country. Case in point. My nephew graduated with a degree in meteorology from an Ivy League College last year with a debt load of about $125,000 dollars. He financed the loan for twenty-five years. By the time he finishes paying the loan, his education will have cost him $420,000 dollars. Is that obscene or what?"

"I feel sorry for him. He'll hard-pressed to join the ranks of the middle-class saddled with such a huge debt load. It's not only obscene, it's outrageous!"

"The slave masters of the U.S. plantation spare no effort to keep our feet planted on the debt treadmill in pursuit of the illusory American Mirage. They've got to keep us busy paying off financial debt so we're too distracted to keep tabs on wasteful government shenanigans."

Sandra's eyes looked up and away from his and she smiled. He was about to glance over his shoulder when a stylishly-dressed woman, who looked to be in her forties, parked herself in front of their table, holding a pen and a piece of mauve-colored paper.

Before he could recover, she said to him, "Please excuse this—my rudeness, but could I have your autograph?"

A confused look planted itself on his face. "Don't you want her autograph?" he said, pointing his finger at Sandra.

The lady blushed. "I already have Miss Dowling's. She autographed my copy of her book last summer."

Sandra smiled at this admission.

"Well, this is a first." He grinned and took hold of the pen and paper she held out to him. "What's your name?"

"Rachel Goldbloom." While he scratched out a message on the piece of colored paper, she said, "I was surprised but also pleased with what you said about the Day of Ashura on Miss Dowling's show. I had no idea Muslims commemorate the Exodus with fasting."

He was on the brink of returning her items and stopped himself. "Of course not. The Islamophobes cannot allow the American people to be privy to such truths. This would only serve to remove the divisions they have created between us."

"I think the people are hearing it loud and clear now."

"Contrary to popular perception, Muslims are allies of Jews. We don't believe in the crucifixion of the Messiah."

"We can use allies since the Pittsburgh massacre."

"You probably heard CelebrateMercy, an Islamic charity, raised almost two hundred thousand dollars for the families of the victims. American Jews might have thought they were safe in this country because the haters' attentions were focused on us Muslims. Pittsburgh was their wakeup call."

She seemed to be on the verge of adding to this comment but ended with: "We can only hope better minds will take control of the situation. Well, I've taken up enough of your time. Thank you for your courage, Mr. Giltmore." She turned and walked away.

"It appears your message is having an impact in the unlikeliest places," Sandra said.

"It's all good," he shined.

"Anything that improves Muslim-Jewish relations is a good thing."

"The lady said you wrote a book. Any chance I can score an autographed edition?"

"Only if you do the same for me."

"Consider it done."

"So anything else you wish to share with this *slave of the matrix*?"

"You know, I never experienced prejudice before I became a Submitter. But now I can sympathize with the victims of racism and bigotry to a certain degree, which you, as a black woman, have probably experienced once too often."

She gave her eyebrows a shrug. "Well, as a successful black woman I've experienced my share of racism, but I don't let it distract me otherwise I'd go nuts."

"For a person of color, her skin is her sin. For a Muslim, his belief is his grief."

"Interesting way of putting it. I imagine you've suffered some backlash since you came out of the closet, so to speak."

"You think *so*?" he said with mock humor. "I've noticed the language changes whenever the subject of so-called Islamist terrorism is broached."

"Really? Enlighten me."

"I collected a lexicon from our media reserved for so-called Islamist terrorists. It includes vile words used exclusively to label attacks by putative Submitters," he said with bitterness. "Words such as: Brutal. Barbaric. Bestial. Evil. Savage. Vicious. Uncivilized."

"Those same words describe American drone strikes," she said, hitching in her seat. "But one word is missing."

"Which one?

"Cowardly."

Giltmore jolted. "Say that on your show and you'll be waterboarded."

"They. Don't. Scare me."

"I wanted to pull my frigging hair out when I heard a former pompous president of France characterize the murder of the *Charlie Hebdo* Muslim-baiters as *extraordinarily barbaric*," he said with a French accent. "I wonder how this windbag would characterize the murder of fifteen percent of the Algerian population during the Franco-Algerian war. How ab—"

"Hold on a sec," she said, motioning with her hand. "The French murdered fifteen percent of the Algerian population? That must've been in the hundreds of thousands!"

"One point five million is an official estimate. Mostly civilians. I'd qualify this military action as genocide."

She shook her head in unbelief. "There was nothing barbaric about the murder of those cartoonists. It was tragic and immoral, but nothing exceptional in this crazy world."

"I agree. But such is the Islamophobic temper of our times."

"Islamist murderers are more murderous than others. Didn't you know that, Mike?"

"First, they demean you. Then they dehumanize you. Finally, they destroy you. That was the Nazi playbook for the Jews and now it's the playbook the Islamophobes are employing against Muslims, especially those serving in Congress."

"History is a memory hole for the ignorant and the intellectually lazy," Sandra said.

"Orwell couldn't have said it better."

"Your historical perspective will only have relevance in hindsight. By then it'll be too late."

"What bothers me most about the *Charlie Hebdo* affair is the support in certain Muslim circles for the killers. Those people don't know their religion. The Quran tells us how to respond to verbal provocation."

"I'll take the bait. How should Muslims respond?"

"With something better. Not with violence."

"Words to live by."

"But the hypocrisy of the *Charlie Hebdo* affair is lost on the foaming-at-the-mouth free-speech fascists.

"I wasn't aware of any."

"With the exception of the hashtag hillbilly in the White House, how many Western politicians would defend the free speech of white supremacists gunned down in black Harlem for saying 'not all blacks are criminals but most criminals are black' day after day despite repeated warnings to cease and desist?"

"Not one would dare do so in public."

"Which is every bit as offensive as saying 'not all Muslims are terrorists but most terrorists are Muslim.' You see now how the rules of free speech are selectively applied?"

She bent to the logic of his reasoning. "It's a credit to Muslims they don't jump into the sewer with the Islamophobes and host cartoon contests of Jesus in a KKK costume."

"If they did, the Hebdonistas would be all over it like rats on garbage."

Sandra snickered and continued listening.

"Submitters respect all prophets of God and we are forbidden to malign the gods of other religions such as Buddha and Vishnu," Giltmore said. "We're not hypocrites like the Hebdonistas. Andres Serrano can attest to that."

"I take it you're referring to his *Piss Christ* photo of a crucifix submerged in a glass of his own urine? Did you know he received death threats and his artwork was vandalized? So much for *his* right to free speech."

"If he were murdered for his artwork, how many *Je suis Andres Serrano* rallies would be held here and across the pond?"

"Zero" Sandra mouthed, forming the shape of that number with her thumb and index finger. "You know, as late as 2012, religious organizations were clamoring for the president to denounce the *Piss Christ* photo."

"Of course they would. It's just a matter of whose ox is being drawn and quartered…Uncivilized," Giltmore muttered.

"How do you define civilized, Mike?"

He puckered his brow. "You'll often hear a claim to being civilized staked on technology. But from the Islamic perspective, a person who worships God and only God and not images or idols is the mark of a civilized person. What's your definition of a civilized person?" he asked her, leaning back in his chair.

"How a person treats someone over whom she has power defines a civilized person."

"I'll vote for that."

"Mike, you help me to view things from a different perspective," she said while she rearranged her utensils.

"I do?"

"I get it now. Our victims of terrorism are paragons of heroism while the victims of our military's careless brutality are mere collateral damage or human shields."

"Precisely. It's only our perspective that matters, not the lives of innocent victims killed by our military machine. As a former draft-dodging president once said, 'We don't do body counts.'"

"In the calculus of death, why does one innocent death matter more than another? An innocent death is a death is it not?" she said, anguished.

"Because dead Muslims aren't human beings. They're bloody mindless savages."

"This—this world is going to hell."

"It doesn't have to, Sandra. People need to get off their lazy arses and do their homework. Then they will come to realize Western politicians are at war with the truth. The duty of governments is to keep its citizens ignorant so they can be manipulated. The ruling class use our political and religious beliefs to polarize our perceptions so we can be herded like compliant cattle."

"Where would people begin?"

"The FBI's own website would be a good starting point. According to a terrorism report in the *Reports and Publications* section, so-called Islamist extremists committed just one percent more domestic terrorist acts than communist extremists as of 2005."

"What percentage of terrorist acts did the communists commit?

"A mere four percent, he said. Reading the look on her face, he added, "Here's another surprise. Until 2005, Latino extremists were responsible for the most terrorist attacks in the U.S. at just over forty percent. Ironic isn't it? Despite these facts, you'll never see a headline about Latinos perpetrating more terrorist acts than so-called Islamists. Can't sell as many newspapers leading with such a headline, can you?"

Sandra grabbed a moment to absorb the impact of this myth-shattering news. "The Catholic Church wouldn't be pleased," she thought aloud.

"The Church shouldn't be concerned. Latino terrorism is no more a reflection of Catholicism than terrorism committed by self-proclaimed Muslims is a reflection of Islam. But there's more. The Human Rights Watch organization issued an eye-opener of a report on U.S. terrorism prosecutions not too long ago."

"I've heard of this organization, though I'm sure most of us haven't. Critics have tried to discredit its work with accusations of harboring terrorist sympathies."

"Whenever someone challenges the political status quo, such contemptible charges are levelled. Anyway, this report studied twenty-seven federal terrorism cases and it concluded that most of these cases wouldn't have passed beyond the stage of wishful thinking if not for the assistance and encouragement of FBI personnel. Can you imagine?"

Sandra considered the narrative with mounting alarm. Her apprehension quickly morphed into anger. "Christ, Mike"—she cringed—"Pardon my language. That's aiding and abetting terrorism."

"Not if it's our government doing it."

"I can't believe the FBI is getting away with helping aspirational terrorists become operational. That's entrapment."

"The War on Terror needs casualties or the threat thereof to perpetuate itself. But that's not the end of it. The report also uncovered the FBI often sought people with mental and financial problems then furnished them with the wherewithal to carry out their aborted *terrorist* crimes."

"So the FBI grooms patsies to bolster its Chicken Little narrative."

"You can't sell any umbrellas on a sunny day any more than you can sell Islamophobia without a cloud of phantom 'Islamist' terrorism roiling above, ready to burst. Law enforcement fabulists have to conjure up menacing tales to justify their terrorist apparitions."

"The sky is falling, the sky is falling," Sandra joked. "I wish people would wake up and realize our involvement in foreign wars deliberately distract us from our domestic strife so we can rally against a common enemy. Yesterday it was communism. Today it's Islam."

"You got that right. But it gets better. A former assistant director of the FBI admitted the agency hypes the terrorist threat to the U.S. homeland to protect its budget allocation. 'Keep fear alive,'" he quipped. "How's that for an anti-terrorism strategy?"

"Cheese and crow, Mike. There should be protests from one end of the country to the other about these revelations."

Around them the hoi polloi of Indiana ate and drank. A babel of voices rose and fell in the background with no frequency or pattern. Utensils clinked on plateware and waiters circulated taking orders, refilling goblets of wine and glasses of water. All was merry and bright in la la land.

"Media oligarchs quash these kinds of revelations by colluding with the Deep State," he groused. "When press organs such as the *Wall Street Pravda* and *The New York Izvestia* parrot the agenda of the Deep State, what can you expect?"

"This reminds me of an incident when I was working for a city-wide newspaper at the start of my journalism career. An editor called me into his office and asked me to rewrite a few lines in my article because the publisher's friends in Washington wouldn't appreciate the facts I uncovered."

"I'm not surprised. Left-wing and right-wing media are antagonistic ideological echo chambers for the agenda of the Deep State. The job of the mainstream news is to manufacture consensus around the opinions they want us to hold. This is why news is selected and slanted before it reaches the masses. News is a commodity that has to be modified to make it palatable for mass consumption. People are more concerned with what they put in their bodies than in their minds. God forbid they should consume the truth and realize what the American regime is doing in their name," he said with a sneer. "The fourth estate was supposed to be a public watchdog with a bite. It's nothing but a toothless lapdog of the elites."

"I'm sure politicians don't lose any sleep over the state media gumming them to death."

Giltmore would've laughed if his mouth wasn't full of water. He coughed instead, dousing the table. Between bouts of coughing, he apologized, but Sandra was too busy laughing to care.

"Are you *okay*?"

"I'll live," he said in a strained voice. "Gummed to death. Too funny for me." He dabbed at the water with his napkin and the tension of the moment seeped from his body.

"Glad you liked it." Giltmore was on the mend, so she continued. "But getting back to what you said, since the Reagan era, the separation of media and state has all but disappeared."

Regaining his breath, Giltmore added, "Grave-faced media pundits intone we now live in a post-factual era. That facts don't matter anymore. Only assertions do. And the more *official* the assertions are, the more *credible* they are. Uh, *sor-ry*. The truth is, we've never lived in a fact-based world insofar as the media are concerned. The notion of a free press in the U.S. is as big a farce as free markets. U.S media organs are about as independent as those of Russia, China and Iran. Have you ever read any condemnation of the Zionist insurgents' never-ending illegal and brutal land confiscations and house demolitions in Palestine in any corporate media, whether on the left or the right?"

Sandra gave her head a shake.

"I fear we're slipping into a new Dark Age. An age where politicians and pundits, posing as a neo-medieval priesthood, call the truth *fake news* and a good chunk of the people, already lapsed into ignorance and superstition, go along with them."

"The media are to blame, Mike. They have so debased the currency of truth that an orange-tinted chump in the White House can spout naked lies and still remain in office. Pity the nation that has no regard for the truth."

"There's more, Sandra. According to a joint intelligence report released by the FBI and Homeland Security, between 2000 and 2016, white supremacists committed twenty-nine terrorist attacks, resulting in forty-nine deaths. Greater than any other domestic terrorist group. But here's the kicker. More than three hundred thousand Americans were killed by handguns in this same period. So you are far, far, far more likely to be killed by a non-Muslim than by a Muslim in America. We should ban all non-Muslims from entering the homeland until our country's representatives can figure out what the hell is going on." He sat back with a triumphant look.

Sandra drummed her fingers on the table. "It now makes a whole lot of sense why we're spending trillions of dollars fighting a War on Terror overseas to supposedly protect us from terrorists while here at home we're killing each other with handguns at the rate of *only* thirty people per day."

Giltmore couldn't help but grin at her sarcasm. "It's okay if *civilized* non-Muslim Americans kill each other in the tens of thousands per year, but God forbid an *uncivilized* Muslim American should kill just one of us."

"Didn't you know the God-given right to bear arms is the Eleventh Commandment? Politicians can carp all they want about gun control. This issue won't be solved in the halls of Congress but only from behind the pulpits of America."

"Put another way, a gunman can massacre dozens at a country music festival or slaughter eleven Jews in their synagogue or annihilate six Muslims in a Quebec City mosque and it's not considered terrorism. It's only labelled terrorism when the gunman shouts 'Allahu Akbar.'" He shook his head in disgust.

"Anyone can shout slogans. Murder is murder. Calling it terrorism doesn't change the result," Sandra said. "It only warps our perspective."

Glancing left and right, he said, "It's no coincidence our homicidal culture pervades our country's foreign policy. When the U.S. continent was conquered in the late nineteenth-century with the violent pacification of Native Americans in the name of Manifest Destiny, America began its wars of overseas conquest. Starting with the Spanish-American War. Our country has been at war ever since. It has no choice. We're a nation of blood-thirsty conquerors, like our British cousins.

"Our political masters no longer call this racist ideology Manifest Destiny. They now call it 'spreading democracy.'"

"Yeah. If you don't give us what we want, we'll bomb your country in the name of democracy. U.S. statecraft aside, here's the best. The Justice Department's own inspector general admitted in a 2015 report that the Patriot Act was ineffective in combating terrorism."

"I-can't-believe-I'm-hearing-this."

"It's just the frikking tip of the iceberg, Sandra," he said, rattling the cutlery on their table with his fist.

"Jim Morrison said, 'Whoever controls the media, controls the mind.'"

"Jim Morrison of *The Doors*?"

"Yup."

"Well, flabber my gast. He was right. The Deep State has conjured up images of raving barbarians at our gates to advance their twisted Orwellian agenda. But we needn't be concerned because the barbarians are inside the gates and they support the terrorists in the White House and Congress."

"Fear is a powerful motivator for manipulating people into sacrificing their liberties in return for security. Who has time for sound judgement when you're afraid? Fear is the enemy of reason. It crowds out critical thinking. When you're gripped by state of fear, you want it to go away," she finished, fiddling with her napkin.

"The Turks have a saying: feed the crow so it can turn around and poke your eye out. It's unfortunate the chicken hawks in the corridors of power aren't familiar with this saying, otherwise, they'd stop birthing groups like ISIS and Al Qaeda, the Mad Hatters of the Middle East, who end up biting the hand that feeds them," he said, dabbing his mouth with the napkin.

"This white noise of anti-Muslim rancor has been going on for ages. It's always humming in the background. Like the weather. The never-ending conflicts in the Middle East fuel this hatred toward Muslims. This whole issue just numbs the mind and the soul. Most people tune it out. I know I do."

"Apathy is what the *business-as-usual* propagandists want. So long as the effects of Islamophobia don't impact us, the majority of us couldn't give a crap what our government is up to. The fewer citizens engaged in this issue, the easier it is for the Deep State to advance its end goal of world conquest. The default position of the Deep State's media marionettes is to ignore and excuse crimes against Muslims. We saw it with the Chapel Hill shootings in North Carolina."

"It was disgusting a whole day passed before these murders made the national news. If it had been the other way around, the airwaves would've been saturated with hysterical anti-Muslim diatribes."

"What's more disgusting is Christian leaders didn't apologize for the terrorist actions of the gunman who committed the Charleston Church Massacre."

"You're kidding, right?"

"No-I'm-not," he said with barely controlled fury. "If Muslim leaders are compelled to condemn the actions of a misguided minority, why shouldn't Christian leaders be corralled before microphones to condemn the murderous actions of one of their own?"

"But Roof was a member of the Klu Klux Klan."

"Which is a right-wing extremist 'Christian' terrorist organization whose white-supremacist propaganda motivated his hate crime," he glared at her. "See, Sandra. I, too, can play the role of the ignorant and arrogant religious chauvinist."

Chastened. "I get it. Double standard."

"Precisely. What's good for the Christian goose is good for the Muslim gander—halal of course."

"Unquestionably."

"Equally galling was the state media's linking of Roof's rampage to Confederate nostalgia and not to a radical right-wing 'Christian' ideology. Nostalgia made him do it."

"We Christians don't kill in the name of *our* religion, Mike."

He winked at her irony. "No truly pious person would kill in the name of their religion, unless in self-defence. Anyway, the calumny against the religion of Submission has existed at least since the time of Jesus," he said in a world-weary tone.

"It has?" She perked up.

"Certainly."

"You say this so definitely. What makes you so convinced?" she asked, twirling her glass of water.

He leaned in. "Because the religion of Submission poses an existential threat to the economic interests of the parasitic, self-serving elites: the Anglo-American bankers, financiers, and mortgage lenders," Giltmore said, listing them on the fingers of his hand.

"How so?" She hunched forward. "This I have to hear."

"The Sanhedrin attempted to crucify Jesus because he chased the moneylenders out of the Temple. In Prophet Mohammed's time, the elites of Mecca tried to assassinate him because he proclaimed the worship of God alone and forbade the worship of idols."

"I don't see the connection."

"Money is the connection, Sandra. Let me give you some historical background then perhaps you will."

She listened with rapt attention.

Giltmore explained how the pre-Islamic tribes of Arabia undertook an annual pilgrimage (Hajj) to Mecca to worship some 360 tribal idols. It was a huge influx of people and considerable commerce was conducted during this period. When Prophet Mohammed proclaimed the worship of God alone, the pagan elites feared for their livelihoods. They assumed the pilgrims would stop visiting Mecca. "No idols, no pilgrims. No pilgrims, no commerce. Ergo, no commerce, no power. In a nutshell, monotheism would weaken the elites. And so the pagans tried to kill him," he said. "The irony is the Hajj is a twenty-plus billion dollar industry today."

"But how does Islam threaten today's financial elites?"

"Modern capitalism is a debt-based communist financial system," he pointed out to her.

"What!"

"Private property taxes, the progressive income tax and central banking are major planks of the *Communist Manifesto*," he counted on his fingers. "Planks that are anathema in Islam."

Sandra's jaw dropped.

"Debt is the new capital, and the hand that dispenses debt rules the world. Banks issue money created out of thin air which then must be paid back with interest." He took a sip of water and continued. "The religion of Submission forbids receiving or paying usury. In an Islamic financial system, the owners of capital have to assume the same risk as the borrower when drawing up a loan contract."

"I'm intrigued. How does this work?" she asked, cupping her chin in her hand.

"Do you have a mortgage, Sandra?"

"No."

"Aren't *you* lucky," he said. "If you *had* a mortgage, what would happen if you ceased making payments?"

"I'd lose my home."

"Not just your home. You'd also lose the principal you paid. The lender forecloses on your property *plus* the equity accrued. Heads they win, tails you lose. Is this fair?"

"I never thought of it that way. No, it's not fair at all," she said, slapping the table. "So how does Islam compete with our financial system?"

"In an Islamic financial system, banks are legally obliged to issue interest-free loans to qualified borrowers. When buying a home, the bank purchases the house and the lender makes at least a twenty-percent down payment then pays the bank a combination of rent for the house plus principal, on a sliding scale, until the principal is paid off, typically within fifteen years." He concluded with, "Once the mortgage is retired, the property deed is transferred to the borrower."

"I appreciate the fairness of this system, but what happens if you can't repay the entire mortgage?"

"You lose the house. But here's the catch. The bank keeps the rent you have paid for living in the house but it is legally bound to return to you the principal paid. Again, is this fair?"

"You're damn right it is. We should adopt such a system."

"An Islamic financial system would have prevented the financial collapse of 2008," he said. "The moneylenders wouldn't have sold homes to all those people who had no business buying them. As we now know, the speculative housing market imposed a financial risk too burdensome for the mortgage lenders' business model to bear and so it crashed. Islamic finance is structured to prevent speculation in financial markets," he finished.

"Then how come Dubai experienced a financial crisis every bit as severe?"

"There are no Islamic countries on this planet that implement *shari'ah*."

"Not even Saudi Arabia?"

He gagged. "Hereditary monarchy alone is an affront to the egalitarianism inherent in Islam. The only thrones monarchs are worthy of sitting on are made of shiny white porcelain."

Sandra convulsed into laughter. "Mike…you sure…have…a way with words," she said through her giggles.

"And I'm being generous."

"Stop it," she said between gasps, her hand across her chest. "Oh, God, I needed that."

"You won't read or hear anything I'm saying on network or cable television. Truth is too volatile for the masses to handle."

"I'm receiving a flashback of something I read on one of those independent news websites."

"You surprise me, Sandra."

"Confession time. In my meager spare time I like to indulge my curiosity for news that offers a point of view at odds with the lamestream media. Anyway, I read NATO bombed Libya to prevent Gaddafi from establishing a gold-based banking system in the African Union. Do you know anything about this?"

"You're on the right track. NATO attacked Libya because Gaddafi was going to demand payment in gold from the Europeans for Libyan oil, which would furnish the gold for his proposed monetary system. European heads of state wouldn't stand for such a transfer of wealth. Especially the British whose Exchequer sold half of Britain's gold reserves for a song at the turn of this century. Anyway, long story short, British and American Special Forces heisted 144 tonnes of gold bullion from the Libyan central bank during the NATO incursion. That was the real reason for the Libyan operation and not the justification purveyed by the White House's

Ministry of Truthiness and Propaganda. Gold has intrinsic value. Money isn't worth the paper it's printed on."

Sandra sat there with a stunned look on her face. "How deep does the rabbit hole go?"

"Deeper," he said with an artful grin. "Saddam Hussein was snuffed out because he planned to sell Iraqi oil in euros, not dollars, which would have crashed the American economy because it rests on the petro-dollar currency. His oil-for-euros plan was the only weapon of mass destruction in his arsenal as we later learned. Which is why the U.S. still has troops in Iraq and everywhere else in the Middle East for that matter. The Deep State can't allow the Arabs to sell *their* birthright, that is, their oil, for Euros instead of American pesos."

"Dare I say the word *conspiracy*?"

"It *is* a conspiracy, Sandra," he said. "Anyone who challenges the regime's official narrative is labelled a conspiracy nut or a traitor by White House stenographers who masquerade as independent journalists. It's a devious way of discrediting the message and the messenger to suppress the truth," he said.

"You know, you're right. It happened to that former CIA employee who fled to Russia and to that former U.S. army whistleblower who reassigned his gender," Sandra acknowledged. "It's obvious the Deep State and their media puppets don't welcome plebes who speak truth to Power. People should be concerned by the uniformity of lamestream media reporting, whether on the left or the right."

He signalled his agreement with a firm nod. "This is why governments have an Official Secrets Act on their books. It prevents their citizens from knowing what their governments are doing behind their backs. Which is why the penalty is so harsh when whistleblowers speak to the media about government misdeeds. There will always be deception in this world. Hopefully, there'll always be brave souls like those two individuals you mentioned who risked their personal freedom to expose the crimes committed by our government. If not, this country is doomed.

"You make it sound so gloomy."

"I can't help it, Sandra. Our capitalist system is in its death throes. It has reached the stage of criticality," he said. "The West blew its capitalist load in an orgy of debt-based financial speculation this past decade. Don't be surprised when the financial house of cards implodes. The interest-bearing debt banks are carrying on their books can never be repaid because the world economy is shrinking, not growing despite the lies of the U.S. regime's reporting agencies." He added, "Capitalism is a pernicious ideology for which every modern war has been waged, including the so-called War on Terror."

"You shouldn't say this in public, Mike. It's considered heresy."

"Capitalism is the true religion of the West, Sandra. Notice how the ruling class in this country is always warning us *our* sacred way of life is under attack. What the ruling class means by *our* way of life is actually *their* way of life. There is no *you* and *I* in *our*. The ruling class couldn't care less about *us*. *We*, the great unwashed, don't enter the consciousness of the ruling class except as debt slaves, cannon fodder and bagmen."

"You have a dark view of humanity, Mike."

"I depict the world the way it is. Not how people wish it to be. My beef is with the financial elite, the bloodsuckers who manipulate money to create more money producing nothing of value. Unless social misery is a value."

"You mentioned all modern wars have been waged to protect the capitalist system. Does this include the Cold War?"

"Marx was opposed to usury. I'd quote him but his tirades against usury are laced with anti-Semitism. Yesterday, it was an ideological war against communism. Today, it's a recharged ideological war against Islam. The war for the capitalist elite persists."

"It's doubtful communism will ever rear its ugly head again. It has been so discredited as a mode for organizing a society."

"At least the Marxist version. But not the religion of Submission. It's much more than a political and economic system. Islam is a way of life, both inner and outer. The West has been trying to discredit and destroy this religion for centuries. It will never succeed."

"Are you implying the war against terrorism is at root a war against Islam?"

"No, Sandra. I'm saying the War on Terror is an effing crusade against Islam and 9/11 was the inciting incident that reignited this crusade. Didn't a former president preach a crusade against terrorism?"

"It was a slip of the tongue."

He raised an eyebrow at her as if to say, "Puh-lease." He paused to decide whether to debate this point. His conclusion was no. "The U.S. launched a life-or-death struggle for the financial and banking interests of the Anglosphere. Once communism was defeated, the U.S. and its vassal states unleashed its propaganda apparatus and war machine on its age-old enemy, Islam. This will be a war to the death. But the West has lost the war. It has yet to accept defeat."

"You believe Islam is *winning*?

"Islam is the fastest growing religion in Europe and North America because the West is morally bankrupt. The West can only offer the world a nihilistic foreign policy and a debauched culture." He folded his hands. "Failed states are the harvest of the West. As Jesus cautioned, 'You shall know them by their fruits.' And what is on offer in the rotten fruit basket of the West? How about the funeral pyres of Somalia, Sudan, Afghanistan, Iraq, Libya, Syria, Palestine, Yemen and Ukraine," he said, answering his own question. "Burnt offerings to the folks whose support the ruling class needs to achieve world conquest."

"You have a point. I can't think of one major U.S. foreign policy success since the Korean War."

"Excluding the U.S. invasion of the superpower Caribbean island nation of Grenada, there isn't any."

"So this whole anti-Islamist military campaign is a sham?"

"Sandra, it's a propaganda war for control of our minds," he wanted to shout. "The first rule of war is to demonize the enemy and exaggerate its power. This is for homeland consumption. It galvanizes public support for war. It's the old media-manufactured *us versus them* paradigm."

"You're either with us or we bomb you," Sandra said in a withering tone.

"Do you remember a month before the start of the second Gulf War against Iraq when Homeland Security issued an alert for a potential terrorist attack involving chemical and biological weapons?"

"Yeah, fear was at its height. People were scrambling in the stores. It was worse than Black Friday."

"Did you dash out to the local hardware store in a panic to buy duct tape and plastic before they ran out?"

"My personal assistant did," she sheepishly admitted. She twirled a tendril of hair with her fingers.

"See what I mean? Iraq had no capability to project its military power beyond its borders let alone across an effing ocean. Yet Americans fell for this false alert like a bunch of suckers. They were cowed into line on a road paved with ignorance and irrational fear."

"Did you stock up?"

He backed away from the table. "I passed. I knew the puppet masters in the administration were terrorizing us with a bogus threat." Giltmore added, "We possess the most powerful military and intelligence-gathering system in the world and yet we run around like a bunch of Chicken Littles with our heads cut off whenever the puppeteers in Washington say, 'Boo!' It's so pathetic. We're not worthy of our Founding Fathers' legacy."

"I see now how the threat of terrorism shapes our fears and how our fears mold our perception of it. Comedians had a field day with this false terror alert at our expense."

"We need them to keep us honest."

"Notice how the folks in Washington don't announce potential terrorist threats anymore."

"When you cry wolf so often and the threat fails to materialize, people cease paying attention," he pointed out. "The puppet masters in Washington must have stumbled upon Lincoln's saw about fooling all the people only some of the time."

Looking down at her hands overlapped on the table, Sandra said, "We've gone from a country that pledged to put a chicken in every pot to a coop of chickens whose collective pot is cooked."

"This is because the U.S. military-industrial complex cannot exist in a peaceful vacuum. It needs enemies to justify its existence. Paradoxically, peace is its greatest enemy. So phantom threats need to be conjured to defend our huge military expenditures. Peace is bad for business."

"A connection is forming, Mike. A very disturbing one. Do you think this is why we invaded Afghanistan?"

"We invaded Afghanistan for the same reason we invaded Vietnam," he said in a melancholic voice. "To corner the opium market. Prior to the Taliban seizing power, Afghanistan was the primary exporter of opium in the world. It's the reason the former Soviet Union invaded this country way back in 1979. They fought a war to control the supply of opium and flood the West with heroin, a by-product of opium. When the Taliban threw out the Russians, it consolidated its power over most of Afghanistan. In July 2000, Taliban leader, Mullah Omar, issued a *fatwah* banning the cultivation of the poppy plant, which is used to produce opium. His troops dutifully eliminated the poppy crops in Taliban-controlled territory. It was a hugely successful anti-drug campaign. Then guess what happened?"

She flapped her hands. "You must tell me."

"The U.S. ran out of drug money to fund financial boondoggles like pet gerbils dot com. The money drought brought on the Dot-Com Crash of 2000-2001. Which was followed up with the conveniently timed 9/11 terrorist attack in September of 2001."

"I don't like where this is going," she said and not without a hint of uneasiness.

"Our military forces invaded Afghanistan in October of 2001 and deposed the Taliban in 2002. And now the poppy fields are in bloom once again in Afghanistan. Get this. The Vienna-based United Nations Office on Drugs and Crime reported the cultivation of poppies increased from 100,000 acres to over 400,000 between 2001 and 2013. And from 2016 to 2017, poppy cultivation increased another sixty-three percent to about 660,000 acres. Until 2017, opium production was at an all-time high and American stock markets were on a tear. But this upward trend came to a screeching halt in 2018 due to a reduction in U.S troops in Afghanistan. Opium production fell that year and so did U.S. markets." He asked, "Coincidence? Or cause and effect?"

"Our government is involved in drug smuggling?" she said. "I always questioned the strategic significance of Afghanistan. There's no oil there and it's a landlocked country, but I still find your contention hard to swallow, Mike."

"Why so sceptical?" he said. "The British Empire fought three wars in Afghanistan between 1839 and 1919 to install pro-British vassals to control opium production, all under the guise of containing Russian expansionism in Central Asia."

"What did they want with the opium?"

"To supply the opium market in China, a country against which the British fought two wars in the same century to force the Chinese government to accept the importation of this drug. The sale of opium through the British East India Company funded the maintenance of the British Empire. An empire is a capital-intensive enterprise, Sandra. Military garrisons cost money and taxes can't cover these costs. Our military's eight hundred foreign installations and our intelligence services' endless blackbox operations require an alternative means to finance them."

"I'm beginning to see a pattern forming here," she said warily. "History doesn't repeat itself but it sure stutters."

"The only difference is the British regime didn't need to stage a 9/11-style false flag attack to justify its invasions of Afghanistan and China."

"Seems like investors only need follow the fortunes of Afghanistan opium production to predict the direction of the stock market."

"Good advice. But here's the clincher, Sandra. What was happening in the U.S. in early 2009 following the collapse of the housing bubble?"

She reflected a moment. "Banks were in crisis and stock markets were crashing."

"And how did our government respond?"

She threw him a blank look.

"Our country was facing the gravest financial crisis in its history and the American regime ordered a surge of troops to Afghanistan in February 2009, didn't it?"

"You're right," she remembered. "You've piqued my curiosity now. Sending troops to the Afghan warzone is a peculiar method for addressing a grim financial crisis, at least by my reckoning."

"You're on the right track," he congratulated her. "U.S. banks were illiquid in early 2009 because they were under-capitalized due to military setbacks in the Afghan war theatre. The opium harvest had fallen off a cliff thanks to a resurgent Taliban, starving U.S. banks of much-needed drug money which was used to juice the housing market and boost the stock market. So the regime in Washington ordered a surge in Afghanistan to ramp up opium production and get the drug money flowing once again to U.S. banks and re-inflate the Dow Jones and NASDAQ."

Sandra was floored. "Jesus, Mike. Can the people in charge be so sick?"

"Problem is we assume our politicians and generals are like you and I. Fact is, they aren't. The people in charge of the American Empire are psychopaths. Humanitarians don't rule empires, psychopaths do." He glugged mouthfuls of water before continuing. "Not too long ago our president pardoned a soldier convicted of a war crime by a U.S. military tribunal."

Sandra wriggled in her chair.

"Is this the action of a righteous person?" Giltmore asked.

"Far from it."

"This is the kind of morally-impaired leadership helming our ship of state. Our politicians then wonder why our enemies hate us. What galling nerve," he said, his teeth bared. His blood was up now.

Patrons at other tables turned their gaze toward them. He was conscious of their eyes on him. Careful, Ol' Boy. Venting while Muslim is as dangerous as driving while black in this country. Have to watch how you speak. People might come down with a case of the jihadi jitters and call the authorities…You're being paranoid. Relax. You're sitting with Sandra Dowling, America's Queen of Talk…Yeah, but she's still a black woman and fame only gets a black person so far with the White Man in this country. He heard Sandra's voice penetrating his mental fog.

"—and those to whom evil is done do evil in return," she said. "Revenge is a powerful human impulse."

He dismissed his paranoia. "It doesn't have to be. In the Quran, God prescribes believers to follow up an evil action with a good one."

"Then how come Muslims commit murder in the name of Islam?"

"That's the paradox of the Quran, Sandra." He twerked his nose. "God guides toward the right path those who have good in their hearts and God misguides toward the wrong path those who have evil in their hearts. Just like the Bible does."

"Mike, you're a breath of fresh air," she announced. "I'll never view the world the same way again."

"Save your applause," he said with a smile. "I'm not done yet.

She gave him a look that said, "There's more?"

"The world-wide illegal drug trade is conservatively estimated at three trillion dollars per year. Three thousand billion smackers. A prize worth killing millions for."

"And blowing up office towers."

"You get it!" he said. "This drug money props up the Anglo-American banking system as I just alluded to. Wasn't the HSBC Bank fined almost two billion dollars for laundering drug money back in 2012? And wasn't a JP Morgan-owned ship impounded for smuggling one billion dollars' worth of cocaine in 2019?" Giltmore asked.

"Yeah, I remember these stories. No one went to jail though."

"Of course not, Sandra. The banksters are doing the dirty work of the Deep State. But if you and I were to profit from the drug trade, we'd be sent up the river."

""Something you said before doesn't make sense."

"Such as?"

"If American troops are protecting the opium production in Afghanistan, then why did the President reduce the number of troops there?"

"Because the President isn't privy to this black op. The Deep State didn't bring him onside because he's an outsider who has no political debts and therefore it can't own him. All former presidents had skeletons in their closets which the Deep State leveraged to compel them to do its bidding. The Deep State tried to deny the current president the last election by exposing the skeletons in his closest. When that gambit failed, the Deep State concocted Russiagate and now Ukrainegate to derail his presidency."

"So that's *why* the Pentagon and senior Republicans and Democrats are beside themselves over his troop-reduction plan in Afghanistan."

"They see their fortunes disappearing in a stock market rout.

"The world you're sketching is distressing. I feel like I'm stuck in that Edvard Munch painting."

"It's a manifestation of the disturbing times in which we live," he said. "The Deep State is a mafia, and the Pentagon protects the rackets run by it. Whenever a U.S. puppet balks at bending over, the regime in Washington reams it with 'democracy.' Have you ever read the *War is a Racket* speech delivered in 1933 to the United States Marine Corps by two-time recipient of the Medal of Honor, Major General Smedley Butler?

"I haven't but something tells me I should."

"I encourage you to read it. It's an eye-opener. The more things change...."

Doug returned with platters laden with bounty from the sea, setting them down before Giltmore and Sandra. They lapped their napkins and appraised the feast spread before them.

"I'm starved. This conversation has stimulated my appetite," she said.

"Me, too. *Bon appétit.*" He grabbed a complimentary bun from the wicker basket on their table, tore it open and smeared butter on it.

Between bites she reproached him. "You leveled a severe indictment against the folks in Washington, Mike."

He swallowed a morsel of salmon before answering. "If the truth sucks, then suck it up. The apparatchiks in Washington, with the overt help of the faceless state media cabal, has made Islam the stalking horse in the West to further its economic and political agenda. Behold the distorted perception of Muslims and Islam."

"I guess it's no accident."

"You guess," he shrilled. "Don't be an apologist for your profession, Sandra. People construct their perception of reality from the propaganda orchestrated by state media. Too many people swallow this manufactured misinformation in the belief the media talking heads tell the whole truth and nothing but the truth. Once it's on the TV, it's true. It has to be, doesn't it? State media wouldn't *lie* to us."

"Now hold on a second there, Mike. I hap—"

"State media in the West have conditioned people to adopt negative attitudes toward Islam and Muslims. It's Pavlovian. This is a propaganda model by design, not by accident."

"I was about to agree with you before you cut me off," she said tetchily, her eyes flashing. "We're on the same side."

"Oh. Sorry for misjudging you, Sandra," he said, wincing.

"Mike, learn to come to a simmer, not a boil," she gently scolded him.

He pursed his lips in contrition. "It's tough to be dispassionate in the face of Islamophobia and the human carnage perpetrated in its name. You're an exception to the rule. If you were to raise these issues on your show, you wouldn't be the host much longer. A quisling in the head office would fire you for being a *conspiracy theorist*."

"This would be the proof proving the lie."

"If you mean the lie about the crusade raging against Islam isn't a crusade against Islam, then yes."

"What you're telling me should be broadcast from every street corner in America."

"I have an idea," he said, sitting back and laying down his fork and knife. "Why don't you have me back on your show to do a segment on the synthetic terrorist threat the Deep State is propagating to maintain our sense of paranoia and contaminate our minds about Islam and Muslims."

"An appealing proposal, Mike. However, I wouldn't be able to sell such a radioactive show to my producer. There'd be howls of self-righteous indignation from our corporate sponsors."

"Tell them you're planning a show about the history of the U.S. regime terrorizing us with our own ignorance and using fear to control us. Then we'll hit them between the eyes."

"What history of fear?"

"Do they not teach anything relevant in journalism schools?"

"Apparently not. Time to ask my alma mater for a refund."

Her comment elicited a chuckle from Giltmore. "Ever since the U.S became an empire following the Spanish-American War, the Deep State has conjured up a threat *de jour* to advance its foreign policy agenda. The Red Scare of the 1920s. The Yellow Peril in the 1940s. McCarthyism in the 1950s. The Domino Theory of the 1960s and 70s. The renewed Cold War of the 1980s and 90s and now the current War on Terror and Russiagate. The history of the U.S. is one dreary continuum of combating manufactured enemies to create the impression our country is under constant siege in order to stimulate mass anxiety." He raised his hands. "Behold! I present to you Islamic terrorism. A never-ending terrorism to fill the void left by the expiration of the Soviet Union." He tabled his hands. "It's just one effing existential crisis after another. This constant war footing limits, if not quells, popular dissent against American militarism. This theme can be fodder for an exposé on your show.

"You're asking a lot of me, Mike."

"Someone has to take the bull of propaganda by its horns and wrestle it to the ground. Why not you, Sandra?" he urged. "You'd be doing the American people a huge favor."

"This could cost me my career, Mike. You're asking me to roll some pretty big dice."

"I'm not asking you to put your career on the line for my sake. I don't exploit my relationships for personal gain."

"I'm relieved to know this." She filed the information away in a folder marked *Keeper*.

"All I'm asking is for you to bear in mind the interests of the American people. Consider the hundreds of billions of dollars wasted on this artificial War on Terror that could be used to fund a true public healthcare system and real education programs for our children. We have to eradicate this frontier mentality that keeps us on edge. This mentality that says, 'Be afraid. The savages are lurking just beyond those hills yonder, waiting to kill you.' I'm convinced your viewers will trust you before they believe the presstitutes anchoring lamestream news desks across the land. Do the research, Sandra, and draw your own conclusions," he recommended. "Investigate my proposal while I'm in Istanbul."

"Sounds like a plan to me. Any other simple requests?" she teased.

"Not at the moment. But give me a few minutes and I'm sure I'll come up with one," he said with a wink.

"Do you think we can debunk the dominant narrative of this propaganda war?" She looked at him with a hopeful expression. "I don't want to follow in Sisyphus' footsteps."

Speaking in a confident tone, he said, "I demystified and deconstructed Christianity, didn't I?"

"You sure did."

"I sense a hunger, a craving, in this country for authenticity," Giltmore said, swallowing a forkful of sautéed rice. "At least from those not wedded to the Republican-Democratic two-party paradigm. We suspect but cannot prove our mealy-mouthed political leaders are charlatans and swindlers. I'll demonstrate our suspicions are not unfounded but are in fact warranted. If I lay out the facts on your show as I have done here, the Islamophobes in Washington will be scurrying for cover like cockroaches caught in a bright spotlight."

"I need more convincing."

"The name of the game is perception management, Sandra. An ugly ideology left unchallenged will flourish until it becomes part of mainstream thought. I believe inflammatory propaganda can be extinguished with a deluge of cold, hard facts. Never underestimate the power of truth. It's a potent weapon in the proper hands. The *Pentagon Papers* helped bring an end to the Vietnam War, didn't they?" He laid down his utensils again and steepled his hands. "Too many of us have become sheeple since 9/11. We need to be jolted out of our complacency with the truth. With your show, you can reassure the American people dissent is the highest form of patriotism they can engage in."

"Sheeple? What do you mean by this remark?"

"It means we're a bunch of sheep. The Patriot Act ushered in a state-sponsored campaign of fear and paranoia, casting a pall over political dissent in this country. The Pledge of Allegiance should be recited as follows: Truth is rebellion. Dissent is treason. Obedience is loyalty. Look what happened to that ex-CIA whistleblower," Giltmore said. "He's been labelled a traitor for uncovering our regime's illegal surveillance activities. Congressmen called for him to be hanged. People should be protesting in the streets on his behalf. Instead, they're amusing themselves to death in front of the idiot-box and on social media."

"Madison said, 'No nation could preserve its freedom in the midst of continual warfare.'"

"A wise man with a good head on his shoulders."

"There's a few congress-cretins whose ignoble heads need a good swat," Sandra said, her eyes smoldering.

"I'll supply the gauntlet," he offered with a wicked grin. "These same Congressmen cried salty tears over the deaths of the *Charlie Hebdo* murders. Effing hypocrites."

"They should save their tears. Save them to wipe their self-satisfied smirks from their faces. They only harp about free speech when it suits their agenda."

"The concept of patriotism has been distorted in this country," Giltmore went on. "The Deep State has constructed a grotesque monument to servility upon the ruins of patriotism. Those two aforementioned Americans are the epitomy of patriotism," he said. "Do you know of anyone who was prosecuted for illegally spying on us? And yet our hypocritical politicians want to incarcerate the ex-CIA whistleblower. How effing Kafkaesque."

"You want hypocrisy? The *Washington Post* opposed a presidential pardon for him and yet this same newspaper received a Pulitzer Prize for its NSA leaks journalism based on official papers released by him."

"It's *so* ironic he had to seek refuge in Russia. Once upon a time dissidents were fleeing that country for the West. And it's a gross miscarriage of justice that the re-gendered U.S army whistleblower spent time as a political prisoner in the American gulag." He continued, "Lady Justice wears a blindfold not because she's impartial, but to hide the shame in her eyes for the repeated defilement of her honor by serial rapists in the White House and Congress."

Sandra grinned at his wit. "So long as our politicians had the Soviet Union's human rights violations to carp about, we could ignore the war crimes committed by our own government," she pointed out. "Since the collapse of the Soviet Union, many people inside and outside this country judge the U.S. to be the greatest threat to peace and liberty on this planet. These people are called dissidents—even terrorists— but never patriots. And they're given no airtime in the lamestream media." She took an angry bite of her meal.

"Nero might have fiddled while Rome burned but future historians will note we sexted and tweeted while the Torch of Liberty sputtered and died."

Sandra swallowed. "When Ben Franklin was asked what kind of country the Constitutional Convention conceived, he replied, 'A republic, if you can keep it.' That experiment in government has failed. We now live in an oppressive national security state," she griped. "The republic is dead."

"And in marches fascism swathed in the flag, clutching a bible in one hand, a gun in the other, goose-stepping over the corpse of the republic in glossy black jackboots."

"It's all so bleak."

"How's your seafood?" Giltmore asked.

"Delicious…No pun intended…How's your salmon?"

"Delicious," he echoed, dabbing his mouth with his napkin.

They both chuckled.

Materializing out of nowhere, Doug asked, "How's the food?" as he topped up their water goblets.

Sandra and Mike exchanged looks with one another then said in unison, "Delicious!" They burst out laughing.

"Someone's having a good time this evening," Doug mumbled under his breath as he retreated to the kitchen. "What's Sandra Dowling doing eating with *him* of all people? Must be business," he rationalized.

Giltmore stole a glance at Sandra while she cut another piece of scallop. He watched her eat, the way her jaw moved when she chewed, the way her hands manipulated her utensils, the way the muscles in her arms rippled with exertion. He drank in deeply the sight of her. She was a vision of beauty.

She glanced up. "*What?*" she said, her self-consciousness apparent.

"*Nothing*…So where were we?" Giltmore asked. Almost got busted, Ol' Boy.

"We were discussing patriotism."

"Right."

"I now know why that MIT professor of linguistics has been pushed to the margins by mainstream academia and media despite his being America's greatest public intellectual," Sandra said.

"He's one of my heroes. I'm indebted to his scholarship, especially his seminal work *Manufacturing Consent*. He's a true patriot."

"I studied him in journalism school…You miss teaching don't you, Mike?"

"What makes you say that?"

"Because conversing with you reminds me of my time in university."

"Sorry. I spent a lifetime in academia so I'm used to talking at people. And I'm sure I sound didactic at times, but I'm trying to quit."

She flapped her hand. “No need to apologize, Mike. I’m an earnest student. How if we change the subject? My head hurts.”

“I guess we’ve travelled far enough down the rabbit hole for now.” A sudden realization hit him. “Here I am prattling about geopolitics but we’ve barely talked about you.

“There’ll be time for that in the future.”

She said, future. As in tomorrow. Or next week. I’m feeling optimistic. Why not next year? Sandra’s voice brought him back to the present.

“…dreamy look in your eyes.”

He laid down his fork and knife. “Whew. I’m stuffed. How about you?”

“I’d lick the plate, but we’re in public.”

“You’re full of spunk, Sandra. I mean that in a good way.”

“I’m just getting revved up,” she said with a look of mischief.

“Want some dessert?”

She patted her stomach. “I’m in the mood for coffee and pie but let’s wait until our dinner has settled.”

They conversed about friends and family and of many things, building trust and intimacy one story at a time. And they ordered dessert.

“Any regrets?” Sandra asked.

“About what?”

“Life in general.”

“Just one.”

“Are you going to share it?” She winkled it out of him with her eyes.

He studied the water in his glass. Then he spoke quietly and his lower lip quivered. “When I accepted Prophet Mohammed, peace be upon him, as my prophet and Submission as my religion, God cleansed the black stain of sin from my heart. I was reborn pure, like a newborn baby, but I still have this one pain in my soul.”

“Mike, if God forgave your sins, then you need to forgive yourself too.”

Giltmore traced the pattern woven into the linen tablecloth with his finger. He felt his eyes mist with emotion. “Teresa…She was an orphan," he began. "Her parents died when she was a child. We were engaged. Both in our late twenties. It seems like yesterday. How swiftly time flies." He paused in retrospect and his eyes glistened with the memory of it. "I accepted a professorship at Thomas More. She was supposed to follow, but I let her slip away because I was a hot-shot professor. I thought I could do better than her." He sighed in regret. "That never came to pass."

"My father used to say, 'It's not our losses in life we mourn most but rather the moments in our lives when we failed to give that full measure of commitment to our better selves.'"

"Your father's wise…I pray for a second chance all the time."

"Maybe your prayer has been answered."

"How so?"

"Both my parents are dead. Doesn't this qualify me as an orphan?" her eyes questioned.

"May God's mercy and forgiveness be upon their souls." Her vulnerability swept him away. "So what about you, Sandra? Any regrets?"

"Like you, just one."

He sensed her pain. "I'm listening."

She played with the remains of her half-eaten key lime pie with her fork, then took a deep lungful of air. Her eyes watered. "I…I've been alone most of life because I don't think a man could still love me when this is gone," she bemoaned, swiping her hand down her curvaceous figure.

"No need for concern there, Sandra. I'll probably be dead before that happens," he blurted out in sympathy.

She produced a quick laugh.

He realized his slip of the tongue and his cheeks blushed the color of her dress.

"You say the sweetest things, Mike."

He was at a loss for words.

"You look surprised," she said.

"No one's ever uttered such a testimonial before."

They conversed on about matters both amusing and noteworthy until it was time to leave.

"I'll walk you to your car, Sandra. Too many sharks in the water tonight."

"Thank you, I'd like that." She paid the bill and Giltmore escorted her out of the restaurant.

Sitting at a table nearby, a Homeland Security agent wearing a dark suit withdrew from his table a parabolic listening device, which resembled a common smartphone, and slipped it into the breast pocket of his jacket. He did the same with the wireless earbud as he watched Giltmore guide Sandra toward the exit. He knows too much, the agent worried. Far too much. He can't go public with it. He might become a lightning rod for reform. Or its extreme:

Revolution!

This won't have a happy ending, the agent thought.

They came abreast of her car in the cool evening air. Vehicles zipped by on the busy avenue. "I really enjoyed myself, Sandra. I'm so glad I squeezed you onto my social calendar." He gave her a wink.

"Oh, you're so generous, Mike. It was such a privilege," she replied in jest.

"*Au contraire*. The privilege was all mine."

"Are you speaking French?"

"*Un petit peu*. A little bit."

"French sounds *so* romantic."

He sighed. Looks like French lessons are in my future. The things one does for love. He held her car door for her. "How if we get together again after I return from Istanbul?"

"Sounds like a great idea."

"I'll call you when I return. *Au revoir*, Sandra."

"Take care, Mike."

He shut the door and waved goodbye from the sidewalk as her car pulled away from the curb and merged with the traffic, the tantalizing scent of her still lingering in his nostrils, a fleeting but fragrant reminder of an enchanted evening.

They went their separate ways that night and they both remarked on how effortlessly they had slid into each other's thoughts and lives.

## Chapter Twenty-Two
## Istanbul

Bowled over with amazement, Father Marco and Aysel stopped reading. They stood side-by-side, not saying a word, their solemn silence communicating the enormity of their encounter with the Divine. They didn't need to look at each other to know what the other was thinking.

Father Marco, ready to burst, spoke first, holding his end of the scroll in a death grip. "Holy Christ. This is too much for me!" he exploded, rubbing his other hand back and forth across his scalp. He felt overwhelmed yet exhilarated, used up yet energized.

"The original Gospel. It exists. This is so dream-like. So—surreal!" Aysel said as she rewound the parchment onto its wooden spine with delicate fingers.

"This writing changes everything," he said, releasing his end of the scroll into Aysel's possession, his hair mussed from running his hand through it.

"Jesus wasn't crucified." Her eyes went wide. "Think what this means for the world."

"Me and a lot of other people will have to find a new vocation—*if* the scroll is authentic."

"You mean a real job?" she said. "An institution that protected pedophiles until very recently precludes receiving any sympathy from me. Good riddance to it."

So much for our spirit of *entente*. "We are not enemies, but friends. We must not be enemies. Though passion may have strained, it must not break our bonds of affection."

"Father, that's so lyrical," she said.

It's not lyrical. It's Lincoln. But what she doesn't know won't hurt her. "There's lots more where that came from," he said, trying to further impress her.

"Maybe you can find a new vocation as a writer."

How about as your husband? "Let's not jump too far ahead of ourselves, my dear," he cautioned her. "We need to authenticate this scroll before there's any further talk about changing jobs."

"You're right," she said, patting it. "Did you know Jesus had a scribe?"

"In the Gospel of Matthew, Jesus mentions scribes becoming disciples of the kingdom of Heaven. Now whether these scribes documented his revelation is open to speculation."

"We know that one of them did. From the hands of the Messiah's scribe to our hands. Who could fathom such a random possibility?" Wonder lit up her face. "Do you want to continue reading the scroll?"

"Let's wait until you have validated it. Any objections?"

"I don't doubt its genuineness, but are you done reading it?"

"I've read quite enough to digest for one evening," he said wearily, and he subsided to the ground and leaned his back against the uneven wall of the tomb, his mind tangled up like a ball of wool. He reached for a water bottle and drank deeply. It was easy for him to imagine the scribe filling the scroll with the words of holy revelation by the light of a candle—did they have candles back then?—not knowing the impact these words would have on the future of humanity. His eyes glazed over at the wonder of it all.

A sudden hunch struck Aysel. "Father. Please bear with me for a sec. When did the beloved disciple meet with Jesus?"

He adored the way her face screwed up when she was on the verge of forming an insight. He paused a moment to gather his wits. "The Gospel of John states he met with Jesus after the cleansing of the Temple, which happened at the start of his ministry."

"Darn. Scratch that idea," and her shoulders slumped.

"You're holding out on me. Let me help."

"I surmised that if the first meeting between Jesus and the beloved disciple was close to the Crucifixion, then perhaps Jesus conferred the title upon him and delivered the scroll to him at this meeting."

"Their first meeting occurred too soon in Jesus' ministry for your theory to be plausible. Jesus' full revelation wouldn't have been transcribed," he said.

"You're sure there was no other meeting between Jesus and the beloved disciple after their preliminary meeting in Jerusalem?"

"It's not documented in the Bible."

"The beloved disciple was a member of the Sanhedrin, right?"

"Says so in the Bible."

"So he would've known about Jesus' upcoming trial."

"He petitioned for Jesus to be tried in court. Where are you going with this line of enquiry, my dear?"

"Please indulge my passion for deductive reasoning, Father. It's intrinsic to archeology."

"As you wish."

"When did the Sanhedrin pass sentence upon Jesus?"

"Sunday evening. Five days before Jesus' crucifixion, which occurred on Good Friday." He put the water bottle to his lips again and took a long draught.

"When was Jesus arrested?"

He swallowed before answering. "Roman soldiers apprehended him in the Garden of Gethsemane after midnight on Tuesday. Or early Wednesday morning to be more precise."

"Where did Jesus stay Sunday evening?"

"I must think..." He burped and excused himself. "Jesus roomed Sunday night and possibly Monday night in Bethany at Simon the Leper's house. He was a disciple of Jesus."

"Could Jesus have secretly met with the beloved disciple in Bethany late in the evening on Sunday?"

"Uh, it's possible, my dear, but whatever for?"

"To convey the scroll to his beloved disciple."

"What makes you say Jesus passed the scroll to him?"

"I'm assuming."

"Jesus was a wanted man. I can't picture him sneaking around Bethany in the dead of night, playing a game of cloak and dagger with the Sanhedrin."

"Then who?"

"Why not the scribe? He authored the scroll. And he was unknown."

"Seems conceivable. When did Jesus announce the date of his crucifixion?"

"At the end of his Sermon on the Mount of Olives, Jesus told his disciples the Passover was coming in two days at which time he would be handed over to the authorities to be crucified."

"When did Jesus give that sermon?"

"Sunday afternoon into the early evening."

"So the scribe had one day, between Sunday evening and Monday evening to hand over the scroll to the beloved disciple."

"Why do you think the scribe would wait until the sandglass was empty to present the scroll to him?"

"To ensure the entire revelation was recorded for posterity."

"You're forgetting the covenant of the Last Supper."

"The blood covenant is false," Aysel said. "The scribe wrote Jesus was not crucified. Ergo, no Crucifixion, no Eucharist."

"Provided the scroll is authentic."

"The odds of this scroll being a fake are incalculable."

"Woman's intuition again?"

"Uh-uh. Occam's razor. When deciding among several possibilities, the simplest explanation is typically the right one. In eleven concise words, the scroll issued a repudiation of Christianity and its jumbled mysteries."

"Only eleven?"

"I bear witness the M'sheekha was not crucified, dead and buried."

He conceded her point with silence and his mute testimony confirmed the rightness of her argument.

"I never believed in the Crucifixion, anyway. It smacked of injustice," she said, jamming her fists on her hips. "Where's the justice in crucifying an innocent man so your sins—my sins—can be forgiven? This dogma diminishes the majesty and might of God, who possesses the power to forgive our sins without human sacrifice. Besides, the Crucifixion released Christians from observing the moral law and if it didn't, then what was its purpose?"

Aysel's habit of coming to the point, feelings be damned, endeared her to him. "You're not the only person who holds these opinions, my dear," he acknowledged. "Too often in my pastoral work I struggled to explain the doctrine of vicarious atonement for my parishioners who raised those same issues. I remain uncertain if my explanations dispelled their concerns." Or added to their confusion.

"Christianity has had a long shelf life, Father, but its best before date expired ages ago."

"I hope this scroll is authentic for it will resolve my own reservations which have been festering these past weeks."

"A doubting priest?"

He didn't want to answer her. Her question only forced him to examine his own beliefs. "No offense, my dear, but it's between me and the Almighty."

Aysel paced again then stopped to deliberate a moment. "Let's backtrack a minute. The beloved disciple wouldn't have been present at the Last Supper in Jerusalem, would he?"

"He couldn't be seen in public with members of the Way." He balanced his wrists on his knees, holding the water bottle.

"And he couldn't be seen at Simon's house, either. So the scribe had to have left Simon's house either Sunday night or Monday night to meet with the beloved disciple somewhere in Bethany."

"Why in Bethany, my dear?"

"Time was short and Jerusalem was far away. And the gates of Jerusalem were locked at sunset. People were allowed to leave, but not enter."

"I wonder how the scribe communicated with him," he pondered. "They couldn't meet in public. Too dangerous."

"Perhaps they had a go-between. Someone to pass messages back and forth."

"It's hard to imagine the scribe involved in such a clandestine scheme."

"Don't forget, Father, he was Jesus' scribe so he was under God's protection, I'm sure."

He heaved a wistful sigh. "Oh, to have been present when the scribe passed the scroll to the beloved disciple. How they interacted. What was said? What final words of wisdom and truth were imparted?"

"We'll never know. Another mystery known only to God."

"Or until another artifact is found."

"I'm still curious how the beloved disciple ended up here in Istanbul."

"Maybe he fled Jerusalem when the Jews revolted against the Roman Empire," he ventured.

"A conceivable theory."

That's one mystery we won't be able to solve, my dear."

"It's not important. But there remains a mystery that still is."

"Which is…"

"Who is the final prophet named *The Praised One*?"

"Your guess is as good as mine, Aysel."

"Guessing won't get us very far." She glanced at the roll of parchment. "So what do you want to do with the scroll?"

"Can you use the AMS dating process without damaging it?"

"I must cut out one small blank section. A square inch will be enough."

"Why is it necessary to damage the scroll?"

"A section must be combusted to measure the amount of carbon-14 in it."

"I see."

She must have read his expression for she said, "No need to be concerned, Father. I'll remove a piece of the scroll from the end. Will be hardly noticeable."

"Be extra careful."

"And I can sample the ink from different places on the scroll without damaging it."

"You have my blessing, my dear."

"You won't regret it."

"The scribe dated the scroll using the Jewish calendar. Shouldn't be too difficult to determine the corresponding date in the Gregorian calendar using Google."

"That aside, the AMS dating process isn't precise."

"With computer technology, you would think it'd be kindergarten easy."

Aysel gave him a benevolent smile. “The process is accurate to within a plus-or-minus margin of about eighty years at worst and plus-or-minus forty years at best.”

“That’s quite a wide margin of error. Why such a disparity?

“It’s related to the amount of a radioactive isotope, carbon-14, in an organism. Organic material contains carbon-14 atoms which, due to their inherent instability, decay into nitrogen at a constant rate when an organism dies. Dating this isotope is problematic because, although the rate of decay, or half-life, of carbon-14 atoms is constant, approximately 5730 years, the amount of carbon-12 atoms in the atmosphere against which carbon-14 is measured has not been constant throughout history. We have to correct for this uneven constant using a calibration curve. The pro—”

Father Marco held up a forestalling hand. “You lost me at radioactive isotope. Do the best you can.”

Unfazed. “Okay. I’ll collect the bone sample. We must be sure what we found is authentic.”

“Take what you need to perform your assay of the scroll, my dear.” As an afterthought, he asked, “How will you transport the scroll and the bone sample?”

“Plastic freezer bags” she replied. “I always carry them in my toolkit.” Father Marco helped Aysel insert the scroll and femur bone into separate extra-large plastic bags. She sealed them tight. “This should do it.”

“Help me re-cover our brother, Aysel.” Together they drew the folds of the shroud over the skeletal remains. “May God bless you with a peaceful repose,” he said. “You’ve earned it.”

“I second that.” She glanced around. “I guess this wraps things up. No pun intended.”

“We’d better get this ladder back to Dimitri. He’s probably wondering why I’ve needed it all this time just to restock shelves.”

“Dimitri doesn’t strike me as the suspicious type,” she said in defense of his caretaker. “How if I climb the ladder and wait for you up top.”

“Good idea.”

She mounted the ladder, carrying the plastic bags, which she deposited on the floor away from the edge of the hole before climbing out of it. He followed her up, carrying the lantern. She stood topside, waiting for him. He set the lantern on the floor near the plastic bags then climbed out. "Can you help me pull the ladder out of the tomb?"

Hearing no reply, he glanced at her. Aysel stood immobilized, staring past him, her face pale with fear, her mouth labouring silently. "What's the matter? You look like you've seen a ghost."

"Not a ghost, but a man," a deep voice spoke.

Father Marco whirled in surprise. "Dimitri?" He noticed a gun in Dimitri's steady hand and felt his heart lurch. "I don't understand," he said, and his head spun in bewilderment.

"This tomb was first discovered at the end of the tenth century when an earthquake struck Constantinople during the construction of this church," he began. "When the earthquake occurred last month, I considered it a good omen. I wasn't wrong," and Father Marco thought: So that's why he smiled when I told him an earthquake had hit us. Dimitri continued his narrative. "For centuries, the legend of this tomb has been passed down through generations of my family. I will tell you a story now."

Marco and Aysel weren't in any position to argue, so they indulged him.

"It all began the day the earth shook here on October 25, 989. And an auspicious day it was."

*In a generous act of piety, His Imperial Highness, Basil II, the "Slayer of the Bulgars" and the Emperor of the Byzantine Empire, having won a three-year battle against his restive nobles in Asia minor, commissioned the construction of a new house of worship near the Hagia Sophia, the largest church in Christendom. But the emperor's church would be much more modest in design; necessarily so, because the treasury had been depleted by decades of warfare fighting enemies on the borders of the empire.*

*Within sight of this hallowed architectural wonder of the medieval world, common laborers and expert craftsmen milled around in small clusters in the contracting morning shadows of sparse trees on an empty plot of land, waiting for their foreman to show. There was a spirit of excitement in the warming air. For the new church would be raised on the very spot where the men were killing time. It meant years of paid labor as well as an opportunity for the remission of sins—so they believed—if the Lord accepted their toil performed in His behalf.*

*A tall, dark-bearded man with a weather-beaten face approached the clusters of men, accompanied by a wizened priest.*

*"Everyone gather round," the Greek-speaking foreman ordered. "Before we stick a spade in the ground, Father Comenisus will bless our work and this sacred spot." He turned to the white-bearded priest and said, "Father, if you please."*

*The priest began the rite of consecrating the ground with holy water. Some men yawned while others toed the dirt, actions at odd with their eagerness to commence building the church to earn their place in Heaven. If he noticed their indifference, his features revealed no telltale sign of it. He concluded his ceremonial act and the troop of men uttered a perfunctory chorus of "Amen."*

*The foreman extended his gratitude to the priest. They watched him leave. Then, pointing to colored stakes poking out of the ground to delineate the footprint of the future walls of the church, the foreman said to the laborers: "You men need to dig a trench three feet wide and ten feet deep. Questions anyone?" He waited. "Get to work then," he ordered in a stern voice.*

*The hours passed quickly by. Though it was late October, the sun, now high in its arc, beat down upon the sweat-soaked workers without mercy. The water bearers were kept busy slaking the thirst of the perspiring laborers who, due to social decorum, were prevented from working shirtless.*

*"I wish there was an easier way to earn my eternal home in Heaven," a worker named Theodosius grumbled to his wiry companion, wiping the perspiration from his forehead with the back of his meaty hand, leaving behind smudges of dirt.*

*"What else would a man with the smarts of a bag of rusty hammers do?" Marcion said, smirking, working the earth with his*

*spade, the matted hair of his sinewy forearms thicker than the hair on his scalp.*

*"In a word I could pulverize you with one of those hammers, you dog's breath you."*

*"That is more than one word."*

*"Like a bag of hammers, I cannot count."*

*"Aye, you could strike me but you would then be just one of many amusements for the wild beasts in the coliseum."*

*Although Theodosius was a head taller and a hand span wider, Marcion wasn't intimidated by him.*

*Like most citizens of Byzantium, Theodosius had witnessed many a spectacle of criminals and barbarians torn apart by lions and tigers in the great public arena.*

*Theodosius leaned on his shovel. "Perhaps you are right," he replied and resumed digging. Unexpectedly, his shovel rang out against the ground, hitting what seemed to be solid rock. "Damn. Can't be." He had only dug down three feet.*

*"What is it?"*

*"Not sure. Might be bedrock." He shook his head in dismay. "But we shall see about that."*

*Theodosius grabbed a large chisel and motioned to Marcion. He handed the tool to him. "Hold it tightly against the rock." Marcion held the chisel with both hands in a vise-like grip. Theodosius took hold of a large sledge hammer and pounded the chisel over and over. The rock eventually split. "Hah! I knew it was not bedrock."*

*Theodosius ditched the sledge hammer and seized a solid iron pry bar thick as his wrist and long as he was tall. He worried it into the crack as far as it would allow.*

*"Help me, Marcion."*

*They put their backs into it. Their muscles bulged and veins writhed like purple snakes beneath their skin and their contorted bloodshot faces were fit to explode with the effort. The rock gave way unexpectedly, the pair of them staggered backward and fell in a tangled heap in the confines of the narrow trench.*

*"Get off me you flea of a dog," Theodosius barked.*

*"Gladly. You reek of a low-life latrine."*

*They stood up and brushed themselves off.*

*"Would you look at that," Theodosius said.*

*"Let me see," Marcion said, pushing his companion aside. "Oh."*

*They both gaped at the black hole before them.*

*Theodosius spoke first. "We need to tell the foreman of this setback."*

*"That would be best. A genius I am not but the ground in this spot may not be as rock-solid as needed to support the walls of the church."*

*Theodosius went to fetch the boss.*

*"Where is the hole?" the foreman asked.*

*The other men working in this section of the trench stilled their shovels and picks, probably wondering why the foreman was inspecting the trench so early in its excavation.*

*Theodosius pointed to it.*

*The foreman jumped into the trench to take a peek. "What in God's blazes is this?" He scratched his beard, then said, "We need a torch, a coil of rope and a length of cord." He faced Theodosius. "Go to the tool keeper and fetch these items for us." To the idling men he roared, "Why are you standing around like a bunch of washer women? Return to work and put your backs into it."*

*The men bent to their toil with alacrity.*

*Theodosius handed the torch to his foreman who threw it into the pit; it hit bottom in the blink of an eye. The foreman kneeled and peered into the glowing cavity. Then he rose in a flash and hurriedly crossed himself, from right to left.*

*"What is it?" Theodosius said.*

*"There is a stone ossuary in there. I do not like this one bit. It is an evil omen. We have disturbed the grave of someone of social prominence."*

*"How do you know?" Theodosius asked.*

*"You offspring of a donkey. Who but a person of status is laid to rest in a full-length ossuary inside a tomb?"*

*He pulled a face at the boss.*

*"This is a calamity," the foreman muttered to himself. "A day's work lost."*

*"Perhaps not," Marcion offered. "This area needs to be excavated for the future church's archive. Today's digging can be considered a head start on that project."*

*"Yes, but the entire perimeter needs to be shifted now," the foreman replied.*

*"But how far and in which direction?" Theodosius asked.*

*The foreman swung his eyes to them.*

*"Theodosius and Marcion, descend into the tomb and take some measurements."*

*They glanced at one another then back at the foreman.*

*"I have no desire to enter a tomb," Theodosius said in a firm voice.*

*"If you do not, you shall have to find work elsewhere." The foreman added with a devilish grin, "The army always needs fresh meat to fight the infidel Turks in the east."*

*They weighed their choices.*

*"Tis better than a kick in the arse with a pointy boot," Marcion decided.*

*One at the time, Marcion and Theodosius shimmied down the rope, and the ossuary lay silent in the torchlight, its eerie presence unnerving the intruders. They each crossed themselves in the superstitious belief doing so would offer them Divine protection.*

*Theodosius gained his bearings from the foreman who instructed him in which direction to face in the tomb.*

*"Marcion, take hold of this cord and pull it until it touches the wall opposite me."*

*Cord threaded out of Theodosius' hand until Marcion touched the end of the cord to the far wall. Theodosius tied a tight loop knot on his end of the cord to mark the distance between himself and the wall. He was re-coiling the cord when the ground began shaking—violently. Above ground and below, everyone fought to keep their balance. The rattling of the earth went on for what seemed like an eternity then became still, as though nothing had occurred.*

*Theodosius and Marcion fought for self-control in the tomb. A contorted face poked into the hole above them. It was the foreman's. "Are you all right?" he called down to them.*

*"Hold fast the rope," Theodosius shrieked. "We are leaving this forsaken tomb." He glanced one last time at the ossuary; its lid had fallen to the ground and broken in two. "Please forgive us," he prayed to the corpse.*

*They scrambled up the rope faster than rats fleeing a burning ship.*

*"Lord save us," a worker near them wailed, pointing toward the Hagia Sophia Church.*

*They turned to look where he was pointing and their eyes went wide with horror. An arch of the patina-stained copper dome of the church had collapsed. Other workers in the trench took up the cry.*

*"This is an evil omen, indeed," the foreman said in a low voice. "We have disturbed the grave of a holy person."*

*"May the Lord forgive us," Theodosius said, still catching his breath.*

*"He was nobody important. There is no shrine marking his grave," Marcion said, a little winded.*

*"Get the stonemasons to cover up this hole. And say no more about it or you will both be dismissed," the foreman ordered. "I will speak to the architect about this, ah, setback."*

*"You have my word," Theodosius said.*

*"Gladly," Marcion said.*

"Fortunately for us," Dimitri said, "oaths made under duress are rarely honored despite the best of intentions. The oaths of Marcion and Theodosius were no exception. From loose lips and imaginative minds, a legend was born."

Dimitri's eyes held a glazed look. "Little did my ancestors know," he said. He gazed with covetousness at the scroll on the floor. Then his features became menacing. "The legend will remain a part of history. And so will both of you."

A sudden memory struck Marco. "It was *you* who was spying on me the night I entered the tomb."

Dimitri answered with a vulpine smile.

"So I wasn't imagining things."

"I could've ended this affair that night but I didn't know who you had discovered. I'm glad I waited. And now it is time to finish what I started."

"W-What do you plan to do?" Father Marco asked. He could scarcely breathe for fear clutched at his heart.

"This scroll is worth a mint on the black market."

"You want to sell a document that belongs to posterity for a few pieces of silver?"

"Enough! Pull the ladder out of the hole and drag it over there," he motioned with the pistol.

They complied without protest.

"Marco," he ordered, "put the key to this room on the floor where you're standing. Then both of you back into the tomb. And don't make any sudden moves. I'm a good shot with this," and he wiggled the gun at them.

He plans to kill us. Father Marco's face burned and conflicting emotions warred within him. He spied the bone lying on the floor between himself and Dimitri and his brain clicked into gear. It's worth a shot. He placed the key as requested then, as he walked toward the hole, he flicked the bone with his right foot, flinging it at Dimitri's chest, who, out of reflex, raised his hands to catch it.

It was all the opening he needed. Before Dimitri could recover his wits, Father Marco closed the distance between them in a flash of movement and delivered a kick to Dimitri's solar plexus. He made a wheezing sound as he doubled up into a fetal curl on the floor, struggling for air. The battle was over before it had even begun. The wind knocked out of him, there was no fight left in him. Father Marco took possession of the gun and verified the safety was off.

"Still think you could give you what for, my dear?"

Dimitri was still in no shape to respond.

Father Marco took charge of the situation. "Aysel, call the police."

She had remained speechless the whole time. She couldn't believe how fast he had moved. His words stirred her to action. "Uh, sure, Father," she said in a state of semi-shock. She yanked her mobile out of her hip pouch and gave a report to the police. "They're on their way."

"Please grab the scroll and the bone and my key." Turning his attention back to Dimitri, he commanded him to get on his feet. He struggled, holding his stomach.

"You know your way to the front door. Now march."

Father Marco told the police Dimitri had tried to steal church property and had threatened to kill him and Aysel when caught in the act. Aysel backed him up. After the police had escorted the caretaker off the premises in handcuffs, Aysel said, "Unbelievable."

"I'm as astonished as you are. I've known Dimitri almost two decades. My faith in humanity is shaken. For the sake of crummy lucre, he tossed aside our relationship like it were a dog bone."

"It happens out there in the real world, Father," Aysel said, tossing her thumb over her shoulder toward the church's double doors.

"What do you mean?"

"It's a different world out there. People hide their evil side in this holy domain."

Except in the confessional. Fondness in his eyes, he held her upper arm and said, "I'm grateful to the Lord for protecting you."

She averted her eyes and shyness overcame her. Changing focus, she said, "You weren't kidding when you said you found someone who would rock Christendom."

His hand dropped to his side. "I never imagined finding what might be the Holy Grail of Christianity."

"It sure beats a wooden chalice."

"I'll drink to that."

"I've gotta ask you," Aysel said. "What was that move you used on Dimitri?" She executed her best imitation of it.

"The foot strike I used is called a push-kick in the Wing Chun Kung Fu fighting style."

"Like Bruce Lee?"

"Sort of." He shifted the conversation. "I have an important favor to ask of you, Aysel."

"Ask away," and she pulled a curious look at him.

Stone-cold serious, he said, "I want you to swear on the Bible you won't tell Baki about this discovery."

"Why should I swear such an oath?" she demurred.

"Tonight's episode with Dimitri has shaken my confidence in people. My gut is telling me to trust no one but you. Can you do this for me? Please."

A gulf of silence stretched out between them. And there was awkwardness in it. Aysel stood still, her face impassive, weighing his request, uncertain what to say next.

"I'm not asking you to choose between Baki and me, my dear." He wished she would. "Postpone telling him until we've determined the authenticity of our find and have placed the scroll in the hands of the proper authorities. Agreed?"

"You've been through a lot, Father. Where's the Bible?"

They retreated to his office.

Done swearing her oath, she fell silent for a few moments. Then she said, "Well, I guess we've had enough excitement for one day," her mood brightening.

"I don't want to stare down a gun ever again."

"You were brave."

"Something tells me our lives will never be the same," he said with a grimace.

"If this scroll is genuine, then your Church, my Church, everyone's Church will cease to matter."

"We must keep this discovery to ourselves for the time being. What we've stumbled upon will impact every Christian on this planet."

"This secret is almost too heavy to bear." She clasped her hands in front of her chest. "But bear it we must."

"That's the spirit. There's no predicting how people will react to this discovery, if it's genuine."

"Father, my nerves are shot. I'll drop these items off at the university and put them under lock and key. Then I'm going home."

"Good idea. Have yourself a peaceful evening, my dear. God be with you."

"And with you."

"I'll walk you to the door." He made to move from where he was standing but Aysel held up her hand.

"It's okay, Father. I'll let myself out."

He watched her leave and a piece of him left with her. With only his meditations for company, he flopped into his chair and stared off into space. He could no longer ignore the dreadful thought lurking in the recesses of his mind. The scroll will transform the Church—even destroy it! A troublesome realization jolted him. Maybe this job isn't so bad after all...And it will be taken from me when news of my discovery is announced. What will I do for a wage? Where will I live? Where will I work? He glimpsed his future fading away into an uncertain and unfamiliar place.

He teetered on the edge of a mental abyss, staring into a great yawning space, a pit of existential angst. A sensation of helplessness overcame him much like when his mother and sister were killed. O Lord, I need your help now more than ever, he supplicated, his inner being fraught with anxiety.

He got up and paced the floor of his office, the prospect of revisiting the turmoil of secular life unsettling him. A life of uncertainty and unpredictability. The Church had been his refuge for most of his adult life. A refuge from the nihilistic world he had turned his back on decades ago. The Church sheltered him from the day-to-day turbulence that buffeted his flock. His well-ordered life, revolving around prayer and pastoral work, would be irretrievably lost with the release of the scroll. For the first time in his pastoral calling, he felt what many of his parishioners had possibly suffered at least once: a visceral fear of an unfamiliar tomorrow.

Lord, I've always been your dutiful servant. I worship you faithfully. I help the poor and the downtrodden. I'm humble toward my fellow man…Be honest. You need to work on your humility…I don't ask for much. I have nothing but the priesthood to sustain me. He stopped before his desk, impotent rage building in him. He clenched his hands and pounded his fists on the desk.

"What do You want from me that You haven't already taken from me?" he screamed.

He moved around the desk and crumpled into his chair, emotionally spent. Ungrateful wretch that I am.

Please forgive me, Lord.

Spying the Bible on which Aysel had sworn her oath, he opened it to a random page and read the first passage of Scripture his eyes landed on:

> *If anyone wishes to come after me, let him deny himself and take up his cross and follow me. For whoever wishes to save his life shall lose it, but whoever loses his life for my sake will save it.*

A refreshing wave of relief washed over him. Thank you, Lord, for your holy guidance, he prayed.

A conundrum popped into his mind. I have to give a sermon tomorrow. How can I look my congregants in the eye and speak with conviction the words I've written? I'd be telling them a lie…Never stopped you before. Shut up…He pondered his options then he hit upon an idea.

"Thank you so much, my dear." Father Marco hung up. Glad that's settled. His deacon accepted to deliver the Sunday sermon. Without thinking, he got up, grabbed the bag containing his soutane and shoes and locked up the building.

He walked home feeling like a free man released from a prison whose walls had been wrought from fear and insecurity. A feeling of renewed purpose intensified in him as the church melted into the dark background of the night. For the first time in his life, he strolled rather than raced along the streets of his district. Calm had descended upon him. He was done running from his past. It was a pleasant experience not having the world rush by.

His thoughts wandered back to his days in the old neighborhood. I wonder where the boys are now. Are they dead? Alive? Sudden alarm intruded upon his meditations. Where's my soutane? He panicked. Without his soutane, he felt naked, vulnerable. Then he remembered the bag he was carrying. What's happening to me? I never walk in public without wearing my soutane. He stopped a moment to contemplate this change in habit. Surely my faith is profounder than a piece of cloth…Did I exchange the security and support of my gang for that of the Church? He knew the answer to his question. He had joined the Church because he had been lonely and afraid and in need of stability. But he had now come to an awareness that the Church had wobbly foundations which might not be worth shoring up. This deeply rutted path I have been travelling on most of my adult life is pointed in the wrong direction.

He resumed walking, taking his time, his new understanding of himself invoking a sense of serenity. Discovering a hidden truth about himself on a deep level was a soul-satisfying experience. He inhaled the algae-scented air blowing off the Sea of Marmara. He glanced to his right and saw ships' navigation lights blinking and bobbing above the turbulent waters, giant fireflies in flight. We're not much different from those vessels, he ruminated. They'd be floundering like flotsam if not for the steady hands of their skippers. We, too, have a steady hand at the helm of our lives, but oftentimes we detour from the path the good Lord has plotted for us. When we run aground, we have no one to blame but ourselves.

He strolled by cafes and restaurants buzzing with locals and tourists, their conversations spilling out onto the street, and he wondered if the tourists appreciated the historic character of Istanbul as much as he did. He didn't pine for the ubiquitous chain stores whose garish neon signs contributed to the visual pollution back home. Old Istanbul had eschewed the commercial vulgarity of the West to preserve its old-world charm.

He drew abreast of a hole-in-the-wall newsstand he had never noticed in his travels. A single naked lightbulb washed a rack of newspapers in stark yellowish light. Above the fold of the *Hürriyet Daily News*, Turkey's principal English-language daily, a headline caught his eye: "Professor Michael Giltmore to Host Interfaith Conference in Istanbul."

Father Marco stopped and picked up the newspaper for a closer reading.

> Michael Giltmore, retired professor of theology, controversial author, and recent convert to Islam, will host an interfaith conference at the Four Seasons Sheraton Hotel on September 22-23.

Next week, he remarked.

The article went on to discuss the ongoing controversy surrounding Giltmore's notorious book and provided highlights of the upcoming conference. He replaced the newspaper and continued toward home.

He's a Muslim now. How about that. I guess remaining a Catholic wasn't an option for him. He gave way on the sidewalk to a passel of gregarious tourists, and their boisterous voices faded into the gloaming. Maybe I'll pay him a visit at the conference. Wouldn't Giltmore be interested to learn of what I've discovered?

## Chapter Twenty-Three
## Byzantium - 63 CE

Who is calling at this time of the day?

The beloved disciple rose and shuffled to the entrance of his home. He fumbled with the handle of the heavy iron-bound door and swept it open. His vision blurry, old age having had its way with his deteriorating health despite his vocal but futile complaints, he squinted at the silhouette of a large man filling the doorway. Then a shock of red hair and a beard of the same color came into focus. These features belonged to but one man. He smiled warmly as he greeted his guest.

"Brother Ignatius, peace unto you."

"And unto you peace, Brother Daniyyel," he replied, a grave air about his ruddy face.

"Do come in. It has been too long." He led him to a crudely-built settee. "Please sit for a spell."

The settee groaned beneath his substantial bulk. He gulped for air.

"You appear ready to burst, Brother."

"A messenger arrived with news from Rome. There was a great trial last month," he gasped.

"Catch your breath," Daniyyel urged, planting himself on a sella across from him. "There is no hurry."

"Forgive me, Brother. The journey from town was short but hot. May I have a libation to slake my thirst?"

"Where are my manners," he said, somewhat mortified. "Rachel," he called out over his shoulder. He waited for her acknowledgement from the other room. "Refreshment for our guest, if you please."

"Aah. Thank you, Brother. Much revived I am now," he said as he wiped his mouth with his sleeve.

"You mentioned a great trial in Rome."

"You shall be pleased to know the false prophet is dead. At the behest of Jewish authorities in Rome, he was arrested for preaching a

Law-less Gospel to the Jews. Death by beheading was his punishment."

So Paul met an ignoble end. Would that he had listened to me. I warned him his false preaching might bring down ruin upon him. He sensed a lightness in his soul as though a great load had been wrenched from him. He raised his eyes to Brother Ignatius. "The death of a human being is no occasion for pleasure no matter the kind of man he was. May God the Most Merciful save us from such a fate."

"Amen," Brother Ignatius said as he hung his head in contrition.

"The Christians shall make a martyr of Paul no doubt. I pray this trial is not a harbinger of measures more wicked to follow. Emperor Nero harbors much ill-will toward the Christians."

"I have heard rumors the emperor is given to spells of violence. Members of his inner circle tread delicately around him. They seek not to incite his unpredictable wrath."

"Absolute power reduces a person's character to that of a beast. We need possess moral restraint to rise above our brutish nature. The M'sheekha's Rule provides the moral check on our worst impulses," Daniyyel said, wagging his finger.

"The Rule is not found wanting, just its application."

"Unfortunately, the Rule cannot trump Nero's brutality towards a religious minority."

"Brother Daniyyel, thank you for your hospitality. Please forgive me but I must go now." He stood up.

"So soon?" he said. "I do not receive many visitors these days." He rose slowly from the sella and his joints creaked with age.

"Please forgive me, Brother Daniyyel. I must announce Paul's execution to the Christians in the agora. They shall no doubt be distressed at this news."

"But the truth of his execution shall be lost on them," he said. Daniyyel clapped his hand on Ignatius' broad shoulder and guided him to the door. "Thank you for coming by. God be with you, brother."

"And with you, brother."

He closed the door and returned to a settee where he sat thinking. For the first time since he had escaped his enemies in Jerusalem, he would no longer have cause to fear in a public space. Over ten years had passed since he fled his homeland. The harrowing journey he, his wife and fellow passengers had endured crossing the Middle Sea still gave him nightmares on occasion. Recalling the memory of this treacherous sea journey gave him a frightful shudder he could not repress.

Although many years had elapsed since his escape, his enemies had not forgotten him. It was but a few years ago when several strangers, passing through Byzantium, discreetly enquired about a man who called himself Keeper of the Revelation. He had ceased referring to himself with this honorific when he sailed away from the Judean coast more than a decade ago in the dark of night. Perhaps they shall seek me no more.

A tremor in his chest roused him from his contemplation. He put his hand to his heart. It palpitated. Not again. Please be still my heart. "Wife. Come to me."

"What is it, husband?" she said as she hurried into the room, the distressed tone of his voice causing her concern.

"There is something I have kept from you and I sense now is time to reveal it."

She sat beside him and took his hand in her lap. "I am listening."

"I have withheld a great secret from you."

"There are no secrets between us, husband." She patted his hand.

"There are not?"

"You carry an object beneath your cloak. I feel it when we embrace."

"You *do*? Then why did you never inquire about it?"

"If you had wanted me to know, you would have let me into your confidence."

"You're a good wife, Rachel. I judged it best if you were not privy to my secret. I did not want to put your life in danger."

"My life is in God's hands, husband."

"I have carried the message of the M'sheekha beneath my clothing these past long years."

Her hand shot to her mouth. “Why did you never speak out? You could have halted these Christian heresies in their tracks.”

He shook his head. “The Gentiles would not follow the M’sheekha’s path. The written word would have made no difference.”

“You speak with such conviction.”

“They followed the false prophet, not the M’sheekha.”

“This explains the profound change in you after your final meeting with the scribe.”

“Aye. A solemn burden it has been, Rachel. But God does not charge a soul except to within its capacity. Divine revelation weighs heavy on a man’s mind and tongue. I have lived in constant fear of the scroll falling into the wrong hands, especially when I was in the Temple. Imagine. The very thing the Sanhedrin inveighed against was within its reach.”

“Peculiar how the truth can cause such strife.”

“The Christian sects will not be satisfied until one believes what they believe. They do much violence to one another in defence of their heretical doctrines. Would that they had believed in the way of the M’sheekha.”

“Killing only begets more killing.”

“The truth is worth dying for but never worth killing for unless in self-defence. I fear there shall always be people who cannot discern this difference. There must be no compulsion in religion, for truth stands out from falsehood.”

“You fought the good fight, husband. But it was not for you to guide people. Your duty was to inform them. Only God the Almighty can change the condition of misguided hearts. May He make our hearts firm on the path of Submission.”

“There is no word but the Word of God and the M’sheekha was the Word of God.”

“Amen.” She paused, mulling. “Does your possessing the message have anything to do with our fleeing Bethany and your changing your name?”

“Wife, your powers of perception never fail to astound me.”

"Praise God who protected you through this long trial of yours. May He reward you for your perseverance and for your dedication to His way."

"Am I a good husband, Rachel? Tell me I am a good husband," he pleaded.

"You are a most pious man and the best husband a wife can ask for."

"Swear by God the Witness."

"I swear by Him."

Contentment smoothed his face riven with lines of worry and old age. "I sense my remaining days are few in number, Rachel. Be sure the scroll is entombed with me. It must never be revealed to the public in our time. The Christians would destroy it, claiming it a fake. Like they will do to the message of *The Praised One* when he comes."

"I shall honor your wish, my husband." Her interest piqued, she said, "May I see the scroll?"

He pulled the leather thong over his head then he reached under his garments and withdrew the scroll. He hesitated before handing it to her.

Her eyes went wide with amazement. "The parchment seems to vibrate."

"A pleasant sensation, no?" Her beaming countenance answered his question. "I have possessed this scroll for almost half my life and, though I have aged visibly, the scroll is as immaculate as ever."

"I see what you mean, husband," she said while caressing the scroll. "The vellum feels and looks as fresh as the day it was cured." She returned it to him.

"The message of this scroll has been a constant source of comfort and joy to me." He added: "Much like your companionship." He smiled at her. Then of a sudden his face froze in alarm and his hand flew to his chest.

"Your heart again?" she asked anxiously.

"It beats rapidly. Difficult to catch my breath." He felt washed-out. "I am weary, dear wife." He shifted himself and laid his head in her lap. "There is no deity but God and Yeshua was the M'sheekha of God," he murmured.

"Rest, my dear husband, rest," and she stroked his hairy face. Unexpectedly, he spasmed then sagged. "Husband?" She shook him. "Most Beloved?" She shook him again and again but the beloved disciple did not awaken.

* * *

The beloved disciple woke as though from a beautiful dream. He sat upright. Calm. Like still waters that run deep. He realized he was no longer in his home. Serenity suffused him and soft glowing light surrounded him. He enjoyed no perception of time or place. He perceived the presence of two angels, floating. He had been expecting them for the M'sheekha had spoken of the trial in the grave presided over by two angels.

"Peace be upon you" he called out to them.

"And upon you peace," one of the blue-black angels answered in a voice that rumbled like thunder and whose eyes flashed like lightning.

He waited.

"We are the Angels of Death," the other said.

"This landscape seems familiar," he said.

"It is your resting place until the Day of Reckoning."

He glanced around the pleasant void once again and his calm increased. "Am I dead?"

"You are dead," an angel answered.

He was content with this response.

"You must answer three questions." The angel glanced sideways at his companion.

The other angel gave the beloved disciple a welcoming look. "Who is your master?"

"God, the Almighty."

"Who is your prophet?"

"The M'sheekha."

"What is your religion?"

"Submission to the will of God the Almighty."

Then a crier called from the highest heaven: "My servant has spoken the truth, so spread a bed for him from Paradise, clothe him in Paradise, and open a door for him into Paradise. So some of its air and perfume will come to him, and a space will be made for him as far as the eye can see."

Then the beloved disciple's grave was widened for him and was made light for him. A broad opening appeared at the foot of his grave. The scent of musk pervaded his nostrils. Delicate warmth caressed his inert feet. A comforting breeze soothed his soul. Birds, twittering and tweeting, flitted and flew by the bright opening in all directions. In the distance, he could see trees whose bark glittered like gold and whose leaves shined like silver, and the ground sparkled with precious gems. My teacher spoke the truth, he thought in wonder.

"Is that what I perceive it to be?" he said, pointing his finger at the foot of his grave, his voice quivering with anticipation.

"Yes, it is Paradise."

He tingled, the angel's pleasing tone comforting his soul like the tenderness of a mother for her newborn baby.

"My Lord is most generous," he said.

The angels replied, "Verily we knew you would say that. This is your place of rest until the Day of Reckoning. You were upon certain faith and died upon it and upon it you will be raised up, if God wills."

"My Lord is Most Just," he said.

"Sleep, servant of God, sleep," they said to him. "Sleep as the newly married sleeps until God raises you up from this place of sleep."

The beloved disciple laid back down, a satisfied smile on his lips. Immeasurable and unfathomable peace of Divine provenance enveloped his soul, so soothing to his heightened self-awareness. He lay in comfort and in calm in his spacious grave filled with faint flowing light. Gentle sleep overtook him, and he dreamed the dreams that only an obedient servant of God could dream.

## Chapter Twenty-Four
## Rome - 63 CE

Without warning, Roman authorities transferred the man from the comfort of a rented home where he had been living under house arrest to a prison cell no better than a pigsty where he now awaited execution. The stench of unwashed bodies and of human excrement spoke to the primitive conditions of the condemned.

The prisoner leaned against the rough, uneven surface of the stone wall and listened to the rustle of rats foraging in the straw strewn on the cold, damp floor of his cell. They didn't object to his company. He wasn't the first inmate to intrude on them nor was he likely to be the last.

The windowless room and the feeble torchlight burning in the corridor beyond the iron bars hampered his ability to see the creatures scurrying in the semi-darkness. Light or dark, there was not much to hold his attention. Although he had no cellmate for companionship, he was not lonely. The M'sheekha, his Lord, was with him in spirit, and his Lord's presence made his involuntary confinement bearable. He recognized his journey on earth had reached its terminus and he accepted this fate with no reservations.

This is my Lord's will, he told himself.

Other cells nearby were occupied. To his right, a man in distress moaned while across from him a prisoner snored. His conscience must not be troubling him, the prisoner thought. Despite his depressing surroundings and the odor of human waste and unwashed bodies, his mood was cheerful.

Though I had done nothing against my people or the customs of my ancestors, yet I was arrested. The one who is righteous will live by faith. For the wages of sin is death, but the free gift of God is eternal life in Christ Jesus our Lord. This remembrance gave him hope.

He reflected on the circumstances of his Lord's death. The M'sheekha's disciples had abandoned him as did my followers. No man stood with me at my trial and now all men have forsaken me as they did the M'sheekha. He scratched his scruffy beard, a telltale sign of how long he had been imprisoned.

He heard indistinct movement at the far end of the lengthy corridor. The sound of leather sandals slapping stone drew nearer. Are they coming for me? So be it. For I am already being poured out as a drink offering, and the time of my departure has come. I have fought the good fight, I have finished the course, I have kept the faith. In the future there is laid up for me the crown of righteousness, which the Lord, the righteous Judge, will award to me on that day. And not only to me, but also to all who have loved His appearing.

Unconcerned, he did not move. Two beefy soldiers emerged from the darkness and stood in faint silhouette in front of his cell. Keys jingled as one of the guards unlocked the door to his iron cage and opened it wide, and it squealed and groaned in protest on its rusty hinges like a mythological Chimera roused from the depths of Hades. The snoring man stirred, smacked his lips together several times, mumbled a few unintelligible syllables and went back to sleep.

"Paul of Tarsus. On your feet and step forward," barked the guard in a tone that brooked no defiance.

Not one to be hurried, Paul rose slowly and approached the door, his head held high. Strands of straw stuck to his ragged clothing.

"Turn around," the guard commanded.

He felt rough hands bind his own with a leather thong that bit into the soft flesh of his wrists. The door of his cell closed with a metallic *clang*, signalling a departure from which there would be no return, and the rats did not pause in their foraging. Paul and his jailers marched in silence along the corridor which seemed to stretch forever into the dimness beyond, a guard in front and one in back of him. An unnecessary precaution. There was nowhere to run, but protocols were protocols.

They came to a stone staircase. The cold, clammy stairs chilled the soles of his dirty, bare feet and the atmosphere grew brighter the higher they climbed. He bowed his head for the light hurt his eyes. Before long, the three of them burst into stark sunshine. He squinted in the harsh solar radiance.

He found himself in a large grassy courtyard where other inmates were lined up facing a crowd of onlookers who occupied tiered seating. Beneath a covered dais in the bottom tier lounged Emperor Nero, imperious, clothed in a simple white toga, his cranium decorated with a golden *corona civica,* a crown of woven oak leaves. An air of boredom surrounded him. A contingent of the Imperial Germanic Bodyguard stood at attention on the ground, their backs to the dais. These elite personal bodyguards were separate from the Praetorians, the Roman Emperor's main bodyguard. The Imperial Standard ruffled in a gentle breeze. It flew wherever the emperor presided.

An imperial herald read out the charges, one by one, in a raised voice for each of the condemned. The prisoner was then summarily beheaded. "Paul of Tarsus," the herald's voice rang out. Paul's head snapped to attention at the sound of his name. "You have been found guilty on three charges: treason, sedition and heresy. The sentence of death by beheading is hereby decreed in Caesar's name."

His jailers brought him forward and pushed him to a kneeling position and placed his neck on the chopping block. Paul did not resist. This was his fate and so he accepted it with gladness in his heart. Martyrdom. The best death. He stared at the lifeless heads in the woven reed basket below his eyes. Out of the corner of his eye he saw the executioner look to Emperor Nero who gave the thumbs down as though he were deciding a wrestling match. The executioner bowed his acknowledgement. Sunlight glinted off the well-honed axe blade as it rose and fell in a cruel arc. The crowd cheered.

* * *

Paul woke immediately as though from a terrible nightmare. He bolted upright. Disconcerted. He realized he was no longer in the public arena. Panic engulfed him. He did not recognize his surroundings and the lack of perception of time and place added to his panic. In the dim, dusky light he beheld the presence of two beings, floating. He did not know what else to label them. "Who are you?" he called out to them.

"We are the Angels of Death," one of the blue-black beings answered.

"What—what is this unfamiliar landscape?"

"It is your resting place until the Day of Reckoning."

Paul glanced around the menacing void once again and his alarm increased. "What am I doing here?"

"You are dead."

"How—"

"Silence," the angel commanded, the word chilling Paul's soul like an icy wind. "It is we who ask the questions. And there are three." The angel looked sideways at his companion.

The other angel gave Paul a hard stare. "Who is your master?"

"The M'sheekha."

"Who is your prophet?"

"I received revelation from the Lord."

"What is your religion?"

"Worship of the M'sheekha."

A crier from the highest heaven shouted out: "He has lied, so spread a bed for him from Hell, clothe him from Hell and open for him a door into Hell."

A broad opening appeared at the foot of Paul's grave. Stomach-churning smells pervaded his nostrils. Intense flames licked and lashed his inert feet. Scorching wind singed his soul. Sparks as huge as houses flew by the opening in all directions.

"What is that?" Paul said, pointing his finger at the hole, his voice quavering with existential terror.

"It is the Hellfire."

Paul jerked, the angel's barbed voice flaying his soul like a flagrum lacerating flesh.

"This is your place until the Day of Reckoning. You lived upon doubt and died upon it and you will be raised up upon it if it is God's will."

"No," he screeched in horror. "It is not just. The Lord died for my sins."

"God is Most Just," shrieked the angel, flames dancing in his reflective eyes. "The Hellfire is the recompense of the deniers."

Silent, remorseless terror gripped Paul's soul. He struggled to climb out of his grave, but the more he struggled, the deeper he sank. Creatures, some creeping, some crawling and still others slinking and slithering, crowded his grave as it closed in on him and pressed against his ribs, smothering his screams of horror in a dank pit of suffocating darkness.

# Part III

*Dissent to power is the highest form of patriotism and deference to power, the lowest form of treason*

## Chapter Twenty-Five
## Indianapolis

Giltmore had drawn up a list of particulars, itemized by category, he required for his trip to Istanbul. He was double-checking it. He adored lists. They reduced the clutter in his brain which freed up his intellect for more important matters that demanded his full attention. Once he had written something down, he no longer had to dwell on it.

He had a weekly grocery list as well as a weekly to-do list, a list of movies to view, a list of books to read, and a list of man toys he wanted to buy. He even had an inventory list of his personal effects. Giltmore attributed much of his success in life to lists.

His eccentricity recalled Einstein's habit of donning the same clothes for work every day so he wouldn't waste precious time and cognitive function wondering what to wear. Giltmore was a clothes horse so he couldn't adhere to Einstein's sartorial preferences. Every genius indulged in an unconventional whimsy or two that spoke to the requirement for organization and efficiency in their life. So Giltmore believed.

This covers it, he decided. He saved the file and closed the word-processing application, then leaned back in his chair to admire the background on his computer. The picture, taken at sundown, must have been snapped from a boat traversing the Bosporus Strait, for it was of the iconic imperial Suleymaniye (pronounced Soo-lay-man-ee-yay) Mosque in Old Istanbul, which stands proud on the third hill of the seven hills of the Golden Horn and dominates the inimitable skyline when approaching the peninsula from the east.

Giltmore marvelled at the mosque's four slender minarets, thrusting skyward like spears planted upright in the ground, their pointed tips stabbing the heavens, and the mosque's massive dome, curving upward like an enormous Ottoman shield, protecting all those beneath its canopy of lead and stone.

The Suleymaniye Mosque was designed by Mimar "The Architect" Sinan, the chief imperial architect of the Ottoman Empire during the latter half of the sixteenth century. He began his illustrious career as a military engineer, building bridges and aqueducts, and ended it as an architect of unsurpassed skill. Although a contemporary of Michelangelo, his prodigious architectural output far exceeded that of his Italian counterpart. In his day, Sinan designed and supervised the construction of the equivalent of *three* St. Peter's Basilicas—absent vulgar idolatrous artwork and statuary—as well as 474 other major religious buildings and complexes, including schools, hospitals and *hamams*. His remarkable architectural output is unmatched by anyone in any age.

Sinan's genius extended far beyond Turkey. Several of his apprentices helped design the Taj Mahal in Agra, India, and his student, Mimar Hayruddin, designed and built the *Stari Most* (Old Bridge) in Mostar, Bosnia-Herzegovina, in the mid-sixteenth century. Croatian forces destroyed it in 1993 during the internecine Yugoslav Wars and it only reopened in 2004.

He tore himself away from his laptop and picked up the ringing phone. "Hello."

"Guess who?"

"Hmmm. Your voice sounds familiar, but I date so many women I don't want to risk uttering the wrong name," he said, rocking in his chair.

"You're a real kidder," Sandra said.

"Banter is the soul of good conversation. I didn't expect to hear from you until I returned from Istanbul."

"I'm taking a break from work and I had nothing better to do so I decided to call you."

He heard a smothered laugh on her end. "And I had nothing better to do so I answered the phone," he replied in kind. He stopped rocking and crossed his legs.

"*Touché*."

"So what's going on?"

"I was working on my questions for a guest interview with Farryn Ishei."

"I'm jealous."

"No need to be, Mike. He's happily married. Besides, he's not my type."

Ishei's no match for me, anyway. "Who makes your bells chime?" he dared to ask.

"Stick around and find out."

"I might just do that." He smiled into the instrument.

"So what've you been up to?"

"I was reviewing my packing list for my trip to Istanbul."

"Sounds like you're an organized kind of person."

"Right you are. How about you?"

"Well, my career compels me to be meticulous but my personal life is a little messier, shall we say."

She better not be a slob, he willed. He admired his uncluttered desk where every item on it was neatly arranged. "In what way?"

"I like to wing it. I'm averse to planning things too far in advance. I value spontaneity."

So she's impulsive. "Understood."

"Do you like to do things on the spur of the moment, Mike?"

"My social life is so hectic spontaneity must be scheduled." His comment was met with silence. He could sense her disappointment. "Sandra, I'm teasing you again. I have so much free time I can't help but be *spur-ious*." He leaned on the armrest of his chair, his mind in flight. How he liked the soft, feminine rhythms of her voice.

"Clever wordplay." There was relief in her tone. "Are you worried about travelling to Turkey?"

"Turkish security forces are in firm control of the country. Communist Kurdish terrorists have been neutralized along the border."

"So what are your plans for Istanbul?"

"We're bringing Christians with us on this trip to introduce them to Islamic culture and religion and to Ottoman history. The Turks have been at the end of a long and concerted campaign of disinformation by the West since their capture of Constantinople in 1453. We plan to educate the Christians joining us that Western scholarship on the Ottomans and Turks is—to paraphrase Henry Ford—bunk."

"How did your guests come to know about this trip?"

"The Institute put the word out to interfaith organizations with which it is affiliated."

"Mmm. I've noticed Turkey has been in the news much more than usual," she said.

"If Turkey remained an economic and political backwater, there wouldn't be all this handwringing in the West. But because Turkey is a resurgent regional power and has an Islamic government in office that is pursuing a foreign policy at odds with U.S. interests in the region, the Turkey-bashing has intensified."

"And several European countries have called the Armenian resettlement the first genocide of the modern age."

He pressed his lips in anger. "Of course they would," he said, his voice dripping with disdain. "There is no love for Turkey in Europe because of the centuries of warfare between Europe and the former Ottoman Empire. The West's hypocrisy and selective amnesia aside, deeming the Armenian exile the first genocide would be news to the Dutch Boers whose women and children died in the tens of thousands in British concentration camps during the Boer War at the turn of the last century. And let us not forget the Congolese who were massacred in their millions by the colonial government of Leopold II, King of Belgium, in the early twentieth century. I haven't heard any European country passing a law making denial of those genocides a crime as France has done with the Armenian exile. The fact is, Sandra, collective punishment was the global norm prior to the adoption of the Genocide Convention in 1948."

"It's curious the White House has repeatedly declined to qualify the Armenian resettlement as a genocide."

"It's no eye-opener," Giltmore said as he glanced up at the ceiling. "But here's one for you. After the U.S. purchased the Philippines from Spain for $20 million, the U.S. army massacred two hundred thousand Filipino civilians in the conquest of the islands in the Filipino-American War. A war President McKinley sanctioned to 'civilize and Christianize' the Filipinos most of whom were Catholic. That was an act of genocide, which again predates the Armenian exile by nearly a decade. And let's not forget the American genocide against black Africans during the centuries-long slave trade during which an estimated one in five Africans died." He shook his head, miffed. "You see, Sandra, the U.S. has as much blood—if not more—on its hands as any other nation on this planet." He added, "Besides, the U.S. regards Turkey as an important ally. Armenia can be ignored. It has no strategic value. Welcome to *realpolitik*."

"Turkey is a member of NATO isn't it?"

"Necessarily so. But Turkey is an ally of convenience, not common culture. The U.S. needs Turkey to be in the West's orbit. It occupies strategic real estate, particularly the Bosporus Strait."

"What's so important about this strait?"

Sandra was one of those rare public figures who wasn't afraid to reveal her lack of knowledge when the opportunity presented itself. Her unpretentious character was what endeared her to her legions of fans.

"It's the chokepoint through which Russian naval vessels reach the Mediterranean from their Black Sea port on the Crimean peninsula." Giltmore visualized the channel of water that snaked between the continents of Europe and Asia. "We can't have the Turks cozying up to the Russians, especially since the Deep State has reignited the Cold War. Which is why the U.S. tried to oust Ordekan in a military coup several summers ago with its proxy army, the Gülenist Terror Organization. Thank God the coup failed."

"I wish our asinine politicians tended to their own affairs," she complained.

"America is the cold heart of a ruthless and brutal empire, Sandra. It has no friends, just interests, particularly energy interests." He tugged at the crease in his pants so it would lie straight.

"There'll never be peace so long as our country is butting its nose in every country's internal affairs."

"It wouldn't faze me if the Turkish president is on a CIA watch list. His pro-Islamic pronouncements have raised eyebrows in official Washington circles. There's talk from the commentariat about Turkey being *Islamist*. That's dog-whistle for *anti-American*."

"It really burns me how our politicians arrogate to themselves the divine right to base our laws on the Ten Commandments and to call the U.S. a Christian country, and nobody bats an eye. But when any Islamic polity wants to base their country's institutions on Islamic law, our generals start polishing their missiles."

"Here's a bombshell," Giltmore said. "The Ten Commandments are a component of *shari'ah*, which means *path* in English. A path of a Divine Guidance for humanity's benefit in this life and the next. Didn't God reveal the Ten Commandments to Moses?"

"The sophophobic Islamophobes want us to believe *shari'ah* is the coming of the apocalypse," she fumed.

"It's because Islamophobes are like anti-Semites, but without the sobriety or subtlety. They steal their ideas from the discount loony bin during the blue-light specials at the local insane asylum."

Sandra cracked up. "I read the other day Ordekan has a personal doctor who ensures the safety of the food eaten by him. His food and drink are analyzed for poisons and radiation before it's consumed by him at home and abroad."

"The U.S. can't threaten Turkey with democracy and because the U.S.-instigated military coup back in 2016 failed miserably, it'll take the conventional route of assassination if push comes to shove."

"You talk as if this is a done deal, Mike."

He swiveled back and forth in his chair. "The crazies helming the U.S. ship of state wouldn't hesitate to toss Ordekan overboard if he keeps disobeying their orders," he said with conviction.

"I hope such an occasion never comes to pass."

"If it did, the White House would blame such an incident on ISIS or Kurdish terrorists. *Who* doesn't really matter. The uncritical state media will go into overdrive parroting whichever terrorist group or individual our Dear Leader selects," Giltmore said matter-of-factly. "Much as Western sock-pocket presstitutes keep pimping anti-Russian propaganda regarding Putin's legal annexation of Crimea."

"It was sheer madness how the U.S. tried to provoke World War Three with Russia over this issue."

"What's more galling is the complete news blackout of the U.S.'s violent annexation of Puerto Rico and Hawaii and Israel's violent annexation of the West Bank. Putin held a democratic referendum on the issue of annexation which the Crimeans voted in favor of. Can't same the same thing about Puerto Rico, Hawaii or the West Bank where no plebiscites were held."

"The media report only that which supports the Deep State's agenda."

"The Deep State sees the writing on the wall, Sandra. It knows the U.S. is the 'Sick Man' of the West. Which is to say the American Empire is crumbling. Europe has no stomach to fight a war against Russia and the U.S. is no longer favored to defeat China in a conventional war. War with Russia is not inevitable but likely because the U.S. cannot allow any country to challenge its global hegemony."

"The problem with this country's propagandists is they come to believe their own bs. They have no clue how the outside world perceives our country. So when does the war of words end and the shooting war begin?"

"I believe no such thing will happen in the immediate future. The regime in Washington has butted up against Russian's red line in Syria. Putin will never give up Syria. The Russian naval base in Tartus is the only beachhead Russia has in the Mediterranean Sea."

"It's ironic the U.S. once supported the father of Syria's current leader."

"The geopolitical landscape has changed since the death of Hafez Assad. The Syrian government stands in the way of Israel's fanatical lust for a Greater Israel.

"What! If what you're saying is true, I'll have to bang my head against the wall. Sounds like our government is concealing its evil goals with War-on-Terror rhetoric."

"And the aborted Turkish coup was a stupid attempt to bottle up Russian natural gas exports and damage Russia's economy. The U.S. regime was enraged over Ordekan's post-coup deal with Putin to build a gas pipeline from Russia to Turkey under the Black Sea, which now connects to Turkey's gas pipeline that feeds Europe. This pipeline will cripple the U.S.'s plan to ship its much more expensive liquefied natural gas to Europe."

"Mike, you possess an amazing ability to connect these disparate dots on the geopolitical map."

"The landscape changes but the U.S. regime's fixation on securing energy resources remains constant. Including in Syria. This is why the U.S. created ISIS. The Pentagon used ISIS to clear a path to Syria's oilfields so American forces could grab the oil."

"In certain political circles, your talk would be dangerous to U.S. interests," she alerted him.

"What're they going to do? Send someone to shoot me. I don't pose a clear and present danger to the security of this country, Sandra. It's not like I'm divulging state secrets. Besides, I'm practically a senior citizen. Which gives me the right to be grumpy," he said with a chuckle.

"Mike, have you forgotten the life-threatening emails you've received?" she reminded him.

"How can I?" He was untroubled by the number of trolls who had crawled out of their virtual caves to express their hollow threats. "As you predicted, the personal attacks have increased since my interview with you. I now know how the author of *Satanic Verses* must have felt during his early *fatwa* period."

"Please be careful, Mike, if not for your sake then for mine."

Giltmore's gob was momentarily smacked. He couldn't remember the last time someone had expressed concern for his welfare.

"Am I making you paranoid...? Mike?"

The lurch in his chest subsided. "Not at all, Sandra…So I needn't worry about the strange car parked across the street?" he teased as peeked out his office window.

"Are you putting me on?" she demanded.

"You got me." Giltmore sensed her relief.

"Please be more vigilant. You never can tell who's watching—or listening," she cautioned one last time.

"I'll try, but I find it as hard to shut my trap as a politician trolling for votes," he said, hoping to allay her worry.

"I just remembered. Did you see the newscast about an unhinged security guard named Julio Vasquez who cursed you after his DUI arrest a few days ago? Was this the Julio you mentioned on my show?"

"Yes, I saw it. I feel bad for him. Last time we emailed each other he was having marital problems. Nothing to worry about."

"But this Vasquez character blames you for losing his job at the university."

"He asked me for advice. I gave it. He accepted it. Now it seems things have gone awry."

"He was ordered to undergo a psych eval by the court."

"I don't think Julio is crazy. He's an inquisitive young man seeking answers. He's just projecting his anger in the wrong direction instead of taking responsibility for his actions."

"Oh, look at the time," she said out of the blue. "I'd love to linger with you, Mike, but I must finish my interview questions tonight."

There was so much more she wanted to say.

"Don't let me keep you from your work." I wish I could but you've got a career to manage. "Give my regards to Mr. Ishei," Giltmore said.

"I just wanted to touch base with you and wish you a safe journey. Please come back in one piece."

"God willing. Thanks for calling. Take care, Sandra."

"You, too, Mike."

He pressed the phone against his ear. He could almost feel her warm breath. Almost. All in good time.

* * *

Ted Carlyle, Deputy Director of Counterterrorism Operations, looked up from a sheath of papers lying before him on his desk and leaned back in the black leather executive office chair, a cat-that-ate-the-canary expression upon his face. "Your psychological profile of Julio Vasquez is comprehensive, Dr. Bryce."

"Thank you, sir."

Carlyle levelled his cold grey eyes at the man across from him. "Your professional assessment points to his responsiveness to manipulation." The statement was delivered more as a question than as a declaration of fact.

Bryce held his boss' steady gaze. "In his current state of mind, the subject's anger and feelings of injustice can be channeled to produce desired ends." He punctuated his sentence with an ever-so-slight smile.

"How long?"

"A skilled operative can gain Vasquez' trust within a couple of months, or less."

"That will be all, Dr. Bryce." This was his cue to signal the meeting was over.

Bryce gave a nod and stood up.

Carlyle watched the door close. Alone now in his office, he allowed himself a rare smile. The pieces on an imaginary chessboard began to take shape in his mind. If the mission is successful, and it will be, he predicted, the media will report Giltmore's assassination as a crime of revenge. A proud king struck down by an aggrieved pawn.

## Chapter Twenty-Six
## Istanbul - Monday

The radiocarbon testing laboratory at Koç University was deserted as were the other rooms in the building. Not unusual at this time of night. Aysel opted to work in the lab outside normal hours so no inquisitive colleagues would intrude on the secretive nature of her quest.

Seated at a workbench, her hands sheathed in blue latex, she prepared a sterile slide onto which she placed the parchment sample then slid it into the magnifying device. Through the lens of the scanning electron microscope (SEM), she scrutinized the specimen to verify its composition and to identify any exogenous impurities which may have contaminated it. She wasn't expecting any bombshells at this stage of the process. But she had to ensure all the boxes were checked off to satisfy and survive any potential challenges to her scientific findings. Despite her attention to detail, she anticipated with certainty there'd be at least one challenge: the Catholic Church. Because it stood to lose the most from this momentous discovery should it prove to be genuine. This she did not doubt.

"Awesome," she said to no one in particular. The parchment was made from calfskin, which boosted the religious significance of the scroll, for calfskin was the material of choice of Jewish scribes for preserving sacred writings. I can't get over how pristine this vellum is, she marvelled. It's as fresh as the day it was skinned. Aysel couldn't scientifically account for the immaculate condition of the scroll. Miraculous, she presumed.

The microscopic evaluation completed, she gave the vellum specimen a sequence of chemical washes with organic solvents to dissolve any foreign carbon-14 particles which might have come from sweat and dirt due to human handling. She cut the piece of vellum in two with a sterile knife and put both fragments in a petri dish she had sterilized earlier.

Finished with the parchment, she washed the femur with ordinary tap water for the same reason as she had cleansed the vellum. The bone and parchment samples had to be pristine. Any contaminants would skew the final dating results.

Next, Aysel ultrasonically cleansed the bone with distilled water. Then, using a sharp tool fashioned from tungsten, she scraped off the outermost layers of the bone as she grimaced and gritted her teeth. The sensation of metal scraping bone was like dragging fingernails through wet gravel. When done, she wiped her forehead with her sleeve, relieved.

*What an ordeal. Glad I'm not a butcher.*

After grinding the remaining bone into powder, she treated it with a series of chemicals to extract uncontaminated samples of chemically-isolated collagen, free of the humic and fulvic acids which typically corrupt ancient bones. Following this, she placed the collagen particles in a separate sterile petri dish.

The next step in the process involved the conversion of the vellum and collagen samples into carbon dioxide through combustion. Once a gaseous state was achieved, the $CO_2$ gas could be converted into graphitic carbon. To achieve this gaseous state, Aysel inserted the samples into separate quartz combustion tubes containing copper oxide and strands of silver wire. She hooked up the tubes to a vacuum line to suction the air out of them. She watched the needle on the gauge. Within seconds, it showed a vacuum state had been achieved in the tubes. Aysel grabbed a mini-blowtorch and flame-sealed the tubes. She then put them into a muffle furnace for high-temperature combustion where they would remain overnight, converting from solids to $CO_2$ gas.

Stretching her arms above her head, Aysel exhaled a well-earned yawn, and her shoulder joints cracked. It had been a long evening spent hunched over a workbench.

*Whew. Glad this is over. The first phase of this process is complete. Tomorrow I'll have the samples analyzed in the accelerator mass spectrometer.* The thought of it made her pulse race.

She left a note on the door of the furnace that instructed her colleagues not to disturb the contents combusting within. She tidied up the lab to leave no trace of her labors. Should curiosity get the better of her coworkers, she'd tell them she was radiocarbon dating a parchment recovered from her dig at the Van Castle.

With flagging enthusiasm, Aysel regarded the scroll that lay on the workbench. One more mystery to unravel before I call it quits. Despite her fatigue, she gathered up the scroll and made her way to the dressing room to don a protective outfit in preparation for accessing the archeology department's cleanroom facilities.

She pushed open the door to the room and strode across a Tacky Mat, relieving the soles of her shoes of any foreign particles that clung to them. She walked with effort as though she had tiny suction cups attached to her feet. Before donning her protective gear, she removed the scroll from the plastic bag, slipped it inside a clean Ziploc bag and vacuum sealed it. She then cleaned the external surfaces of the bag with an approved decontamination wipe as well as the counter on which she placed the bag.

Aysel was no stranger to the cleanroom. Toiling in it, though, wasn't something she did often. Typically, a doctoral candidate performed the investigative work she herself would undertake this evening.

Although the step-by-step instructions for donning the special protective gear necessary to enter the cleanroom were posted on the walls of the room, she knew the dressing sequence by heart. She tossed the latex gloves in the garbage and slipped on a pair of booties followed by a hairnet. After this, she slid on a facemask and snugged it over her nose and mouth. Next, she donned the first pair of gloves. Then she pulled on a hood followed by a pair of safety glasses. A pair of coveralls selected from the rack matched her height. She stepped into them and zipped them up. Lastly, she donned a second pair of gloves which covered the sleeves of the overgarment. She was now suited up and ready for the cleanroom.

Mr. Clean has nothing on me, she joked to herself.

Snatching the Ziploc bag off the counter, Aysel entered a small, glass-walled anteroom where, once again, she stood on a Tacky Mat. She pressed a button marked Vacuum. Instantly, she felt a tug on her outfit as the air was sucked out of the sealed space. The decontamination process had to be completed before she could open the second set of doors to the cleanroom. She pushed a button marked Open and a whooshing sound issued forth as the airlock slid open. She stepped into the cleanroom at last, free of contaminants, and the overhead positive ventilation system whirred as it purified the air circulating inside the room. The Turks take archeological authentication seriously.

Aysel approached a worktable on which lay the equipment she needed to assay the age of the ink. She removed the scroll from the bag and unrolled a foot-length section on the table's surface. Grabbing a hose connected to a central vacuum unit, she decontaminated the end of it then brushed it over the parchment to remove any invisible dust particles. She replaced the hose. With a fine-tipped stainless-steel needle, she extracted flecks of ink from random spots on the scroll which she then deposited on a sterile slide. This was inserted into a special microscope whereupon she examined the specks of ink using polarized light microscopy (PLM), a contrast-enhancing technique that detects color.

All the ink fragments are uniformly black. This indicates a single type of ink was used. Excellent. A favorable first sign, she noted.

Next, she studied the flecks of ink using both scanning electron microscopy (SEM) and transmission electron microscopy (TEM) to gather visual data on their composition and to determine their source. Ancient black inks were typically carbon-based, composed of soot and Arabic gum, which acted as a bonding agent. Aysel tinkered with the controls on the device.

Splendid. The basic elements matched scientific norms as well as her hopes. Another box checked off.

She sat erect on her stool and rolled her shoulders to relieve the tension that had crept into her neck and upper back. Done, she reached over and put the needle in a tray marked for cleaning. She rose from her perch and replaced the scroll in the Ziploc bag. She vacuumed the slide, placed it with the needle then she vacuumed the counter. The scroll in hand, she exited the cleanroom, light on her feet. After putting her protective garment in the laundry bin, she returned to the main lab with the scroll in her possession.

This has been a productive night, she congratulated herself.

Spotting her oversized handbag on a workbench, she stowed the scroll in it. With nothing left to do, she turned off the lights in the lab and swiped her access card through the slot in the electronic reader. She waited for an LED to turn from red to green before tugging on the door. All entry and departure times of employees were electronically recorded and a video camera monitored access to the lab. Security was robust for this particular laboratory due to the valuable equipment stored within. Aysel was grateful for these security measures because they made her feel safe when she worked alone late at night.

She set off toward the elevators along a dimly lit corridor bathed in an eerie bloodshot hue. To conserve energy, only red emergency lighting illuminated the hallways after 10:00 PM. Passing by the Processing Lab where artifacts are cleaned, catalogued and, if necessary, repaired, she noticed a light glowing behind the frosted window of the door.

That's odd.

She retrieved her pass from her purse, swiped it and the electromagnetic lock made a metallic click as the locking action released. She opened the door and poked her head into the room whose workbenches were cluttered with ancient objects in various stages of processing.

"Hello, anybody there?" Aysel called out. She waited a few moments then repeated herself. No reply. Someone must have forgotten to turn off the lights before they left. Funny, I don't remember seeing the lights on when I arrived this evening. My head must have been in the clouds, she rationalized. Still holding the door, she reached over and flicked the switch. She ducked out of the room and let the door close automatically.

It clicked shut, a reassuring sound as she continued on her way to the bank of elevators. The artifacts collected and curated in this lab are historically prized as well as intrinsically valuable, she told herself. Priceless was too parsimonious a word to quantify the value of these artifacts to human culture. It's puzzling there's no security camera monitoring this lab. The artifacts are of far greater value than lab equipment. They're rare but, more importantly, they're irreplaceable. Back assward priorities. She shook her head. I need to mention this oversight to the security administration.

She filed this away for later retrieval. Reaching the elevators, she pressed the down button and her mind wandered to thoughts of Baki. Knowing him, he's likely asleep by this time, she bet, glancing at her watch while the elevator doors closed quietly on her.

* * *

Crouched behind a workbench, Baki expelled his breath in a sigh of relief when he heard the door shut with a resounding click. That was too close for comfort. What the heck is Aysel doing here this late? Must be working on something important, I bet. He reflected upon this for a moment. I'll get Cemil to look into it. Time to flee the coop. He had what he needed to fulfill his part of the contract. If his client demanded more tablets, he could always sneak back.

He peeked over the top of the workbench and faint red light glowed in the window like an evil eye. Good. The coast is clear. Unwelcome questions exploded in the dark corners of his psyche. So Baki Boy, could you have done it? Could you have pulled the trigger if she had caught you in the act? A cold, malevolent wind blew in his head. He squeezed his eyes shut for a few beats to ward off the murderous images that strobed at the edges of his sanity.

He pushed aside his gun with silencer attached and yanked a flashlight out of his knapsack, which also held several of the tablets he had helped Aysel crate just weeks ago at the Van Castle site. Led by the beam of the flashlight, he walked in stealth mode toward the door. When he reached it, he stowed the flashlight and then withdrew from his jacket pocket an electronic device at the end of which was a flat piece of metal in the shape of a credit card and swiped it through the reader. The LED turned green. He opened the door and stuck his head into the murky corridor. Not a soul in sight.

He made his way to the stairwell at the end of a long corridor, descended the stairs two at a time to the main level and left through an emergency exit he had used earlier to gain entrance above which a web-based camera he had hacked into months ago looped phoney video of a closed door.

"The security business sure has its advantages," he said into the dark, a smirk on his face as he strode away into the cool night air.

## Chapter Twenty-Seven
## Istanbul - Monday Evening

Giltmore's Sunday flight had been pleasant and uneventful. While his plane circled high above Istanbul, he noticed from his window seat how green the city appeared, a city of fifteen million people. He recalled a story on the president of Turkey claiming credit for directing the planting of an inconceivable three billion trees in the country over a twelve-year period in government. He made a quick calculation: 250,000,000 trees per year. That's over three times the population of Turkey. He didn't have time to perform an accurate count from his perch in the sky but the sylvan carpet peppered with red-tiled roofs undulating to the distant horizon was all the proof he needed.

He also noticed the absence of swimming pools from the air. As the plane descended, he realized why. Next to no single family homes. Just block after block of condos and apartments. With such a dense population, three-quarters of which lived on the European side of the city, making Istanbul the largest European city, these living arrangements made sense.

His accommodations in Istanbul were the epitome of opulence. He now knew how a portion of his donation dollars to the Institute had been spent when he checked into his hotel room Sunday afternoon, his shoes sinking into the thick pile of plush Turkish carpeting into which was woven an intricate and vibrant floral design. The space was well-appointed with elegant furniture and fine draperies. A four-poster king-sized bed lay against one wall and a highly polished writing table supported by Queen Anne legs abutted another while a buttoned leather wingback armchair stood in a corner. Tall windows bathed the room in natural light and afforded a view of a central courtyard decorated with trees and flowers as well as hosting an open-air dining area. A nice locale for a honeymoon, he thought, as he admired his sumptuous surroundings. You're getting too far ahead of yourself, Ol' Boy.

* * *

Giltmore and his guests invited by the Institute had spent the whole of Monday visiting historic sites and shops mere blocks from their hotel. Evening had since fallen and now they were dining on a rooftop terrace which overlooked the Sea of Marmara and was within sight of the Blue Mosque. Colored lights strung around the multi-level restaurant lent a festive spirit to the setting.

As normally happens in a large group of people, cliques had formed and so people split up among separate tables. A refreshing breeze blew in from the west across the open water, a welcome respite from the oppressive heat of the day, and beneath a star-bright sky ships plied the sea lanes, their bobbing navigation lights a sign of turbulence in the expanse of black water.

Delores, a single, middle-aged woman, her long, auburn hair streaked with silver, remarked in a nasal accent, "It's such a charming view from here. Coming from the landlocked Midwest, I don't have the pleasure of such coastal vistas to enjoy," she sighed.

Seated to her left, Giltmore turned to her and asked, "Where's home?"

"Sioux Falls, South Dakota."

"That explains your accent," Jermaine joined in, who was sitting across the table from her. An ex-Marine officer and still built like one, he had allowed his black woolly hair and beard to grow out, a mute gesture of protest from the former strictures of military discipline. "We're long-distance neighbors, Delores," he grinned, his gums as pink as his teeth were white. "I live in Cedar Rapids, Iowa."

"And I'm from Salisbury, Delaware," Martha chimed in, tortoise-shelled glasses perched high on her prominent nose. She was sitting next to Jermaine.

Detecting a lull in the conversation, Giltmore cleared his throat and dove in. "Now that we're acquainted," he said, "how if you folks share your reasons for coming on this trip." He paused a beat. "Who wants to go first?"

"I came here on a fact-finding mission," Delores began. "I have a degree in cultural anthropology so I want to observe Turkish society up close and personal. To try to discover the *peace* in the religion of peace."

Giltmore didn't fail to detect the sarcasm in her tone.

Jermaine patted his still trim waistline and said, "I heard Turkish cuisine is to die for, so I couldn't resist," provoking a round of laughter. "Seriously, though, I wanted to visit an Islamic country that the U.S hasn't bombed. Pretty hard to do these days."

That raised a chuckle from all but Delores.

"What's that supposed to mean?"

Surprised at Delores' challenging tone, Jermaine said with a tight smile, "Sometimes exaggeration is used to emphasis a point of fact."

"The U.S. has a right to protect itself from terrorists. We kill them overseas so they can't kill us back home."

Jermaine was about to retort, but Giltmore interjected with, "And what's your reason for coming here?" He directed his question at Martha.

"Like a majority of Americans, I had never left the country," she confessed. "I researched Turkey on the Internet and concluded fifty million annual tourists know something about this country I don't. So here I am."

"Thank you for sharing your motives," Giltmore said. "Did all of you watch *Midnight Express* as requested by the Institute?"

They answered in the affirmative and waited for him to pick up where he had left off.

"What impression did this movie leave you with?" He turned to Martha, who sat shyly in her chair. "Would you like to go first?"

She sat up straighter. "Honestly, the film gave me second thoughts about coming here."

"Why was that?" Giltmore asked.

"Because the Turks behaved like wild beasts in the movie. They enjoyed inflicting pain on people," she said, puckering her brow.

"Jermaine, you're eager to speak," Giltmore noticed. "Give us your impression."

"Right-o," and he nodded his thanks to him. "The movie portrayed the main character as a hard-luck American hero. He was smuggling drugs for Chrissake. That loser deserved a good beating in my books," he said, smacking a cantaloupe-sized fist into his other hand.

"And your impression of the Turks?" Giltmore asked.

Jermaine reflected a moment. "They didn't seem to possess any humanity. They were cruel to the point of sadistic."

Without prompting from Giltmore, Delores said, "I was enraged with the harsh verdict rendered by the corrupt judicial system and by the random punishment dished out by the prison guards," she huffed. "The drug dealer didn't receive a fair trial."

Jermaine said, "In Singapore, he would've been hanged so he should count his lucky stars he was arrested in Turkey."

"So you believe the lesser punishment was just?"

"Delores, the guy was caught red-handed with a large stash of hashish taped to his body. And his story also led to discrimination against Turkish Americans. Unbelievable."

"Didn't the screenwriter for *Midnight Express* admit to have taken certain liberties with the script?" Martha asked.

"He did," Giltmore answered. "Back in 2004 he made a trip here to apologize to the Turkish Minister of Culture for how the movie painted an appalling portrait of Turks and Turkish society." He added, "Only in our country could you create a sympathetic victim out of a convicted drug smuggler while making soulless villains out of his jailers," he said, his tone full of disdain. "The Turks couldn't win for losing."

"Sad, very sad," Martha said almost to herself.

"It comes as no surprise your impressions of Turks were negative," Giltmore said. "The movie was a wholesale indictment of Turkish society.

He shifted his body before continuing.

"I put it to you the Turkish way of life is not so different from ours. Turkey has differences no doubt owing to the fact it's an Islamic country, but are Turkish values alien to ours? Is the rule of law upheld here?" He looked around at his guests. "Didn't the Turkish people defend democracy with their lives during the attempted coup several years ago? You've been in this country only a couple of days and I know this isn't a long time, but what are your impressions of Turks?"

They all tried to speak at once.

"Delores, why don't you go first," Giltmore suggested.

"I hate to say this but Turkish shop owners are aggressive. They won't leave you alone."

"I think the shopping experience is unique. The shopkeeper I visited served me apple tea while we bargained over the price of pottery," Martha said with gaiety. "That was a hit with me."

"Definitely not the down-home experience," Jermaine said. He stroked his beard. "I noticed people line up for the tram here. It's not a free-for-all like many other countries I've visited. There's no pushing or shoving."

"So I'm sure you're aware now how this scandalous movie deliberately shaped your perceptions of Turks," Giltmore said to them.

Heads nodded in agreement.

"Several friends of mine uttered jokes about Turks and sodomy when I mentioned to them I was planning a trip to Istanbul," Jermaine piped up.

Murmurs of disapproval erupted around the table.

"More than a few of these friends have advanced degrees," he scoffed. "I guess it's because they know more and more about less and less."

"It's fair to say you believed the biased and unfavorable portrayal of Turks in this film because it reflected your innate perceptions long nourished by a steady diet of misinformation propagated by Orientalists in Western academia and media," Giltmore argued. "This movie has warped our attitudes toward Turkey for generations just as the movie *Lawrence of Arabia* did for an earlier generation," he said in an amiable tone, taking some of the sting out of his provocative words.

Martha raised her hand. "What's an Orientalist, Mike?"

"A Western scholar who studies Easterners employing a fixed set of racist stereotypes covered by a thin veneer of academic jargon that gives it an intellectual gloss. Col—

"A fancy word for white supremacism."

Giltmore acknowledged her comment with a smile before continuing. "These stereotypes are labelled *Orientalism,*" he explained. "It's no coincidence *Midnight Express* exhibits the cinematic devices of Orientalism."

"I don't see it," Delores said, unconvinced by his argument.

"Orientalism is the racist lens through which Western academics view Easterners. It is a set of reductive propositions and intellectual tropes which stereotype the eastern *other* as backward, exotic, lustful, misogynistic, uncivilized, given to capricious violence and incapable of developing democratic values," Giltmore said.

"Have you observed any evidence supporting the constructs of Orientalism in your travels thus far?" he asked, glancing around the table to verify he had their attention. "Does the Turks' behavior mirror these stereotypes?"

"Not here in Turkey but look what's going on in Libya, Iraq and Syria. Muslims killing Muslims," Delores said.

"Those countries only experienced those extreme levels of violence after they were illegally invaded by our armed forces, which destroyed their civil institutions and infrastructure and which flooded those countries with weapons," Jermaine said.

"Delores," Martha cut in, "We're discussing Turkey, not the entire Islamic world. Muslims aren't killing each other in Malaysia and Indonesia nor are they killing each other in this country. I wonder *why*?"

"The fact that the Turkish people stood up to treasonous army units during the aborted coup speaks to their love of Islamic-based democracy," Jermaine said, folding his hands on the table.

"The shopkeeper asked about my family and their health. The question took me by surprise," Martha said.

"Maybe you should shop in South Dakota," Delores said. "I receive friendly service there."

Martha ignored her. Giltmore leaned forward in his chair. "Here's the thing. Orientalism is the lens through which the West views the East, particularly Muslims," he said definitely. "The purpose of Orientalism, as with all forms of propaganda, is to create an intellectual reflex that automatically dismisses conflicting information. Orientalism tells you who you should hate, why you should hate them and how to deal with this hatred. It muzzles your critical faculties because it defines your reality for you," he pointed out.

"Our media and universities have started portraying Islam and American Muslims in a more positive light," Jermaine said. "But it still has a *long* way to go before you can say the public treatment of Muslims is fair and balanced."

"Agreed," Giltmore said. "The thing with Orientalism, or any other *ism*, is it constricts one's mind rather than expands it. We don't call ideologues *narrow-minded* for no good reason. Orientalism is a form of mental automatism for the lazy and the wilfully ignorant. The logical fallacy 'all Muslims aren't terrorists but most terrorists are Muslims' is a prime example. Case in point, between 2005 and 2015 only 94 Americans were killed by self-proclaimed Muslims but over three hundred thousand Americans were murdered with handguns in this same time period."

"People want to believe the worst about Muslims," Martha said.

"What can we expect from our media who whip up the flames of hatred against Muslims and Islam?" Giltmore said. "Islamic countries have no monopoly on violence. We only need to review the last seventy years of Western history to prove this assertion. The Holocaust, the atomic incineration of Hiroshima and Nagasaki, the Algerian genocide, the Vietnamese and pre-Khmer Rouge Cambodian genocides, the Bosnian genocide, the Iraqi genocide and the ongoing Palestinian genocide," he listed. "The West has no claim to the moral high ground. They should remove the forest of trees from their own eyes before they complain about the specks of sawdust in their neighbors' eyes."

"But we don't use children as soldiers," Delores shot out.

"When a besieged people are desperate, they will resort to desperate measures. Jewish children fought the Nazis to the death in the Warsaw ghetto during World War Two. Do you have a problem with that?" Jermaine said.

He and Delores glared at one another. A ship's horn lowed forlornly in the night.

Jermaine broke eye contact with Delores and spoke up. "There's substance to what you say, Mike. Some American media outlets have been commandeered by demagogues and fear mongers. They excuse and validate the violence of our government's foreign policy and they inoculate us from the truth of our government's war crimes. I've experienced it firsthand."

"Our government never acts, it reacts. It doesn't sow dissension and discord, it promotes peace and security. Yeah, and Saddam was hiding weapons of mass destruction under his bed," Martha said.

They chuckled.

"So that's why we couldn't find them," Jermaine carried on, smacking his forehead. "Who would have thought?"

Their laughter intensified.

"They didn't check under the bed because they were afraid of the Muslim bogeyman," Martha deadpanned.

They convulsed with laughter while Delores sat stone-faced.

Settling down, Giltmore said, "The problem is too many of us passively consume news that anchors our personal opinions and ridicules opposing views. We don't challenge it. Once we've found a comfortable stance that confirms our biases, we park our brains there and rarely do we shift from it. Habit is a powerful inhibitor of change." He cautioned them. "Too many of us are incurious. We don't investigate and analyze political discourse. We just accept the party line. This is why America is sinking into despotism and dragging the world down with it."

"I somewhat understand what you're driving at, Mike," Jermaine allowed. "I served two tours in Iraq, but what I experienced there was nothing like what was portrayed in the *American Sniper* film."

Giltmore, surprised enough to let it show, said, "Please enlighten us, Jermaine."

"I mean, the Iraqi people are nothing like the cardboard savages depicted in this movie," he said. "We need to be frank. Our country illegally invaded Iraq so we shouldn't bemoan the absence of Iraqis singing *Kumbaya* in the streets."

"What are you talking about?" Delores said. "Iraq was responsible for 9/11."

Jermaine exploded. "Have you been living under a frigging rock? No one with a brain in their heads believes in that myth anymore. Saddam Hussein had nothing to do with 9/11. The 9/11 Commission Report proved it. That frat-boy president sold us a whopper and we fell for it because we allowed our unthinking patriotism to crowd out our reason. Sounds like you're still falling for it. Maybe you'll hit bottom one day and wake up."

Heads turned toward their table.

Delores threw down her napkin as though she were throwing down a gauntlet and shot to her feet. "I've had enough of you terrorist sympathizers," and stalked off.

"What planet is that woman living on?" Jermaine wondered out loud.

Giltmore held up his hand. "Let's not backbite. God says in the Quran that backbiting is like eating the flesh of your dead brother. May God guide her to the truth."

"Generous words," Martha said.

"So where were we?"

"We were talking about the *American Sniper* film," Jermaine reminded Giltmore.

"Yes, well, I don't think *American Sniper*, despite its box office success, will have the same impact as *Midnight Express* did," Giltmore wagered. "This film holds up a mirror to our venomous Arabophobia. It doesn't break any new ground. It just feeds into the dominant Islamophobic narrative so deeply embedded in Western consciousness. Unintentionally, the movie gave voice to the unspoken homicidal id of American culture."

"I watched the movie with a new pair of eyes. It incensed me how the movie made a sympathetic hero of the sniper and monsters of his victims. A brilliant propaganda coup. I enjoyed positive interactions with Iraqis when I served in Iraq. They are no different than us."

"*American Sniper* is the Pentagon's dream picture," Giltmore said. "The Department of Defense's Entertainment Media Office backs Hollywood productions that portray U.S. foreign policy in a positive light because these films can then be used to recruit missile fodder for our next military adventure."

Jermaine said, "You're right, Mike. Enrolment in the U.S. Navy has skyrocketed since the release of the *Top Gun* sequel."

"The sad reality is we need killing machines like the sniper," Martha said.

Changing subjects, Giltmore said, "By now you should realize how Hollywood employs these Orientalist propositions and tropes to justify our intervention in Islamic countries under the guise of promoting freedom and democracy," he said. "Muslims should be wary of our politicians bearing gifts of *democracy*."

Snickering broke out around the table.

"Both these movies reveal more about the mentalities and agendas of their producers than they do about the foreigners portrayed in them. The producers must think we're a bunch of ignorant dupes," Jermaine said. "Some of us are, but not all of us."

Martha weighed in. "The problem is, Mike, some people don't want to know the truth because they can't stomach it. They're in deep denial. They believe in the Hollywood-contrived hologram because it usually depicts us as the good guys. This is a consequence of their skewed sense of patriotism."

"With the rise of a self-confident and resurgent Turkey whose leader is challenging European and American dominance on the world stage, the racist agenda of Orientalism is failing," Giltmore said. "When President Ordekan embarrassed our former president into commenting on the assassination of three American Muslim students in North Carolina, we can say the tide of Orientalism is waning."

Martha said, "It was shameful it took that president three whole days to acknowledge that hateful crime."

"Because Muslim lives don't matter," Jermaine pointed out.

Giltmore affirmed his remark with a nod. "Notwithstanding Orientalist propaganda, we can agree Turkey is the model of a successful Islamic society. This is because it's the sole Islamic country never colonized by the West," he informed his small audience.

"Is that right?" Jermaine said. "You may have a point there, Mike."

Giltmore indulged him with a smile. "The Turks developed their own civil and governmental institutions with minimal interference from the West. They didn't have a puppet *democracy* imposed on them at the point of a gun by the West. It developed organically, from the bottom up, as well it should."

Before anyone could comment, the waiter came, took their orders and left.

"From what I've seen, Turkey represents what can be achieved without our government's meddling," Martha said.

"I use to wonder when our government would interfere in Turkish affairs," Jermaine said. "I got my answer with the failed military coup."

"Why would you say that?" Martha asked.

"Because a successful and peaceful Islamic country is a threat to U.S. interests," he replied. "Turkey is the opposite of a failed Islamic state. It is democratic and militarily powerful, but most importantly, it's Islamic."

"I see your point," Martha said. "Turkey's a showcase nation other Muslim countries could emulate. Turkey undermines the perception that all Muslim countries are ruled by corrupt dictators."

"You folks are on the right track," Giltmore encouraged, unable to hide his delight with what he was hearing. Shifting course, he submitted, "I sense our conversation caused you a measure of discomfort at the outset." He gave his dining companions a serious look. "This was intentional. But I wager you've been re-educated."

A ripple of soft laughter broke the silence. Giltmore's discourse had given his dinner mates many uncomfortable truths to digest.

Her laughter ended, Martha said. "To be fair, our country's exceptionalism isn't unique in history. The ruling class of every empire, whether it be British, French or Japanese, believed in the rightness of its mission to oppress peoples it considered inferior."

Her table mates nodded in agreement.

"The Turks have a saying: Wolves prefer foggy weather," Giltmore said to them. "The wolves in Washington befog our minds with half-truths and outright lies. We're fortunate to have cast off our mental blinders so we can recognize the fog of propaganda that clouds our vision. But now we need to help others escape their mental prisons constructed of ideology, racism and wilful ignorance."

"Ignorance is its own best friend. It seems natural for a people to claim they're superior to another people. But this mindset presents a real danger when it infects our foreign policy," Jermaine weighed in.

"Here's the crux of the problem. Our stupidity hasn't increased. It's the quality of education that has diminished. Reality has been dumbed down to the lowest common denominators: imagery and emotion. It's only independent news sites that stand up to Authority whether it emanates from the left or the right," Giltmore griped.

"Authority deserves a can of wumpass," Martha added.

Giltmore and Jermaine collapsed in laughter.

"Martha's on the right track," Giltmore said. "The backlash against independent news sites has begun. Corporate media recognize they no longer possess a monopoly on the 'truth,' so they've taken to calling independent news entities purveyors of *fake news*."

"Mike, it seems we've solved the world's problems," Martha said.

"It's been an eye-opening experience so far. I'm glad I came on this trip," Jermaine said.

"Ditto for me," agreed Martha.

They talked on, sharing personal stories. Giltmore leaned back in his chair, enjoying the ensuing conversation. They get it, he beamed, pleased that his dinner companions grasped the power of propaganda to sway and corral popular opinion. An ugly ideology can only spread when the voice of reason remains silent. Maybe, just maybe, the hype and hysteria fanning the flames of Islamophobia can be extinguished with a deluge of cold, hard facts. He could only hope so.

"So, Mike, why did you convert to Islam?" Martha threw out. "Islam is such a prescriptive and restrictive religion."

Giltmore paused a moment to gather his thoughts. "Do you have children, Martha?"

"Yes, I have three adult children who are living successful, happy lives as far as I know." Her eyes twinkled when she said it.

"Did you teach your children what behaviors were acceptable and unacceptable?"

"Of course."

"And when they misbehaved, what did you do to them?"

"I didn't believe in spanking, so I sent them to their rooms and gave them extra chores to do."

Giltmore continued with his Socratic enquiry. "So you taught your children right from wrong?"

"Most definitely."

"Did you teach your children how they should address you?"

"What do you mean?"

"Well, were they allowed to call you names or swear at you?"

"Certainly not."

"Why did you do this for your children?"

"I don't understand the question."

"Did you raise your children to be respectful towards you and others out of love or to prove you were the boss?"

"I never really thought about it. I just did it…I'd have to say I did it out of love. I didn't want my children to grow up to be monsters."

"As a parent you had obligations to your children. You brought them into this world, so you were obliged to feed them and clothe and educate them, right?"

"Yes."

"And you taught them to be grateful to you for feeding, clothing and educating them, right?"

"Yes."

"So how would you feel if your children started to praise and thank your next-door neighbor instead of you for all the things you provided them?"

Without thinking, Martha replied, “I wouldn’t be happy and I would remind them that it was *me* who provided these things.”

“Do you believe God created human beings?”

“I do.”

“Do you believe God is a loving God?”

“I do.”

“So just as you taught your children right from wrong out of love, wouldn’t it be peculiar if a loving God left his human creatures to stumble around in the dark from pillar to post, wreaking havoc on themselves and on each other?”

She thought for a moment. “I see where you’re going with this.”

“God gives us life, He provides for our needs and in return all He expects from us is that we praise and thank Him and only Him and not an idol, an image or a human being in His stead. Agreed?

“Yes.”

“So if we thank someone or something other than God, He has a right to be angry with us, doesn’t He?”

“He does.”

Giltmore smiled. “Islam instructs the human being how to address and worship God in a manner prescribed by Him and Islam instructs the human being how they should deal with themselves and with every other creature on Earth, human or otherwise, in every facet of life. Is this Divine Guidance the action of a loving and caring God?”

Martha’s eyes watered. “It sure is.”

“God gives us a choice. Follow His commands to avoid falling into grave trouble or ignore them at our peril. It’s really that simple, Martha. I choose to obey the teachings revealed by God in the Quran and to follow the way of Prophet Mohammed, peace be upon him, because taken together they are comprehensive in every sense of the word. Prophet Mohammed was a husband, a father, a cousin, a companion, a brother-in-law, a businessman, a spiritual leader, a general, a negotiator, a judge, a healer and a head of state. So if we want to know how to act in any of those roles and more, we should look to Prophet Mohammed’s life. And the Prophet’s wives, peace be upon him and them, are role models for women.”

"I read somewhere Mohammed was a pedophile," Jermaine said.

Giltmore jolted and his face flushed scarlet. He took a sip of water to cool his nerves. "Child brides were once acceptable in the West because of low life expectancy. Child bride marriages only became taboo when Westerners began living longer due to better medical care. The urgent need for procreating at puberty lessened as life expectancies increased. In the Semitic culture of the seventh century, when a female child reached puberty, she became a woman and therefore could marry. That said, if Prophet Mohammed's marriage to a young bride raised a moral issue in his times, his enemies would have pounced on it, wouldn't you agree?"

"I suppose."

"In the Quran God mentions the derogatory names used against Prophet Mohammed by his enemies. They called him a forger, a poet, a magician, a madman and a soothsayer, but they never ever called him a pedophile. And if you were to search the historical records of that era, you won't find any such accusation."

"I think I've just been schooled," Jermaine said.

"This type of accusation is the lowest of cheap shots propagated by know-nothing Islamophobes who, unable to defeat the Prophet's message, slander his reputation instead." Giltmore clasped his hands on the table. "The Prophet's marriage to Aisha is only a problem for people of this era. It's best to explore both sides of an argument before coming to a conclusion about it."

"It's easier to pass on a lie than it is to investigate its source. Thanks, Mike. You'd make a good preacher," Jermaine said.

"I'm still a work in progress and not worthy of preaching to people."

"Aren't we all," he agreed. "Aren't we all."

He waved off Jermaine's gratitude with a flap of his hand.

"Look. Here comes our food," Martha said.

Jermaine rubbed his stomach. "Enough talking. Let's eat."

## Chapter Twenty-Eight
## Istanbul - Tuesday Morning

Despite the late hours Aysel had kept last night, she was in her office at her usual time this morning. The anticipation of what the day had in store had deprived her of deep sleep, and her foot had lain heavier on the gas pedal when she raced her car along the flower bedecked boulevards on route to the university campus.

She checked her emails before going to the lab. Nothing urgent. Relieved, she entered the lab, greeted her colleagues already immersed in their own work and made a beeline to the furnace. She noticed her note was still taped to the door. The timer on the furnace had expired so the vellum and collagen samples should've combusted. Using a pair of forceps, she withdrew the small quartz tubes from the furnace. As expected, the substances had converted to carbon dioxide and water overnight.

One by one, Aysel hooked up the tubes to a device that separated the $CO_2$ from the water and released the gas into a series of glass pipes which then transported it to individual bottles at the other end of the line. Once a bottle filled with gas, the apparatus automatically sealed it. She labelled each bottle she disengaged from the machine.

The next step was to manufacture graphite for each bottled sample of $CO_2$. This involved mixing the captured gas with liquid hydrogen inside a graphite reaction vessel that contained powdered iron. Aysel hooked up each bottle of captured $CO_2$ to a vacuum line which drew the gas into the vessel. When the mixing was completed, she withdrew a quartz tube containing a mixture of $CO_2$, hydrogen and iron from the reaction vessel. She then connected the tube to a device which heated the mixture to a high temperature.

After the combusting was finished, she disconnected the tube from the heating device. The iron, which had acted as a catalyst during the combusting of the gas and hydrogen, held particles of pure graphite. She worked in silence, repeating this procedure for each bottle of captured $CO_2$. Her colleagues, too preoccupied with their own work, were unaware of the fateful toil occurring under their noses.

Once Aysel had produced all the graphite possible, she cut open each tube and deposited the graphite specks into cone-shaped containers which she had labelled earlier. When done, she marched the containers over to the accelerator lab where, with reluctance, she handed what she considered were her babies now to Cemil, a youngish, bespectacled, tousle-haired technician popular with a few of the younger women in the department. Only authorized personnel were permitted in the accelerator lab, so only he could complete the radiocarbon-dating process for her. With nothing left to do, she returned to her office to await the results, and her heart pulsed with nervous excitement.

## Chapter Twenty-Nine
## Istanbul - Tuesday Afternoon

Cemil mounted Aysel's graphite samples along with blank samples in the accelerator mass spectrometer. The latter were controls for cross-comparison. He activated the accelerator and sat back and listened to the hum of the high-tech machinery do its job of blasting the carbon particles with ions (positively- or negatively-charged atoms), which were then fired through the particle accelerator and separated into their constituent components of ionized $^{12}C$, $^{13}C$ and $^{14}C$ using magnets. Once separated, the machine calculated the number of individual ionized carbon isotopes.

When the work was done, he dialed Aysel.

"That didn't take long. So what have you got for me?" she said with breathless anticipation.

"Before I give you the results, what were the original samples composed of?"

"The Sample A specimens were calf vellum and the Sample B specimens were human bone." Her curiosity piqued, she said, "Why do you ask?"

"I've been performing mass spectrometry analysis for over a decade now and I've never seen results like these."

"Results like…"

"There's something peculiar, almost supernatural, about the Sample A you sent me," he said with a tone of wonder. "Let me explain. As you know, no graphite sample is chemically flawless. There's typically isotopic fractionation between $^{12}C$ and $^{14}C$." He was referring to the phenomenon of isotopes from a carbon element having different isotopic ratios due to minor differences in the atomic mass of each isotope.

Anticipating Cemil's next statement, Aysel blurted out, "There's no isotopic fractionation in the sample is there?"

"How did you guess?"

"Woman's intuition."

"What was the parchment sample taken from?

"I'm not at liberty to say. But I *can* say we're witnesses to a miracle. It makes sense when you consider the source of the parchment."

"Well, I'm glad it makes sense to you because it makes no sense to this dude," he confessed. "You're not even going to give me a hint?"

She dropped her voice in a conspiratorial tone. "Sorry, Cemil. It's top secret," she said. "If I tell you, I must kill you."

Baki won't be happy. Can't say I didn't try, he thought in frustration. "Since you put it that way…"

"Do you believe in a higher power?"

"I believe in what I can see."

"So you're a materialist?"

"My beliefs are personal."

"Uh, sure, Cemil."

"Well, it's been real, Aysel."

"Science can't explain every phenomenon."

"Perhaps. Anyway, I'll email you the full report."

"Could you send it right away?"

"…I suppose I could."

"Can't thank you enough, Cemil. You've been a big help."

"Yeah." You might not be so grateful if you knew how much I'd like to help myself to you.

* * *

Aysel waited a few minutes before checking her email. Unable to wait any longer, she clicked the Send/Receive icon and Cemil's email popped into her Inbox. She browsed through the reports until she found what she was searching for. So the beloved disciple died about 63 CE. He outlived Jesus by three decades—give or take a few years. The last human link to Jesus. She reclined in her chair and briefly savored the moment. Time to make history. She picked up the phone.

## Chapter Thirty
## Istanbul - Tuesday Afternoon

Staring out his office window with a haunted look, "Likewise, my dear," Father Marco said, his mouth gone dry as dust. With a shaky hand, he hung up, his expression mirroring the silent commotion of his mind.

The scroll is authentic!

Aysel's galvanizing words ricocheted in his skull. He massaged his temples to relieve the anxiety churning inside him. She might as well have shouted "Two thousand years of Christianity have ended."

Alarm stabbed at him. How suddenly and irrevocably his life had transformed with a simple phone call. He thought he had prepared himself for this not-so-unexpected news, but one is never really prepared when confronted with reality. The fate of the Church—maybe even humanity—was at stake! His alarm transmuted to panic, and he felt his chest tighten. O Lord, please give me strength.

Father Marco prayed until the wave of anxiety subsided, leaving in its wake a vacillating soul, tortured by conflicting ideas, uncertain which path to choose. I could make this go away. The only other person privy to my discovery is Aysel. He clenched and unclenched his hands on the desk. Is the past worth clinging to? He mulled it over. He couldn't in good conscious keep this information secret. People needed to decide for themselves…Sometimes folks have to abandon the thing they hold most dear for the sake of truth.

He wrestled with his conscience, tossing ideas left and right, weighing the practicalities of each. Then, unbidden, a maxim his mother had taught him at a young age leapt to the fore: When you're on the verge of committing a wrong, don't look around, look up. He submitted to his mother's wisdom and glanced heavenwards. *You*, my Lord, know.

Only days ago, he had made a life-changing discovery on letting go of his fears and putting his trust in his Creator. What was he supposed to do?

This state of affairs has gone way beyond my personal concerns, he scolded himself. What about all those misguided souls who are sleepwalking to a destination in Hell? Don't they deserve to hear the truth? I can't have them on my conscience, he resolved, nodding to himself. What they do with the truth is their business. I can convey the truth to people but I can't make them believe.

He reclined in his chair and let his mind range. Another perspective sprang into view. How short-sighted of me. He shot forward. The scroll can bring peace to the Holy Land. It puts to bed the theological differences between Christianity and Islam over the issue of the Trinity. And the Jews are off the hook for the Crucifixion. Fundamentalist Christians can no longer blame them for crucifying Jesus!

Mind-boggling.

Father Marco identified what he had to do next. Providence had set him on this path for a reason. There was no turning back. He could only go forward and fulfill his destiny. But he couldn't manage this affair alone. He was a nobody.

But the Church wasn't. Only the Church possessed the resources to announce this Divine gift to humanity and could explain its potential for promoting peace between Muslims, Jews and Christians, he concluded.

The moment of decision was upon him. He could postpone his duty to humanity no longer. I must contact Rome. But whom? He puzzled over this question. A name from his past popped into his mind, a broad smile spread on his face. Vitto. Of course! They had been fast friends in seminary college where they shared the same sense of skepticism about the doctrines of Catholicism. But Vitto had been more ambitious and, thus, had risen high in the Church hierarchy despite his weak conviction.

This will destroy the only life I have known, but I can't live a lie. Having resolved his moral dilemma, he picked up the phone with a steady hand, aware his destiny and the destinies of millions, possibly billions, of his fellow humans were about to be upended. To what degree? His guess was as good as another. He tapped his foot while he waited for the call to go through.

"The Congregation for the Doctrine of the Faith. How may I direct your call?"

"I wish to speak with His Eminence Cardinal Petrelli," Father Marco said.

"Whom shall I say is calling?" the priest secretary asked.

He gave his name and added, "I'm the parish priest for the Santi Giuseppe Church in Istanbul."

"His Eminence is out of the office. May I take a message?"

"The future of the Catholic Church is at stake." He surprised himself how the words escaped his mouth without any forethought. This should get his attention.

"Not another sex scandal."

"Worse."

A pause came down the line.

"What could possibly be worse?"

"My report is for His Eminence's ears only."

"I *see*," he said when he did not see at all. He loathed the least whiff of exclusion from the affairs of his cardinal.

"His Eminence needs to contact me as soon as possible," Father Marco insisted.

"I will pass your message to him," he replied with barely concealed annoyance. He didn't appreciate being a mere messenger.

"Thank you. Our Lady's blessings upon you." He didn't know the secretary's name.

"And upon you."

Father Marco leaned back in the chair, kneading the knobby knuckles of his hands, staring a thousand yard stare, as his mind struggled to come to terms with this newfound reality.

## Chapter Thirty-One
## The Vatican - Tuesday Afternoon

His Eminence, Cardinal Vittorio Petrelli, stormed along the shiny wide corridor in the Palace of the Holy Office, home to the *Congregation for the Doctrine of the Faith*, his footsteps pounding on the marble, his scarlet moiré soutane billowing like a bonfire and his scowling mien telegraphing the fury that raged within.

Gifts and qualities to offer Christians, he harrumphed, the Pope's conciliatory words toward sodomites and sapphites ringing in his ears. As if the Church doesn't suffer enough the scandals of pedophiles and homosexuals already staffing its ranks, the cardinal mused through gritted teeth. Why is His Holiness revisiting this issue? The last Synod tabled its decision on human sexuality. But His Holiness persists in deepening the moral rot that has seeped into the foundation of Catholic doctrine.

Like all heads of dicasteries, he served at the pleasure of the Pontiff and so he exercised polite discretion when in disagreement with him. He had refrained from expressing his vitriol out loud but he had communicated his displeasure with the Holy Father's strategy with as much tact as he could muster. Cardinal Petrelli had survived numerous doctrinal dustups in the Roman Curia, the central governing body of the Catholic Church, by engaging in duplicitous diplomacy and navigating shifting alliances. A consummate insider, he was the repository for countless secrets for he knew where the skeletons were buried.

His Holiness must be desperate to fill empty pews if he is seeking to invite homosexuals into the Catholic family. If the Church hadn't lost its way in the moral quagmire of modernism, all would be well, he reasoned. Ultra-conservative, Cardinal Petrelli had been reappointed by the new Pope. His was an inspired decision designed to mollify the concerns of conservative bishops who took issue with his liberal outlook. This was one view. Another view held the Pontiff liked to keep his friends close but his enemies closer. Regardless of which view was correct, the cardinal was an operative who knew how to ingratiate himself with his colleagues and, more importantly, with his superior, the Holy Father.

Whispers circulated about Cardinal Petrelli becoming the next pope. His many allies viewed him as a bulwark against the rising tide of liberalism lapping at the doors of the Church which threatened to erode centuries of Catholic teachings. The cardinal encouraged this whispering campaign, but he was careful to leave no traces of his involvement so he could claim plausible deniability. Overtly seeking power was the quickest route to exile in the Roman Curia.

As though leading a royal procession of one, he swept by his secretary, Father Angelo Cajoli, stationed in an anteroom, into his sumptuous office decorated with antique furniture, hand-woven Persian carpets and silk wallpaper. A life-size painting of the Annunciation dominated the wall opposite his baroque desk. His workplace silently but ostentatiously reflected the unquestioned privileges of his sinecure. As Cardinal Prefect of the *Congregation for the Doctrine of the Faith*, he was the second most powerful man in the Roman Curia and was not afraid to wield his power when circumstances dictated.

Cajoli darted out from behind his desk. "Your Eminence, can I get you something?" he asked in a servile tone.

"You are inestimable in your abilities, Angelo," he said, paying his secretary a rare compliment. "But can you conjure up a new pope for me?" he asked, glancing at the papers arranged in a neat row on his desk in order of importance, his jowls merging with the fleshy wattle beneath his chin.

Father Angelo took the compliment at face value, for his features didn't register any change. He had been at the cardinal's side since his election to the College of Cardinals over twelve years ago. They had both studied at the *Collegio Romano*, or the Roman College, as had five popes. He was the sole person Cardinal Petrelli trusted in the Roman Curia. And he could trust Father Angelo because the cardinal possessed several edifying photographs of his subordinate's proclivity for engaging in forbidden sex acts with fellow priests.

"Was the conference with His Holiness not to your liking, Your Eminence?" He twitched before the cardinal's desk.

"Your hunch is precise, Angelo." Cardinal Petrelli said.

"What has so upset you, Your Eminence?"

"Later this week the Pope will once again call for further inclusion of homosexuals in the Catholic family. How his intention will be implemented—if ever—will be discussed in the coming Synod." Cardinal Petrelli held his secretary's eyes in a level gaze. "Perhaps, Angelo, you could advise His Holiness in this matter since you, ah, have more experience in these matters than I do," he goaded him.

Cajoli blanched and twitched in discomfort. "I—I'm certain Your Eminence is quite able to manage this issue in your own way."

"I knew you would see it my way," he lorded over him. "Make sure my *allies* do, too. If any of them balk, remind them where the bones are buried. *Capisce*?" he said, a wolfish grin on his plump lips.

"Thy will be done, Your Eminence."

"Is there any urgent matter that requires my attention before I dine?" he asked with an attitude that implied: Better not be.

He seemed to debate with himself. "There is," and he cringed before the cardinal's glowering demeanor. "A priest from the parish of Santi Giuseppe Church in Istanbul called earlier with a disturbing message."

"Out with it," Cardinal Petrelli commanded as his hunger increased and his patience diminished by the minute.

Father Angelo flinched, he spoke in a rush. "The priest said he had information that would"—he paused, endeavoring to remember his caller's words—"affect the future of the Mother Church," he recalled, the words tumbling out.

"What could possibly threaten our future?" He answered his own question. "Not another book by that heretic American professor?" he said with a grunt.

His secretary remained impassive. "He didn't divulge the reason, Your Eminence. He said his message was for your ears only."

"What is the name of this priest?"

"Father Marco Arrigoni."

Cardinal Petrelli blinked and then his face broke out in a rare grin. Images of himself and Marco sneaking out the seminary late at night to paint the town red screened in his mind. His secretary coughed, blanking his mind. "What time is it in Istanbul?"

Father Angelo broke eye contact to think. "Istanbul is two hours ahead of Rome."

"He can wait and so can the future of the Church," the cardinal said, exercising his unspoken assumption of authority.

"As you wish, Your Eminence," Father Angelo oozed.

Cardinal Petrelli patted his ample stomach. "Appetites must be satisfied, shouldn't they, Angelo?" he said, restrained menace in his tone. "Perhaps some more discreetly than others," he ended with a knowing wink.

Father Angelo reddened in response to the subtle threat. "Yes, Your Eminence," he replied smoothly, bowing his head in obeisance, as his sybaritic cynosure rushed by in his finery.

## Chapter Thirty-Two
## Vatican - Tuesday Late Afternoon

Cardinal Petrelli and Father Marco spent several minutes on the line catching up and laughing about their youthful escapades. Then there was a lull and it was time to get to the matter at hand.

"So my old friend, what makes you think the Church is in danger?"

Father Marco brought his superior up to date with his chance discovery.

Aghast, Cardinal Petrelli pressed the instrument against his ear and squirmed in his chair, unsure if he had heard Father Marco correctly. "Scribe of Jesus? Beloved disciple?" he exhaled, unable to believe the enormity of what had been communicated.

"That's what I said, Vitto," his caller enthused, ignoring the protocol that required him to address his superior by his proper title.

His Eminence Cardinal Petrelli gripped the phone tighter, his knuckles whitened, and the tightness in his chest made it difficult to breathe. A silence of annihilating dread conducted through the air.

"Is something wrong, Vitto?"

"No, no. This is startling but happy news," the cardinal said, stifling his alarm.

"I have scientific proof of the scroll's authenticity from Koç University located here in Istanbul," Marco said, forgetting his promise to Aysel.

"And how did you secure this proof?"

"Before I go any further, Vitto, you have to promise me what I'm about to tell you can never be divulged because it will jeopardize my friend's career.

"I swear by Our Lady I shall never say a word of this to anyone." You can be sure of this.

"A few years ago I befriended a professor of archeology at Koç University whom I met while assisting on several archeological digs during my summer vacations."

"Does this archeologist have a name?"

"Aysel Bigili."

"A female?" he said salaciously, and he flicked his tongue like a serpent.

"God as my witness, my relationship with Professor Bigili is professional and platonic," he said without guilt. "Moreover, she is in love with another man."

"You say that with a tone of regret."

"Is it that obvious, Vitto?"

He could hide the depth of his feelings for Aysel from himself but not from Cardinal Petrelli's shrewd powers of perception.

"No need to worry," the cardinal replied. "We may wear the cloth but we're men after all—most of us, anyway."

They shared a laugh.

"Where is the scroll now, Marco?"

"I have it," he said. "Aysel dropped it off earlier along with a radiocarbon-dating report."

"Can your, ah, archeologist friend keep a secret?"

"I compelled her to swear on the Bible to say nothing until the scroll is made public."

"Brilliant idea. You appealed to her Christian conscience," he congratulated his subordinate. Then he asked, "What does this scroll state that is so threatening to the Church?"

"I only read the first few paragraphs. I plan to read the rest later," he added. "But the little I read confirms the Islamic conception of God and of Jesus," he continued. "The scroll reveals Jesus wasn't crucified nor resurrected and it makes clear Jesus was only a human being and not the son of God. It also describes the oneness of God as absolute and indivisible. We can only conclude from these statements that the Crucifixion, the Resurrection, vicarious atonement and the Trinity are false doctrine."

The temperature in the cardinal's office seemingly plunged. A chill spread outward from the pit of his stomach. Dizziness overcame him. The room spun, and he fought for self-control as a man would whose world was crashing around him. The cardinal swallowed hard. "Now I understand the urgency of your call." Then he had a disquieting thought. "Are there copies of the report?"

"There might be copies at Koç University here in Istanbul." He asked innocently, "Is this a problem?"

"No, no," he replied. "The least number of people who know about this discovery for now, the better."

"I agree with your assessment. The Church will need time to prepare a proper response to these astonishing developments." Then he blurted out, "Imagine what this could mean for peace in the Holy Land. Jews are exonerated from crucifying Jesus and it corroborates Islamic monotheism. The message in the scroll bridges the theological rifts dividing Muslims, Christians and Jews."

"You think far ahead, Marco," he said. "I hadn't considered these positive ramifications."

"How do you wish to take possession of the scroll and its supporting documents?"

"We use a diplomatic courier in special circumstances such as this," the cardinal explained. "A Father Giovanni will meet you at your apartment tomorrow afternoon at 2:00 P.M. Is this convenient for you?"

"It's fine, Vitto. I'll ask the deacon to manage the affairs of my church while I wait for the courier."

"All is arranged then. Again, your discovery is a monumental blessing for the Church and for the advancement of world peace. May Our Lady bless you and all that jazz," he said with a grin.

"You, too."

Cardinal Petrelli hung up, but he was no longer smiling.

* * *

Father Angelo grunted. So that's what's at stake, he worried, as he gingerly cradled the phone extension. What will His Eminence do now?

## Chapter Thirty-Three
## Istanbul - Tuesday Evening

Murat was lounging in his favorite booth at his favorite underworld club with his favorite Russian girl, Natalya, seated in his lap. Techno-pop blared from hidden speakers. Business was slow, but the night was still young and hot. So was his date. She had to shout in his ear to be heard but he didn't care. For he liked the whisper of her minty breath on his face.

His smartphone vibrated, intruding upon their amorous *tête-à-tête*. He wished he could ignore the vibration he felt next to his chest but someone was probably calling for his services. He retrieved the phone from his inner breast pocket and read a message sent by Red Bird, a wealthy individual whose true identity was unknown. Tonight? he said to himself. "Double my fee and consider it done," he texted back.

"Agreed," came the reply.

"Tally-Babe, I have a job to do," he told her, his voice full of regret.

She pulled a face.

"Don't pout," he warned her. "Remember who pays for your clothing and your rent." He lifted her up and deposited her none too delicately onto the leather banquette.

Motivated to return to his good graces, she smiled coquettishly. "Try not to be late, Murat."

"I'll wake you if I am," he said as he caressed her bare arm and gave her a lecherous wink.

She made to say something but he had already turned and walked away. Another evening left alone. Murat didn't see her mouth settle into a moue as she watched him go.

## Chapter Thirty-Four
## Istanbul - Tuesday Evening

Murat's contact at Turk Telecom came through for him. Everything was for sale when the price was right. He now had the personal information he needed to locate his intended quarry. Seated in his sports car, he started the powerful engine, shifted it into gear and rolled in the direction his smartphone tracking software specified.

He drove up the tree-lined campus road and parked his vehicle in the shadows. The virtual tracker showed his target was in the building looming up ahead in the darkness.

The security guard at the front counter stood up to greet Murat when he entered wearing a ball cap pulled down low.

"Your identification card."

"Of course. Where is my focus tonight?" Murat said with an air of distraction. He reached into his jacket and withdrew his silenced gun. "I don't have an ID card, but I have one of these," he said, waving the weapon in the man's face. "It's my universal access card. I never leave home without it." He smiled a dolphin smile.

Before the guard could react, the gun spat twice in his chest, the force of the bullets propelling him backwards. He bounced off his still-warm chair and fell to the cold floor dead as an autumn leaf.

Murat came around and pulled the body close to the counter so it could only be seen by someone leaning over the counter. I should charge extra for this hit. He picked up the phone and dialed his quarry's smartphone.

"Hello."

He eyeballed the security guard's name tag pinned to his shirt. "This is Taner at the front desk."

"Yes?"

"I'm just checking in with you. Is there anything to report?" A dead body perhaps?

"Uh, no."

"I need to confirm your location." He noticed a clipboard on the counter with her name and signature on it and a male guest's name beside hers. She has company? I must ask for an increase in my fee. Bullets aren't free after all.

"I'm in the Processing Lab on the second floor."

"Excellent. That's what's indicated on the sign-in sheet. Have yourself a safe evening, Professor Bigili."

"You, too."

Murat searched the guard and stole his security pass.

This might come in handy.

## Chapter Thirty-Five
## Istanbul - Tuesday Evening

Up in the lab, Baki turned and asked, "Who was that, Treasure?"

Her brow furrowed in puzzlement. "It was building security. They were checking in with me."

Catching her expression, Baki asked, "Is that standard procedure?"

"It's the first time since I've been working here," she said, mystified. "Something new, I guess," she tossed out as an afterthought. Aysel pushed herself away from the workbench. "I forgot a folder in my office." She grabbed her purse in reflex before leaving.

Baki nodded his head in acknowledgement. Why do women have to take their purses with them wherever they go? he wondered. Must be a woman thing, he settled on. The door clicked shut. He glanced over his shoulder. Alone. Finally. He reached for his knapsack and stuffed into it more of the ancient tablets from the crate at his feet. Have to keep the client happy.

He heard the door open. "That was quick," he said without looking.

"I intend to be," a deep male voice replied in Turkish.

Baki whipped around. "Who the hell are you?" he said, trying to conceal his unease at the sight of a silenced gun in the intruder's hand.

"I'm your friendly neighborhood assassin," Murat answered, as though he was a mere clerk at the checkout lane. "Where is Professor Bigili?"

"Go screw yourself," Baki said as he dove for the floor, his hand clutching his knapsack.

A bullet whizzed overhead and smacked into the opposite wall.

Baki retrieved his gun from his knapsack and crawled to the end of the workbench. Massive fear palpitated his heart and churned his bowels. He peeked around the corner. The space was vacant. He had endured his share of scrapes in his risky career but he had never been shot at.

"You have nowhere to go. I'm the man with the gun. The odds are against you," the killer crowed.

Baki replied with a gunshot in the direction of the voice. "How do you like the odds now?"

The bullet went wide.

Aysel's in danger from this guy and he's between me and her.

Baki arrived at the only decision possible. He stood up and fired at the gunman, keeping him pinned down while he made for the door. He carried his knapsack in his left hand as he fired his gun. Then he transferred the weapon to his left hand and searched his pocket for the card key.

Big mistake.

The gunman, taking advantage of the temporary lull, fired a round and nailed Baki in the shoulder just as he swiped his device through the card reader. He fell into the hallway, alive but gravely wounded, and his gun flew out of his hand and clattered on the floor. He thrust himself away from the door with his feet, seeking the safety of his pistol.

* * *

At the far end of the murky corridor, Aysel was returning from her office. She saw the door to the lab fly open and briefly illuminate the figure of Baki stumbling into the corridor. Why is he lying on the floor? she asked herself, as if the answer was forthcoming.

The door to the lab flung open again and another man stepped into the rectangle of light holding the shape of a gun in his hand. The hallway returned to darkness when the door snicked shut, and the click of the locking mechanism sounded like a firecracker in the tense silence.

"Baki. Get away," she screamed, but no sound escaped her constricted throat. She choked on her words and her eyes went wide with fear.

"I will ask you one last time. Where is Professor Bigili?" he roared.

Baki jolted alert. "What do you want with her?" he said. "If you want artifacts, you can have them." He slid his knapsack toward the killer with his good arm. "Take what's in here."

"I don't want your useless relics. I want Bigili and the documents related to the scroll she found. If you do this for me, I'll let you live."

The killer's words hit Aysel as though she had been slapped. How does he know about the scroll? her mind shouted in panic.

"I don't know anything about a scroll. I swear," Baki said in a pain-filled voice.

"Wrong answer."

Aysel saw the man point his hand at Baki who jerked once. The gunman then turned to scrutinize her end of the corridor. She pressed herself against the wall and backed away, blending with the shadows. Her nerves soon got the better of her, and she bolted toward her office. A bullet whizzed behind her and nicked the wall on her left, spitting debris at her. She turned the corner and ran for her office. The door was unlocked. Relieved. Thank God I forgot to re-lock it. She slammed it shut. No sooner had she set the deadbolt when someone rattled the handle which tore at her frayed nerves.

"Go away," she screamed. "The police are on their way."

Bullets pierced the solid wooden door. Her threat had failed to diminish the killer's resolve.

She was trapped.

Then she remembered her smartphone was in her purse which she still clasped in her hand. She fumbled with it. Get control of yourself, Aysel commanded while she frantically dialed 911.

The opposite end picked up and her words erupted in gulps. She repeated herself several times before the operator understood the seriousness of her predicament.

"Please stay on the line, Miss Bigili. The police are their way."

"Ple-e-e-eze hurry. He-he's shooting-me-the door. He-Baki-killed-he's dead," she jabbered.

Sirens soon wailed in the distance.

All was quiet on the other side of the door. Minutes passed. She heard loud voices approaching. A sudden rap on the door startled her.

"Miss Bigili...? Miss Bigili? It's the police. It's safe. You can unlock the door."

"Operator. Someone is banging on my door claiming to be the police. Can you confirm their arrival?"

Seconds elapsed.

"The police are at your location."

Aysel crawled to the door, released the deadbolt and backed away. Heavily armed police stormed into her office. They helped her to her feet.

The questions came hurtling at her. "Are you all right? Are you hurt? Were you shot?"

The effort to question her was wasted. She refused to answer and pushed past her interrogators, walking hesitantly toward her injured lover, still unsteady on her feet. Her pace quickened as her courage returned. She broke into a run. "Baki! Baki!" she called out to him, her voice striking a note of hysteria as she ran, sobbing.

Medics were attending to him. A uniformed man leaned over Baki's prone body, pumping his chest.

What the hell are they doing to him? They're hurting him. "Get off him," she screamed as she tried to tear the paramedic away from her lover.

A policeman grabbed her from behind and gently restrained her.

Aysel tore loose from his grasp and went to Baki. "I love you, I love you, I love you...Why...? Why did he...do this to you?" she wept, the words gushing out in spurts.

The paramedic stopped pumping Baki's chest.

"Why are you stopping you fool?" she shrieked. "He's not dead, not dead, not dead." A soft voice seemingly far away penetrated her fog of sorrow, telling her nothing more could be done for him. Someone tugged lightly on her arm, pulling her back to reality. A protest came to her lips but remained unexpressed.

"Miss Bigili, I'm Detective Beygolu. Is there someone we can call for you?" he asked.

She stifled her grief and focused. Mother can't be of any help at this hour. Then she thought of Father Marco. "I want a lift home."

"Before you go, I need to fill in the blanks to get a full picture of what happened here. So I'd like to ask you some questions, if you're up to it."

"I'll try."

"What is the name of the deceased?"

He tapped her answer into his smartphone and studied the screen. Aysel saw a look of concern cross his features.

"What is your relationship to him?" Again, he entered her answer in his device.

"Did you get a look at the person who shot your boyfriend?"

"It was too dark. Things happened so fast. It was all I could do to reach my office alive."

"Did Baki have any enemies...? It's a standard question, Miss Bigili."

"I've only known—knew—" She stifled a sob. "I met Baki a few months ago."

"We found this next to him," an officer interrupted, indicating the victim with a toss of his head.

Beygolu turned back to her. "Did this belong to Baki?"

Aysel recognized the black knapsack he held in his hand. "It resembles his."

He reached into the bag and withdrew a clay tablet. "There are several more in the knapsack. Is this the property of your boyfriend?"

Aysel fixated on the tablet. "No." What were you up to, Baki?

"Miss Bigili, it's probably a bad time to mention this but Baki was known to us."

"What are you implying?" she asked. Conflicting emotions tore at her heart.

"We believe he was smuggling antiquities. We could never catch him with the goods—until now. This crime looks like a settling of accounts."

The blood in Aysel's veins congealed like cement. She didn't hear Beygolu's assumption about the motive for Baki's murder. Her countenance assumed a lithic expression. The nebulous contours of unease which had been niggling at her subconscious since Baki had come into her life burst into bold relief.

"Is something wrong, Miss Bigili?"

Caught in the grip of extreme emotion, she raged in silence as she struggled for control of her rational mind. "No, detective," she said icily as she fought back tears. Fooled again. All this time her lover had been nothing but a callous buccaneer using their lovecraft for personal gain. Battered by waves of bitterness, she struggled to maintain a steady emotional keel while her dreams sank beneath the turbulent waters of betrayal. "Everything's as smooth as still waters."

## Chapter Thirty-Six
## Istanbul - Wednesday Afternoon

Father Marco fidgeted in his chair, waiting for the courier to show up at his apartment. Better get here soon, he raged in silence through clenched teeth. Kuffing horns are driving me crazy. Don't know how much longer I can stay put. He gazed anxiously at the large package lying on the kitchen table.

Poor Aysel, he thought. I can't imagine what she must be going through. A strong woman if there ever was one. Thank God she had the presence of mind to warn me earlier about the shooter.

He felt guilty he didn't have time to go to her. But every minute he waited was one more the killer had of possibly finding him...I can't understand how he learned of the scroll. He racked his brain for a logical explanation. Aysel swore she told no one...Could the killer be an ally of Dimitri's? He didn't want to hang around to find out.

Although the scroll was worth dying for, so was staying alive. More than a few items remained on his bucket list he wanted to cross off. Dying a hero wasn't one of the—

The doorbell went off, detonating the tense atmosphere in his apartment. Marco bolted upright in his chair.

Must be the courier. So he deigned to show up. About damn time.

Hurrying toward the front door, he welcomed a surge of relief.

It didn't last.

An obvious question rattled his brain: What if it's not him?

Marco froze and time with him. The living room seemed to shrink and fade away until nothing but the front door loomed before him. If he remained still, maybe the caller would give up and leave.

The buzzer detonated again; he jumped out of his skin.

Caught in the amber of indecision, Marco fixated on the door, knowing there was no going back once he opened it.

His senses on full alert, he found his courage and reached for the deadbolt with utmost effort, as though in a nightmare, and at that same moment a shudder ripped through him—the fuse on the most explosive secret in history was about to be lit.

He stopped himself mid-motion.

Would the killer announce himself?

His need for resolution overcame his paranoia.

Best take a peek.

He put his eye to the spyhole. A man in a dark suit and tie stood before him.

"Looks harmless enough," he murmured to himself. "Who is it?" he said in Turkish through the door.

"It's Father Giovanni," the man replied in immaculate Italian. "His Eminence Cardinal Vittorio Petrelli sent me to pick up a package."

Arrigoni's tension-filled body relaxed.

Thank God he finally arrived.

Although it was unusual for a priest to be dressed in civilian clothes, his dress code didn't set off any alarm bells in Father Marco's head. For the sake of decorum, he himself wore informal priestly attire for the meeting: a black shirt and pants and, of course, his ecclesiastical collar. As Marco reached for the handle, he realized he was about to change human history forever.

Swallowing his anger, he opened the door to his caller. The dark-haired courier stood with his hands clasped in front of him, eyes welcoming and full of warmth.

"Are you Father Marco?" the man said in a pleasant tone.

He detected a Sicilian accent. "I am," he replied in his mother tongue.

A hint of a smile bowed the man's fleshy lips. "Sorry I'm late."

Reassured, Father Marco let down his guard. "You made it. Please come in." He stood by the door as Giovanni passed him.

"Forgive me for saying so, Marco, but were you expecting someone else?"

"I—forget it," he said, closing the door. He came around to him. "Can I get you something? Tea? Coffee?"

"Kind of you, but I'm in a bit of hurry," he replied. "I'm double-parked."

"So you're responsible for the traffic jam below."

"Guilty as charged," he confessed, placing his palm on his chest and smiling that thin smile of his again.

Dimly, a warning sounded in Arrigoni's mind, but he ignored it. He stood there, assessing his guest. Not the typical behavior of a priest. *But who am I to judge?*

"I don't mean to rush you…"

Father Marco gave a start and blinked. "Right. The scroll. Please have a seat. I'll be only a moment." He turned on his heel and went to the kitchen. Returning to the living room, he froze and his eyes saucered in fright.

*Not again.*

Evil had slithered into his presence under a guise of innocence. His guest stood in the middle of the room, pointing a pistol at him with silencer attached. Blood fled his brain.

And that quickly, Giovanni unveiled his true persona. "The shock on your face is priceless. You've made my day," he taunted, holding back a smirk.

Time moved with the viscous horror of a nightmare. The sight of a gun targeting him caused a surge of adrenaline to course through his bloodstream like electricity conducting through a wire, intensifying his fight-or-flight mechanism. His heart raced and plasma pounded in his skull. "What are you doing?" Father Marco asked, playing for time while he wrestled with his fear.

"Nothing personal. Just business. Put the package on the sofa," Giovanni motioned with the gun. "Then turn around."

He took his time doing as ordered. *So this is how it ends…But not without a fight.*

"The Church hasn't survived all these centuries through God's grace alone. Sometimes He needs our help when the Church's interests are threatened," he said. "Extreme measures for extreme causes. Now get down on your knees and clasp your hands behind your head," he commanded, no pity in his tone.

He heard Giovanni approach him from behind. He looked over his shoulder. Giovanni was standing an arm's length away, the gun pointing at the back of his head. *The hunter and the prey.* Something instinctive stirred him—the will to survive. Sometimes a cornered prey strikes back, no matter the odds. He knew what to do.

"Face the front," Giovanni barked. "Once I'm done with you, your friend the archeologist is next. My client wants no loose ends."

Father Marco almost lost his composure. You'll only get to Aysel over my dead body you bastard. He began to tremble. His martial arts skills, which hadn't rusted though he had been a peace-loving priest for so many years, slid into gear. If there was ever time for a miracle, my Lord....

"Ah. You had me fooled," the courier said with cheer. "I thought you would die fighting and give me the pleasure of killing you. But you're weak like the rest of them," he gloated. "Any final words before I give you your last rites?"

We all have a plan until reality smacks us upside the head. "Just two. Screw you!" Hardly had he spoken when his right heel shot backwards and upwards, connecting with his would-be executioner's right kneecap, smashing it.

Giovanni tumbled rearward onto the carpeted floor beside the sofa, howling in agony, but still he gripped the gun. He managed to fire a shot but his aim was off, and Father Marco had already rolled to his left by the time the weapon discharged, protected by the heavy, old-fashioned sofa. Giovanni, his body flooded with blinding pain, fired at the sofa again and again. Stuffing erupted from ruptured cushions, but the shots were high, ineffectual.

"You're a dead man," he bawled, his voice tinged with pain.

Father Marco, his nerves frazzled by the *zing* of muffled gunfire, slithered behind the sofa. He stayed low and drove himself forward with his legs and forearms. "How do you like your last rites?"

Giovanni lashed out, firing his gun without proper aim.

Father Marco peered around the other end of the sofa and saw his assailant's head. Just where I want you. He wiggled himself back. He got into position and waited. Sensing a lull in the shooting, he sprang upwards and shoved his shoulder against the top edge of the heavy sofa which teetered then toppled onto Giovanni who didn't have time to react.

He screamed in agony. The substantial piece of furniture had landed on his body, pinning him. Father Marco scrambled to his feet and stood gazing down at his attacker's thrashing head.

"Tough luck, buddy. I changed my mind. No clock for you." Instead, he clocked the courier's skull with his foot. It stilled.

The stress of having bested his assassin made him tremble—for real this time. My life has been spared. I'm still alive. Alive! O Lord, thank you for delivering me from death, he prayed. He slumped into an armchair to let his stress bleed away. Having dodged a bullet—several of them—literally and figuratively, he ruminated on his next course of action. A staggering realization jolted him. This—this assassin was sent by Vitto. The horror of his friend's betrayal floored him…I spoke with him only yesterday afternoon. Then it dawned on him. This hitman is likely the same guy who shot Baki and the security guard last night. He had to be their killer. The coincidence is too great.

He got up and flipped the sofa upright. He stared at his assailant with unbridled contempt. "Scumbag. Did you and your crony think you could thwart God's will?"

Perturbing questions pricked his curiosity.

Why would Vitto want Aysel and me dead?

I was willing to give him the scroll, no strings attached.

Did he covet the limelight for himself?

Before long, he dismissed the last question. In his estimation, Vitto wasn't the type to seek publicity. Wait a minute. There are rumors of his wanting to be the next pope. Wheels spun furiously in his brain. He doesn't want to publicize the scroll. He wants to suppress it! His brief spell of intuition chilled his blood, but it also strengthened his resolve to ensure the truth would never be entombed again. He stared into the near distance. Nearly all men can stand adversity, but if you want to test a man's character, give him power. You messed with the wrong guy, Vitto. I now possess the power to destroy you and so I shall, God willing.

Anger whirled in his mind. Vitto's treachery was the last thread in the fabric of lies woven by the Church.

I will stand with anybody that stands right, and stand with him while he is right, and part with him when he goes wrong. Once again, the Church hierarchy has placed its interests before the greater good. How can I remain a priest in such a corrupt and self-serving institution? I gave the Church a chance to act on behalf of humanity and instead it chose the path of self-preservation, as it always has. This is the consequence of my misplaced trust. Never again. The Church is finished and I with it!

Father Marco surveyed his tight quarters. He felt trapped, the need to flee overwhelming him. He was about to lay down some shoe leather but then stopped himself. With a sense of urgency, he stooped to grab the package. From nowhere a smartphone chimed. He pulled it out of the dead man's suit coat. It soon stopped ringing. He hesitated, gave a shrug and pocketed it.

A worried countenance froze his face. He grabbed the killer's wrist to check for a pulse.

Nothing.

He frantically checked his neck.

Flat.

What've I done? A shudder of remorse passed through him. Please forgive me, God. Murder was not in my heart. His sorrow was short-lived. Don't fret. You did what you had to do. He had it coming. He deserved his fate.

On the verge of fleeing, his sense of moral obligation pinged his conscience. Shouldn't I contact the police? He debated with himself. It's the right thing to do otherwise I'll look guilty. He placed the call and made a brief report.

What happened next was a foggy nightmare. He scooped up the package and flew out the door. He scarcely recalled tearing out of his apartment and descending the stairs two at a time while his fear raced on ahead of him. It was all a blur, events merging in a confusing jumble. First Baki and now him. He had to escape—and fast. The hitman might have an accomplice.

I won't let them win, he vowed.

In his rush to get away, he brushed by a stranger sporting a ball cap, windbreaker and dark sunglasses on his way out of the lobby.

Father Marco mumbled a perfunctory apology to the man who stared after him. Outside, he snaked his way through the tangled mass of cars that crept raucously along the street. I should have paid more attention to these horns. They were warning me something was up. Too late now.

Beneath a gray shell of a sky, he raced northeast toward Sultanahmet Square, leaving behind the honk-and-beep commotion of his neighborhood. He didn't know why he headed for the square—safety in crowds?—but he needed to be surrounded by people.

The square, once the ancient site of the Hippodrome of Constantinople, was now an open plaza that fronted the Sultanahmet Mosque, known popularly as the Blue Mosque. The crash of riotous cheering, the beat of horses' hooves, the slap of leather and the whir of chariot wheels filled his imagination. The squeal of an excitable child returned him to the present.

Only the Constantine Obelisk, the Serpentine Column and the Obelisk of Thutmose III remained of the one-hundred-thousand seat stadium, less-than-impressive memorials of the once-majestic Byzantine Empire.

Hastily navigating the sea of humanity in the vast public space, he picked his way through knots of tourists, some milling about, others snapping pictures of these historic monuments. They took no apparent notice of him. He checked behind himself, desiring to put as much distance between himself and his apartment as fast as he could. He surveyed the crowds of people as he dashed by. Expressions of appreciation were writ large on their faces as they marvelled at the ancient structures standing tall in the square.

What're they smiling at? Those monuments are nothing special compared to the package. Just piles of stone.

A distant wail of sirens grew louder, ending his spate of reflection. He felt the urge to run, but he didn't want to draw attention to himself, and he tightened his grip on the package tucked under his arm. An inexplicable tickle in his nose caused him to sneeze explosively. The unanticipated jerk of his upper body saved his life; a silenced bullet whizzed by and struck a woman strolling in front of him. Screams erupted.

Out of instinct, he dove for the ground, rolled to his left and bumped up against the German Fountain. It was a gift given by Kaiser Wilhelm II to Sultan Abdulhamid II and the city of Istanbul in 1898 during his second visit to the capital of the Ottoman Empire. The neo-Byzantine styled structure had undergone extensive restoration work back in 2013.

Bullets nicked it, spraying him with fragments of concrete. Heart pounding, he scrambled around the fountain to place it between himself and the shooter hot behind him. Nerves jangling and breath coming in gulps, he realized he was trapped. On his haunches, he leaned against the base of the octagonal structure to gather his wits.

"You're never more…alive…when Death is breathing down your neck," he rasped, breathing heavily. "Now I know how a fugitive in a thriller feels."

The walls of the fountain were tall. So he peeked around a corner to locate the gunman. Sight-seers were running pell-mell, except for a man wearing a ball cap and dark sunglasses, and he was moving toward him with the determined gait of a predator.

Chrissakes! It's the guy I bumped into in the lobby. Giovanni's accomplice. He must have discovered the clock had run out on Giovanni. These guys deserve an "A" for persistence.

Father Marco glanced around for something to use against the shooter. In the game of cat and mouse, bare hands against a gun wasn't a fair fight. Fortuitously, Sultanahmet Square, blanketed with security cameras, was located just up the street from a main police station.

Out of nowhere, police cars with sirens blaring and lights flashing roared into the square like cavalry of old. Policemen hopped out of their vehicles with weapons drawn, pointed at the gunman. Maybe he was suicidal, but Mr. Ball Cap fired his gun at the police officers, refusing to recognize the gig was up. Given no choice, they mowed him down. Dead men don't talk after all.

With the sudden release of tension, Father Marco exhaled audibly. He was that rare man: he had cheated death not once, but thrice! Using the chaos to his advantage, he snuck away on rubbery legs and melted into a curious but nervous tangle of people that had begun to congregate. He might yet save the scroll from its enemies. But he kept his optimism in check. His plan to disappear was now at a dead end. He could no longer run and hide. The police would be looking for him. Who could he turn to for help?

Footsteps away he came abreast of Divan Yolu Street, the main thoroughfare which ran through the heart of Old Istanbul. He stood at the edge of the wide sidewalk and watched the torrent of humanity rush by him in both directions. The moment of danger over, he felt the rapid thumping of his heart begin to fade.

Moving toward him, the familiar bell of the commuter train grew louder, and the ground beneath his feet vibrated as the heavy red-colored rolling stock trundled by, its metal wheels screeching in protest at the steel rails. The chain of cars rolled down the hill past the monumental Oriental Plane tree that stands proud between the opposing rail lines then heaved out of sight around the corner past the fifty-foot high stone walls of the Topkapi Palace, former seat of the Ottoman sultans and their harems.

He waded into the stream of pedestrians, crossed the street, careful not to step on the rails for no explicable reason other than a phobic habit, and plunged back into the moving current of humanity on the other side of the avenue, weaving through it like a man pursued. He marched northeast while he tried to figure out a different plan.

Desperate restaurateurs stood at the threshold of their modest eateries, practically accosting passersby to sample culinary delights cooking within while animated merchants peddled their wares on the sidewalk. Like every big city, commerce competed for people's attention and money.

Eyes darting left and right, a bold advertisement posted on a message board cluttered with posters for maritime excursions and indoor *hamams* caught his attention. He stopped to read it. Serendipity. He came up with a new plan which would take him behind the Blue Mosque and the Hagia Sophia.

Damn. The square must be crawling with cops. What could he do about it?

He dropped into the nearest men's haberdasher and drew curious glances from the shopkeeper when he donned a shirt and hat immediately after paying for them. He left the store and marched in haste toward his objective. Not the best disguise, he told himself, but it's better than standing out like a belly dancer at a baptism.

His prediction proved accurate for the square hummed with cops and well-armed paramilitary personnel. Father Marco hugged the edge of the square opposite the German Fountain. Then he ducked down the side street that passed between the Hagia Sophia Church and the Blue Mosque, which led to the lower town.

Streets thronged with tourists here as they did uptown. Merchants must be doing a brisk business hawking their wares, he judged, noticing numerous shoppers clutching large bags. They can't help themselves, he sympathized. Turkish ceramics and pottery are so artfully handcrafted. Even he had purchased a framed tiled mosaic which showcased a twining flower motif. It had once hung on his living room wall. Then the earthquake struck. Now it was in pieces, decomposing in a distant dump.

As in every bustling tourist hotspot, pedestrians competed with cars for rule of the road, but the warren of ancient narrow avenues of Old Istanbul weren't laid out to accommodate heavy vehicular traffic. Drivers had to have the patience of Job to navigate the constricted streets and foot-travelers had to be as quick and nimble as Jack to stay alive.

He didn't have far to go after turning left onto Kabasakal Street. The next corner should be the street I'm looking for, he assured himself. His sight latched onto a signpost. It was the name he sought. He hung a right onto Tevkifhane Street. The Four Seasons Hotel, once a former prison and now a luxury hotel, was easy to spot up ahead on the left. The conspicuous pastel yellow building and its distinctive Turkish architecture of exposed eaves made this exclusive lodging a landmark in the neighborhood. Unlike the guests of old whose stay in the former crowbar hotel was involuntary, guests of this current establishment were free to check in and out anytime they liked.

Father Marco entered the luxurious lobby and his shoes clunked on the marble floor as he approached the front desk. “I’m late for the conference with Michael Giltmore. Could you direct me to it?”

The female clerk gave him an inquiring look what with the way he was dressed. “Take the elevator to your left, sir, and go to room 211.”

He thanked her then made his way to it. The doors glided shut, encasing him in sumptuous silence. He appraised his compact quarters. The elevator was better decorated than more than a few of the upper class homes he had visited.

A bell chimed and he stepped out of the well-appointed compartment into a richly carpeted hallway. He studied a brass plaque on the wall which displayed a range of room numbers. The conference room number was in the range whose black arrow pointed to the left. He hurried along the corridor, rounded the corner and spotted in the distance a stout man in uniform guarding the entrance to what was most likely his destination.

*Must be my objective. Admission probably isn’t free. I’ll fight my way in if I have to. Too much is at stake.*

## Chapter Thirty-Seven
## The Vatican - Wednesday Late Afternoon

Why haven't I heard from Murat? Cardinal Petrelli worried while he sat at his polished, hand-crafted antique desk, fingering his rosary. There had been no news from the courier since he had texted him. Murat should have completed his mission by now. He checked his watch again. The deadline had passed hours ago. It was not like Murat to be late in communicating the success of an assignment. Cardinal Petrelli stared at the smartphone on his desk, willing it to ring. His salvation was in sight, but just out of reach.

Unannounced, his secretary barged into his office, interrupting his fretful state.

"Forgive this intrusion, Your Eminence. Have you seen the latest news?"

"What news can excuse your impudence?" he asked, his tone brimming with menace.

"A gunman tried to kill the priest you spoke with yesterday," he said breathlessly, ignoring the cardinal's menacing attitude.

"And who would that be, Angelo?" he replied. "I speak to many priests daily."

"Father Arrigoni. From Istanbul."

"No!" He composed his face in an expression he hoped was appropriately aghast. "Heaven help us," and his pulse quickened.

"Do you suppose this has something to do with his dire message?" Father Angelo said.

"When I spoke with him yesterday, he didn't sound frightened. Is Father Marco still alive?" he asked, pretending to care.

"He is but the gunman is dead. Father Arrigoni must have put up a hell of a fight," he answered with unmistakable disappointment.

Cardinal Petrelli paled. Blood chilled in his veins. The rosary slid from his hand and clattered on the hard surface of the desk like falling marbles. Murat has failed. The Church is doomed. I mus—

"Your Eminence, you appear unwell. I'm sorry if this news has upset you. Is there—"

"Leave me at once," he said, smacking the desk with his hand. "I wish to be alone."

"I'm sor—"

"Out," his face dark with fury.

Father Angelo turned on his heel and scurried out of the office with almost comic haste.

Cardinal Petrelli's stomach churned, his thoughts gyrated. The room swirled before his eyes. Troubling questions ran through his brain in quick succession:

Can they link the courier to me?

Does Marco know?

Am I a suspect?

He buried his face in his hands. I will be the next pope. Nothing will stand in the way of my life's dream, he vowed with blind certainty. His head shot up, his eyes blazed with fiery zeal. I must move quickly but quietly. The police might be on their way. I can't sit here, trusting in my luck. He picked up his office phone and pushed a button.

"Yes, Your Eminence," Father Angelo spoke in a timid voice.

"We're going on a lengthy journey. Pack accordingly. Bring my car around to my apartment. I'll wait for you there. Now move," he ordered. I have an important score to settle.

* * *

Father Angelo looked at the phone before cradling it. Long journey? The prospect of travelling with the cardinal made the rite of self-mortification seem downright enjoyable in comparison.

## Chapter Thirty-Eight
## Istanbul - Wednesday Late Afternoon

Giltmore stood at the podium at the front of the conference room and gazed upon the audience like a shepherd surveying his flock. The large turnout pleased him. Seated before him were several hundred people a minority of whom were his fellow travelers. The balance were paying guests.

My reputation precedes me. Praise God.

He adjusted the microphone before speaking. "*Salaam alaykum.* Peace be upon you," he began, offering the traditional salutation of God's prophets. "Thank you for coming here this afternoon. For those of you who arrived with me several days ago, I hope you're still enjoying your stay thus far. The Turks are known for their warm hospitality." Giltmore observed many nods of approval.

"As you're aware, today's lecture is titled, *The Conquest of Constantinople: Causes and Consequences*. Before we begin, a show of hands from those who support President Ordekan." Many raised their hands. "A show of hands from those who support him but want no one to know."

Laughter erupted in the hall. No one raised their hand.

Always a good idea to loosen up the crowd with humor before plunging into a serious topic, Giltmore professed to himself. "Before I delve into today's topic, I congratulate the Turkish people for re-electing President Ordekan," and he led the audience in a round of polite applause. "Turks must do everything in their power to protect President Ordekan and his government against foreign influences," he said in a raised voice. "You may not know this, but the American regime is no friend of Turkey and its people."

Vigorous applause ensued, and he waited for it to subside.

"Now let us begin," he said into the microphone. "In May 1453 Constantinople, considered by Christians of that age to be the Second Rome, fell to the armies of Mehmet the Conqueror, the Ottoman Sultan. When news of this catastrophic defeat reached Rome, church bells pealed in a spirit of mourning. But the Islamic world rejoiced. One battle, two opposite reactions. The Christian response is understandable. The loss of the last remnants of the majestic Byzantine Empire, which had stood invincible for one thousand years, was a shock to the collective psyche of European Christians. For the Muslims, however, this martial victory meant an end to the existential threat posed by the Crusaders who had staged the majority of their invasions of the Holy Land from Constantinople since the First Crusade was preached by Pope Urban II in November 1095."

He paused to take a breath.

"That's a brief sketch of the Christian and Muslim reactions to the Conquest. Any questions?" Seeing no raised hands, he continued with his lecture. "Now for some background on the cause of the First Crusade before we continue with the Conquest. As a diversion to the political tumult roiling Christendom since his election as Pope in 1088, Urban called on European Christians to take back the Holy Land from the Turks who he claimed were attacking pilgrims visiting Jerusalem. There was no al Qaeda or Taliban or ISIS to rally against back then. Turks were the Muslim bogeyman of that age. They were a convenient punching bag for medieval Islamophobes. At any rate, recent scholarship shows Pope Urban's claim to be bunk. It is true bandits attacked pilgrims trying to reach Jerusalem. But the bandits didn't care what religion the pilgrims followed. They were equal opportunity outlaws. Muslim, Christian and Jewish pilgrims were plundered and murdered. Booty was booty. Unfortunately, dead pilgrims couldn't talk but anti-Muslim propagandists of the time did. And they shouted far and wide across Europe to rouse anti-Muslim hatred to a bloodthirsty peak. Sound familiar? So you see folks Islamophobia isn't a new phenomenon. It has a long history. It's the same old poison in a new bottle with the words *Suck It Up* on the label."

Many heads in the audience nodded their understanding.

"Once Constantinople had been conquered, the land of Islam was safe from European invaders. For close to four hundred years, the Ottoman Empire protected Muslim lands from the depredations of Christian Crusaders. But as the Ottoman Empire contracted during the nineteenth-century until it finally ceased to exist in 1922, the rapacious Anglo-French Crusaders came storming back to lop off the juiciest morsels from the Ottoman carcass. From Morocco to Iraq, the Crusaders conquered one Muslim country after another. No Muslim power could stop them then or now. In present times, only Turkey and Iran stand against the combined might of the neo-Crusader armies and their insatiable lust for other nations' treasures."

He paused to take a question when the doors at the back of the room burst open and banged against rubber stoppers mounted in the floor. A man wearing a hat rushed in and halted just beyond the threshold. Giltmore gave a start at the unexpected intrusion.

"You must be Professor Giltmore," the man said in a halting voice, gulping for air as he approached the lectern.

All eyes followed the intruder as he raced up the central aisle.

Giltmore took his time replying. Before the doors automatically swung shut, he saw, with concern, the security guard planted on his hands and knees in the hallway. Then he noticed the stranger was carrying a bulky yellow envelope under one arm. What's this? The man's ecclesiastical collar peeked out from his overshirt and what appeared to be bruises on his face further aroused his interest. Has the rebellion within the Church been joined? he jested to himself. "You've found him. What can I do for you?" he demanded.

"I don't have time to explain. Everything you need to know is in this envelope," he said, handing it to Giltmore. "Guard it with your life." He hesitated. "And please extend my apologies to the security guard." His aspect conveyed remorse.

Giltmore reached to take possession of the bulky package. No sooner had he done so when the priest turned and fled in the same direction as quickly as he had arrived. Giltmore examined the label on the envelope handwritten with a thick black marker: **The Congregation for the Doctrine of the Faith**. What have I been pulled into? he wondered as a worm of worry wiggled its way into his brain.

Addressing the audience, "I'm sorry for the intrusion," he said. "I've never witnessed a priest moonlighting as a mailman. I guess he needs the extra income."

The audience cracked up.

"Could someone—preferably Turkish—see to the condition of the security guard," he asked.

A man got up.

"*Teşekkür ederim.* Thank you," he said to the retiring man. Giltmore turned his attention back to his lecture notes. He spent the next hour riveting his listeners with the major outcomes of the Conquest.

At the end of his talk, Giltmore invited audience members to take part in the Question & Answer portion of the lecture.

"You did a swell job of bashing Christianity. So how about explaining to the audience how Islam was spread by the sword," a female voiced shouted from the back of the conference room.

"The short answer to your assertion, Delores, is that it is patently false. The lo—"

"No it's not," she shrilled. "The Ottoman Empire spread Islam by the sword."

"May I respond, Delores?"

"Go ahead. No one is stopping you."

"Thank you." He grasped the edges of the lectern. "You anticipated tomorrow's topic, so I'll only touch briefly upon it today. We must separate the Islamic empire from the religion of Islam. It is historical fact the *borders* of the Islamic empire were expanded through force of arms. However, modern Western historians have thoroughly debunked the Orientalist myth that the *religion* of Islam was spread by violence. Notwithstanding the Quranic prohibition against compulsion in religion, there *were* forced conversions, but these were a minor exception rather than the rule. The spread-by-the-sword accusation sprang out of Crusader polemics against Islam to explain its rapid growth in formerly Christian lands.

"One example of forced conversions was the Ottoman *devshirme* system established in the late fourteenth century wherein Christian children were snatched from their homes in the Balkans and raised as Muslims to serve in the Sultan's personal army or to work in the civil service. This system clearly violated the Islamic proscription against religious coercion.

"Sadly, the *devshirme* system foreshadowed Canada's residential school system (1876-1996) wherein Indigenous children were ripped from their homes and raised in Christian boarding schools in a program of coerced conversion and assimilation '*to kill the Indian*' in them. History *does* repeat itself, to the detriment of humanity.

"That aside, Western scholars admit without reservation the success of Islam lay not in the wielding of the sword, as it did for Christianity, but in the wielding of justice for Muslim and non-Muslim alike. Islam spread primarily through honest trade, missionary work, intermarriage and its appeal to equal justice for all, regardless of religion." Giltmore paused before issuing his final remarks. "The philosopher Spinoza wrote: *Minds are not conquered by arms but by greatness of soul.* To this end, Islam spread by conquering souls, not cities. And this is because Prophet Mohammed, peace be upon him, was the greatest of human souls."

More questions ensued.

"If there are no further questions, we can wrap up this meeting." Hearing silence, Giltmore said, "Thank you for participating in this most fruitful discussion. Turkish refreshments are available on the tables to my right. Please help yourselves." He ended his talk with the same words as he had begun "*Salaam alaykum.* Peace be upon you."

His contribution to the day-long conference over with, he regarded the package resting on the lectern with unbearable curiosity while guests shuffled their way toward tables laden with food and drink. It required all of his self-control to stop himself from tearing open the package there and then.

I can't wait to—

"Professor Giltmore," a voice broke in. "I was wondering if..." and Giltmore turned to face his interlocutor.

## Chapter Thirty-Nine
## Istanbul - Wednesday Night into Thursday Morning

Giltmore sailed into his unlit hotel room brimming with anticipation. Moonlight filtering through the sheer curtains bathed the room in an ethereal glow. Shadows writhed on the carpet, swaying to an indiscernible rhythm. He laid the package on the bed and turned on the bedside lamp. Shadows disappeared to dimensions unknown, the dance over. He walked to the television stand, picked up the channel menu and found the number he was searching for. On the remote, he punched in the three-digit number for ANN TÜRK. A glance at his watch informed him the top of the hour was still a few minutes away.

Perched on the edge of the wingback armchair, forearms resting on his knees, he listened to a sordid tale about a Turkish starlet and her latest brush with the law. Why do these talking heads suppose the conduct of these celluloid bimbos is of interest to the public? he wondered. So much easier to pander to our voyeuristic impulses than to appeal to the nobility within each one of us. He shook his head in disgust. The tabloid segment fizzled to a merciful end.

"We turn now to local news."

His ears perked up. He hoped to learn more behind today's bizarre encounter with the priest in disguise.

"We have a report tonight concerning the discovery of a deceased male who is suspected of committing the double murders that occurred at Koç University yesterday evening." The newscaster narrated the details of the murders while a picture of the suspect remained in the top right corner of the screen.

"The suspect was taken to the city morgue to determine the cause of death. A police spokesman confirmed rumors the alleged killer belonged to the Turkish underworld."

The TV screen showed a picture of the morgue where presumably the assailant had been taken.

"Confidential sources revealed the suspect was found by police in an apartment belonging to Marco Arrigoni, a serving Catholic priest and an American citizen."

A dated picture of Marco replaced the suspect's face and video showed the entrance to his apartment building cordoned off by a yellow ribbon of police tape. Giltmore leaned in for a closer look and sucked in his breath.

"Arrigoni is still at large. Istanbul police are asking people to contact them with any information on his whereabouts. Police say he is a material witness and is wanted for questioning.

"Turning to today's tragedy in the Sultanahmet Square, a female tourist from Korea was shot to death and her killer was gunned down by police. The tourist's name has been withheld pending notification of her family. Investigators believe the gunman was an accomplice of the university killer. Surveillance video from Sultanahmet Square captured footage of Arrigoni walking through the square at the time of the shooting. Investigators presume he was the intended target of the deceased shooter."

What in Hades have I become entangled in?

Giltmore shut off the television, crossed the room and sat on the edge of the bed, one leg dangling. The tinkle of tableware and the murmur of conversation wafted into his room from the courtyard restaurant on the soft blowing breeze, and the bedroom curtains billowed and sagged, inhaling and exhaling with dreamy pleasure. He stared at the package for a few moments, tentative.

Will I break any laws if I open it? he wondered.

Overcoming his trepidation, he carefully tore open the large, padded envelope, reached inside and pulled out a sizable scroll and then a sheaf of papers. The documents were titled:

**Koç University - Department of Archeology**

Intrigued, he drank in the words. Minutes ticked by. The papers quivered in his hand. Done reading the Executive Summary, Giltmore let out his breath in a long whistle. "Glory to God," he whispered as though afraid of being overheard. He gazed in anticipation at the scroll.

Can it be true?

He pored over the entire report. A shiver rippled up his spine when he finished. He glanced around. Of course no one was watching. He reached for the scroll and slowly unwound a section of it on the bed. His pulse accelerated as a feeling of awe grabbed hold of him.

He read, transfixed by numinous words transcribed for eternity on ancient parchment. A growing sense of unreality seized him. Time passed unnoticed. He was in transport. The room seemed to shrink and fade away. The moon rose and fell while insects chittered and chattered in the evening air. Muffled voices sounded in the corridor then died away. Such was the scroll's hypnotic hold on him, wild beasts couldn't tear him away from it. Words swam in his watery eyes. His mind reeled by the time he came to the end of the scroll.

The Crucifixion was a ruse! Rumors about the Crucifixion having been faked had circulated down through history but could never be authenticated. But here was the truth in black and white! This scroll affirms the *ayat* (verse) in *Surah an-Nisa* (Chapter of the Women) of the Quran wherein God states a look-alike was crucified in place of Jesus.

Christianity rests on a foundation of lies!

The enormity of this truth and its repercussions seized hold of him. His senses tingled at the prospect of revealing this earth-shattering news to the world. No longer will the Church conceal the truth and Islamophobes will have to find another outlet for their vile hatred. I staked my reputation on an unpopular position and now I have been vindicated by this discovery. My tattered reputation will be made whole again. My quest for the truth has been fulfilled! This was all the lift he needed to take action against his critics and enemies. With this knowledge, he could alter the course of humanity's destiny.

He caressed the scroll with an affection reserved for a lover. His self-congratulatory thoughts were buoyed by another dose of pleasant reality. Jesus revealed his successor by name: *The Praised One*. The Islamophobes are doomed and so are their days of prosecuting crusades in Muslim countries. His face assumed the misty look of an ancient warrior savoring his triumphs in battles past. What a game-changer this is.

Just then the phone on the bedside table rang to life. He flinched. He glimpsed at his watch. Who's calling at this ungodly hour? Maybe it's Sandra.

He unclogged his throat before answering. "Hello."

"Professor Giltmore?" the male voice said.

His Italian accent sounded familiar. "Speaking."

"I apologize for calling so late, but I guessed you'd still be awake. It's most extraordinary isn't it?"

Cagey. "What is?" he said.

"The scroll. I trust you've read it by now."

Something in Giltmore's mind clicked, like a lens sliding into place, and the day's jarring events came into steady focus. "You're the priest I met earlier today."

"Ex-priest."

"Why are you contacting me? You're wanted by the police," he let drop.

"God as my witness, I committed no crime. I plan to turn myself in later this morning and give an account of what occurred yesterday afternoon in my apartment," Marco said. "I called to warn you your life might be in danger. Sinister forces are involved."

"Because of the scroll?"

"What do you think, Professor? Who would kill to possess that scroll?"

The man had a point. "Off the top of my head. The Vatican. Secret societies. Private collectors."

"True. But as of today there are only five people alive who are privy to the scroll's existence. You, me, my friend, Aysel, who prepared the archeology report, the caretaker of my church, who is in jail, and the head of *The Congregation for the Doctrine of the Faith*."

"Cardinal Petrelli?"

"None other."

"Now I know why you sought me out."

"Truth, like politics, makes for strange bedfellows."

"Got that right. But what's the cardinal's role in this affair?"

Marco ignored the question. He had one of his own. “What do you plan to do with the scroll?”

“I’m going to contact a friend in the U.S. media and convince her to broadcast the message of this scroll to the entire world.”

“Do it. You have my blessing. The political and religious insanity poisoning our world has to end before we annihilate one another. Once this scroll’s message goes public, the warmongers will have to devise some other way to divide and manipulate us. Its impact on future interfaith relations is incalculable.”

“Good point.”

“Watch your back, Professor.”

“Should I be worried?”

He paused to consider Giltmore’s question. “The enemy has played its hand and lost. Keep this matter under wraps until you speak with Turkish authorities. The sooner, the better.” The connection broke.

“Hmph.” He stared at the phone for a moment. “That was rather abrupt,” Giltmore muttered before he cradled it. He reviewed the conversation. Questions popped into his head.

What’s Cardinal Petrelli’s connection to this mystery?

Why wouldn’t Arrigoni tell me?

Where is he hiding?

Stumped, he settled under the weight of these questions. Something doesn’t fit. He spied the envelope lying on the bed. Only the name of the dicastery overseen by the cardinal was written on the label. He went over the timeline of events reported in the newscast. Nothing significant jumped out at him.

He examined the envelope again. No destination address. No return address. No postage. Strange. It appears Arrigoni didn’t plan to mail this package. He tapped the envelope while he gazed at the billowing curtains. Faint light glowed in the courtyard from lights bordering the footpaths. Arrigoni wouldn’t trust the mail system with so valuable an object. Who in their right mind would?…Send it by courier? But there’s no address…A Turkish mobster was found dead in Arrigoni’s apartment suspected of killing a security guard and the boyfriend of the archeologist who authored the report...Arrigoni wants me to divulge to the world a document that will destroy his Church. He couldn't put his finger on it, but somehow the cardinal was involved. None of this adds up. It's starting to resemble a politician's campaign promises. He sighed. As Mom used to say, "It will come out in the wash."

Giltmore reached for the phone. I wonder what this call will cost me. Then he remembered his mobile. He hung up and retrieved his unit from his suit jacket. He scrolled through his contacts until he found the name he was searching for. He placed the call through *WhatsApp* and checked his watch. Too early for her to be in bed, he judged.

## Chapter Forty
## Indianapolis - Wednesday Late Evening

With legs seemingly made of cement and feet made of bricks, Sandra clambered from the depths of sleepfulness to the heights of wakefulness, a state where she recognized the source of the strident sound resonating in her brain was of an external, not internal, origin. The urgent ringing of a telephone returned her to awareness. As she reached above her head for her mobile, a Quran slid off her lap and landed on the living room floor with a *thunk!*, startling her. She realized she had dozed off on the couch in her jammies in the midst of indulging her newfound curiosity about Islam.

"Hello?" she said, her voice still muzzy with sleep.

"Sandra, did I catch you at a bad time?"

His voice hit her like a glass of cold water. Wide awake now, she asked, "Mike, is everything all right? Are you okay?"

"No need to be alarmed, I'm fine."

Her stomach fluttered at the timbre of his voice. "What time is it there?"

"It's 3:23 A.M. Thursday morning," he said. "San—"

"What're you still doing up?"

"I was feeling lonely and I wanted to hear the sound of your voice," he half-kidded.

Her heart skipped a beat. "It's good to hear your voice, too."

"Yes, but more importantly—"

"More importantly?" she broke in, the disapproval in her tone vying with expectation.

"Just-as-importantly, I have the scoop of—of—since history began," he blurted out. "It relegates the 9/11 inside job to a cyclone in a saucepan."

Her interest aroused, Sandra swung her legs and planted her red toe-nailed feet on the polished wooden floor. "I'm all ears." She fussed with her hair.

"I ran into a priest—ex-priest. Actually, he ran into me but—His name is Marco Arrigoni. He's American. Have you seen him in the news?" Giltmore couldn't think straight, the excitement building in him like a pot of water on the boil.

"I'm too busy with work to watch television."

"You'll hear of him shortly and so will millions of others."

"What's got you so worked up, Mike?"

"The end of Christendom as we know it."

"I don't understand?"

"I don't expect you to. I'll tell you when I get home. You never know who's listening."

## Chapter Forty-One
## Istanbul – Early Thursday Morning

After dropping off the package at the Four Seasons Hotel, Marco made his way to Aysel's condo located north of the city. He had no choice. A wanted man, he needed shelter and she was his only friend.

Although more than a day had passed, Aysel had recovered somewhat from the initial shock of Baki's murder. His betrayal eased her tossing him down the memory hole—like flicking away a dead bug. Lucky for him, the assassin robbed her of the occasion to avenge his duplicity. Death had rescued him from her boundless wrath.

Well past midnight, Marco sat beside Aysel on a loveseat, holding her hands, happiness mingling with sorrow in his eyes. He found himself in a peculiar position. The woman he secretly loved was now available. So was he. No barriers between them remained, except his own anxiety and shyness. But he possessed the proper sense to know it wasn't the time to leap for joy but the time to console. He mustn't rush it, mustn't ruin the dignity of this moment. She was vulnerable, her psychological wounds raw. Her vulnerability wasn't his to exploit. Such a tactic could backfire on him. Her face exhibited a strained composure, like she was holding back volatile emotions. He would proceed with patience. Time was on his side.

"Twice I almost lost you, my dear. Praise God who saved you." He gave her hands a gentle squeeze.

"Your concern means a lot to me, Father. I'm glad you came."

"I'm…I'm sorry about Baki. He didn't deserve to die. May God's mercy be upon his soul." Afraid she could read his thoughts, he lowered his eyes and examined her hands. My rival is out of the picture so how come I don't feel content?

Aysel seemed touched by his heartfelt concern for her but she didn't share his sympathy for Baki. Her bitterness had recast her romantic image of her ex-lover.

"It's easy for you to be charitable, Father. You weren't the one deceived," she said, sourpussed.

He raised his eyes to hers. He saw deep emotional pain in them. "Baki's death was an outcome with no moral victory attached to it. Try to forgive him. You'll feel much better if you let go of your resentment toward him."

"That lying, deceitful bastard! He…He—" Overwrought, Aysel buried her face in his shoulder, and she abandoned herself to her anguish. Her body convulsed with waves of grief and anger, and her tears dampened his shirt. Marco awkwardly put his arm around her and did his best to comfort her. After several minutes of expending her misery, she composed herself.

"Sorry, Father." She sniffled and sat up again. Shimmering dampness clung to her long curved lashes.

He yanked a tissue from the box on the table and offered it to her. "Don't call me Father anymore."

She gaped at him with wide-open, mascara-smudged eyes, as if she had been slapped.

He bit his lower lip. Damn. "Forgive me for being short with you, my dear. I…I don't consider myself a priest anymore."

"You abandoned the priesthood?" she asked, dabbing her eyes with the tissue.

"Unofficially. Can you blame me?"

"No—Marco," she said in a mild tone. "And please call me Aysel from now on."

They were now on an equal playing field. His former occupation no longer stood between them.

He explained to her the killer's connection to the cardinal and how it was the final nail in the coffin of his Catholic faith.

"We've both been through an emotional wringer. We need to take stock of our situation," she said.

"Agreed. Tell me, Aysel. Did you mention the scroll to the police?

"Of course not."

"God bless you for keeping your word."

"At least one of us did."

Marco blenched. "I didn't break my promise to you on purpose. It sort of slipped out in the enthusiasm of the moment. Who would have guessed a high-ranking cardinal kept hired assassins on his payroll?"

She threw him a look that said, "You're forgiven this time, buddy." Then she adopted a more sympathetic expression. "Well, it's not your fault Petrelli's a snake."

He smiled and said, "I need to make a call. Is that okay with you?

"Be my guest."

He got up and paced while he spoke. He noticed Aysel out of the corner of his eye looking up at him with—appraisal?

His call ended, he returned to the loveseat.

"Who was that?"

"I was talking to a new friend. He has our scroll."

"Good riddance to it. It brought us nothing but bad luck."

"I can't imagine what you've been through, Aysel…But the word of God is a blessing, not a curse."

"We *are* still both alive, so I guess I should be grateful to God," she allowed.

"That's the spirit." He fiddled with another smartphone.

"Why do you have two phones?"

"One's mine, and this one"—he waggled it in his hand—"belonged to the killer. I snatched it before I fled my apartment."

"You took his *phone*?"

"The hitman wasn't in a position to argue…Ho-*lee* Mother! Your name and number are listed."

"But my number is private."

He showed her. "Petrelli likely gave the killer your name. How he got your number is anyone's guess." He resumed searching through the list of contacts, which were many.

"So that's how he located me. He tracked my smartphone."

Marco stopped scrolling and shot her a bewildered look.

"There's an app that allows invited parties to locate you via your mobile phone."

"Is there no privacy anymore?"

She rolled her eyes at him.

"It's nobody's damn business to know where I am," he said, and he continued scrolling.

"Any luck?"

"No bites yet." His thumb paused. *Kırmızı Kuş*. Turkish for red bird, he translated. "How clever," he said aloud.

"You found Petrelli's number?" Eagerness lit up her face.

"I suspect so. The killer entered his name under *Red Bird*."

"The cardinal is a red-colored bird. Bravo!" She clapped her hands. "Maybe the police can trace the number."

"Good idea. But I need to do something first."

"Such as…?"

"Contact Petrelli."

"What?" She beheld him as though he were a fugitive from a padded cell. "This psycho hired assassins to kill us and now you want to speak to him."

"Listen and learn."

## Chapter Forty-Two
## Greece – Early Thursday Morning

After taking the ferry from Brindisi, Italy to Igoumenitsa, Greece, Cardinal Petrelli and his driver, Father Angelo, drove with few breaks. Travelling on diplomatic business for the Vatican was a rare event for him but above suspicion. He had informed His Holiness of an urgent matter in Istanbul concerning the provenance of an ancient relic, for he couldn't leave the Eternal City without notice. His absence would be too conspicuous to ignore.

His Holiness wouldn't endorse my journey if he knew what I was up to, I'm sure, Cardinal Petrelli mused as he gazed out the window of the car while the Greek countryside rolled by. Wind whistled past them as they plunged in and out of verdant valleys, several cordoned by cloud-capped mountains. They stopped more than a few times on the rollercoaster ride to allow flocks of sheep to traverse the road from one field to the next.

The unexpected ring of his personal smartphone jolted him out of his meditative state. He withdrew it from his pocket and checked the Caller ID. "Impossible," he swore under his breath. He hesitated to answer it…Maybe the caller is an associate of his.

The instrument rang like an alarm bell in the tense atmosphere of the sedan.

Cardinal Petrelli made eye contact with Father Angelo in the rear view mirror.

He yielded at last and answered the ringing phone, disguising his voice. "Who is this?" he said in Italian.

"Guess who, Red Bird?"

He sucked in his breath and fear crept into his belly.

"You made your move and now I will make mine. *Capisce*?" the voice said, deathly calm.

The line went dead. Somewhere in the future lay a fateful meeting with his nemesis, a meeting that would decide both their fates. In his twisted mind, Cardinal Petrelli believed good always prevailed over evil. This certainty brought him a measure of comfort despite the knot of worry in his stomach.

"Who was it, Your Eminence?"

"An enemy of the Church." He added, "But not for much longer." He hoped he sounded more convinced than he felt. Fury boiled inside of him. Holy Mother, grant me revenge against those who seek to destroy your Church. He looked at his phone. Could it lead the police back to him? He removed the SIM card and pocketed it, then he lowered the window and threw away the phone. No loose ends.

## Chapter Forty-Three
## Istanbul - Three Weeks Later

Building to this moment for weeks, the American News Network had been saturating social media and the airwaves worldwide with breathless promos of a world-shattering television event billed as *The Last Miracle of the Messiah*. People, agog at the cryptic clues circulating on news sites, remained glued to their mobile devices. Anticipation was at a boil. Speculation was rampant. Bookies took bets on the substance of the miracle. Persons stopped in the street, often unmindful of their location, to check their Twitter and Facebook feeds, risking life and limb. Then the day of the big reveal finally arrived. And the world held its breath.

Giltmore, wearing a bespoke charcoal gray suit and red-patterned tie, and Sandra, outfitted in a smart black jacket and matching skirt, fidgeted in their seats, waiting for the signal to begin the show. The studio audience buzzed with excitement, its sense of expectation almost too great to contain. Tension permeated the air.

"Any predictions for this evening, Mike?"

"Tonight giants will fall—far and hard. For too long, the autocratic Catholic Church has quarantined the truth. The propagation of theological truth will resume once I'm done."

"Is the world ready for the truth?"

"Too bad if it isn't."

"Then let's make history together."

The studio manager signalled to Sandra off-camera and gave her the thumbs up.

"To all our viewers and listeners, welcome. We have a special show for you this evening," she said in a voice giddy with delight. "We are live at our affiliate studio here in Istanbul with retired Professor Mike Giltmore, who needs no introduction by now." Sandra turned to him.

"So, Mike, let's jump to the finish line. What is the last miracle of the Messiah?"

He cleared his throat. "Since the early 1900s, Bible scholars have hypothesized the Synoptic Gospels—Matthew, Mark and

Luke—were based on a so-called *Q document* because of their internal textual similarities. This primary document has remained elusive." He left the point hanging there in space for a pregnant moment. "Until now!"

The audience jerked, relieved of some of its pent-up tension.

"Turns out this hypothesis is factual beyond any doubt."

"I assume this so-called Q document is with us today?" Sandra said, prolonging the expectations of billions of viewers."

"Moses had his stone tablets and Jesus had the Gospel."

The audience wriggled in their seats, waiting with unbridled anticipation.

"What could this document be?" she teased.

Giltmore opened the lid of a shiny lacquered box sitting on a low table in front of them and withdrew a large scroll from it.

"To answer your question, it is the scroll of Jesus' beloved disciple!" He held up the scroll for the audience to see.

People jumped in their seats, shocked by his revelation.

"And, unlike the man-made Bible, this scroll is genuine," Giltmore said with conviction.

"What's the proof of this claim?"

"Aysel Bigili, a professor of archeology at Koç University here in Istanbul, radiocarbon-dated the scroll using accelerator mass spectrometry."

"And what did this analysis determine?"

"Pay attention ladies and gentlemen," he said. "When an organism dies, whether it be a tree or a bird, its carbon atoms decay at a measurable rate. That is how we can determine with great accuracy the age of ancient relics." He paused for effect. "This scroll is made from calfskin."

"So how old is it?" Sandra said, posing the question on every viewer's mind.

"It is two millennia old!"

"Which fits with Jesus's timeline," Sandra said over the loud murmuring emanating from the audience.

"Preserved for humankind with his most beloved disciple," Giltmore said.

"We'll come to the identity of this disciple in the second half of this show," Sandra said. "Before we go any further, the Turkish Ministry of Culture plans to reveal sections of this scroll in a special televised venue in several weeks' time. Happily, the ministry has allowed us to divulge a couple of salient points from the scroll to prevent us from going mad with curiosity. Mike, take it away."

"Thank you, Sandra." Turning to the camera again, he said, "The message in this scroll is a series of dos and don'ts as well as a collection of parables. There is no itinerary of Jesus' supposed travels nor any lists of his family lineage as mentioned in the Gospels.

"In my book, I advanced the theory Jesus survived his crucifixion. I was wrong." He smiled conspiratorially. "I was wrong because Jesus was not crucified!"

This revelation brought down the house.

"Someone else took the place of Jesus on the Cross. The scroll does not identify this person. Whoever he was, may God's mercy be upon his soul."

"Amen," Sandra said.

"Notwithstanding the scribe's message, we don't have to stretch our imaginations to believe the crucifixion of Jesus was a hoax," Giltmore said. "There's evidence in the Bible that undermines the Crucifixion story when we examine the testimony of those who witnessed the post-crucifixion Jesus."

"Patience, folks," Sandra instructed the restless audience. "Mike is coming to his conclusion."

"None of the witnesses mentioned any wounds on Jesus' face or body. We only have doubting Thomas asking to see Jesus' hands and to touch his side, and this account is only in the Gospel of John. The other three Gospels are silent on this topic.

"It bears mentioning the four Gospels were composed at least a couple of decades *after* the letters of Paul had gone the rounds in Asia Minor and *after* the destruction of the Second Temple in 70 CE," he emphasized. "Paul's theology of a crucified and resurrected Christ enjoyed a head start of at least two decades in the Greco-Roman world before the human-inspired Gospels entered the scene.

This explains the theological disconnect between the Gospels and Paul's letters."

"So what's your point, Mike?" Sandra asked, prevailing on him to conclude his monologue.

"What I'm trying to get at is when a martyr for God is resurrected, he or she will be resurrected bodily with the marks of martyrdom on his or her figure before entering Paradise blemish-free. If Jesus had been resurrected, there would have been more than nail marks on his hands and a scar in his side. Remember, he had been scourged. The story of doubting Thomas was an invention by the author of the Gospel of John in support of Paul's false theology."

"Invention?"

"The Gospel of John can't have it both ways. If Jesus was crucified and resurrected, he'd be unrecognizable because of his wounds. If Jesus wasn't crucified, he'd be blemish-free. Take your pick."

"So what is the truth according to Giltmore?" Sandra asked in a playful voice.

"It's conjecture but please indulge me one last time," he appealed.

"Okay," Sandra interjected. "Just this once," and the audience chuckled.

"Thomas wasn't seeking evidence of Jesus' crucifixion. He was seeking evidence of Jesus' having not been crucified." Giltmore remained silent for a moment to let his point sink in. Then he continued. "Think on this, folks. It was night time when the Roman soldiers, carrying torches, supposedly seized *Jesus* in the Garden of Gethsemane. Torchlight is not nearly as bright as modern electric lighting. Anyone resembling Jesus could have been nailed to the Cross and no one would have been the wiser. The Bible specifies not one of the twelve disciples witnessed Jesus' crucifixion."

"Your argument is intriguing but academic, Mike, since we now have this scroll in our possession."

"I wanted to demonstrate to the people how easy it is to be bamboozled when we accept conventional truth without critical and unbiased analysis."

"So you did. Now let's jump to the second point," Sandra urged. "It concerns the Good News that Jesus transmitted to the Jews."

Looking at Sandra, Giltmore said, "In the Gospel of John, Jesus tells his disciples he must go so he can send his successor." He added, "And no it wasn't Paul the Gnostic."

Scattered laughter erupted in the studio.

Turning back to the audience, he said, "Before I reveal the identity of Jesus' successor, I want to reach out to Christians and advise them of something before they form any judgement. For millennia, Christians have denigrated the Jews for denying the Messiah. But Christians are in the same position vis-a-vis Jesus' successor as the Jews are regarding the Messiah."

"Sounds like a classic case of the tires calling the pavement black," Sandra slipped in.

"There are none so blind as those in state of denial." He stopped speaking to allow his statement to sink in. Then he resumed his talk. "In this scroll, Jesus identifies his successor by name. His name is *The Praised One* in English. It means *Ahmed* in Arabic." He paused again for effect. Then he cried out, "Ahmed is also another name for *Mohammed* which means *Praised One* in English."

The audience reacted as if a bomb had exploded.

"Mohammed is the final prophet of God," Giltmore shouted. "This affirms the prophecies found in Deuteronomy, chapter 18, verse 18 and John, chapters 14 and 15, verse 26. For 1400 years, Islamophobes have been denying and ridiculing the designated successor of their supposed savior."

"Folks, we need to reflect on the impact this revelation will have on Jewish-Christian-Muslim relations," Sandra counselled. "Christians and Muslims are now coreligionists," she said, putting her reputation on the line. Someone of stature had to lead. Why not her? "Christians can no longer accuse the Jews of crucifying the Messiah and they can no longer deny the oneness and indivisibility of God, the foundation of Islam."

The audience acknowledged her brave declaration with a round of applause.

"Which brings us now to the second part of this show," Sandra informed, hoping no white supremacists back home would lynch her. "For two millennia, Bible scholars have puzzled over the identity of the most beloved disciple of Jesus. Because of our next guest's good fortune we know who this disciple was." Standing up, she said, "Please give a warm welcome to Marco Arrigoni."

A storm of applause burst when Marco strode onto the stage, wearing a dark suit and an open-necked white shirt. (He would've worn a tie but he didn't know how to knot one.) Giltmore rose to shake his hand. Marco exchanged handshakes with both of them, then settled into his chair.

"We're fortunate you could join us this evening, Marco. Can you share with us what has transpired in your life?"

Marco shifted to the edge of his seat. He took a deep breath and let it out, giving him time to center himself. "Two assassins sent by a high-ranking official in the Holy See tried to murder me so they could steal the scroll I found."

The audience collectively gasped and Mike's jaw dropped, recalling his conversation with Marco on the hotel phone. The wash had been hung out to dry.

"But, thanks to God, I got the better of the exchange with one of the assassins who lies dead in the city morgue. The other assassin was shot by the police as I'm sure you've all heard by now."

"I gather you've cleared up this unfortunate episode with the authorities?"

"No charges were laid against me. I pleaded self-defense. The public prosecutor accepted my plea."

Boisterous applause rang out.

"You mentioned the assassins were in the employ of the Holy See. Have any arrests been made at the Vatican?"

"None," he said without resentment. "There is no material evidence linking the assassins to the Holy See. Legally, a person cannot be arrested based on someone's accusation alone."

"For the record, a Vatican spokesman denies any involvement of the Holy See in this sordid affair. We would expect such a statement," Sandra said. Marco had more to get off his chest so she let him continue.

"Because of the message of the scroll and my Church's long-standing moral corruption, I abandoned the priesthood." A hint of sadness clouded his eyes which was swiftly replaced by a squinty expression of anger. "I could not remain a member of an institution that has sought, and continues to seek, to preserve its well-rehearsed fictions and privileges at all costs." He paused. His face then conveyed gentleness. Turning to the cameras again, he said, "If any of my parishioners are watching, I urge you to consider what has been discussed here today. After much soul-searching, I renounced Catholicism and I am exploring the religion of Submission now. I invite you to do the same."

Giltmore reached over and patted him on the shoulder. "If you have any questions...."

"We wanted to give you the honor, Marco, of revealing the identity of Jesus' most beloved disciple since you discovered his tomb," Sandra said. "But before we do where is this disciple's tomb located?" she asked, prolonging the suspense.

"Why, right beneath my former church."

Eyeing the cameras, Sandra disclosed, "Before you rush over to the Santi Giuseppe Church, the tomb is closed to the public. The Turkish police have instituted round-the-clock surveillance of the tomb. She added, "According to Turkish law, any historic artifact found on Turkish soil belongs to the state."

"There's no telling what the Church would do with his remains," Marco said in an ominous tone.

"What does the Turkish government plan to do with his tomb?" Sandra inquired.

"The Minister of Culture informed me the tomb will be sealed in concrete and will be video-monitored to prevent any unpleasantness. Catholics have a penchant for praying over the bones of so-called saints. This practice will not be allowed," Marco said matter-of-factly.

"So what are your plans for the future?"

"I need to find a new job."

"You're a hero," Giltmore said. "You shouldn't have any trouble finding one."

He smiled shyly. "It has been over twenty-five years since I applied for a job."

"We wish you the best in your new life, Marco," Sandra said, clapping her hands with gusto. Looking toward the audience, she reminded, "The Turkish Ministry of Culture is planning a worldwide television event in the coming weeks. The scroll will be publicized at this event. Please check your local stations for further information." She returned her attention to her guests. "How if we reveal the beloved disciple's identity?"

"I'm game," Marco said.

"Take it away," Sandra said.

Just as he was about to speak the lights went out and gunshots erupted in the studio. Above the ensuing pandemonium, a man screamed, "Death to the Illuminati. The scroll is a forgery. The Church will destroy those who get in its way."

When the lights came back on moments later, Giltmore was lying on top of Sandra, shielding her with his body, and he clutched the scroll. Marco was hugging the ground, staying as low as possible. People swarmed the exits, clambering over and tearing at one another, desperate to escape the bedlam. Plainclothed security personnel appeared out of nowhere with weapons drawn, seeking the gunman. Too late. He had fled the scene before the resulting panic ensued.

Sensibly, the network cut to commercial for people were too busy scrambling for their lives.

Believing the moment of danger had passed, Giltmore helped Sandra to her feet.

"I, uh, hope I didn't crush you."

Her tongue planted firmly in cheek, she gamely replied: "Don't worry about it, Mike. I've had rougher dates than this."

She glowed at his willingness to protect her with his own body.

"I hope we can do that again—but without the gunshots," he blurted out. Realizing his gaffe, he backpedalled. "I mean, I hope we don't have to go through *that* again. Not that I didn't mind. I mean—"

Sandra and Marco dissolved into fits of laughter while Giltmore's face silently communicated his embarrassment with a deep shade of scarlet.

When the humor of the moment had passed, Marco said in a more serious vein, "These fanatics won't give up. We must remain vigilant."

"I pray this was their last attempt to prevent the inevitable," Giltmore said with a faraway look in his eyes, "but something tells me it won't be."

## Chapter Forty-Four
## Istanbul

Cardinal Petrelli and Father Angelo endured each other's company in the residence of the Bishop of Istanbul since arriving in town several weeks ago. During this period, the cardinal had stepped out twice in civilian dress, ostensibly to inspect the affairs of the diocese in disguise. He returned from the second trip with a walking cane.

Ever imperious, Cardinal Petrelli had worn out his welcome with the bishop who was only too happy when His Eminence left the residence to attend the unveiling of the scroll in Old Istanbul. In the bishop's estimation, not since the time of Job did a man have to endure such trials in forbearance.

The limousine came to a stop in the VIP parking lot. Father Angelo shifted the transmission into Park.

"Wait for me here," Cardinal Petrelli ordered.

Father Angelo watched the cardinal limp away, leaning on a cane. Since when does His Eminence use a cane?

* * *

Cardinal Petrelli moved like a man on a mission. There was determination in his uneven stride as he limped southeast on Divan Yolu street devoid of pedestrians. Shops were shuttered in the security zone. A dusk curfew was in effect for local residents. He nodded to the security personnel on his way to the venue in Sultanahmet Square. They stared back at him as he shuffled by on the sidewalk as though assessing his potential to be a threat.

When he was out of earshot, a security guard spoke *sotto voce* into his throat mike: "Red Bird is approaching. Stand ready."

A roar of applause and chanting erupted while the cardinal stood in line waiting to pass through the x-ray scanner before entering the VIP section. His turn came. He showed his ID and handed his cane to an attendant who took hold of it by its shaft. He passed through the scanner without incident and picked up his cane on the other side. As he made his way toward the VIP section, his cane beating *tap*, *tap*,

*tap* on the pavement, the object of his hatred could be seen up on the stage. Cardinal Petrelli abandoned himself to his mania for revenge and mounted the stairs to the stage, no limp in his step now.

* * *

In the twilight of a fading day, Giltmore stood proudly on the promontory that is Old Istanbul, visualizing his position on a map. Bounded by the Sea of Marmara in the south, the Bosporus Strait in the east and the Golden Horn River in the north, towering above the coursing waterways far below, the peninsula on which Old Istanbul reposed in historic splendor rose gradually from the shoreline where the waves rolled in and hurled themselves against the rocks again and again with Sisyphean single-mindedness. For seventeen hundred years this headland beyond the reach of the pounding sea had been the locus of Roman and Byzantine emperors and Ottoman sultans, leaders of vast armies before whose vast might many an enemy had once trembled in terror.

How times had changed, Giltmore ruminated. Istanbul was no longer an imperial capital. Hadn't been for almost a century. Gone were the royal trappings of empire. What remained, however, were sacred architectural wonders—imposing monuments which spoke to this former imperial glory—dotting the skyline of Old Istanbul laid out before him. These colossal edifices, composed of brick and stone and marble, summoned to mind the faded grandeur of a glorious past. Though Istanbul had ceased to be the capital city of an empire, which had influenced world civilization every bit as much as the Roman Empire had, its heart still thumped to the beat of a martial cadence.

Just as bygone empires had their day in the sun so had human-inspired religions. Totems, talismans and amulets were sprinkled throughout archeological sites worldwide. Tangible souvenirs of pagan beliefs which had once held undeserving sway over the credulous minds of great swathes of humanity.

People of this age have no qualms sanctimoniously judging the unenlightened beliefs of their ancestors who had once assigned great spiritual value to these artifacts all the while kissing and bowing to statues of religious figures that could neither see, nor hear, nor speak.

Giltmore sighed at the hypocrisy. The unconscious conceit of so-called *modern* people.

Whoa, Ol' Boy, not so fast. It wasn't too long ago that you yourself were an idol worshipper, his inner voice reminded him. Giltmore winced at the reminder. So true, he mouthed to himself.

Happy to be back in Istanbul after several weeks spent stateside preparing for the momentous celebration about to unfold this evening, he stood once again between the former Hagia Sophia Church, erected in 537, now a museum, and the Sultanahmet Mosque, also known as the Blue Mosque, completed in 1616 on the site of the former Great Palace of Byzantine, which had fallen into ruin by the time Mehmet the Conqueror entered Constantinople in 1453.

He inspected the elaborate stage constructed in the shape of a bridge which linked those crowning achievements of sacred architectural genius. It suggested a connection, a continuity between those two towering monuments of religion: Christianity at one end and Islam at the other. The sun, however, was setting on the former and a new dawn was beckoning for the latter.

Huge screens, erected on either side of the stage, would provide simultaneous translations in Turkish, Arabic, Russian, Italian, Spanish, French, German, Greek, Hindi, Japanese, Malay and Mandarin, permitting the major regions of the world to be witness to a new chapter in the history of humanity waiting to be written, not in the blood of martyrs as so many others had been written, but in the spirit of brotherhood and sisterhood. That was the hope.

Security was omnipresent and tight as a sailor's knot. Anonymous threats had been leveled against this venue for there were many who could not accept the new reality thrust upon them, preferring instead the *status quo ante*. The enemies of truth, who might try to sabotage tonight's special gathering for their own selfish ends, did not operate within the boundaries of moral law and so lethal force was visibly deployed. Ready to counter any desperate assailant, alert and armed-to-the-teeth security personnel ringed the stage, fingers on the triggers of their weapons. Dogs, trained to detect explosive materials, and their handlers roamed the premises, seeking, always seeking.

People entered the venue through x-ray scanners like those used in airports. Armed drones—lethal electronic eyes in the sky—hovered silently in the no-fly zone above Istanbul, like birds of prey, waiting to unleash pinpoint death with a microwave beam at a moment's notice. The drones' fourth-generation Forward Looking Infrared (FLIR) cameras blanketed the security zone in overlapping rings of harmless electromagnetic radiation, seeking concealed sources of heat which might indicate sinister intent. Vehicles were forbidden within half a mile of the venue, creating extraordinary headaches for motorists but peace of mind for security personnel.

Beneath a star-filled inky sky, dignitaries, comprising heads of state and representatives of principal religious orders, were seated in the grandstand behind the stage where Giltmore stood, imposing, redeemed. He radiated self-assurance, savouring his moment back in the spotlight. His reputation had been rehabilitated, his detractors thoroughly discredited, hoisted with their own fatuous *pétards*. He projected an air of rejuvenation, like he had been revivified and given a new mission in life, a mission replete with potential dangers. He was resigned to his new path in life, a life to be lived in the service of promoting religious conciliation to his fellow man and woman.

It would be easy to gloat, Giltmore thought, as he surveyed the assembled crowd, a convocation of the truly hopeful. He had been vindicated, his detractors thoroughly rebuked. Justifiably so. But that was then and this is now. He had won and they had lost. A hunger for revenge had been gnawing at his gut but it had been assuaged by an act of forgiveness. "Magnanimity is the better part of victory," Marco had counseled him. So it was in this spirit he proceeded.

He approached the podium while his stomach fluttered with excitement. This must be how Jesus felt at the Mount of Olives when he addressed the multitudes.

He surveyed the audience like a rock star at a concert. "People of the world. Welcome. In the words of Moses, Jesus and Mohammed, peace be upon you," he greeted those in attendance, and his voice boomed over the loudspeakers.

The applause rose steadily, building in strength like a cresting tsunami of sound. On and on it rose to a pulsating crescendo, washing over him, invigorating him. He recognized the applause wasn't meant for him but for what this evening represented for humanity—a chance to come together as one global family. Giltmore buzzed with the thrill of solidarity before this emotive sea of humanity. He grinned like a five-year-old gifted with his first bicycle.

I have achieved my life's dream. I pursued the truth and, by God, I found it!

His excitement rose with the tidal wave of applause. "Thank you…Thank you. I detect a sentiment of great anticipation in your applause," he said above the crash of clapping hands. "Your expectations will not go unrequited but will be fulfilled beyond your imagination!" he promised.

If it were seemingly possible, the applause increased in intensity and volume. He held up his hands for silence. A semblance of order was soon restored.

"This is a humbling experience. Who could have dreamed humanity would ever be witness to this historic moment," he wondered aloud.

Rapturous applause erupted in the open air of Sultanahmet Square again.

It had taken two thousand years for humanity to arrive at this moment in history. What was a few minutes more? He waited for the applause to subside.

"Time is a swift flowing stream," he began. "Therefore, we cannot stand in the same moment twice. So let us seize this historic moment in time before it passes us by," he urged. "Now is the time for reconciliation, not recrimination. The time for building bridges, not barricades. The time for creating alliances, not divisions. The time for solidarity, not dissension. The time for celebrating what has been found, not grieving for what has been lost. The time for valorizing what unites us, not what divides us. The time for celebrating common ground, not occupying the moral high ground.

This-is-now-the-time for a new beginning, a beginning that promises hope, a hope that will lead to harmony among humankind."

Frenzied clapping ensued, drowning out sporadic voices of protest, the majority of the audience swept away by his soaring oratory.

To hell with the script. Time to sow the wind and ride the whirlwind, he decided. "Now is the time for the citizens of every country whose leaders are flouting international law to rise up and toss the leaders of these rogue regimes in jail. Power to the people! Power to the people!" he yelled into the microphone, and the audience took up his chant. "Unleash the revolution for truth. Let the manipulators of truth tremble in their shoes!"

The audience went wild and the dignitaries squirmed in their seats. Rebellion was in the air and he was their standard-bearer.

He reverted to the script once the crowd had calmed down. "I want to draw your attention to this distinctive stage on which I am standing. It was built in the shape of a bridge to represent a shared link between Judaism, Christianity and Islam," he explained. "And what is this link?" He answered, "It is none other than Jesus the Messiah whose message is the link between Moses' and Prophet Mohammed's revelations, the bookends of rational monotheism."

Once again Giltmore had to pause his speech for the hand clapping and cheering were too deafening to hear him.

"After Jesus, God sent one last prophet, not just to the Arabs, but to all of humankind. Prophet Mohammed was the only prophet sent to preach a universal message to all of humanity and not to a single tribe, people or ethnicity. As you will soon hear, the message of the scroll has a resounding echo in the message of the Prophet, peace be upon him."

Boisterous applause broke out.

"So here we are peacefully assembled in a spirit of brotherhood and sisterhood, an assembly made possible by Divine Power," Giltmore continued. "We are on the cusp of a new era in global human relations. Instead of religious fratricide, we can look forward to a period of religious fraternity. For the first time in almost two thousand years, we are witnesses to the words of the prophet and messenger of God whom humanity has known as Jesus the Messiah. And like the message of Mohammed, Jesus' message of Submission is the cure for, not the cause of, humankind's afflictions.

"On these giant screens you see to the left and right of me, facsimiles of the Messiah's scroll will be displayed. The Aramaic text will be highlighted as it is translated. For those who can read Aramaic, you'll have the unalloyed pleasure of reading the text in the Messiah's native language, as I have.

"For security reasons, the scroll is not present with us this evening. It's stored away for it's a prize that belongs to posterity. Nonetheless, I've heard rumors there are plans afoot to exhibit the scroll in venues around the world in the near future," he said, smiling conspiratorially.

Applause exploded from the crowd.

"For all the doubting Thomases out there," he shouted into the microphone.

A chorus of laughter issued from the audience.

"For centuries, Christians and Muslims have been at odds with one another," he said with chagrin. "At the center of this clash was a theological dispute over the person of Jesus the Messiah. This dispute no longer exists with the discovery of the scroll." His tone was contrite, not condescending.

"This shocking reality is difficult for the followers of Jesus to digest. As a former Christian, I know. But it's the truth according to the message of the scroll, and so Christians should accept this newfound truth in a spirit of humility and respect. To do otherwise is to reject the words of Jesus and of his Lord.

"And to my fellow Muslims, out of respect for your Christian brothers and sisters whose world has been upended, you should be charitable and adopt a tone of humility rather than a note of triumph in this matter," he advised. "So, in the enduring words of the Messiah: 'Do unto others as you would have them do unto you.' And in the eternal words of the Prophet: 'Desire for others what you desire for yourself and you will be the most just among mankind.' Who can dispute the wisdom of their immortal words?

"Furthermore, God said in the Quran: and surely you will find nearest of them in affection to Muslims, those who say, 'We are Christians. That is because among them are priests and monks, and that they are not arrogant.'

"Moving now to the scroll, Jesus attests to submission to the will of God as his path and the path of the prophets just as we read in Matthew 12:48-50, Mark 3:35 and Luke 8:21, all of which communicate the same message: whoever does the will of God is my brother and sister and mother. Imagine. With the stroke of a reed pen, Jesus unwittingly but decisively removed the source of animosity and division between Christians and Muslims."

He waited again for the deafening applause to diminish.

"Not surprisingly, the scroll is silent just as are the canonical Gospels about the central tenets of Christianity—original sin, baptism, the Trinity, vicarious atonement and the Resurrection. So we can conclude that these rituals and practices are nothing more than inventions," he pointed out. "The scroll also refutes the notion of the Trinity by preaching the absolute oneness of God and His not conceiving a son. Regarding the Crucifixion, the scroll mentions it was not Jesus who was crucified but someone who resembled him. Finally, the Ascension of the Messiah is recorded in the scroll. This tells us Jesus is alive in Heaven and awaiting his return!"

Cheers of joy rose up from the crowd.

"Let me conclude my introduction to the scroll by saying, there is no longer an *us* and a *them*. For we are all beings created by one God in all of our wondrous colors and hues."

Vigorous whoops and whistles resounded in the square.

"Without further ado, please welcome to the stage a hero for the ages," Giltmore said, as he gestured to his right.

A huge roar erupted from the crowd which rose as one, and the phalanx of cameras arrayed in front of the stage swung as one in the direction of Giltmore's arm. As Marco approached the podium, camera flashes went off like the opening volley of cannon fire in the Battle of Constantinople. They pumped hands before Giltmore took his seat with the dignitaries. Temporarily dazzled, Marco had trouble seeing the text of his speech laid out on the lectern, and a gentle breeze ruffled the pages of his address. He smiled nervously at the cameras. This was his moment. He had earned it. If not for the grace of God, he wouldn't be here.

Should I blow them kisses? Knock it off, he ordered himself.

He patted the air in a silent appeal for calm. The audience, in its enthusiasm, ignored him. TV cameras, trained on him, their cyclopean glassy eyes monitoring his every movement and nervous tic, made him self-conscious even though he was used to public speaking. After all, he had been a priest. But this. He now had an inkling of what it was like to be in the spotlight, and Marco knew he would never forget this moment for as long as he lived.

He waited for the audience to quieten down before delivering his first line. "Welcome. *Salaam alaykum.* Peace be upon you. My name is Marco Arrigoni," he humbly informed the audience.

"Mar-co!" the assembled crowd chanted over and over.

He blushed with embarrassment. I seek refuge in you Lord from pride, he prayed in the silence of his heart. Faced with such unexpected adulation, he grappled with his ego to maintain a humble equilibrium. He waited for the chanting to wane.

In a strong voice quiet with conviction he began his address to the peoples of the world. "Several weeks ago, I was an anonymous priest toiling away in obscurity, doing my best to save souls and make this world a better place for my flock," he said. "Little did I know what life-altering plans the Almighty had in store for me. It was only through Divine intervention I found the scroll. An earthquake isn't a natural phenomenon that typically produces a happy ending, but the Almighty, in His unfathomable power, transformed something destructive into something constructive. For just as an earthquake shakes the ground on which we stand, the discovery of the scroll has shaken the world in which we live!"

A torrent of applause descended.

"There's no doubt these are times whose temper test men's souls just as these are times whose trials temper the souls of men. Let us put an end to the old world of divisiveness so that a new world of inclusiveness waiting to be born can take its place. We—"

He had to pause once again for the audience to express itself.

"We are fortunate to be witnesses to this miraculous birth of friendship and goodwill among diverse peoples. We are met in this great gathering of humanity to bear witness to the message of a humble carpenter and a prophet and messenger of God who lived two thousand years ago. A message reminding the people of that age what their obligations were to their Lord and to each other. These obligations were neither new nor onerous, simply voluntary.

"God commands our humble submission to His will, but we can choose to obey or disobey Him. Submission is a simple covenant between creature and Creator every adolescent understands. It entails no mysteries to be demystified by a priestly caste, no incantations to be intoned by initiates and no consumption of flesh and blood whether they be transubstantiated or consubstantiated. The convention of suspending one's reason for the sake of contrived and convoluted beliefs is finished."

Marco paused for breath while the audience applauded triumphantly.

Swiping a wayward lock of hair, he picked up where he had left off. "Centrifugal forces beyond our control have been pulling humanity apart for ages. Then, like a bolt from Heaven, the message of the scroll appears miraculously in our midst, appealing to the better angels of our natures. As you will soon learn, its words radiate the power to draw us back together with the compelling authority that only Divine revelation can exert on our collective consciousness. Tonight is a rare opportunity for global peace to take flight, a peace that enshrines tolerance for good and intolerance for evil. The time when war followed war like waves upon the sea is surely over."

"Peace not war," someone yelled repeatedly and the audience took up the chant.

Marco waited for the chanting to dwindle. He continued. "In the ledger of life, we are the sum of all our yesterdays and our tomorrows are but the sum of our hopes and fears of our todays. So let us pledge from this day forward that our tomorrows will be greater than the sum of our todays so that when the final sum is tallied, our fears will be vanquished and our hopes will be victorious."

Enthusiastic applause supervened.

"I conclude this brief address by paraphrasing the words of the man known to history as the Great Emancipator, who, like the beloved disciple, did not live to witness the fruits of his labor. So I ask your indulgence, ladies and gentlemen, as I channel my inner Abraham Lincoln."

The audience fell silent in anticipation.

Marco glanced heavenward. This is for you, Mama. He coughed into his hand before continuing. "In the name of God, the Entirely Merciful, the Especially Merciful," he invoked. "We are gathered in a city having known religious warfare throughout its long history but likewise it is the final resting place of a prophet's disciple so it is altogether fitting and proper that the first step of this noble journey on which we are embarking this evening should begin on this hallowed site.

"To ensure the success of this journey, we must dedicate our efforts toward the reconciliation between the People of the Book, that is, between Christian, Muslim and Jew. In so doing, we must acknowledge our unpayable debt to the beloved disciple who dedicated his life to safeguarding this scroll upon which this great effort of reconciliation lies. We know not what personal trials he bore to secure its survival for the benefit of posterity but we do know what trials humanity has borne in the absence of the scroll's message. The beloved disciple did his part for humanity and now it is up to us to ensure this effort of reconciliation can long endure.

"In the great scheme of life, however, we cannot honor the beloved disciple's dedication if our deeds contradict our declarations. For if our actions belie our words, then the sacrifice of this humble disciple will have been in vain. Therefore, if this great effort of reconciliation we have conceived is stillborn for lack of proper care and constancy, then posterity shall remind us and long condemn us for the unfinished toil begun here. It is, therefore, binding upon us to continue to light the way he forged so long ago so he shall not have died in vain. It is for us, therefore, to be committed to the difficult task remaining before us—that, to honor the dedication of this disciple, we stay true to that just purpose for which he gave the last full measure of devotion—that this world, under God, shall enjoy a rebirth of Submission, wherein the religion of God, by God and for God, shall be submission to the will of God on His good Earth."

A thunderous roar of applause erupted, threatening to awaken the heavens.

"Let us turn now to a number of passages from the scroll and listen and learn," he said, concluding his brief address. He gathered the pages of his speech, squared them edgewise, then tucked them under the laptop computer which lay on the lectern. Marco heard loud voices behind him as he raised the screen of the laptop. He peered over his shoulder and did a double-take.

So you dared show up.

Cardinal Petrelli, his scarlet soutane flapping with each unyielding stride, marched toward Marco like an angry squall. Guards ran onto the stage, shouting for him to stop. Onward he came, like a thundercloud ready to burst, his face a roiling mask of fury, manifesting his state of inner turmoil.

The sight of his treacherous friend stoked a white-hot rage in Marco; the instinct for revenge consumed him. He sprinted toward the cardinal, still several yards away.

Petrelli had but one shot to fire. "Vengeance is mine, I will repay," he bellowed, and he pointed his cane at Marco just as he slid to the ground.

A single gunshot exploded from the end of the walking stick. The open square amplified the report, the danger it signified.

Screams erupted from the crowd.

A bullet whizzed above Marco who kept sliding on the slick wooden stage until he connected with the cardinal, knocking his feet out from under him. It was as though two worlds had collided: one timeworn and backward-looking, the other confident and forward-looking. Security forces ran pell-mell onto the stage and pounced on Cardinal Petrelli.

Cheers erupted from the audience.

Marco scrambled upright. Cardinal Petrelli, yanked to his feet by guards, glared at Marco who said, "I only turn my cheek to a true believer." Then he added with a smirk, "A nice pen has been prepared for you, Red Bird. It's called prison. Birds who flock together are caged together."

Cardinal Petrelli reacted maniacally. "I am the next pope," he screamed over and over, as he tried to break free from his captors who were just as determined to see him meet his well-deserved fate.

Marco returned to the lectern somewhat shaky on his feet. He smoothed back his hair and gripped the sides of the lectern. He swallowed the lump of anxiety in his throat and spoke evenly into the microphone. "Ladies and gentlemen, please remain calm. Order has been restored. It appears there are still members of the old guard who cannot accept the new world order that has been thrust upon us." He kidded, "The organizers of this ceremony promised us fireworks this evening. I'm sure this is not what they had in mind." He hoped he sounded witty if only to disguise his own fright and to soothe the audience.

Nervous laughter rippled through the crowd.

"I think I speak for everyone when I say we've had enough excitement for one evening. So let us return to the program." He reached for the remote. The words *The Last Miracle of the Messiah* appeared on the large video screens to his left and right. A smaller screen rose from the stage behind him for the viewing pleasure of the dignitaries.

Cheers exploded from the crowd.

Marco waited for the cheering to abate. Without introduction, he launched into the scroll. His audience, hushed in silence, sat spellbound in their seats as he recited words of majesty recorded by the scribe of a holy prophet. The perception of time vanished. Minutes turned to hours as he read portions of the scroll. When the end of the reading approached, he stopped speaking and scanned the audience. They held their breath, their eyes riveted on him.

He peeked at his watch. Glory to God! Over three hours had elapsed since his recital began. "And so we arrive at the final verses of this message. Let us hold fast to these words for the sake of generations to come," he pleaded. Then he recited:

My teacher said before he departed:

In the last days there will be learned men who teach abstinence in the world but will not be abstinent themselves, who will teach men to take delight in the next world but will not take delight in it themselves, and who will warn men against coming before rulers but will not refrain themselves. They will draw near to the rich and keep far from the poor; they will be pleasant to great men but will shrink from humble men. Those are the brethren of the devils and the enemies of the Merciful.

Do not hold on to me because I am ascending to my Lord. Go instead to my brothers and say to them, 'I am ascending to my Lord and your Lord, to my God and your God.'

It is to your advantage that I go away, for if I do not go away, the Advocate will not come to you; but if I go, I will send him to you. When the Spirit of truth comes, he will guide you into all the truth; for he will not speak on his own, but will speak whatever he hears, and he will declare to you the things that are to come. He will take what is mine and declare it to you.

Whoever hates me hates my Lord also.

And their saying: 'We killed Christ Jesus the son of Mary, the Messenger of God,' but they killed him not, nor crucified him, but so it was made to appear to them, and those who differ therein are full of doubts, with no knowledge, but only conjecture to follow, for of a surety they killed him not. No, God raised him up unto Himself and God is exalted in Power, Wise.

And I am not over you a guardian. And follow what is revealed to you and do persevere until God judges for He is the best of the judges.

Indeed, for those who do not believe in the Hereafter, We have made pleasing for them their deeds, so they wander blindly.

Those are the ones for whom there will be the worst of punishment, and in the Hereafter they are the greatest losers.

And to God belong the unseen of the Heavens and the earth, and toward Him is the return of the affair—the whole of it. So worship Him and rely upon Him and your Lord is not heedless of what you do.

Surely for those who believe and do good, for them are Gardens of Paradise as an entertainment: they shall abide in them and they shall not seek a change from there.

And should anyone of them say: 'I am surely a deity besides Him,' then such a one, We shall reward him with the Hellfire. Likewise we requite the wrongdoers. Glory be to God, far high is He above what they associate.

And whoever calls upon any other deity with God, he has no authority about it, so his reckoning is only with his Lord. Surely the deniers shall not succeed.

And whoever invokes besides God another deity for which he has no proof—then his account is only with his Lord. Indeed, the deniers will not succeed.

> All praise belongs to God alone, He has no partners, and He is Lord of all the worlds.
>
> The sending down of the Scripture is from God, the Exalted in Might, most Wise. We have indeed revealed the Scripture to you with the truth, therefore, worship God, making the religion exclusive for Him.
>
> So keep your duty to God, and obey me. God, He is my Lord and your Lord. So worship Him. This is the right path.
>
> And truly it is the Certain Truth. Therefore, glorify the name of your Lord, the Most Great!
>
> Amen

After a poignant pause, the giant video screens went blank. Then the air was rent by the high-pitched sirens of multiple rockets launched. Fiery trails arced across the inky sky before exploding in a series of booms in a glittering array of colors, painting the firmament in a kaleidoscope of colorful patterns. Thousands of eyes shifted heavenward in rapt attention.

O Lord, may these bombs bursting in air be the sole kind we witness from this day forward, Marco supplicated as he took his seat beside Aysel in the VIP section. He reached for her hand and they exchanged tender glances. Together they watched bright eruptions of sparkling colors flare up and fizzle out in the sky above them.

## Endings

Weeks later…

**Vatican City**

"We're going live now to St. Peter's Square in Vatican City where our ANN correspondent, Angela Salvadori, is standing by. Angela, can you hear us...? Angela?"

"Hi, Connie. Yes, I can hear you now," she announced, holding her microphone in one hand while she pressed her earpiece with the other.

"Angela, can you tell us what's happening there? It sounds boisterous in the background. What's the mood like?"

"The crowd is angry. People are seething, demanding answers from their spiritual leaders. Behind me, the Swiss Guard has been called out. Soldiers are lined up in front of the gates that lead to the Papal Palace."

"We can hear the crowd around you chanting a slogan. What are they chanting?"

"They're chanting, '*Il Papa non ha i pantaloni, Il Papa non ha i pantaloni*'"

"You're Italian, Angela. What does that mean in English?"

"It means, 'The Pope has no pants, the Pope has no pants.'"

"Any idea what this chant is referring to?"

"I'm guessing it's alluding to Hans Christian Andersen's story *The Emperor's New Clothes*."

"Lucky one of us is culturally literate. Sounds like things could get ugly. Please keep us posted, Angela."

* * *

## Washington, D.C.

"What can you tell us about the crowd surrounding the White House and the Congress, Tom?"

"This is unlike anything I've seen since the anti-Vietnam War protests, Connie. The American people have awoken. Professor Giltmore has the crowd howling for blood." The camera switched briefly to Giltmore galvanizing the crowd on a podium in front of the Capitol Building before switching back to Tom. "His third television appearance with Sandra Dowling last week exposed the War on Terror as nothing but a modern-day crusade for securing energy resources in the Middle East that has bankrupted our country and made us a pariah nation. Administration officials are running for cover."

"I see protesters holding signs. What's written on them, Tom?"

"The message on the majority of signs reads: 'The tree of liberty must be refreshed with the blood of this regime's tyrants.'"

"Jeffersonian but with a twist. Tom, has anyone from the White House commented on this protest?"

"The President's press secretary made a statement." He read from a notepad. "I quote: 'The people have a right to peacefully assemble and express their grievances vocally but the people should be aware that the government will not tolerate any violence from them.' Unquote."

"Smacks of hypocrisy. The President has no problem supporting populist uprisings in Hong Kong, Venezuela and Iran, but not at home. Stay out of trouble, Tom."

"I'll do my best, Connie."

* * *

## Indianapolis

The rust-gutted brown car rolled to a stop across the rain-splattered street from the house located near the Geist reservoir. A *For Sale* sign decorated the well-groomed lawn. The vehicle was out of place in this upscale neighbourhood. The driver drained the last of a beer and flung the can crashing into the pile collecting in the passenger foot well. The house address matched the one provided him by a newfound buddy who had understood his need to get even. They had become fast friends over the past couple of months. He reclined his seat, crossed his arms and slouched down to wait.

Worried, the driver hoped the neighbors wouldn't get suspicious and call the cops.

He waited, and the rain beat a rattling tattoo on the roof of the car and flowed in rivulets down the windows. Periodically, he rubbed off the fog on the driver-side window with the sleeve of his jacket. Few cars passed by him in this chic residential district. To relieve the tedium of his vigil and to drown out the annoying sound of the rain, he turned on the radio.

"…A spokesperson for the Islamic Society of North America has reported curiosity about Islam has mushroomed and visits by non-Muslims to mosques have spiralled upward as well. Not surprisingly the Quran is climbing the bestseller charts. Turning now to international news…"

The driver's patience was soon rewarded. A luxury car splashed through the rain, spraying water in every direction, and pulled into the driveway of the home he was surveilling.

A car door swung out and an umbrella popped open. A tall man alighted from the vehicle.

The driver came alert.

Umbrella Man came around to the other side of the car and opened the door. A female passenger stepped out. Together they approached the entrance to the home.

The man's hand visibly shook as he fumbled with the key to the front door. After several heroic attempts, he inserted the key, unlocked the door and swung it wide open.

The woman stepped hesitantly into the house followed by her companion. The door shut.

"I'll pack some things to take back to your place," he called out to her as she retreated down the hall toward the living room.

The woman entered the bright living room furnished in dark wood and black leather, tasteful and masculine, but with little personality, much unlike the man who had purchased them. She removed the clips from her hair and tousled her mane, loosening the long, silky tresses, while her eyes roamed the pictures hanging on the walls. A large glass picture frame hanging above the fireplace mantel grabbed her attention. She puzzled over it.

"Hon, can you come here for a second, please?"

Moments later the man came up beside her and put his arm around her. She was a few inches shorter than he now that she wore more modest and sensible footwear. "You summoned me?"

"What's *that*?" she asked, pointing to the large picture frame.

His cheeks reddened. "I was on this talk show once, and a special woman touched me on the arm during the interview."

She reflected for a moment. "Go on."

"When I arrived home after that show, I cut off the sleeve of my suit jacket at the elbow to preserve it for posterity," he explained. "It's a sacred totem of my love for her. I suppose I should remove it now that I have you as my lawfully wedded wife."

Her hand went to her mouth. "You romantic fool," she chided him, clapping him playfully on his chest.

"I may be a fool but I'm a fool only for you."

Sandra turned to Giltmore. "I love you," she whispered, her eyes glistening.

"I love you, too," he replied solemnly.

"Is that the doorbell I hear?" she said with a frown, mid-kiss.

He cocked his ear. "Can't be the police. They stopped patrolling last week. I'll take care of it, love." He released her. "Don't go anywhere."

Giltmore peeked through the peephole. "Oh," he said involuntarily, a tic of surprise in his voice. He unlocked and opened the front door. "Uh, hi."

"What? No, 'Nice to see *you*.'"

The caller's sneakers squelched as he shifted his weight from one sodden foot to the other while his hands remained tucked in the pockets of his rain-streaked windbreaker.

"This is a surprise," was all that escaped from Giltmore's throat.

"Do you remember the advice you gave me way back when?" he asked, his glassy eyes unfocused.

"Of course I do."

"You told me to stop going to church and to worship God only. Next thing I knew, my wife up and left me and took my baby girl with her," he blubbered.

"I'm sorry for…for your loss. But what does this have to do with me?"

"I trusted you, Mike. I—things have gone to hell now. They fired me. I have no security guard job. No wife. No kid. Because of you!"

"Calm down, Julio. You can find a new wife and a new job."

"I don't want another wife," he yelled. "I want my old life back." He hit his rain-plastered skull with the heel of his hand. "Shut up. Shut up. Shut up...Friggin' medication they put me on causes me to hear voices," he sputtered.

"Relax, Julio, relax."

Julio yanked his other hand from his pocket, brandishing a small revolver. "This"—looking at the weapon with crazed eyes—"is going to help me relax."

Giltmore sensed Sandra behind him. "Who's at the door, Mike?" she asked, a nervous edge in her voice.

"Get back. He's got a gun," he yelled over his shoulder at her, and she let out a scream of horror.

P-tap P-tap P-tap echoed as she flew down the hallway. Giltmore staggered, the force of the bullets propelling him backwards. He collapsed in the vestibule.

Sandra turned. The doorway was empty. Giltmore lay sprawled on his back on the cold ceramic tiles. Three ugly, red wounds stained his pressed white shirt, like spots of burgundy wine on a starched white tablecloth. She crumpled to the floor. The sound of tires squealing on wet pavement faded away.

"Mi-i-ike," she keened, crawling to where he lay panting. His breath came in labored wheezes and sobs from deep within wracked her body. She cradled his head in her lap. He struggled to speak.

"Ssh, Ssh," Sandra said in a soft voice. "Don't try to speak. Save your energy." His lips quivered. She bent her ear closer to him, her tears dampening his face.

"I-I was r-r-right...I w-wo-won't get t-to see...y-you grow ol-d...and wr-inkly, my love."

"Don't say that, Mike. The ambulance is on its way."

"They…they kill-ed m-me…but they…they can-'t kill…the truth," he struggled. "D-Don't let…them w-win, my love."

"I won't, I won't."

Giltmore rallied himself. "There is…no g-g-god but…God…an…and Mo…hammed i-is His prophet."

"Hang in there, Mike," Sandra wailed as she rocked back and forth, clutching him for dear life.

* * *

**Istanbul**

"Aysel," Marco called out to her, his voice ringing with urgency.

"I'm coming, I'm coming," she hollered from the next room. Aysel dashed into the living room of their secure location and saw him huddled in front of a laptop computer.

"What is it?"

"Something terrible."

She stood beside him and her eyes bulged at the banner headline. "They killed Mike."

"He posed a danger to the Deep State."

"Any regrets?"

"About what?"

"Leaving the Church and embarking on this crusade for the truth."

"None," he replied without reflection, as he reached for her hand. "I thought I had no more lessons to learn but life has proven me wrong. Secluding myself in the Church provided security and no risk. I spent a lifetime running from emotional attachments because they involved both reward and loss. But, praise Allah, I realize now the reward for loving someone is greater than the risk of losing someone."

"How about you?" he asked in return. "Any regrets?"

"None," she said firmly. "You're a dreamboat of a husband."

He shot her a quizzical look.

"Don't ask. Inside metaphor…So what do we do now?"

"Are you ready to pick up the banner of Truth that Mike waved so fearlessly?"

"I'm ready if you are."

Marco smiled. "It's better to die on our feet as free-thinking people than live on our knees as docile slaves like so many of our fellow men and women do."

* * *

**Washington, D.C.**

Deep within the labyrinth of the Department of Homeland Security the Deputy Director of Counterterrorism Operations was putting in another late night.

The urgent ringing of a telephone startled him. He glanced in the direction of the sound. Someone was calling him on the red phone, an ultra-secure line that was constantly swept for hacks.

"Yes," he spoke with authority into the communication device, the jagged ridges of his craggy face limned by the glow of his computer screen in the darkened office.

"Director, Operation Thomas More was concluded successfully."

"Gilmore is dead?"

"Confirmed."

"The people will have to find another Pied Piper to lead them," he said. "What about the shooter?"

"Vasquez is still at large."

"Did he not suicide per the psychotropic medication protocols?" he asked, massaging his temples with his thumb and index finger.

"No, sir."

"Terminate him with extreme prejudice," the Deputy gritted out. "And make it appear a suicide."

"Yes, sir."

"Don't compromise this mission."

The director broke the connection before the agent could answer.

He removed his glasses and squeezed the bridge of his nose. "The people won the first battle in the war for peace but little do they know peace is bad for business," he said into the dark. "I wonder who the genius is who dreamt up the name of this operation. He must have read *Utopia*."

A former professor of political science, he quoted out loud with relish a memorable passage from Thomas More's book:

> "Therefore, I must say that, as I hope for mercy, I can have no other notion of all the other governments that I see or know, than that they are a conspiracy of the rich, who, on pretense of managing the public, only pursue their private ends, and devise all the ways and arts they can find out."

He smirked into the darkness.

"Just as More had to be executed, so did Giltmore. We can't have rebels upsetting the natural order of things."

**THE END**

## Author's Notes

The maxims introducing Parts I, II and III are from my own hand.

This novel is dedicated to the victims of racial and religious bigotry and injustice in all its guises the world over.

I encourage you to Google and read Major General Smedley Butler's *War is a Racket* speech. Those who are ignorant of evil conspiracies in the past will be dupes of evil conspiracies in the present.

I composed this novel as an antidote to the virulent Islamophobia poisoning Western politics and international relations. Just as the right-wing extremism of Nazi Germany found its wicked expression in anti-Semitism, we see in the current age the right-wing extremism of Western countries, particularly in the United States, finding its evil expression in Islamophobia. Could America end up as Nazi Germany did? Only time will tell.

Thomas More was Chancellor to King Henry VIII. More was executed for taking a stand against the King's separation from the Catholic Church and for refusing to annul the King's marriage to Catherine of Aragon. He is a model for dissidents in every age who speak truth to Power.

So who was the Beloved Disciple mentioned in the Book of John? I deliberately left his identity a mystery so you could arrive at your own conclusion based on the clues sprinkled throughout this novel.

The Ottoman-Armenian civil war sprang not from the religion of Islam but from Turkish nationalism as historian Arnold Toynbee pointed out in his book *Turkey: A Past and a Future*.

For further reading on Armenian-on-Turk killings and Kurd-on-Armenian killings during the breakup of the Ottoman Empire, read the end of Chapter 5 in *The Ottomans: Dissolving Images* written by historian Andrew Wheatcroft.

The reference to the youth volunteering to take the place of Jesus (chapter 12) is based on Ibn Kathir's *Qisas Al-Anbiya* (*Stories of the Prophets*). An earthquake did strike Constantinople on October 25, 989 CE, and an arch of the Hagia Church did collapse in consequence (chapter 22).

Prophet Jacob's house of worship is the present-day Al Aqsa Mosque. It is true the Sanhedrin of Jerusalem had no legal jurisdiction in Damascus, which had its own Jewish governing council; therefore, Paul could not have received any letter from the Jerusalem Council authorizing the arrest of Christians (chapter 17).

The number of terrorist attacks committed between 2004 and 2015 by white terrorists (18) versus "Muslim" terrorists (9) is taken from a study conducted by the New America Foundation (www.newamerica.org) (chapter 21).

I documented three questions that, according to a narration of Prophet Mohammed (peace be upon him) will be asked of every human soul at the point of death (end of chapters 23 and 24). The archetypical responses to these questions given by the Beloved Disciple and Paul are not to be taken literally. Their responses are merely provided to illustrate their consequences, for better or for worse.

Koç University in Istanbul exists. The accelerator mass spectrometer and cleanroom facilities do not.

The Santi Giuseppe Church and the University of Thomas More (in Indiana) do not exist.

## Suggested Websites

For those wishing to escape the propaganda matrix of corporate lamestream news, the following websites will be of great help.

https://www.aljazeera.com/
https://www.alternet.org/
https://www.davidicke.com
https://www.democracynow.org/
http://glenngreenwald.net/
https://www.globalresearch.ca/
http://www.hurriyetdailynews.com/
http://www.informationclearinghouse.info/
https://www.rt.com/
https://www.zerohedge.com/
Youtube: JFK to 911 Everything Is A Rich Man's Trick
Youtube: Aaron Russo Interview with Alex Jones
Youtube: From Freedom to Fascism

# Appendix

**Islamic Creed-612 CE**

There is no deity but God.

God has no partner and there is no one worthy of worship but Him.

Mohammed is the Prophet and Messenger of God.

**Niceno-Constantinopolitan Creed-382 CE**

We believe in one God, the Father Almighty, Maker of heaven and earth, and of all things visible and invisible.

And in one Lord Jesus Christ, the only-begotten Son of God, begotten of the Father before all worlds, Light of Light, very God of very God, begotten, not made, being of one substance with the Father; by whom all things were made; who for us men, and for our salvation, came down from heaven, and was incarnate by the Holy Ghost and of the Virgin Mary, and was made man; he was crucified for us under Pontius Pilate, and suffered, and was buried, and the third day he rose again, according to the Scriptures, and ascended into heaven, and sitteth on the right hand of the Father; from thence he shall come again, with glory, to judge the quick and the dead; whose kingdom shall have no end.

And in the Holy Ghost, the Lord and Giver of life, who proceedeth from the Father, who with the Father and the Son together is worshiped and glorified, who spake by the prophets.

In one holy catholic and apostolic Church; we acknowledge one baptism for the remission of sins; we look for the resurrection of the dead, and the life of the world to come. Amen.

**Athanasian Creed-Late Fifth or Early Sixth Century CE**

Whosoever will be saved, before all things it is necessary that he hold the catholic faith. Which faith unless every one do keep whole and undefiled, without doubt he shall perish everlastingly. And the catholic faith is this: that we worship one God in Trinity, and Trinity in Unity; neither confounding the Persons, nor dividing the Essence. For there is one Person of the Father; another of the Son; and another of the Holy Ghost. But the Godhead of the Father, of the Son, and of the Holy Ghost, is all one; the Glory equal, the Majesty coeternal. Such as the Father is; such is the Son; and such is the Holy Ghost. The Father uncreated; the Son uncreated; and the Holy Ghost uncreated. The Father unlimited; the Son unlimited; and the Holy Ghost unlimited. The Father eternal; the Son eternal; and the Holy Ghost eternal. And yet they are not three eternals; but one eternal. As also there are not three uncreated; nor three infinites, but one uncreated; and one infinite. So likewise the Father is Almighty; the Son Almighty; and the Holy Ghost Almighty. And yet they are not three Almighties; but one Almighty. So the Father is God; the Son is God; and the Holy Ghost is God. And yet they are not three Gods; but one God. So likewise the Father is Lord; the Son Lord; and the Holy Ghost Lord. And yet not three Lords; but one Lord. For like as we are compelled by the Christian verity; to acknowledge every Person by himself to be God and Lord; So are we forbidden by the catholic religion; to say, There are three Gods, or three Lords. The Father is made of none; neither created, nor begotten. The Son is of the Father alone; not made, nor created; but begotten. The Holy Ghost is of the Father and of the Son; neither made, nor created, nor begotten; but proceeding. So there is one Father, not three Fathers; one Son, not three Sons; one Holy Ghost, not three Holy Ghosts. And in this Trinity none is before, or after another; none is greater, or less than another. But the whole three Persons are coeternal, and coequal. So that in all things, as aforesaid; the Unity in Trinity, and the Trinity in Unity, is to be worshipped. He therefore that will be saved, let him thus think of the Trinity.

Furthermore, it is necessary to everlasting salvation; that he also believe faithfully the Incarnation of our Lord Jesus Christ. For the right Faith is, that we believe and confess; that our Lord Jesus Christ, the Son of God, is God and Man; God, of the Substance [Essence] of the Father; begotten before the worlds; and Man, of the Substance [Essence] of his Mother, born in the world. Perfect God; and perfect Man, of a reasonable soul and human flesh subsisting. Equal to the Father, as touching his Godhead; and inferior to the Father as touching his Manhood. Who although he is God and Man; yet he is not two, but one Christ. One; not by conversion of the Godhead into flesh; but by assumption of the Manhood into God. One altogether; not by confusion of Substance [Essence]; but by unity of Person. For as the reasonable soul and flesh is one man; so God and Man is one Christ; Who suffered for our salvation; descended into hell; rose again the third day from the dead. He ascended into heaven, he sitteth on the right hand of God the Father Almighty, from whence he will come to judge the living and the dead. At whose coming all men will rise again with their bodies; And shall give account for their own works. And they that have done good shall go into life everlasting; and they that have done evil, into everlasting fire. This is the catholic faith; which except a man believe truly and firmly, he cannot be saved.

**Chalcedonian (Trinitarian) Creed-451 CE**

We, then, following the holy Fathers, all with one consent, teach people to confess one and the same Son, our Lord Jesus Christ, the same perfect in Godhead and also perfect in manhood; truly God and truly man, of a reasonable [rational] soul and body; consubstantial [co-essential] with the Father according to the Godhead, and consubstantial with us according to the Manhood; in all things like unto us, without sin; begotten before all ages of the Father according to the Godhead, and in these latter days, for us and for our salvation, born of the Virgin Mary, the Mother of God, according to the Manhood; one and the same Christ, Son, Lord, only begotten, to be acknowledged in two natures, inconfusedly, unchangeably, indivisibly, inseparably; the distinction of nature's being by no means taken away by the union, but rather the property of each nature being preserved, and concurring in one Person and one Subsistence, not parted or divided into two persons, but one and the same Son, and only begotten, God the Word, the Lord Jesus Christ; as the prophets from the beginning [have declared] concerning Him, and the Lord Jesus Christ Himself has taught us, and the Creed of the holy Fathers has handed down to us.

**Apostles' Creed-Ecumenical Version**
I believe in God, the Father almighty,
creator of heaven and earth.
I believe in Jesus Christ, God's only Son, our Lord,
who was conceived by the Holy Spirit,
born of the Virgin Mary,
suffered under Pontius Pilate,
was crucified, died, and was buried;
he descended to the dead.
On the third day he rose again;
he ascended into heaven,
he is seated at the right hand of the Father,
and he will come to judge the living and the dead.
I believe in the Holy Spirit,
the holy catholic Church,
the communion of saints,
the forgiveness of sins,
the resurrection of the body,
and the life everlasting. Amen.

CPSIA information can be obtained
at www.ICGtesting.com
Printed in the USA
BVHW061055190820
586801BV00016B/503

9 781644 38468